DARK RAIN

Dana Duthie

Matchstick Literary
1-888-306-8885
orders@matchliterary.com

KEY WORDS

Straight out of today's headlines! The U.S. fighting
forces battle Iranian terrorism in the skies. A must
for fighter pilots and fighter pilot wannabees!

PREFACE

Obviously this book is fiction. However, I have attempted to portray real Air Force fighter pilots and their lives to let you know what it is really like. Many of the incidents really happened – to me, and to the men and women I worked with and around for over twenty four years. Some of the characters may be familiar to those who served and flew with me through the years. These folks obviously impressed me enough in my Air Force career to remember them, and I hope I have offended no one by describing them, albeit with a slightly different name. The intent is to entertain, but to add as much realism as possible.

"Dark Rain" combines some of the drama and threat of the Cold War 80s with terror related issues of today. The military specifications and tactics may be a little dated since my time in the Air Force ended over 25 years ago. The reader might believe that the events in the book are a bit far fetched. Could there really be "moles" from a terrorist sponsoring country buried within American society? Could pilots from those families really be imbedded in the Air Force or Navy? We certainly hope not, but would it be possible to take over the cockpits of four airliners at the same time and fly them into buildings in New York and Washington or into a field in Pennsylvania? We didn't used to think so.

Dana Duthie

CHAPTER ONE

SUNDAY DECEMBER 5, 1230 HRS - OFF THE COAST OF NORTHERN VIRGINIA

"Wolf, let's split for an intercept. One's the bogey. Maneuver when line abreast."

"Two."

Colonel Brad Mitchell was leading a two ship air to air training mission of F-16s from the 121st Fighter Squadron of the 113th Air National Guard Wing flying out of Andrews AFB, Maryland. Other than pulling air defense alert with a flight of two F-16s ready at all times, most of the wing's flying was done during the weekends. Most of the pilots were what many called "weekend warriors," pilots who had other day jobs. Many were airline pilots, but there were defense contractors, lawyers, even a United States Congressman assigned to the wing as a fighter pilot. The work load of the Air National Guard had ramped up significantly after 9/11. In fact, the 121st squadron had just returned from a four month deployment to Quatar where they flew in support of U.S. and Kurdish troops in Syria.

Brad Mitchell's position as the wing commander was a full time job. Although he was in the Air National Guard, he had "retired" from the active Air Force last year after 26 years of a very action packed and colorful career. He had won the Silver Star for valor after leading a multi-aircraft raid on a North Korean nuclear facility. He was a squadron commander in South Korea and was shot down during the raid and an unsuccessful attempt to rescue UN inspector hostages held at the facility. His escape was the thing of legends. In fact, there were so many "legends" involving Mitchell that the Air Force had basically put him out to pasture and sent him around the country on speaking engagements. That's when Mitchell read the handwriting on the wall, confirmed with his bosses that he was not going to be promoted to General, and decided to take the job offered at Andrews. More than likely his propensity to call a spade a spade and reject "political correctness," had a lot to do with his absence on the promotion list. In fact, Brad had been sought after by the Guard Bureau when it became clear they were going to have to fire the wing commander at Andrews, Brad's predecessor. There had been some discipline problems in the wing, and being the "showcase" outfit that the 113th Wing is, with Air Force One and all the publicity and notoriety that comes with its basing at Andrews, the Air Force and the ANG needed to make some changes. Colonel Brad Mitchell was brought in to "clean house," and he had done a good job so far.

There was another reason the Air Force and the Pentagon wanted Brad Mitchell close at hand. He and his wife Melanie were tagged as team players in a very close knit and close hold project team that consisted of special operations folks - Navy SEALS, Army Green Berets and Air Force special ops paramedics. They, along with CIA, FBI and Homeland Security personnel manned a "Black Ops" cell that met very infrequently and operated directly out of the White House. Melanie Mitchell was onboard because of her background in North Korea and as a CIA operative in the Middle East before "retiring" to marry Brad Mitchell and start a family.

Mitchell and his wingman split up and headed toward opposite ends of their training area. The scenario was set up that once at their respective starting points, they would turn around and head towards each other. As the "bogey," or target, Mitchell was to maintain 18,000 ft until the two were line abreast. Then he could maneuver once he had a visual on his "attacker." Wolf 2 could maneuver at any altitude he wanted as long as he didn't pass through 18,000 ft when within 5 miles of his leader. Once they started maneuvering they would transition to BFM (Basic Fighting Maneuvers) to try and get the offensive advantage on the other guy. Starting off as the target, and locked into one altitude, Wolf 1 had a disadvantage and the normal transition, assuming the two pilots had similar talents and experience, was for the wingman in this instance to achieve missile parameters, or at least a close in gun solution.

As he headed north to his turn point, Mitchell's flight suit pocket vibrated. It was his cell phone. Normally he wouldn't bother answering it while flying, but today he expected a call from his wife Melanie. She was waiting in the wings of a local hospital where her best friend was on her last legs, dying of breast cancer. Brad expected bad news. He had the earplugs hooked up to the phone, stuffed one bud up into his ear under his helmet, and put the phone on speaker.

"Colonel Mitchell"

"Sir, this is Lt. Colonel Ellis we have a situation." It was Don Ellis, squadron commander of the 121st squadron. "Sir.... who is your wingman?"

"What do you mean 'who is my wingman?' It's Captain Hanes. Is this some kind of joke?" Mitchell was not happy with the use of the phone. "And why aren't you on the radio?"

"Sir, Johnny Hanes was just discovered stuffed in a closet in the personal equipment area with his throat cut. He's dead sir, but all of his gear - helmet, harness, g-suit - are missing"

Holy Shit Mitchell thought. *What the fuck ... then who AM I flying with?* He thought back. After briefing the mission he drove out to the flight line with his staff car because he carried all his gear with him in the car. He sometimes flew with other units on the base and it was easier than keeping his gear in one squadron PE room. Hanes (or whoever this is) came out later in the crew bus and he had his helmet on, visor down when he stepped off the bus. Mitchell couldn't see his wingman's jet from where he was parked but he supposed either the guy had done the preflight with his helmet on, or the crew chief simply didn't recognize him as an imposter. Neither scenario was all that strange. The crew chiefs certainly didn't know all the pilots, and in fact the real Johnny

Hanes was a relative newcomer. When the weather was cold some pilots wore their helmets as soon as they got outside.

"Don, I guess I have no clue who this is on my wing, but I'm going to join up now and RTB (return to base). In the meantime, put the alert birds on cockpit standby. I'll keep this line open as well." The air defense alert crews were housed in a separate facility with their airplanes and normally had a 5 minute response time requirement. Putting the crews in the cockpit cut that time to just 2-3 minutes. Mitchell didn't have a clue what was going on, but it was obvious the guy he was flying with was up to something, and being this close to Washington, the Andrews alert force was often called on to intercept planes penetrating the closed airspace around the White House.

"Yes Sir. Will do. I'll also have the Security Police meet you in the chocks." Ellis was a sharp guy and hopefully he had notified everyone up and down the chain of command of whatever possibility might be in store.

"Wolf, let's knock it off. I've got some minor electrical issues. Join up on me and let's head for the house. I'm at Flight Level 180, holding 350 knots." Brad wanted to get his wingman in sight as soon as possible.

"Two copies. You need any help sir?"

Yeah I need some help. I need you to tell me who the fuck you are and what you're planning. "No everything seems to be ok except I'm getting a flickering left gear down and locked light. Slowing to 250 knots. Join up and check me out when I lower the gear." Brad had decided that the best way of keeping control of this guy was to have him land on the wing in a formation landing. That was not foolproof. After all, the other pilot was flying his own airplane and there was no way to completely control him.

"Two copies. I have a visual. I'm at your 3 o'clock, 4 miles and closing" Brad looked out and saw the geometry of the join-up unfolding.

"Roger. Starting a left turn toward base and an easy descent. Let's go to Approach Control, channel 13."

"Two." Mitchell switched the UHF radio to Washington Approach Control and watched as his wingman traded altitude for airspeed with a beautiful barrel roll and slowed to match his speed, joining up like a pro on the left wing.

"Washington Approach this is Wolf 1, flight of two F-16s, 30 miles east of Andrews to land tin formation, requesting vectors for a VFR approach. Wolf check" The weather was clear and beautiful and Brad wanted to get this flight on the deck as soon as possible.

"Two." His wingman checked in on UHF, and then switched to the squadron FM channel. "Wolf 1 your landing gear look to be up and locked."

"Copy that, standby. Gear down - now!" Mitchell lowered the landing gear and his wingman did the same to maintain formation with the gear hanging. Brad knew of course there was nothing wrong with his gear, but the standard procedure with a potential malfunction was to test it out at altitude before really needing it and finding out they wouldn't all three go down. "Showing two steady green here, but the left one is blinking." Brad lied. His wingman slid over to the left side and snuggled up close to see any malfunction.

"Looks good from here One."

"Roger - let's raise 'em and try again later with a little g. Gear up - now!" They raised the landing gear and proceeded inbound. Brad increased the speed to hurry up the process. The landing gear limiting speed was 250 knots, and that would take a while to get home. "Wolf 1 is showing all up and locked with a blinker." He lied again.

"Wolf this is Washington Approach, you are cleared for visual approach Runway 01 at Andrews. Descend and maintain 5000 ft. Altimeter 30.15. Be advised Air Force one is 40 miles south, inbound to land. You will be Number One in front of him."

"Roger, out of 16,000 for 5000, altimeter 30.15." *Shit! Air Force One! Could that be what this is all about?* Brad thought to himself. Their F-16s weren't carrying any live ordnance, but the jet itself could make for a deadly weapon. Witness the Twin Towers and the Pentagon on 9/11. He got his phone out of his lap.

"Lt. Colonel Ellis, you still with me?" Mitchell called the squadron commander.

"Sir, Colonel Ellis is on the line with the National Command Center. This is Major Smiley sir. Can I help you?" Mitchell thought - *good, Ellis is talking to the right folks, but...*"

"Smiles, get him on the horn to the Air Defense Sector Command and suggest launching our alert birds to escort Air Force One. She's 40 miles out and I have no clue what this guy on my wing has in mind." Brad was the commander of the alert force, but he did not have the authority to launch them. That was up to a higher pay grade in the Air Defense Sector hierarchy. "In the meantime, we are coming in for a formation landing with me faking a gear indicator failure. Be sure the Security Cops are there to jump on Wolf 2 as soon as he's in the chocks."

"Ellis here boss. Copy all. The alert birds are launching now. Be advised Air Force One is carrying the First Lady and others. The President is in the White House." Lt. Colonel Ellis had returned to the comm.

"Copy that. Good work." Brad made a note to himself to congratulate Ellis for handling things on the ground. He assumed the Vice Commander and the Director of Operations (the other two full bird colonels in the wing) were not on base. "By the way sir, I've called Colonels McCall and Wycoff, and they are on their way in." Brad tried to smile. Ellis was reading his mind.

"Copy." then he switched to the radio. "Washington Approach, Wolf One is leveling at 5000 ft. Andrews in sight, request visual maneuvering and immediate clearance lower." Brad looked toward his wingman. Rock solid and steady with 3 ft wingtip clearance. "Two move it out to a loose root for now." He said on squadron common radio while shaking the rudder pedals, the visual signal to loosen the formation. Wolf Two moved out about 3 wingspans off the wing and about 30 degrees back.

"Wolf flight you're cleared to descend at your discretion and cleared for the approach. Be advised the alert force is rolling on a scramble, should be no factor. Air Force One is 25 miles south. No other traffic." The alert aircraft were rolling east and would be clear of the runway shortly, then turning south to intercept Air Force One.

"Copy that. Wolf Flight let's go Channel 3." He switched to the tower frequency and checked in his wingman. Then on FM, "Wolf, standby for gear. Gear Down - now!" They lowered their landing gear together and Brad showed three steady green lights.

"Andrews Tower, Wolf flight of two F-16s 11 miles west for straight in formation landing. Be advised Wolf One has intermittent gear indications, left side. Request emergency response scrambled." Brad lied about the gear, but he wanted the firemen and cops out there if anything at all went wrong. Normally if there was a gear problem, making a formation landing would not be a good idea. If his landing gear collapsed on touchdown there would be a good chance of veering into the wingman. But Brad was the Wing Commander and no one was going to question his plan. Besides, the experts on the base were in the squadron and they knew he was faking it.

"Wolf One, Andrews Tower, roger that. Cleared to land Runway 01. Winds 075 at 10 knots, altimeter 30.15." The klaxon went off at the fire department and they rolled within two minutes with five fire trucks, a foam truck (to aid in fire fighting), an ambulance, and other official "lookie-loo" vehicles.

Brad keyed the FM radio. "Two, I'm going to porpoise the jet here to see if the light will steady up." Again, standard procedure with an unsafe gear light. He pulled and pushed the nose up and down a couple times to put G on the gear. Obviously, nothing changed.

"Two copies. No change noted. Gear looks down and locked."

Brad lead the formation on a straight in approach at about ten knots over the minimum final approach speed, making it easier for the wingman to maneuver. He rocked his wings gently - the signal for his wingman to collapse to close formation again. He used hand and head signals to open the speed brake as they started down the glide path, using the visual glide slope lights beside the touchdown point of the runway. They crossed the threshold and he gently pulled the power back more and raised the nose to establish a smooth but firm landing. Out of the corner of his eye he saw that his wingman had landed with him and kept his nose up to slow down to achieve nose-tail clearance. Brad lowered his nose and let it roll out for separation before coming up on the brakes. With about 4000 feet of runway remaining Brad slowed to turn off at the next intersection, expecting his wingman to follow.

Suddenly, out of the corner of his eye he saw the F-16 coming on fast. His wingman had lit the afterburner and blew by him like a scalded ass ape. *Holy Shit!* He immediately thought to follow, but he had turned too far onto the taxiway and it would have been impossible without rolling over the grass beside the taxiway.

"Wolf Two, what are you doing?" Brad yelled over the squadron common FM frequency at about the same time the Tower did over UHF. "Wolf Two, we see your go around. Do you need assistance?" pause "Wolf Two, Tower." Silence.

CHAPTER TWO

SAME DAY, AURORA, COLORADO

"Buckley Tower, Rider flight of four vipers, 20 east for initial." The flight lead of four Air National Guard F-16s from the 120th Fighter Squadron at Buckley was leading his flight back to base after a successful low level and bombing range training mission. The squadron was at the tail end of a three day "surge," generating and flying as many sorties as they could, testing the maintenance and flight crews. It had been a good exercise so far.

"Roger Rider, the pattern is all yours. Buckley landing runway 14, winds are light and variable, altimeter 29.92. Report initial." They were in the middle of the second mass launch of the day, so most of the rest of the squadron was still on the range or in the air to air training areas. Rider flight had the traffic pattern to themselves. The normal visual approach procedures for Air Force fighter and trainer squadrons was to join the traffic pattern on a downwind leg of a rectangle, staying at 1000 or 1500 feet above the ground. The flight lead led the formation at 300 knots airspeed to a left turn onto what is termed the "initial" approach about 6 miles west of the air base, and headed directly over the runway on runway heading.

"Rider's initial with four for low approaches followed by individual SFOs to a full stop." The flight lead was telling the tower the plan was to split up for overhead approaches, followed by individual climbs to 7000 feet over the runway. From there they would each fly simulated flame out (SFO) landings, simulating that the F-16 had lost all power and was setting up for a gliding "dead stick" landing. SFOs were routinely practiced so that if the real thing ever happened and the aircraft was anywhere near a runway, the pilot would have the choice to try the dead stick approach or to bail out. Obviously saving a multi-million dollar aircraft was preferable, but only if everything was near perfect. As they crossed the threshold of the runway at their 1000 foot altitude the leader gave the signal to pitch out with three second spacing to an inside downwind and approach to land - one after another with about 5000 foot spacing. Each pilot brought his jet to within 30-40 feet of the touchdown point, then increased to full power, raised the landing gear, and climbed out to a 7000 ft perch above the runway, maintaining spacing from the aircraft ahead.

"Rider One is high key." That was the call to the tower that the first aircraft is leaving his 7000 ft perch for a spiraling descent to land. Rider Two and Three each mimicked the call and followed their leader down the spiraling flight path. "Rider One is low key, gear down, full stop." The leader was now about abeam the touchdown point on a downwind leg at about 2500 feet and descending.

"Roger Rider Flight, cleared to land, winds 070 at 5 knots." Again Riders 2 and 3 mimicked the calls, configured their jets to land and followed the leader to touchdown.

"Break Break - Rider Four say your intentions." The tower operators had lost sight of the fourth F-16 - not an easy target to see 7000 feet up anyway - and he had not made the high key radio call.

Abdul Sadir kept climbing through 7000 feet after his flight-mates started their descent to land. He kept his power up, leveled off at 11,000 feet and increased speed to 450 knots. He turned south, leaving Buckley airspace heading toward Pikes Peak, which he could see 60 miles to the south of Denver.

"Rider One Tower. Your number four did not initiate an SFO. We don't have him in sight but radar shows him heading south at a high rate. What are his intentions?" The chief tower operator had taken over the radio.

"I don't have a clue Tower." The leader made an uneventful landing, lowered the nose to establish spacing for his wingman behind, then got back on the radio. "Rider 4, Rider 1, what are your intentions?" Then he switched to the squadron common FM frequency and tried it. "Rider 4, Rider 1." "Rider 4, Rider 1, what's going on?" Nothing. No response. Back to Tower. "Tower, Rider 1, I don't know what he has done, but you need to let the command center know, as well as Denver Center. I'm going straight to the chocks and will call from the squadron."

Sadir had no intention of answering anyone. He kept his radios on to determine what, if anything, the Americans were going to do about the fact he had just stolen their F-16 and was heading towards his destiny. He turned off his Identification Friend or Foe (IFF) system to make tracking him on radar a little more difficult. The radar operators in the Denver Center complex, as well as the approach controllers in both the Denver and Colorado Springs areas could still "paint" him as a target and monitor his flight path, but they would have no idea of his intentions.

Abdul Sadir was Rod Crawley to his squadron mates, a Captain in the Colorado Air National Guard. He has been in the squadron for a little over a year, after a regular Air Force stint of 5 years, all flying the F-16. His personnel folder said he graduated from Air Force ROTC at Purdue University with a BS in mechanical engineering, and was originally from Indianapolis. All that was true. In fact, his background could be verified back through high school. His parents were bi-racial. His mother was from Turkey and his father was black. Abdul's father, with the American name of Robert Crawley ran a printing business in Indianapolis and his mother was a school teacher. Abdul also had a twin brother, Mustafa, also known as Mike Crawley, currently flying F-18s in the US Navy, deployed on the USS Abraham Lincoln, a nuclear carrier near the Straits of Hormuz. Nothing in their backgrounds would indicate any issues at least back 15 years. Beyond that however, if one was to dig deeper, the Crawleys would not be who they pretended to be.

The Crawleys, or the Sadirs, were part of a group of operatives trained in Iran, starting 15 years ago. The members were selected from many backgrounds and ethnicities, with the only common denominator being they were converts to radical Islam. Their training included schooling, and exposure to the American way of life. The village they trained in was like a moderate size American suburban town appropriately named Starkville, where everyone dressed, played, ate, drank, and virtually led an American way of life for years. When the powers at be determined they were ready, they were sent out to their new lives in the U.S. and they became model U.S. citizens. Fingerprints, photos, passports, IDs were all expertly managed so that a normal background investigation to join the U.S. military would uncover nothing but good news. That's why after graduating from Purdue, Abdul became a second lieutenant in the US Air Force and went to pilot training, and his brother Mustafa graduated as well, though becoming an Ensign in the US Navy through Navy ROTC.

There were more of these "Americans." Their operation had only started to unfold.

CHAPTER THREE

SAME DAY, EAST OF CHEYENNE, WYOMING

Mary Cogswell and Joe McMann had been on their shift as Intercontinental Ballistic Missile officers since 6 AM. It was a 24 hour shift and everything had been normal…. so far. They preflighted their missile as much as missile officers can preflight the beast. They basically follow the same checklist that the operation had used for decades. Then they went through the hand off process from the previous crew and settled in for a boring day and night. Except this shift would not be boring.

Prior to 10:30 AM, Joe, whose real name was Ali Jabara, had set the plastique explosives he had snuck in in his backpack around the entrance to the complex and as close as he could get in the silo to the missile's warhead. Sneaking the new high-tech explosives in through the security checkpoint had been nerve racking, but relatively easy. They were cleverly disguised in tooth paste tubes, as well has hair gel and other products that Ali and Leona Mir-So (his partner known as Mary Cogswell) had in their overnight bags. They had been through several communications checks already this morning and were waiting for the daily exercise where they would go all the way up to turning the keys to simulate launching the missile. There was always a no-notice test run on every shift, initiated by the Strategic Command Operations Center in Omaha, Nebraska. Since it hadn't happened yet, it wasn't likely to happen today after Ali and Leona initiated their "coup."

Jabari and Mir-So were originally Chechens who converted to Islam, then had come from Starkville, Iran, and moved into their American way of life when they were teenagers. They were as caucasian looking as they could be. Leona was a strikingly beautiful blonde and Ali was a big, strapping football player type. They were the All-American types, Leona went through the US Air Force Academy and Ali had played quarterback and went through ROTC at University of Nevada Las Vegas. They had matriculated into the U.S. in high school, Ali in Fort Collins, Colorado and Leona in Salt Lake City. They had worked for months to be paired up as a team. Their keepers had studied the system and had inserted Ali two years earlier than Leona. He was on his last year of the assignment and had become a training instructor. So when Leona came aboard it was relatively easy to pair her up with one of the few instructors. Ali was also the squadron scheduler, so ensuring they would be on duty today was easy.

At 10:30 they shut down all communications systems from the outside that they could from the inside. They did not respond to any calls from their home base, F.E. Warren AFB in Cheyenne, or from Omaha. However, Ali used his cell phone and called the command post to relay a scripted and chilling message. **"Security at Mission 960425 has been compromised. There are explosives set at the entrance and on the missile. They will be detonated if any attempt to breach the silo is made. We are prepared to die for our cause. Let the will of Allah be."** If they were able, they would launch the missile, probably starting WW III, but the "fail safes" on the system assured that it was impossible for a couple of Air Force captains to launch their "toy."

The command center at F.E. Warren immediately reacted by sending a unit of AF Security Police to the site. It was close to a 2 hour drive from the base to the "boondocks" where the silos were actually located. Omaha also went into panic mode, activating various checklist scenarios and linking communications up to and including the Pentagon and the White House. The immediate questions from the President were: "1. Can they launch the missile? and; 2. Will an explosion trigger a nuclear accident - ie: can they set off the bomb?" The answer to the first question was "no" because of the fail safes in place. The second answer was a bit more complicated.

Because the U.S. ICBM force had been severely underfunded, especially since the end of the Cold War in the early 90s, there were several upgrades to security and operations that were neglected, at least until more recently. With the escalating degradation in U.S. - Russian relations over the past few years, and especially with the Russian incursion into Crimea, the "thaw" in the Cold War had all but ceased. In fact, the U.S. had secretly re-inserted tactical nuclear weapons into air bases in Germany, Italy and the United Kingdom. The nukes in South Korea had been beefed up as well, and the Navy had re-deployed four more nuclear armed submarines to the waters closer to Russia. There was a refurbishment project ongoing in the ICBM force, but not yet at Mission 960425. As a result, depending on where the explosives were located and how they were designed, complete destruction of the missile and its weapon was not only possible, but likely, and a low level yield of radiation and destruction was not out of the question.

Ali and Leona had set themselves up as martyrs to the cause and had called their handler to tell him they were ready. There was no intention of surrendering to the security forces. In fact, the deed would be done before the Air Force cops even arrived. In the meantime, they were both on their knees, facing Mecca and reciting their prayers. The "will of Allah" was about to reign down on the hedonistic Untied States with devastation on several fronts.

CHAPTER FOUR

SAME DAY, USS ABRAHAM LINCOLN, STRAITS OF HORMUZ

Navy Lieutenant Mike Crawley gave the thumbs up signal and a salute to the "Yellow Shirt" on the deck of the nuclear aircraft carrier USS Abraham Lincoln. Then he pressed back into the headrest of the ejection seat in his FA-18 Hornet and pushed the power all the way up and lit the afterburners. The big jet shook and strained until the crew chief gave the signal to the "pit" where the catapult operator pinched the activator and the steam powered catapult pulled the jet from zero to 150 knots in about two and a half seconds. Crawley pulled back on the stick and at first there was a sinking feeling as the fully loaded F-18 settled a bit immediately after leaving the deck of the Lincoln. Then she started a steady climb out with her six 500 pound bombs and full arsenal of missiles and gun. Crawley was number two in a flight that was supporting the U.S. and Kurdish fighters locked in a fierce battle with ISIS fighters north of Aleppo in northern Syria. Crawley's flight lead had launched off just seconds before him on the other of the Lincoln's two catapults.

But rather than continue the climb and join up on his flight lead's wing, Mustafa Sadir had another mission in mind. It had been very difficult for him to drop bombs on his ISIS comrades in previous missions. In fact, whenever he could get away with it he managed to miss, but not enough so as to arouse suspicion of his flight mates or those tasked with battle damage assessment. Today was different. His mission would be very short, and he hoped the death and destruction he was about to bring the American Navy would more than atone for his past actions. He had been in the Navy for seven years, the last two in the attack squadron attached to the Lincoln. They had been on this deployment for ten months, almost all of it supporting U.S. Army and Marine forces in Iraq and Syria. On a previous deployment he had operated in both Afghanistan and Iraq. He had joined the Navy after graduating from Purdue with his twin brother and after commissioning as an Ensign from ROTC. His brother had gone through AF ROTC, spent five years in Air Force fighter squadrons, and was currently flying F-16s for the Colorado Air National Guard. Mustafa had no idea what his brother Abdul was doing today. None of the "stars" of the day's activities knew anything about the overall plan and who was doing what. They only knew that today was the day and they had all been called by Allah to martyrdom by raining death and destruction on the American infidels.

Mustafa leveled his F-18 off at about 1000 feet above the water, let the jet accelerate to over 500 knots, still in full afterburner. He started a 60 degree bank turn to the left, grunting back the G forces, and looked back over his shoulder to pick up the Lincoln. After 180 degrees of turn, he leveled the wings, reached down and armed up his bombs, and a delivery mode that would allow his release of the bombs from about a twenty degree dive.

"Gator Two say your position." Mustafa's flight lead had looked for him to join up and not seen his left turn maneuver that basically took him behind and under the lead aircraft's flight path. Mustafa had no intention of answering. "Gator Two, Gator One?"

"Lincoln, Gator One, do you have my wingman in sight?" The leader queried the ship for help.

"Roger Gator, looks like he might have a problem. He leveled off and is in a hard turn back toward the Lincoln. Do you know his intentions?" The Air Boss, a Navy Captain and senior pilot on the bridge of the Lincoln just became interested. He assumed the F-18 had some sort of malfunction and was trying to return to land. "Break Break! Gator Two this is the Lincoln, are you having problems? Are you aborting sir?" The Lincoln's junior controller tried to raise the the pilot of the obviously crippled jet.

Mustafa waited until he was almost abeam of the Lincoln heading the opposite direction and resumed his hard turn in toward her. He re-checked all switches were armed and his bombs were "hot." He leveled off about four miles out and started a 20 degree climb. He held it for a few seconds, saw the altimeter pass through 3000 feet, rolled inverted and pulled back down to a 20 degree dive, rolled right side up and centered the midship elevator of the Abraham Lincoln in his sight. He locked the computer sight onto the ship and mashed the "pickle" button on the left side of his control stick.

The Air Boss watched the maneuver and wondered what in the world the Lieutenant was up to. The squadron had just watched "Top Gun" in their Ready Room last night, and he wondered if Lieutenant Crawley was about to take a Tom Cruise joy ride maneuver to buzz the Lincoln's superstructure. Just in case, he put down his cup of coffee. He didn't want to wear the coffee on his uniform as the jet stormed by. He picked up his binoculars and zeroed in on the jet barreling toward them. "Oh my God!" he yelled as he saw six bombs separate from the F-18 heading right for the Lincoln.

"Take Cover. Prep for attack." The 20 year Navy Captain could only watch in aghast as the Lincoln was under attack. There was no time for the ship's defenses to react. Although the guns were manned at all times in this theatre, they certainly were not honed in on one of their own who everyone thought was either in trouble or trying to be a hot dog.

Mustafa felt the bombs release with a jolt. He then pulled hard into a full loop so he wouldn't out run the bombs. He leveled off back in a dive with the ship in his sights, used the thumb switch to call up the 20 millimeter canon in the FA-18's nose, pulled on the trigger, holding it in for the rest of his life.

Four of the Mk-82 bombs were on target in a string of 50 foot spacing. The first two impacted the water just below waterline of the carrier, the second one blowing a hole in the side of the hull. The next two bombs flew into the hangar deck through the gaping hole under the elevator that was used to bring the aircraft up to the deck. The destruction in the hangar was complete and the secondary explosions of munitions stored either on ready jets or stockpiles of bombs and missiles blew massive holes in the lower decks up to and including the area of the nuclear reactors. The last two bombs impacted on the deck of the Lincoln, one of them a direct hit on an armed AF-18 that had just been brought up on the elevator. Human carnage was everywhere. The bullets from the gun sprayed the deck, the elevator, and even some of the superstructure. But the largest explosion came when the FA-18 carrying the martyred soul of Mustafa Sadir plowed into the elevator and through the hangar deck.

Secondary explosions went off for almost 15 minutes as crews tried desperately to fight the fires that had been started and tend to their dead and wounded. The Lincoin had taken a major hit and within 30 minutes she started listing to the starboard side. She was basically powerless off the Iranian coast, taking on water and completely out of commission.

A flotilla of Iranian gunboats that had circled out of radar range of the Lincoln before was now inbound at full throttle. The Lincoln's battle group of a cruiser and two destroyers responded as quickly as they could. Three flights of FA-18s that had been launched and were outbound to their targets were immediately called back. Most of the attacking gunboats were repelled or sunk, but two were able to get through on kamikaze missions of their own. With guns blazing they strafed the Lincoln and any sailors who were in the water. Then with explosives stored in their bows, plowed into the stricken carrier, delivering the death blow.

The USS Abraham Lincoln sank two hours later. Many of the crew went down with the ship, but those who had survived the attacks were all picked up by the task force. All totaled, at least 1200 of the over 5000 men and women onboard the carrier were new members of Davey Jone's locker.

—

CHAPTER FIVE

ANDREWS AIR FORCE BASE, MARYLAND

Mohammed Solar touched down with his flight lead, the wing commander, in a perfect formation landing. He held the nose of the F-16 up and watched has the leader lowered his nose and rolled out to get nose-tail clearance. Mohammed gently lowered the nose, raised the speed brake and rolled out for about 1000 feet before starting the next phase of this flight. When he saw that the leader had started a turn off at an upcoming taxiway, he stroked the afterburner to full power and concentrated on a takeoff with plenty of runway remaining. The F-16's greater than one-to-one thrust to weight ratio made short takeoff runs easy. He raised the nose to about a 20 degree climb and made a hard turn to the northwest. He was heading straight for downtown Washington D.C.

Solar was not like the other "stars" of today's show. He had visited Starkville, Iran once, but he was not one of the "graduates." He was a regular Iranian Air Force Captain and fighter pilot who had recently spent a stint on an unofficial "exchange tour" with the Turkish Air Force. It was "unofficial" because it was all done on the QT. The Iranians paid Turkey a handsome amount to train Mohammed in their F-16s making sure that Turkey's NATO allies, and especially the U.S. didn't hear about it. He went through an extensive two week upgrade to the Viper and then returned to Tehran for his final training for today's mission. Originally one of the Starkville graduates was slated for this mission, but two months earlier the man was caught in a relationship with a USAF enlisted woman. He was busted in rank down to second lieutenant and assigned to non-flying duties, ironically as a security policeman.

Mohammed Solar travelled to the U.S. two weeks ago, rented a car at Kennedy Airport in New York, drove down to Maryland and checked into a motel outside the gate of Andrews AFB. He spent hours of several nights scouting the perimeter of the base until he found a weak point in the security surveillance and a good place to cut the fence. Two nights ago he did just that, leaving his rental car and belongings at his motel. He managed to hike into the area of the fighter squadron building, broke into the building last night and read the schedule of today's missions posted on the squadron scheduling board. He selected the flight most likely to fit his timing parameters, and found a nice quiet closet in the personal equipment room to wait. He had no idea who any of the crew were and certainly did not know that his flight lead would be Brad Mitchell, the Wing Commander. He was only interested in the wingman anyway. In the long run, it didn't really matter anyway who his leader was and what the mission was all about. Once he got airborne the hard part was over. He could have left the formation at any time during the flight, but because his leader was the wing commander who had a good reputation as a great fighter pilot and for getting things done, Solar decided to stick with him until the last moment before breaking away. He figured he'd be dodging alert aircraft. He didn't want to add to the fray by evading some gung ho American colonel. Since the flying schedule was light, he had a pretty good idea when Captain John Hanes would be coming in to suit up. He had located Hanes' locker and positioned himself to be able to surprise him. He'd managed to pilfer a couple patches off flight suits and jackets left lying around dand except for his dark complexion, he looked just like any of the squadron pilots. He also brought with him a hasp and screws and attached it to the outside of his closet door, placing a padlock in his pocket.

Colonel Mitchell and Captain Hanes finished up their pre-flight briefing and when it was time to step to the jet, Hanes took one last leak to empty his bladder prior to pulling a bunch of Gs, and went to the PE room to suit up. Solar was an expert in hand to hand combat and especially adept at handling a knife. He quickly approached Hanes from the back and reached around and cut deep into the American's throat with a very sharp knife, much resembling a Bowie knife. He let Hanes fall back into his arms, stuck the knife deep into Hanes soft belly, and quietly dragged him back into his closet, closing the door and wiping up the little bit of blood that had spurted or flowed onto the floor. He threw the bloody rags into the closet and then closed and locked the door with his padlock. Hopefully this would stall anyone snooping around the PE room.

Mohammed quickly put on Hanes' G-suit, combat vest, and parachute harness, pulled on his helmet, lowered the visor and stepped out of the building into the waiting crew van for transport to his jet. When he unloaded he could see his flight lead getting out of a staff car next to a near by F-16. Mohammed saluted his crew chief, placed a small duffel bag in the cockpit - one that could normally carry mission materials like checklists and maps, and then did his "walk around" check of the jet. He was impressed that the American F-16s were in much better shape than those he flew in Turkey. This crew chief obviously took pride in keeping his jet "ship shape."

Ground operations and taxi were normal and Solar was able to breath a sigh of relief when they took off on the mission. That was a little over an hour ago. Now after abandoning the formation landing he accelerated and climbed out to about 5000 feet and headed directly toward the middle of D.C. - 1600 Pennsylvania Avenue to be exact. The distance from the Andrews runway was only 10 miles as the crow flies (or in this case, the Viper). There was no time for anyone to react, except the Secret Service personnel stationed at the White House. They did not get any advanced warning of an aircraft penetrating the "No Fly Zone" that encircles the White House, but they were able to visually acquire the incoming jet. Two operators on the White House roof acquired the Viper with their heat seeking shoulder firing missiles, but because the aircraft was at 5000 feet and not flying in an offensive pattern, they simply followed him as a target until he disappeared to the northwest.

They assumed some throttle jockey at Andrews got lost and would get his ass chewed when he got back to the base

Solar let the city pass under his nose and then started an easy left turn back around to the south, keeping his airspeed at about 500 knots. His radios were blasting off loud and clear. The tower, the squadron, Air Traffic Control, all were calling him on their frequencies and even the Guard emergency frequency, reserved for airborne emergencies and special announcements. His radar warning (RHAW) receiver was squawking and lighting up as well. He could tell when the "White House" defenders were locked onto him, and he could see that other aircraft and ground radars had him as well. This RHAW equipment was a lot more sophisticated than the ones in the Turkish jets. The Americans weren't giving away all their secrets, but Mohammed had read enough intelligence briefings and technical papers to be able to interpret the signals fairly well.

"Hook," flight of two F-16s were the Andrews alert birds that were launched prior to Wolf flight's recovery. They were vectored immediately by the Air Defense Sector to intercept and escort Air Force One. It was a quick pickup on their radar and a sweeping turn to taxi up behind and then beside the big blue and white Boeing 747. They matched configurations to slow down with AF-1 when she lowered her multitude of wheels to land. At the same time, the flight lead was able to acquire the rogue F-16 that had just taken off from Andrews after a formation landing. Hook flight had switched over to an FM frequency that AF-1 monitored, so he couldn't talk to his squadron. But he could still talk to the sector controller. "Mother Goose, Hook one, I have contact on the runaway. Looks like he's over D.C. at 5000 feet and departing."

"Roger Hook, this is Goose. Stick with Air Force 1 until five mile final. Then if there is still no threat to her we'll clear you off and give you vectors to intercept the bogey." Everyone was concerned, not knowing what the F-16 now in a turn back to the south had in mind. Not even knowing who was flying the jet, but especially with the discovery of the real Captain Hanes' body, the "bogey" was considered hostile.

Mohammed Solar rolled out of his turn heading south, keeping the Potomac River off his left wing. He went about unpacking his small duffel bag. In it were packets of plastique explosives, enough to cause enough of an explosion to level a building the size of the White House. *Hmmm. Wouldn't that be nice?* he thought to himself. That was the plan, but Mohammed didn't plan on sticking around to find out. Mohammed was not so radical an Islamist that he was prepared to die for Allah. He was a soldier. Granted, he had orders and he had a plan, but he was not the Starkville graduate he replaced on this mission, a brainwashed idiot who would fly this jet directly into a building, dying for the cause. Besides, knowing what he was briefed about the defenses around the U.S President, he doubted he would be allowed to get that far anyway. He did plan however, to make as big a splash as he could and definitely get the attention of Washington D.C.

"Hook flight Mother Goose, you are cleared to depart and begin intercept on the bogey. He's at 170 heading from you, 40 miles, heading 120, level at 5000 feet, 500 knots." The sector controller pointed the posse at the renegade and hoped for the best.

"Hook copies. Goose this will be a lengthy tail chase, even if we bust the mach. Suggest you scramble the Langley alert force as well." The leader of the Hook alert flight could do the geometry and see that they were 40 miles away and could close only slowly without breaking the sound barrier. Since the bogey was not a threat right now he assumed that blowing out a bunch of windows on the ground by busting Mach 1.0 was not called for. He was correct.

"Roger that Hook. Langley is scrambling as we speak. Keep your speed below mach and continue the intercept." Hook lead also knew that by staying out of afterburner, which he would need to fly much faster than he was, he'd conserve fuel, maybe even enough to see this mission through.

Brad Mitchell had jumped out of his jet in the chocks and headed directly to the wing command post to join Jim McKay and Len Wykoff, his wing Vice Commander and Operations Group Commander. They had every radio tuned to appropriate frequencies and had a moving map display up showing the rogue F-16 and the two tail chasing alert birds. Colonel McKay had brought in the Office of Special Investigations and they had also contacted the FBI. Security Police personnel had located a spot in the perimeter fence where it looked like someone had snuck onto the base. Perusing all the camera footage strung around the base, they had discovered film of an individual snooping around the squadron building two nights ago. There were no fingerprints on the knife in the real Captain Hanes' belly, nor on the hasp and padlock found on the closet door. A quick survey of gas stations and buildings immediately near where the fence had been breached discovered camera footage from a gas station showing a shadowy figure several nights in a row coming out of a motel parking lot and crossing the highway into the brush and bushes close to the Andrews fence. The FBI and Prince Georges, Maryland County Police were en route to the motel to search for clues.

Mitchell got on the horn to the squadron commander, "Don, has anyone contacted Johnny Hanes' wife yet?"

"No sir. I wasn't sure how to do that without knowing what the situation was. I suppose it might be possible that Johnny knew his attacker?" Lt. Colonel Ellis replied. "I can go over and take my wife to be with Linda if you think we should yet."

"Good Point. Tell you what, I'm going to send our OSI chief and Colonel McKay. You pick up your wife and mine and be there after they quiz Linda and give you the ok. I'll call Melanie and tell her you're coming. In the meantime, get with maintenance and prep at least two more jets fully armed to launch if we need to relieve the alert force. Assign two of your best pilots to brief up and step to the cockpit."

"Already in the works sir. Maintenance tells me they'll have four jets ready in 10 minutes." Once again, Ellis was one step ahead.

Mohammed Solar waited until he saw the Chesapeake Bay coming up and then started another gentle left hand turn back towards D.C. Just before the turn he had radar contact with two fast moving targets coming up from the southeast. They were down low and pushing 600 knots. He assumed they were interceptors from Langley AFB. They would be fully armed F-22s, as would the two F-16s now in a tail chase. He started an easy descent as he rolled out of the turn - 1600 Pennsylvania Avenue in his computer and on the nose, 45 miles away.

Magic, flight of two F-22s had scrambled off alert at Langley AFB in Hampton, Virginia. They were briefed that their target was a rogue

F-16 with a potential terrorist pilot but with unknown intentions. They kept the altitude low and their power up, cruising up the west coast of the Chesapeake Bay letting the sound wave of the sound barrier ripple the water. "Mother Goose, Magic, two F-22s inbound for intercept." The flight lead contacted the sector.

"Roger Magic, Goose has you in contact. Bogey is at your 11 o'clock in a left turn, 5000 feet and 500 knots. Be advised we also have Hook flight of F-16s heading south to intercept. They're on your nose for 70 miles." The alert force had the bogey sandwiched, but not having a clue what to do with him.

"Magic copies. Radar contact on the bogey. What is the ROE?" The alert forced need to know the Rules of Engagement, whether they were to simply monitor the F-16, or bring lethal force.

"For now just monitor and see if you can get his attention. We can't get him to respond to any radio calls." The Sector Commander on duty was an Air Force colonel. He knew that he had shoot down authority when push came to shove, but this was a special case. This could be an American pilot gone off his rocker, with no evil intentions. Then again, it could be much worse. He called his superiors and briefed them in.

Solar turned up the volume on his RHAW receiver and he had both indications of radar lock from his nose and his tail. He was able to lock up the oncoming F-16s from Andrews on his radar as well and showed them coming right at him on a collision course about 20 miles out.

The F-22 has a much better radar than the ANG F-16s. The Langley pilot took command of the intercept. "Hook flight, Magic One, we have you contact as well as the bogey, on your nose, 20 miles." He wanted to be sure the F-16s were on the same page.

"Roger Magic, Hook has contact there descending through 3500 feet. Your ball game." Hook Lead knew the F-22 had full situational awareness on his helmet visor and in the cockpit.

"Roger Hook. Take him head on, close pass. Get his attention, then cleared to maneuver off his left wing. Magic will stay low and off the right wing. We're still 20 miles in trail and closing." The idea was to blow by the rogue close enough to rattle his dentures, then do a high G rolling turn to close back onto the wing as soon as possible. Both squadrons practice maneuvers like this all the time, but not usually this close to the ground.

Solar could see what was taking place. He scanned the horizon to look for his oncoming attackers, checking over his shoulder once in a while for the trailers. He descended on down to 1000 feet and maneuvered to keep D.C. on the nose while streaking up the Potomac. He had turned his radio volume down because all the calls to get him to respond were annoying, but now turned it back up, hopefully to hear what the interceptors might have in mind.

"Hook is five miles out. He's still descending." The leader and his wingman both looked hard on or just below the horizon. The F-16 head-on made a small target - tough to see.

"Hook Two is tallyho. On the nose a little low." The wingman got the first sighting.

"Hook one, tally. Ok two, let's bracket him. Run right by with him between us." A gutsy move. "Two." The two F-16s went blowing by with 1000 knots of closure. They both could see the pilot. He was looking straight ahead, but had both hands above the canopy rail giving them the bird - not usually an official flight hand signal.

"Ok Magic, Hook is off to the west. This guy's not real friendly. He just flipped us off." Hook lead stroked the afterburner and zoomed to the top of an Immelmann like maneuver to rejoin on the left side.

"Roger that Hook. Magic has a visual on you and a tally on the bogey. We are 6 miles in trail right side and closing. Magic Two, burners now!" Magic Lead pulled his engines back to military power and they feathered their speed brakes to nestle up close to the bogey on the right wing. They were 16 miles from D.C. at 1000 feet. Definitely a threat to breaking a lot of rules at least. Magic lead maneuvered his F-22 to within 25 feet of the other cockpit hoping to get a rise out of the pilot. He backed off a bit. F-22 pilots weren't used to flying formation this fast this low. It was a bit bumpy.

"F-16 15 miles southeast of Washington, this is Magic fight on Guard. Two F-22s on your right side. Start an immediate right hand turn, climb and reduce power. State your intentions." No response.

"Hook flight confirm you are weapons hot." Magic wanted to know his potential options.

"Roger Magic. Hook has two AMRAMs and two heaters with a hot gun." Hook had everything greened up and armed.

"Roger Hook. Fall back to weapons parameters and lock him up. Break, Break! Mother Goose. We are in visual contact with Hook in parameters. We show D.C. on the nose. What are your orders sir?" Magic and Hook needed authorization to end this folly.

"Roger Magic and Hook. Maintain your position and as long as he has the Potomac under him, keep trying. Break, Break! Rogue F-16 this is the Washington Air Defense Center on Guard, immediately break off your flight path and turn away from the city, climb to at least 5000 feet. Comply or you will be shot down."

"Magic, Hook. recommend you back off to the side a bit. We are locked on with heaters." The F-16 leader didn't want any collateral damage when they launched their AIM 9 heat seeking missiles.

In the White House Situation Room the Chairman of the Joint Chiefs of Staff as well as the Chief of Staff of the Air Force were monitoring the action. The President was notified and the Secret Service took him to a bunker room in the deepest bowels of the building. It was not as safe as other locations for the President, but they didn't have time to get him out of the building.

Solar was about ready to move. He saw the RHAW warning of the two fighters behind him. He knew they would have heat seeking as well as radar guided missiles. He could see one of them briefly, but then they disappeared below him.

Hook flight descended to about 200 feet lower than the bogey to have blue sky behind him and nothing to divert the flight of the missile. "Hook Two confirm you have him locked up, with a good growl. Fire on my command." "Two." The growl from the missiles acquiring their target in both their headsets was so loud it seemed like the missiles were just itching to fly.

At six miles out, Mother Goose had had enough. With his command structure in concurrence, "Magic and Hook you are cleared to fire. Repeat, cleared to engage."

"Magic copies. Two fall back and lock him up." The F-22 lead wanted to make sure there would be at least four in this gunfight if it came to it.

"Hook copies. Hook fire - NOW. Fox Two, repeat, Fox Two" "Fox Two" was the call that a heat seeking missile was in the air. If it had been one of the radar guided Amrams the call would have been "Fox One." "Fox Three" was the call for the gun, but most pilots simple said "guns, guns, guns." None of these calls were usually used for real in combat. They were used more on training missions to simulate the weapons engagement. The missiles left the rail almost simultaneously and streaked toward the F-16, 6000 feet ahead.

Solar saw the F-22s rapidly slow and fall back. He figured this was it. He trimmed up the jet, and reached down between his legs and pulled the ejection handle. His canopy flew off and the seat fired up the rails. He separated from the seat and immediately felt the tug as the parachute blossomed above him.

"Holy shit!" Hook one blurted out. "He just bailed out." Just then both missiles hit the aircraft and it blew into a thousand pieces, plummeting toward the river. "Kill! Repeat Kill!' Called Hook one.

"Mother Goose, Magic, I confirm the kill. The pilot's in a chute descending into the river. Most of the jet is in the river on the Anacostia side. "Holy Moly, there was just a huge secondary explosion. There looks like damage and fires near the Naval Air Station, even some across the river at Reagan Airport." The plastique that Solar had planted in the cockpit went off and blew destruction for about a one mile radius. Fortunately there weren't too many buildings in that radius, but there were hundreds of people in the open space areas on the north side of the river.

"Mother Goose copies Magic, see if you can monitor where the pilot comes down. Hook flight, cleared to recover at Andrews." The F-16s joined up and went home. The F-22s flew in a circular orbit staying out of traffic at Reagan Airport and watching the parachute descend into the river.

CHAPTER SIX

3000 FEET OVER COLORADO SPRINGS

Abdul Sadir was late. He knew it and he wondered about his brother. He knew that his brother had a mission to accomplish as well, but he had no idea it was the death blow he had delivered to the Navy. Cheyenne Mountain was on his nose. The huge gaping hole where the massive doors to protect the Air Defense Center inside were open - at least the outer set of doors were. There was no reason for the folks inside to think they were under attack. Besides, the inside doors were themselves massive 12 inch thick slabs of steel, and they remained closed at all times. Only a small man-way door was used for occupants to come and go.

On the way south from Buckley AFB Abdul had wired his cockpit with plastique explosives - so much so that there was barely room for him in the cockpit. He had it all in a small duffel bag stashed behind the throttle quadrant while flying the mission with his formation. But now he spread them around the cockpit and on the floor, and wired them all together. He flew basically down I-25 from Denver to Colorado Springs, passing over the Air Force Academy and the western parts of the City. He stayed out of the way of traffic using Colorado Springs Airport until he was abeam of the entrance to the Mountain. Then he turned an easy 270 degree turn to the left, ending up pointing directly at the doors to the mountain complex. When he rolled out of his turn he pushed the power up fo full, lit the afterburner and initiated the explosive sequence.

He held tight to the side stick controller as the jet accelerated and just before impact, closed his eyes.

The destruction inside Cheyenne Mountain was significant, but not total. The mountain was designed and built to take bomb and missile attacks, and although an F-16 loaded with explosives moving at 600 miles per hour was noisy and messy, it did not bring the mountain down. Because it was a Sunday, only a skeleton crew of air defense folks were on duty. The death toll was 34, with another 22 injured.

CHAPTER SEVEN

NEAR FE WARREN AFB, CHEYENNE, WYOMING

Leona Mir-So and Ali Jabara had watched their clocks religiously. Their time had come. They also knew that it would be a matter of time before the AF Security Police coming to get into their silo would break in. On one hand it would be better to wait until the Americans were in the complex before blowing their "surprise," inflicting more casualties. But they had a time table to follow. Their handler had given strict orders that their window to act was now.

They had wired the plastique together. They also activated self destruct mechanisms at their control positions, creating as much destruction as they could. They looked at each other one more time and Leona detonated the bombs. The destruction was as complete as it could be. The missile was melted down to almost nothing in its silo. The warhead was damaged significantly and the entire complex of control room, break room and periphery were in flames. The two Chechen born jihadists were cremated within seconds. Alarms went off all over the strategic forces system. FE Warren, Omaha, the Pentagon, and the White House knew what had happened within seconds.

To say the least, President James McDivitt was pissed. "What the hell is going on around here?" he asked his advisors when he got back up to the Situation Room. "We have a coup if you will in one of our missile holes, culminating in complete destruction, within minutes of some crazy guard F-16 jockey blowing himself to smithereens trying to get here to the White House. Can someone shed some light on this?"

"Mr. President, I'm afraid it's worse - a lot worse." Secretary of Defense Robert Lucroix reported. "One of our own F-18s, loaded for bear just dropped its bombs and then pulled a kamikaze attack on the USS Abraham Lincoln in the Gulf. The Lincoln is listing badly and the Captain has ordered "abandon ship." There are hundreds of sailors dead and thousands floundering in the water. Several Iranian gunboats attacked as well, all but two destroyed by the Lincoln's escorts, but two of them got through to provide the death blow by ramming the Lincoln and setting off explosives at the same time."

"Sir, we have another problem." Chief of Staff of the Air Force Michelle Porter had just arrived and just hung up her cell phone. "An F-16 broke out of the traffic pattern at Buckley AFB near Denver and flew down towards Colorado Springs. He is approaching Cheyenne Mountain now. The initial thinking was it was just a throttle jockey going for a joy ride, but in lieu of everything else today and the fact they can't raise the pilot on the radio, makes me think there will be another incident sir." a colonel came in and rushed to her seat and handed her another secure phone. Porter listened for a moment and said "All right. Keep me posted." She hung up and looked sheepishly at the President.

"Let me guess. An F-16 just turned itself into a missile and plowed into Cheyenne Mountain." The President said, hoping he wasn't correct.

The President sat quietly for an agonizing minute with the staff who had gathered nervously awaiting a typical "McDivitt exhibit" of temper and frustration. Then, "Mike, assemble the whole crew. Joint Chiefs, service chiefs, intelligence community, everybody. Since it's Sunday I suspect some will drag in slowly, but I want a thorough briefing on what we know on all these incidents in one hour. The President directed his Chief of Staff Mike Mulroney to round up the whole herd.

—

CHAPTER EIGHT

THE WHITE HOUSE SITUATION ROOM

The entire team of national security, minus a couple of key folks who were just too far away on a Sunday to respond, were gathered around the table in the White House Situation Room, many standing in the background. The primary players who were not in attendance were represented by their assistants or alternates. Everyone was staring at the multiple TV screens throughout the room, all tuned to the same channel - Al Jazeerah. The speaker was dressed all in black, but there was no ISIS flag or any evidence of who he was representing. None was to come either.

"President McDivitt, distinguished guests, and leaders from around the world, I come to you all with an announcement and a dire threat, not to be taken lightly." The man spoke perfect english with a midwest accent. He could have been speaking from Chicaqo. "Within the past few hours we have rained death and destruction down on the military of the United States, in Wyoming, in Colorado, in the Straits of Hormuz, and in the Potomac River, four miles from the White House." Scenes of Cheyenne Mountain on fire and the Abraham Lincoln just sinking beneath the sea accompanied the rhetoric. "You were very fortunate President McDivitt. The aircraft in the Potomac River was meant for your beautiful White House, but by some grace of Allah you were spared. We can only assume this was the case so you will be able to witness the rest of the destruction we have planned. We have people all over the world, imbedded in your military, your Defense Department, your civilian infrastructure. These people have only one goal and direction - to destroy America. For too long we have watched as you and your puppet Israel and NATO allies have brought inhumane and near total destruction to our homelands and our people. Whereas before we charged our friends from Al Quaeda and Daish to fight back, we are now taking command. There will be no mercy given as long as there are American troops anywhere in the Middle East, and as long as the state of Israel continues to exist. Consider those as terms - pull your troops out of our homelands, and dismantle the Israeli government. There will be no deadline established. We will continue our paths of destruction on your forces regardless, stopping only when our demands are met. You have not quite 24 hours before our next attack." The TV screens went black.

CHAPTER NINE

THE POTOMAC RIVER, ANACOSTIA ISLAND

Mohammed Solar survived the ejection and the fiery explosion of his F-16. His parachute deployed as advertised and he was able to guide it away from the burning, sinking wreckage and get free of the debris. He hit the water fairly hard and the initial shock of the Potomac water temperature in December took his breath away for a few seconds. This was one aspect of his mission he hadn't trained for, or even contemplated for that matter. He didn't really expect the Americans would allow him close enough to the White House to do any damage, but he really hadn't planned on how he would escape. As it turned out, he was fortunate in that because it was a cold day in December, and a Sunday at that, there were only a couple of boats on the water, and their occupants were too busy avoiding the fire and destruction that was raining on them from above to see a man in a parachute or subsequently, a man swimming for the shore. He became aware however of a fighter jet swooping down close and orbiting over his position.

Mohammed disconnected from the chute as soon as his feet hit the water. There was enough of a breeze that once loose, the parachute drifted a little downwind from him. He took quick stock of his surroundings and saw that he was about 50 yards off shore of the open space and park on Anacostia Island. There were willows and bushes on the shore and he swam for them to use for cover. It took a couple of minutes for him to cover the 50 or so yards to shore. He watched for anyone that might see him and swam quietly, basically using an easy breaststroke to create very little splash. He crawled into the bushes on shore and then just crouched there, shivering in the cold for a few minutes to be sure he was still undetected. He removed his flight jacket and flight suit. Under it he had worn a pair of jeans and a moisture wicking shirt. Although they were still quite wet, at least he didn't stand out as an Air Force pilot. When the F-22 overhead had departed and it seemed the coast was clear, Mohammed crawled out of the bushes and walked toward the end of the park, joining in where groups of tourists had formed to look at the wreckage and destruction. Eventually he got to the edge of the area, pulled out his cell phone and called for an Uber ride. A few minutes later an Uber driver showed up in a nondescript Toyota Camry. The driver could have passed as one of his countrymen, a middle easterner from Iraq as it turned out. Mohammed spoke only in english, using a little Italian accent, apologized for being wet, explaining that he had slipped running from the explosion. He had the driver take him to the motel he had stayed in before sneaking onto Andrews AFB.

Mohammed had the Uber driver stop short of the motel, tipped him $20 and went into a neighboring Starbucks initially, looking for any law enforcement personnel around the motel. Good thing too. There were county sheriff cars and a couple of big black SUVs parked in the motel parking lot, and Mohammed could see that there were swarms of agents in and around his room. He waited around with a leisurely cup of latte and then quietly departed, walking up the street away from the motel. He again took out his cell phone and called the one number he was told only to use in a dire emergency - his handler - the man who expected all of the people in this scenario to have died for the cause. The phone number was only given out to use if there were problems setting the missions up, not after the fact. However, the handler knew that to have a "loose canon" like Mohammed out there in the open could lead to the discovery of him and of the overall mission. He advised Mohammed to make his way to the Turkish Embassy in D.C. and gave him the number of a contact there. Mohammed decided to walk to the nearest Metro station and then took several subway trips around Washington, eventually getting off near the embassy.

He did a little shopping for a change of clothes and personal hygiene items, found a nearby hotel and settled in for a relaxing afternoon and evening. The television in his room was showing the results of the day's destruction around the world. Mohammed smiled and congratulated the "graduates" of Starkville on their successful missions. He would make contact at the embassy tomorrow, Monday.

———

CHAPTER TEN

THE WHITE HOUSE SITUATION ROOM

President James McDivitt was livid. He had just watched some unknown terrorist threaten the United States and the entire free world, and no one in his intelligence community could tell him even who this madman represented. "So who is this asshole? ISIS, Al Queada, some Mexican drug lord?" He asked his assembled so called experts.

"Sir, logically I would say he's ISIS, but he described them as his 'friends who had done the deeds of the past' and said 'THEY were taking command'." responded Richard Henry, the White House National Security Advisor. "He also didn't display the ISIS flag or any symbols of unity. ISIS typically likes to show off in these videos. By "taking command" we're thinking this guy represents the sponsor of all these groups - Iran?"

"What I don't understand is how did the Air Force and the Navy allow these pilots and missile operators get away with this? Were there no background checks done on these people? And what about this guy who just dumped one in the river here? Is he alive? Have we found him? Is anybody in this room working today?" The President was getting more and more agitated.

"Mr. President to your first question," General Porter, AF Chief of Staff responded, "I can't speak for the Navy, but I have people digging into the backgrounds of the pilots from Buckley and Andrews, and the two captains from FE Warren, the missile crews. We've called personnel folks in from all over - the Air National Guard, Strategic Command, the Guard Bureau and our Military Personnel center in San Antonio. We don't have anything yet, but I'm keeping them at work until we do."

"Ok Michelle. Thanks. Admiral Rogers, how about your F-18 pilot on the Lincoln?" The President looked at Admiral "Buck" Rogers, CNO of the Navy.

"We're working on it sir." the Admiral answered. "Our emphasis has been on recovery of the Lincoln's survivors and finding a place for her airborne jets to land. We have found one interesting fact though. It seems the pilot who we believe was flying the F-18 into the carrier has a twin brother who is stationed in the Buckley Air Guard in Colorado. We're trying to ascertain if the brother is the one who plowed into Cheyenne Mountain." He looked at the AF Chief, who just about came out of her seat.

"That's the first I've heard of this Admiral. Do you think maybe I might like to have known about this?" the general countered.

"Sorry Michelle. I just heard about it myself." the Admiral said defensively.

"Ok gang, hear me well." the President stood up and addressed the whole room, but looking especially at the heads of the Air Force and the Navy. "I assume you all were listening when this dickhead told us we have less than 24 hours until the next event. I don't want any petty territorial bullshit here. You'd better all be on the same team, working together and for one cause - to stop this maniac and whatever he has planned. Do I make myself clear?" There was a moderately enthusiastic, "Yes sir."

"Good. Now, where are we on finding this guy supposedly taking a swim in the Potomac. What have we discovered about his identity and do we have him in custody?" The President looked at his Chief of Staff.

"Sir, the alert pilots from Langley were not able to track him after he apparently swam ashore on Anacostia Island. We are checking all available cameras near there. The Andrews Security Police, the county sheriff, and now the FBI have converged on a motel we think he stayed at over the past couple of nights. The FBI has taken the lead. There is camera footage of a man crossing the street towards the Andrews fence.

A hole in the fence has been discovered with the weeds and bushes beaten down where it looks like he got on base. There is also footage and evidence showing he broke into the fighter squadron building night before last." Chief of Staff Mulroney relayed. "His room has been wiped clean of fingerprints, but the FBI crime scene folks are going through it with a fine tooth comb. We also have a pretty good face shot from the gas station camera" A shadowy figure photo appeared on the TVs in the room. "He looks to be mid-eastern or latino. We are running facial recognition investigations through Homeland Security and all local law enforcement agencies. We'll go out to Interpol, Mossad, and MI-6 as well."

"Ok. See if we can enhance that photo to something more recognizable and put it out on the web and to the media. We need to find this guy. Since by design none of the other perps survived their attack, we need to find out why he was any different and who's pulling the strings." The President stopped and pondered the situation for a minute. It was like a pregnant pause. Everyone wondered who was next to take it in the shorts. Finally, "Ok, every department head in this room do what you have to do to resolve this problem. Leave someone here to relay information or stay yourselves and get your staffs working the issue. I want an update every hour on the hour and I want you all back in this room for the 9 PM update. By then I expect full background checks and results on who these people were, where the attacker in the river is now, and our best guess as to who is pulling the strings here and what can we expect next." The President rose to leave, motioning for everyone to keep their seats. "Mike, I want you, CIA, FBI, SECDEF, General Adams and the Vice President in the Oval Office in ten minutes."

The White House Chief of Staff Mike Mulroney, Secretary of Defense Robert Lucroix, Director of Operations at the CIA Robinson Genoa, Chairman of the Joint Chiefs, Marine General Andrew Adams, and Director of the FBI Jon Bridges were all in the Oval Office, standing around nervously when the President walked in. "Ok, are we all here? Where's the Vice President?" He also looked curiously at Robby Genoa.

"Sir Vice President Valdez is enroute from Texas. She was in San Antonio for a charity event. And Mr. Robinson Genoa is here for Director Axel. Ms. Axel is inbound from Israel and a meeting with the Mossad." Mulroney explained a couple absences. "Mr. Genoa is the Chief of Ops at the CIA."

"Ok. No problem. Now folks, I want a clear course of action when we clear this room. I think it's time to activate and call in our Tango Team. Give them all the resources this country can provide, working out of this building initially, with only one thing in mind - to find, stop, defeat, and annihilate the enemy in this case. No due process will be adhered to. The Rules of Engagement will restrict no tactics. They will have a free hand to deploy any method of investigation, interrogation and operation necessary. They will not exist to anyone outside this room. You will give them everything they need to bring this enemy down. I want this team assembled in five hours." The President looked at Robby Genoa. "Mr. Genoa, if my memory serves me you were a Navy Seal. Is that correct?"

Genoa nodded, "Yes sir. I retired from the Navy four years ago, but I still train with the Seals and keep up to speed. In fact sir, we have three special operator teams that operate under the code name 'Viking' in our black ops program. One of them is allocated to Tango."

"Interesting. Never heard of Viking. But I guess that's a good thing. If I haven't heard of them maybe Congress and the media haven't either." The President sat behind the desk and looked hard at Robinson Genoa. "Mr. Genoa, you will lead this operation. Now everyone - get out of here and set about assembling Tango." The President rose and said, "Robbie, hang back a second."

The rest of the participants left the room. Even the Chief of Staff caught the hand signal from his boss - clear the room. Robbie Genoa stood at a relaxed parade rest, waiting for the President to speak.

"Robbie, what do you think? Any ideas before we get started?"

"Well sir, I believe it is critical that we find the pilot who dumped the jet in the Potomac. Hopefully he can lead us to his handler. Someone had to pulling the strings to make these attacks go off so close in time and or sequence." Genoa had done a lot of thinking about a plan already. "If we then can get to the handler, hopefully we can find out who is behind all of this. Tango has two of the best agents in the FBI. We'll also need their crime lab experts, and their long arm of the law. I believe you know Colonel Brad Mitchell, the wing commander at Andrews sir? He and his wife are also on Tango and will be extremely useful here. Mitchell was flying lead in the formation when his wingman departed and pulled the semi attack here today. More importantly though, Colonel Mitchell has a history with dealing with terrorists. He was shot down over North Korea back a few years ago during the attack on the North's nuclear facilities. You will remember we tried to rescue the UN weapons inspectors. I was one of the Seals on that mission. Mitchell successfully evaded the Koreans and made it to the shore where we pulled him and what was left of his team out via sub. He also has valuable flying experience and is knowledgeable about recovery operations. I think I'll want him on this team."

"Fine. I've met Colonel Mitchell - just about every time I land out at Andrews on Air Force One, he or his deputy always escort us to and from the aircraft. If I'm not mistaken, his wife Melanie is an ex-CIA operative? Is that why she is on Tango?"

"Yes sir. That is correct, though we have tried to keep her past under wraps. She too has some valuable skills we might use."

The President got up and escorted Genoa to the door. "Bring them all on board, and anyone else you need. See you in a few hours."

CHAPTER ELEVEN

9 PM, THE WHITE HOUSE SITUATION ROOM

The President entered and all who weren't standing already immediately got to their feet. The room was packed. All of the primaries had returned to Washington except the CIA Director who was still en route from Israel. The Vice President occupied the chair to the President's immediate left.

"Ok. Let's have it." The President commanded. "First, what's the status of the Lincoln's crew?." He looked at Admiral Rogers.

"Sir, they have all been picked up by the task force ships and choppers. A head count shows 4322 survivors, some in critical condition. That leaves 1217 killed or missing in action. Only a few bodies have been recovered. We will resume searches when the sun comes up, but we assume most went down with the ship. Sir, that includes Captain Rick Sutherland, the Skipper. He had shoved off the last life boat and had jumped overboard as the stern went under, but the crew in the life boats were not able to locate him." The CNO responded with an emotional finish.

"OK Buck, thanks." The President said. "Get me a list of names and next of kin and phone numbers. I will call everyone of them myself. What about casualties in Wyoming, Cheyenne Mountain and on the river?" The President looked at the Air Force Chief of Staff.

"Thirty four dead at the Mountain sir." General Porter replied. "With 22 injured. Only the two missile operators were killed in the

Wyoming silo. Apparently it was a suicide mission as well. There were about a dozen folks injured or burned slightly on Anacostia and the river, but none seriously. I'll get you names and numbers of the next of kin in Colorado Springs sir."

"Thanks Michelle. Carmen, I want you to fly out to Colorado tomorrow and visit all the injured there. Give them my regards and tell them I will be out to visit as soon as I can." The President said to the VP. "By the way, what is the status of Cheyenne Mountain? Is it functional?" He looked back at General Porter.

"We don't know yet sir. He started a pretty good forest fire that is also threatening homes in the area. Mandatory evacuations are in effect. Our best guess is that although most of the inside of the mountain will be intact, communications will likely be degraded." General Porter responded.

"Great!" The President quipped. "What's next? Carmen, plan on staying a few days and touch base with the firefighters and local shelters. Spread the good word."

"Ok. Where are we on finding our Potomac river rat?" The President looked around for who to ask first.

Jon Bridges, FBI Director spoke first. "We have him sort of surrounded sir, surveillance video…"

"Sort of surrounded? What the fuck does that mean?" The McDivitt temper flared.

"Sir, surveillance video showed a middle eastern or latino man in civilian clothes getting into an Uber car about 20 minutes after the pilots lost him. He was not in a flight suit, but he looked like he was wet. Capitol Park Police found his flight suit stashed in some willows where we think he got out of the water. Anyway, we were able to find the Uber driver, and he dropped his passenger off at a Starbucks across the highway from the motel where we think the pilot stayed. Later surveillance of cameras at the subway station nearby shows the same man boarding the Metro. He evidently stayed underground for about an hour or so, but then we got him surfacing at the Metro station near Embassy Row. Then we lost him. We are combing the area and Secretary Wisnewsky is polling the embassies?"

The President looked at the Secretary of State. "Any luck there Paul? Which embassies are near there anyway?'

"No luck so far sir and since it's a Sunday all I'm getting is lot of stonewalling and underlings preaching diplomatic immunity doctrine." The SECSTATE responded. "The closest embassy to the Metro station is Spain. France, Norway, Italy, Turkey and India are all within easy walking distance. We have surveillance set up with cameras on all the embassies and all of their entrances. If he's not already in one, we should see him go in."

"Ok, fine, but Jon get a couple quick reaction teams out there. We need to stop him BEFORE he enters an embassy for obvious reasons. Also, touch base with Robby Genoa and get a couple of his Tango Team members out there. He is down in the Vice President's office." The President looked at the VP. "Sorry Carmen, we have commandeered your office for a while." Vice President Valdez looked a little flustered but she knew better than to say anything other than, "Yes Mr. President."

The President rose. Everyone else did as well. He motioned for them to sit. "Stay seated. I have energized a smaller team of operatives to deal with this matter. Many of you know of them, most do not. Rest assured that if we deem your knowledge is necessary you will be brought into the loop. In the meantime you all need to stay working on this problem. We need to identify who the enemy is, where he is, and what he has planned next. Any ideas or clues you come up with should go directly to your principal who has access to the Tango Team. We need to also bend over backwards for the people hurt so far in this war. And let there be no doubt, WE ARE AT WAR! Anyone who talks to the media without my personally expressed ok will be fired and jailed immediately. I will deal with the Congress myself. Political Correctness is not a term I want bantered about here for now. Are there any questions?" The President looked directly at everyone in the room one by one.

"Good, Then - those of you who need to meet in the Vice President's conference room know who you are. Ten minutes." The room was very quiet as the president left.

CHAPTER TWELVE

WING COMMANDER'S HOUSE, ANDREWS AFB

Brad Mitchell got home about 6:30. He had been through the day's activities several times with everyone on his staff and more. He walked through the PE room at the 121st squadron, interviewed the crew chief who launched the rogue aircraft, surveyed the fence and squadron building break in damage, been briefed by is own security police and the FBI at the motel outside the gate. He debriefed the Air Defense Sector hierarchy as well as the Guard and Air Force chains of command. He had also been over at Johnny Hanes' house and visited with his wife and children for a while, leaving his own wife Melanie there to help out as much as one can help a grieving widow with little kids. He was tired, but more than that, he was pissed. Brad's own daughter, Kristi was home and she new something was going on. They ordered a pizza and Brad sat her down and told her what he knew. At 15 Kristi was a smart kid with her mom's looks and brains, and Brad's drive and ambition. The phone rang.

"Colonel Mitchell." he answered.

"Brad, this is General Porter. The President has activated the Tango Team. You and Melanie are needed at the White House as soon as possible. 2030 hours at the latest." the Chief of Staff of the Air Force said.

"Yes ma'am. Melanie is with the widow of our captain that was murdered today. I'll pick her up and we'll be there within an hour."

"UnnH!" the Chief uttered. "I forgot about that. If you need any help on that front let me know. Bring names and contact information for Mrs. Hanes as well. The President is going to want to visit with her."

Brad got off the phone and immediately called Melanie on her cell. She understood because along with being a wife and a mother, she is a professional. She arranged for the vice commander's wife to come over and help out at the Hanes' house. Brad talked to Leonard Wycoff, his Ops Group Commander and took Kristi to their place to spend the night before picking up Melanie at the Hanes' house. On the way he "shook the stick" of command to his Vice Commander, Colonel Jim McCall. Brad had a feeling he was going to be "out of pocket" for a while.

—

CHAPTER THIRTEEN

WHITE HOUSE OFFICE OF THE VICE PRESIDENT

Tango was assembled. All together there were 17 men and women from several walks of life, all having some experience in special operations, or at least a special talent necessary to conduct what was to be a massive manhunt and search and destroy mission. There were Navy SEALS, Army Rangers, Air Force special ops pilots and PJs, FBI, CIA, and Homeland Security personnel with unique and somewhat "dark" histories. There was a convicted computer hacker of world renowned talents, and there was Brad and Melanie Mitchell. At the head of the VP's conference table and in charge of it all was Robinson Genoa, Operations Director of the CIA.

"Ladies and Gentlemen, find a seat. We have a lot to cover before the President comes in." Genoa ordered. There was a bit of shuffling and confusion while those assembled tried to decide whether they or someone more senior need to be at the table or in the background. "Ok. That's the first thing we need to do, establish a pecking order." Genoa said. "There is no pecking order here. I am Tango One, and you all will be assigned call signs before we leave here tonight - or more like tomorrow morning. However, while we are in meetings together everyone will have an equal say and expected to participate as a peer with equal authority to speak. When we send a team out for a mission there will definitely be a team leader and a team hierarchy commensurate with the task at hand. So - to get started, I believe that all of you have a nickname or tactical call sign that you go by in your respective units. That's just the way it is in special ops. If for some reason you don't have a specific "handle" then make one up and you will go by that name in this operation. In fact, I don't want you to introduce yourselves to even one another by your real name. Only I and selected investigators at my disposal will know those names. I will use them to thoroughly vet everyone here and you all will be assigned top secret and above clearances immediately in order to get this job done. If in my vetting I find that someone in this room doesn't belong here, I'll take care of it. There will be absolutely no discussion or disclosure to anyone outside of this room about what we are doing, where we are going, or who we are with. That includes wives, husbands, mothers, or even bosses. I will take care of communicating with your bosses to be sure you're free to do the job. To that end then, I need you each to write down your name, call sign/nickname, social security number, and current place of employment and give it directly to me so I can get started on the vetting. In the meantime, let's go around the room and introduce yourselves with your call sign and unique talent for this special operation. My handle is "Columbus," ex-SEAL and current CIA." Robby nodded to the man seated next to him.

The attendees squirmed a bit in their seats, not used to any exposure, but went ahead.

"Cretin" CIA, ex-SEAL"

"Bingo" CIA, ex-Army"

"Nitro" CIA, Army explosives"

"Baldy" FBI, ex-SEAL" Baldy had hair in a braid halfway down his back.

"Hairy" FBI, ex-Air Force PJ" Hairy was pool cue bald, obviously a team mate of Baldy.

"Shooter" FBI, ex Army sniper."

"Longbow" FBI, ex Army Ranger sniper and medic." Longbow was also a gorgeous blonde.

"Geek" Best I could come with. I'm a convicted hacker on sorta .... loan?" Columbus nodded and smiled.

"Watchtower" Homeland Security computer gal." Also a female - about 35.

"Yusef" CIA Mid East Desk." Yusef looked the part - Iraqi descent.

"Jihad" CIA Mid East" She also looked the part, habib and all.

"Flygirl" Air America pilot." About a 40 year old African American woman.

"Red Baron" Her co-pil;ot" He nodded towards Flygirl.

"Conan" Air Guard F-16 pilot" Brad offered.

"Athena" Ex CIA, current wife and mom." Melanie added.

The last guy just sat there and looked at Columbus for guidance. He wasn't much of a talker and obviously had something to NOT share.

"We'll call you "Ebola" for this operation." Genoa explained. "That's all anyone needs to know. If and when we get to use Ebola's talents the appropriate team will be notified." Ebola was a "retired" professional assassin.

"All right, for right now, Cretin and Bingo, and Baldy and Hairy you all know about the investigation the FBI and local cops are into trying to identify and bring in the pilot of this afternoon's crash in the Potomac. I need you to leave right now and get down to Embassy Row and the Metro station, meet up with the FBI on scene commander and position yourselves near the Turkish and Indian embassies. Hopefully we can nab this guy before he goes in one of the embassies, assuming that's his intention, and assuming he isn't already there. At any and all cost, bring him in alive. Contact me directly and I'll tell you where to take him. Everyone in the room will now be issued the very latest in communication gear." As Columbus was speaking, Watchtower got up and handed out interesting looking cell phones - a little fatter than a current I-Phone, and with a couple more buttons on them.

"These phones are scramble secure satellite radios." Watchtower explained as she distributed them and a list of all the numbers and who got what to each member of Tango. "Suffice it to say they jump frequencies every second and will be synched up to whoever you are calling. They are the closest things anyone has ever come up with to a secure comm device. However, they do have GPS installed, but only if you turn it on with this small button on the bottom." She pointed out a typical on/off cell phone button. "So only turn it on if you want to be located. You guys leaving now, I'll go out with you and check you out completely. The rest of us will go over it later." Watchtower left the room then with Cretin, Bingo, Baldy and Hairy.

Genoa proceeded to bring everyone up to speed on the day's activities and where everything stood. He explained that they had been hand selected to work this problem, that they worked under direct authority of the President, and that there would be no holds barred and no expense withheld to defeat the enemy. "Let there be no doubt. This is a war. You only have to look at the footage of the Lincoln going down in the Gulf or the destruction at Cheyenne Mountain to understand that. Supposedly we have about 20 hours before the next 'event,' and we don't know where to look. That is also why some of you are here. Geek and Watchtower when she gets back in here, you need to be working now to identify the speaker of the video we all saw a few hours ago. You also need to do a top to bottom scrub of the backgrounds of these three pilots and two missile operators. Middle East folks, get in deep with your contacts to ferret out any traffic about who we're dealing with and what's next. Everyone else pitch in to help where you can." Right on cue, the door opened and the President walked in, followed by his top aides and brass. Genoa called the room to their feet.

"Please be seated folks and thanks for responding so quickly." The President greeted. "Unfortunately as I'm sure you are aware, we weren't quick enough and we are playing catch up with a deadly hot potato. Robby, is everyone up to speed?' He looked at Genoa.

"Yes sir and we just dispatched two two-man teams to the scene on Embassy Row. Sir, with all due respect to them, I need you to tell me who of the folks you have brought in here with you should be read into our operation." The cabinet secretaries and generals were a little put out, but looked at the President for his guidance.

"Good Point. Ladies and Gentlemen, this is the Tango Team." McDivitt waved his hand around the table. "Their leader is Mr. Genoa. None of you will be required to be in attendance for their operation unless it is for a meeting I have specifically called. However, CIA, FBI, NSA, SECDEF, SECSTATE, Homeland, and the Chairman of the

Joint Chiefs, need to understand that they will be operating within your realms of responsibility. They will have the full authority of my office and I expect you to give them the highest priority of cooperation. Let there be no mistake, some of what they do may not be either politically correct or even in accordance with the rules of war. That's why for example, the Attorney General is not in the room. There will be no such thing as a "war crime" committed. All methods of interrogation and persuasion will be on the table. That's all I'm going to say on that matter. Are there any questions?" Once again, the President looked everyone in the room directly in the eye. He paused for a second when he saw Jihad in her habib, Brad Mitchell with a hint of recognition, and Melanie. He paused for a long time when he looked at Ebola who stared back with cold, black eyes. The President almost shivered.

No one had any questions and the President dismissed all but Tango. Genoa went around the room and introduced each member by their call sign and their expertise. When he got to Ebola Genoa whispered in the President's ear. McDivitt nodded and shook the man's hand without saying anything. Ebola just nodded. Brad Mitchell was close enough to see Genoa mouth the word "assassin" in the President's ear.

"Good to meet you folks. I'm going to leave you to it now." The President started toward the door. "Robby, I'm going to do what's necessary to brief the Congress and then try and get a little sleep. However, if you capture our rogue pilot or come up with anything definitive as to who's behind this or what's next, have the Secret Service wake me up. Otherwise, let's get together about 6 AM."

CHAPTER FOURTEEN

———

TEMPELHOF AIRPORT, BERLIN, GERMANY

Barak El-Kamani deplaned from the Quatar Airlines 747 in Berlin. He had boarded at Dulles International outside Washington, flew tourist class to maintain as low a profile as possible. He checked luggage and carried a laptop on board, even though it was completely devoid of any communication pertaining to the last few days' activities or his real status in life. He collected his luggage, rented a car at the airport, and drove into the city, checking into a moderate hotel near the Banhof (train station). He made a point to pay for parking at the hotel and even had the bell hop unpack the suits and jackets in his luggage to hang them in the closet.

El-Kamani was the handler - the man in charge of the operation in America. His real job was the Chief of Operations for the Iranian Revolutionary Guard. He reported directly to the Ayatollah Khamanie in Tehran. He had full authority over the operation and his actions were fully sanctioned by the IRG and Tehran. He had travelled to the United States three months ago, surveyed his "targets" surreptitiously, set up his communications net, and made contact with the Starkville "graduates" who were to carry out his jihad. When the F-16 pilot stationed at Andrews screwed up and got involved with an American woman, El-Kamani was furious. He came close to terminating the man right then and there, but he realized that would throw a wrench into the whole plan if an investigation to the man's death uncovered any aspect of the mission. He simply reprimanded the "idiot" and ordered action back in Iran that would assure the man's silence. The IRG sent a team to his relatives' home, murdered his father and grandparents and took photos of his mother and sister being raped and sodomized, keeping them stowed away in an IRG operated prison. El-Kamani showed the photos of his dead family members and his mother and sister to the Starkville "alumnus," and issued a dire warning. Not only would he be killed, his mother and sister would join the rest of the family but only after a long and painful death.

El-Kamani went about unpacking his belongings except for a small kit of essentials, set up the room to look like he was definitely using it, changed into a dark turtle neck and slacks, and slipped out a back exit to the hotel, being careful to avoid any cameras that he could detect. He took a round about route to the central Bahnhof, and took a train to the northern city of Dresden. There he took a taxi into the city to one of the nicer hotels. He got out of the cab just short of the door and after the taxi drove on, he walked back the other way and ducked down the first alley. From there he made his way to a large parking garage near an office complex. He searched around while avoiding any cameras in the facility, looking for a nondescript car that was unlocked. He located an Opel sedan that was an ugly brown color and expertly hot wired it to start in just a few seconds. He drove out of the garage and out of the city toward the south. Destination - Spangdahlem AFB, an American air base in western Germany, just north of the Mosel River and near the Belgium border. Only then did he activate his communications gear and he called his team of operators in a small town outside of the base.

"Allah's will is ours to serve today." El Kamani spoke into the phone. Expecting no response, he paused, then hung up.

Four members of the Iranian Revolutionary Guard were holed up in a country house in a small village outside of Spangdahlem Air Base, and had been for a few days. Three of the men were of Chechen descent and were as German looking as the locals. The fourth was actually an East German who had been radicalized immediately after the Americans bombed Afghanistan in 2001. He had moved to Iran, joined the IRG and participated in a training program to indoctrinate the Chechens and others to the German language and customs. All four of the men had melted into the town, one actually finding a job as a mechanic at a local auto dealership, two others working as a waiters in local restaurants that catered to Americans on the base. Their situation was not all that unusual. American enlisted men often got together to rent houses off base to avoid life in the barracks on base.

When the call came in from their handler the fourth member immediately contacted the other three at work. The men made excuses to their bosses that they needed to take a break and then joined the fourth in their home. Two of the men changed into Air Force fatigue uniforms with the badges of Air Force firefighters. They also donned vests laden with C-4 and enough destructive capability to level a city block. The other two dressed as security policemen and they all immediately got into a car they had purchased earlier. In the car they had stashed their weapons in the lining of the roof - Air Force issued sidearms for security policemen and a German made long rifle with a powerful scope. They drove toward the base main gate. Because they were in uniform and had appropriate ID cards they were passed through the gate. At the security level the base was currently observing, vehicle searches were random and the luck of Allah was with them today. Even if they had been stopped, by common practice the car would possibly have been swept for explosives, but other than checking their ID cards, the men themselves would not have been searched. As it turned out, every U.S. military base in the world increased their security level about two hours later when the Pentagon came to work on Monday and the decision was made to beef up security in response to the threat issued over the weekend. Once again - luck was with the IRG.

Spangdahlem is a large base, housing the 52cnd Fighter Wing and three fighter squadrons. The squadrons are spread out up and down the runway complex, and nestled near one squadron was the Quick Reaction Force (QRF). The QRF was kept under wraps as much as possible. It consisted of 6 Tab Vee concrete igloo shelters, each with a fully armed F-16 Falcon with a B-61 nuclear bomb strapped to one wing pylon.

Until the early 1990s, when the Cold War was in full swing, the US and allies equipped several air bases in Europe with tactical nuclear weapons, each aimed at targets in and around the Soviet Union. Pilots sat "Nuke Alert" on two to three day stints to be able to get airborne in 15 minutes. The mission was a low level navigation flight avoiding defenses as much as possible and releasing the bomb from a climbing "loft" delivery. The idea was for the bomb to jettison in a climb, then descend with a parachute and detonate either on or above the surface. Immediately after the bomb released the pilot would make a swooping dive and turn of 180 degrees accelerating as fast as possible to escape the detonation. There supposedly was deconfliction from other nuclear detonations (NUDETS), although most of the pilots knew that this was probably a one way mission. Even if they did return through the bombs going off all around them safely, chances are their base of return wouldn't still be there. Everyone knew that the Soviets would respond in kind and the devastation would be catastrophic.

When the Berlin wall came down and the USSR folded, the Cold War officially "thawed," so to speak. Pacts and agreements were made and nuclear weapons were removed from Europe. The U.S. closed several bases in Germany, Spain and England, and consolidated their German air wings at Spangdahlem. Lakenheath Air Base in the United Kingdom, and Aviano in Italy were also kept active, but with only conventional weapons and flying training missions.

That was then, and the case until just within the last few years. When the Russians invaded Crimea and threatened Ukraine, the hawks in the U.S. Congress and the Pentagon came out of their nests. When the Russians moved in and helped Assad devastate his own country in Syria, and when the Russians were said the have interfered with U.S. elections, the hawks prevailed to a degree. Nuclear weapons were secretly moved back into to the European bases, and the Quick Reaction Force was reactivated. No one kidded themselves however. It is very difficult to move a bunch of nuclear weapons around and set up special activities without the inevitable intelligence apparatus of Russia's knowledge. Threats and accusations, and of course - denials were thrown about, but there were enough other distractions around the world to keep the politicians and diplomats busy. In fact, the Russians also had equipped some of their western bases with nukes. In the meantime, the two F-16 squadrons at Spangdahlem took turns manning the QRF with a fresh set of targets. They were scrambled for practice at least once on each shift up through engine start and ready to taxi before shutting down and retiring to their video games, movies and books. The "Victor Alert" sessions were a great time to study for correspondence courses in advanced and professional degrees.

The IRG members dropped off the two disguised as security policemen in a wooded area about a hundred yards from the closed gate on the taxiway out of the QRF that goes out to the runway. One set up there in the woods with his long rifle sighted in on the real security policeman sitting in a truck just outside the gate. The idea was that one of the fail-safes to a launch was that gate. The security police would have to get a real "go" message as well to open the gate. An F-16 is a powerful machine, but there was no way it could crash through a heavy chain link fence gate and not sustain major damage. The other member started a long crawl through the bushes and empty field as close as possible to the gate and truck. Then they both settled in to wait.

The two "firefighters" made their way over toward the Base Operations building, basically the Air Force version of a passenger terminal and the location of the base weather station and tower facility. They kept as low a profile as possible by driving around the block a couple times, mingling with the crowd at the local MacDonald's, and the Quick Stop convenience store, always staying in close proximity to Base Operations and the Base Exchange (BX).

Barak El-Kamani made his way down back roads to the Spangdahlem area and directly to the house his men had rented for the last few days. He entered and spent the next thirty minutes setting up an elaborate computer and communications center. Soon he had direct comm with Tehran, his men on the base, and Al Jazeerah. The muslim television station then had direct links to all the world's major news organizations and were standing by for the next "bomb" to drop.

—

CHAPTER FIFTEEN

WHITE HOUSE OFFICE OF THE VICE PRESIDENT

The President was somewhat refreshed. He'd managed about four hours of sleep after a longer than he wanted session with the Speaker of the House, the Senate Majority Leader and the two Minority Leaders of each house. Finger pointing and innuendos abounded, and finally President McDivitt got up from the meeting and in no uncertain terms told the politicians (at least the ones in the other party) to "Fuck Off!" He would handle the situation and let them in on what ever information HE deemed they should know. The opposition party members were flabbergasted that they weren't to be consulted prior to any retaliation. They knew enough though to not make a fuss about it in the press.

The meeting at 6 AM with Tango and then following with the full blown "War Council" had been somewhat enlightening. The FBI and Tango teams on Embassy Row had interviewed every hotel clerk in the general vicinity and had identified three suspicious clients in two of the hotels. Hotel clerks could not identify Mohammed Solar from the grainy metro photos or the composite the Uber driver had provided, but three solo men of mid-eastern or latino appearance struck a chord. A review of their guest list information revealed enough for a deep dive in the data bases to try and pin point identities. One of the men was legit, just a businessman from California in town for a conference. The other two were bogus names. One turned out to be a Spanish tennis player who was holed up in a hotel near the Spanish embassy where he was conducting a tryst with the Spanish ambassador's daughter, and using an alias for logical reasons. The third man however was an enigma. He had registered as Roberto Calas from Malta. FBI and Interpol files had no such man alive.

"So have we picked him up?" The President wanted to know.

"No sir. We thought it best to wait for him to move and see which embassy he goes for, if any." Columbus answered. "We believe we need a better ID on him and we want to be sure we can get to his contact. There's obviously someone who organized these four attacks - at least the three here on our soil, and we need to get to him. This pilot is only a minion."

"All right, but don't let him disappear into some embassy under the diplomatic immunity cover. What else do we have?" The President wanted a full dump of every bit of useful information.

Watchtower spoke up, maybe a little too soon for Genoa's liking, but she had the info that was pertinent. "Mr. President, we think we have uncovered at least where these people came from. They have all been serving in the Air Force or the Navy for several years. We obviously don't have anything yet on the F-16 pilot who dumped in the river, but the other five have interesting backgrounds. Their history in the U.S. go back into their high school days, but before that they never existed. Granted, kids don't usually have backgrounds to check, but their parents do. These folks' parents also just seemed to appear about the time their kids were in high school. The man in Wyoming was a football player in high school in Las Vegas. The woman graduated from the Air Force Academy and hails from Salt Lake City. We have tracked down their parents and have them in custody. They are Chechens, converted to Islam many years ago and their story is very interesting. The flyboy in Colorado was the twin brother of the Navy kamikaze pilot who took out the Lincoln. They both graduated from Purdue University and with ROTC entered the Air Force and Navy respectfully. Their mother is from Turkey, and their father is an African American running a printing business in Indianapolis."

"All three sets of parents are talking, though reluctantly. They are of course distraught over the apparent suicides of their children. However, the FBI office in Las Vegas was able to break the mother fairly quickly and the rest have at least not denied her information very vehemently. It seems they all came from a town in Iran with the western name of 'Starkville,' where they were trained and lived as Americans, learning our language perfectly, our customs, and our capitalist ways."

"Yeah. I heard about that earlier from your boss, Director Axel." The President reacted. "I understand the CIA has known about this place for a while and just not done anything about it. How big an operation is it? Do we have more of these imposters in our midst?"

"Sir, the particulars are above my pay grade, but we're working on it." Watchtower answered.

Genoa's high tech phone chirped. It was from Cretin keeping watch at the hotel off Embassy Row. "Columbus here."

"Columbus, Cretin. We have who we think might be our prime suspect on the move. He's dressed differently than last night, and right now he's entering a coffee shop. He seems pretty nervous. He's looking hard for any tails."

"Ok. Keep him in sight. Let me know when he moves."

Genoa briefed the President and the others on the activity. The President said to keep him informed and left for some breakfast. Twenty minutes later the White House chef and staff delivered eggs, ham, pancakes, fruit and pastries for the whole Tango Team. Courtesy of POTUS.

CHAPTER SIXTEEN

DAS BOG COFFEE SHOP, LANCASTER ROAD, WASHINGTON

As Mohammed Solar downed his muffin and coffee he scanned the Washington Post, pleased with the stories of the exploits of the day before. But in reality, he was scanning the scene outside. He was almost certain he had seen at least one person on his tail as he left the hotel. There seemed to be a lot of official looking cars in the neighborhood as well. He decided it was time to get off the streets and made his call to the Turkish embassy. He was directed to go around to the back entrance one block further south. His contact would be there to let him in. He folded up the paper, threw away his cup and trash and left the coffee shop crossing the street towards the embassies.

Cretin and Bingo and the two FBI agents with them saw their subject on the move and fanned out to follow from behind, the side, and in front. Bingo moved quickly up the block on the other side of the street and got in front of Solar by about a half block. He had a small mirror that can attach to a bicycle helmet looped over his ear, so he could see down the sidewalk behind him. Cretin called Baldy and Hairy to head their way and he called Columbus to report in.

"Boss, we've got him boxed in, but he knows we're on to him. He's not heading for the embassies. He's heading south, now turning up the block behind. We're behind the Italian and then the Turkish embassy. They have back doors but they look to be like service entrances." Cretin relayed to Columbus.

"My bet is Turkey, Cretin. Don't let him get that far. Take him." Genoa ordered.

Solar saw two men walking parallel to him on the other side of the road. Then suddenly a man ahead of him stopped and turned around, keeping one hand under his coat. Solar started running and pulled out his phone. Cretin started running as well, pulling out his weapon and yelled "Stop." The two agents across the street tried to head Solar off and Bingo crouched down beside a car with his gun aimed, yelling for Solar to stop.

Suddenly two armed military types ran out from the back of what was probably the Turkish embassy. They sprayed the two FBI agents in the middle of the street with automatic weapons, taking them both down. Solar initially hit the deck, then got up running full speed toward the soldiers. Bingo took down one of the soldiers with a shot to the leg. Cretin had closed to within 20 yards of Solar and the other soldier and saw that he had to keep going full speed to get to Solar before he reached the gate. The soldier leveled his weapon at Cretin and was about to fire when his head exploded. Baldy had rounded the corner 50 yards back, knelt down and squeezed off a perfect shot with his sniper carbine.

Cretin tackled Solar about 5 yards from the gate and had him pinned down, reaching for some flex cuffs when a man came out of the Embassy door with four Turkish marines, their guns leveled at Cretin and Bingo. "Let that man go. He is a Turkish citizen. He has diplomatic immunity." The Turk yelled.

"Unlucky!" Yelled Cretin as he stood Solar up, used him as a shield and backed away slowly. Meanwhile, Bingo and Baldy had come up and also backed out, guns aimed at the marines. "Believe me boys, you don't want a piece of this. Now go back in your little safe haven there and smoke some hashish and everything will be good."

Hairy drove up in a big black Suburban and Cretin threw Solar in the back. They stopped to tend to the two agents bleeding in the middle of the street, but didn't stay long. As soon as help arrived, Hairy broke all land speed records and they were gone.

Cretin called into Columbus, "Mission accomplished. Shit's in the bucket." Genoa directed him to a safe house in NW D.C. and went about determining who he wanted to do the interrogation.

CHAPTER SEVENTEEN

CIA SAFE HOUSE, NW WASHINGTON

Columbus approached the safe house with a team of three others. They all came in at different times and from different directions. With him were Yusef and Jihad, both from the CIA Mideast desk and Melanie Mitchell. Many of the Tango Team wondered what Melanie's part in all this was, but Yusef, Jihad and Columbus knew her background and Genoa had a special plan for her. Brad Richardson stayed back at the White House to work the other issues that Tango had going.

Melanie Mitchell was the daughter of an American pilot shot down during the Korean War and a Korean mother. Her father was Air Force Captain Mike Johnston. He had been shot down while flying a bombing mission near Yongbyon. He was injured in the bailout and was found by Melanie's mother and her Korean family. The captain was in severe pain and couldn't walk due to a compression of his spine from the ejection. The family hid him in their farm house and kept his presence from the North Korean army. Melanie's mother was 22 at the time and was assigned nursemaid duties. One thing led to another and they fell in love. Captain Johnston elected to "disappear" rather than return to the U.S. after the war. In fact, his dog tags were conveniently found near another crash site in 1975 during a U.N. sponsored search for remains. He was officially declared "Killed in Action" in 1976.

Melanie's mother and American father lived in hiding for twenty some years after the war. They had a room behind a false wall in the family farmhouse, and because of the American's injury, he could not get around very well anyway. Melanie was born in 1973 and she had a brother born a year later. Their father basically was a "house husband." He stayed home and took care of the children, as well as two other children belonging to Melanie's aunt. The women and healthy men folk in the household worked the farm and did outside chores. Mike Johnston took care of the home, only venturing out at night, and even then very cautiously. But the secret was too difficult to keep. Melanie and her brother obviously had foreign blood in them. Melanie was fairer skinned and had the round blue eyes of her father. Her brother looked even more American. He was blond. These unusual traits did not escape the neighbors, and when Melanie went to school, the authorities became very curious.

In 1979 a squad of North Korean "special police" broke into the family home and grabbed and tortured the family looking for information. They shot Melanie's grandfather and uncle and raped her mother and aunt. Melanie was in the back room with her father at the time. Her father heard the commotion and realized immediately what was happening. He shooed Melanie out the back of the house and told her to run, and he burst into the front room with a pitchfork, to try to rescue the rest of the family. Melanie stopped and watched through a window as her father impaled one officer and then was shot six times. He died instantly. The soldiers killed everyone else in the house except Melanie's towheaded brother. They scooped him up and took him with them as a prize for the night. Melanie stayed hidden until their trucks were out of sight. She was horrified and scared and completely alone in the world – a six year old Korean-American girl in a world where anything American was hateful and a desecration of the homeland. She ran.

The next farm was two miles away. The family had been very close to the Han family. In fact, they had all been together when the American jet came down. The Liu Hong Chun family had actually helped by delaying the search party while the Han family spirited Mike Johnston away. The word from the Hans was that the pilot had died that night, but Liu Hong Chun never really believed it. So when he saw Melanie peering in their window sobbing and crying, he had mixed emotions about what to do. But they brought her in and she told her story. Liu's wife cleaned Melanie up and fed her rice and porridge. The family discussed their options. If they turned Melanie in they too could be accused of collaboration. Melanie could implicate them just by claiming they helped her. The decision was easy. Liu's teenage son Lee Chun was dispatched to escort Melanie to the nearest seaport and to sneak her on a boat for China. They smeared Melanie's face with dirt and blackened her hair with tar. Her hair was mostly black anyway, but there were some light streaks in it – nothing like her towheaded brother, but an obvious feature not normally seen. Lee's mother packed up a container of rice and some dried meat and kimshee, and they all hugged and pushed the two travelers out the door.

Melanie and Lee made it to the coast in four days. They hid in the heavily forested terrain during the day and traveled at night. Lee found a fishing boat captain who for all the money that Liu Chun had given his son agreed to take Melanie across the Yellow Sea to China. It turns out the captain had other motives and between the two ports of call he and his crew repeatedly abused and molested Melanie. They dumped her off on a pier in a village just over the border from Kusong, North Korea, and sailed away.

Melanie's story from then on was almost as depressing and distressing. She was adopted by a family in China who saw her physical traits as an asset. They traveled with a small circus and Melanie was paraded around as a freak, painted with make up and her hair dyed blond to make her vaguely resemble Shirley Temple, the American child star someone had seen pictures of. When she was twelve, a wealthy Chinese aristocratic woman from Peking bought Melanie as a slave and took her to the big city to be her blond girl in waiting. There Melanie was spotted by a local pimp who convinced the mistress that Melanie was worth a lot more as a whore for middle eastern businessmen, and purchased her services for close to $100 dollars. Melanie was now 14. She was growing into a beautiful girl, tall and with high cheek bones – model like quality. She grew up in a hurry.

After surviving in this life for almost four years, Melanie decided she wanted out. She sweet talked one of her "clients" into taking her back to Iran with him. He was an executive with an Iranian oil conglomerate who had an apartment in Tehran where he worked, and a home two hours away where he lived with his wife and three kids. Melanie was his mistress in Tehran – at least for a while. During that time her sugar daddy educated and refined Melanie, and she learned four new languages. She already knew Korean and Mandarin Chinese. She became fluent in Farsi, and Urdu, and had a good command of English and Russian.

At 23 Melanie had had enough. One day she walked through the doors of the Swedish Consulate in Tehran and the rest is a much more pleasant, if still clandestine story. She was recruited in Stockholm by the American CIA as a language specialist and brought to Langley to work in the Middle East Branch. It soon became evident that with all her experience and her looks, Melanie had a "talent" for manipulating men. She moved rapidly through the training regimen and was out "in the field" in two years. She had been hardened by her experiences and was in excellent physical shape. At 5'8" she was tall for a Korean, and built like a Hollywood movie star. Men were hitting on her constantly, but she never had time. She had one rather torrid affair with a married co-worker. It ended up breaking up his marriage and several hearts, got him fired and Melanie reassigned to the Tokyo office. Through all this time Melanie kept one secret with her – who her father was. Even though the Agency tried to find out more about her background in their personnel screening, she was always able to deflect any questions, claiming her father was a German in Korea who disappeared and left her mother shortly after Melanie and her brother were born.

Six years ago Melanie was tapped by the CIA and defense department for a clandestine mission into North Korea. With her knowledge of the area and her spook background she was ideal to accompany a team of seals sent in to rescue six UN inspectors who were being held hostage in the nuclear laboratory facility where Kim Jong Un was secretly developing a nuclear weapon against the sanctions and agreements in place with the west. The mission was in conjunction with a raid on the facility by the U.S. Air Force and Navy. The facility was destroyed and unfortunately all but two of the hostages were killed, as were three of the SEAL Team. Brad Mitchell had led the raid as the Squadron Commander of the 80th TFS out of Kunsan AB, South Korea flying F-16s. In the attack Brad was shot down by a surface to air missile.

For the next week Melanie and the remaining Seals were able to pull Brad out of the jungle and with the two rescued hostages made their way to the coast where an American submarine was waiting just off shore. Because of Melanie's knowledge of the area, fluency in the language, and expertise as a CIA operative they were able to narrowly escape capture and get away without further losses.

That was the beginning of Brad Mitchell and Melanie's relationship. They were both brought back to the States and stationed in the D.C. area. One thing lead to another and they fell in love and got married less than a year later. Melanie "retired" from the CIA and they adopted Kristi, a beautiful 8 year old Asian-American girl whose parents had been killed in a car accident in Canada. Kristi looked a lot like Melanie and most folks never knew she was adopted.

Melanie kept her hand in the spook business periodically, accepting special assignments in the Middle East, though managing to only be away from home for a few days at a time. She adapted well to the Air Force wife way of life, and was a perfect "Mrs. Wing Commander" at Brad's side, especially when the President and First Lady came through the base to and from the White House on Air Force One.

This morning Melanie was dressed head to toe as a muslim woman, cloaked in a black robe with a hijab over her head and face and with only her eyes visible. After Cretin, Bingo and the FBI guys had their turn trying to get information out of Solar, Genoa sent Melanie in the room alone. Melanie turned into anything but the sweet, kind wing commander's wife. She became Mohammed Solar's worst nightmare. In perfect Farsi she asked, "What is your name Infidel?"

"I spit on you woman." Solar reacted. "You are the infidel or worse. You are a whore for the Americans and a disgrace to the homeland and to Allah."

That's about how it went for the next twenty minutes. Solar was saying nothing and Melanie could almost feel the glare of Genoa's stare through the one way glass as he watched the proceedings. She knew there wasn't much time and she was going to have to step up the technique. Cretin and Bingo did have a little success before Melanie and the others got there. They were able through facial recognition get a hit on Solar as they ran it through Interpol. It seems the Turks did a background check on him when they accepted Solar as a student in their F-16 training session. They had made a mistake though and had not hidden the photo or intel from their regular participation in NATO intelligence sharing. Within an hour of his capture, Tango had Solar's name and enough background information to know he came from Shiraz, Iran where he was an Iranian Air Force fighter pilot. From photo analysis in Iran and Syria, he was identified as a probable member of the Iranian Revolutionary Guard. It was also established that he had a home in the suburbs of Shiraz where his wife, two small children, and elderly parents lived. Melanie was given copies of satellite photos of the house and though a bit grainy, what looked to be his kids and wife outside in the yard.

"I know what your name is Mohammed." Melanie sneered. "I also know where you live, where your family is and what you do for a job." She laid the photos down in front of him and Solar looked at them with only a bit of surprise. "Nice family. Too bad they will die today."

Solar looked up at Melanie and just spit at her, calling her a bitch and a whore. With lighting speed Melanie was on him like stink on shit. His wrists and ankles were chained to the chair, so he couldn't have reacted even if he had time. Melanie brought one knee down into Solar's crotch and basically straddled him as she brought a wicked looking curved knife out from under her robe and stuck it into Solar's right nostril.

"This bitch and this whore will be the last person you ever see Mohammed unless you tell me right now who is your handler and where he is? How many more are there like you in America?"

"Fuck you." Solar said in Farsi. At least that's the closest translation. Literally the words had something to do with sex with a pig. He was bleeding profusely from his nose, so he gathered up spit and blood and let a big wad fly toward this she devil making his life miserable.

Melanie deftly dodged the spittle, slammed the knife point first into Solar's right hand, driving it all the way through and into the chair arm. She left it there and went over to a nearby television set on a stand that Solar could see. She turned the TV on and stood back. A picture came on that was obviously taken from an airborne camera. It showed the city of Shiraz from thousands of feet above. It then zoomed in and as the track moved on to the outskirts of the city, it zeroed in on the house in the photo in front of Solar. His house, with his kids playing in the yard. He could even see what looked like his wife standing in the doorway watching the kids.

"This is live video from a U.S. Reaper drone. It is armed with two very destructive Hellcat missiles and it is closing in on your family. If you do not tell me what I want to know, your entire family and home will be reduced to ashes and rubble. Now - who and where is your contact here in America?"

Solar stared for a long time at the video, but then closed his eyes. He seemed to be muttering a prayer. "You will get nothing from me except the promise that I will kill you personally when the wrath of Allah breaks up this little party of yours."

They stared at each other for at least a minute, neither one flinching or blinking. Then Melanie went over to the TV, pushed a button on what looked like a speaker and said "Fire one Captain."

There was a hesitation for a split second and then the video shook, more like a tremble for a second, and the exhaust trail of a missile came out from below and streaked toward the target. The drone was being piloted by an Air Force pilot at a base in the Nevada dessert with direct communication to the safe house. Solar watched in horror, but then realized the video target had switched to the house next door. Four seconds later the house exploded in a fiery ball and as the drone banked into a turn, the camera tracked as the debris settled to the ground in a crater where once there was a house. Abruptly the camera switched back and zoomed in on Solar's house. He could see the kids running to get indoors and their mother ushering them inside.

"Oops." Melanie said. "I guess we missed. Well, not to worry, we have one more missile. It is actually too bad the children went inside. If they were outside when the missile strikes they may actually survive an indirect hit. Now …. so sorry."

"One last time Mohammed. Who and where is your handler?" Melanie walked back up to the TV and put her hand on the microphone button, ready to initiate the launch.

"Wait!" Mohammed screamed. "If I tell you, what happens to me and my family?"

"Your family lives to help the next door neighbor rebuild what's left of his life. You? I don't know, but I believe the American government might go a little light on you for dumping a multi-million dollar jet into the Potomac River, IF your information pans out. You might even be offered some sort of immunity and a new life in the U.S. No guarantees though. I'd just as soon see you suffer and watch your family go up in flames." Melanie put her finger on the mic switch again.

"Ok. OK. I'll tell you what I know."

Genoa came into the room and nodded to Melanie. She sat and basically translated. Though obviously Solar spoke perfect english, he reverted back to Farsi once in a while. He was very nervous, almost like he was expecting the wrath of Allah to rain down on him with every word. He identified his handler as Barak El-Kamani, a big muckety-muck in the IRG. He didn't know how many other Starkville graduates or replacements like himself there were, but he suspected five or six. He knew that the next big event was to take place in Germany, so he guessed that may be where El-Kamani is.

Melanie walked to the microphone, pushed the button and said "Captain, abort the run but stay on scene. Make sure your drone is replaced when you have to recover. We may need your help yet." Melanie looked hard at Solar and hopefully he got the message. His information had better be accurate or he was soon to become a childless bachelor.

—

CHAPTER EIGHTEEN

ANDREWS AFB, MARYLAND

Tango was deployed without anyone really knowing where they were going or even where they should go. FlyGirl and Red Baron were sent out to Andrews earlier to get the CIA's Gulfstream V ready to fly. As soon as Genoa and Melanie reported back the news about Germany, the thinking was something was going to go down there, and lacking any other evidence to the contrary, whatever the next "Big Event" was might just be some sort of activity in Germany. The President happened to be in the VP's conference room when the call came in from the safe house, and although he was nervous about something else taking place on American soil, he agreed that at least Tango should send a small team to Germany to be on site when or if something happened.

Brad Mitchell (Conan), Nitro (Army explosives), Shooter (sniper), and Ebola (the assassin) were dispatched to Andrews. Cretin and Jihad met them there direct from the safe house. Cretin was the designated team leader. They climbed aboard the luxury "private" jet, settled into the plush seats, and were airborne within minutes. Originally their flight plan showed Frankfurt, Germany as their destination, But everyone hoped there would be more narrowing down of the target and the mission before they actually made it to Europe. That's where Geek and Watchtower made their money back in the White House in front of their computer screens.

The first revelation came within about an hour. Geek hacked into the computer system of a domestic affairs office of the Revolutionary Guard. It was actually an easy task - easier at least than trying to get into the foreign and intelligence affairs system of the IRG. There the Guard had employed the top of the line cyber security and although not impossible, it was much more difficult to dive into than their domestic affairs. What Geek found was a lot of communication and support connected to what turned out to be Starkville, the Iranian town dedicated to training the infiltrators that had caused much of the day's damage. Records showed supplies delivered that were strange, to say the least for an Iranian town. Food, clothing, school books, automobiles, music, even movies were being delivered to an IRG outpost identified only as Site #626, located out in the desert about 100 miles southwest of Tehran. The CIA had ferreted out much of this information already, but as is so typical within the American intelligence community, they hadn't seen fit to let anyone else know about it. It was as if the Iranian government was outfitting a normal town in America with refrigerator trucks, auto transport trucks, and deliveries that looked like Amazon Prime. Based on the information gleaned from Mohammed Solar, and information the CIA had provided, the site was identified as Starkville with at least an 80% level of confidence. Drone surveillance confirmed - it was a typical "American" suburban town.

Geek was also able to hack into the computer system at Starkville itself, in particular personnel records and the comings and goings of the "students" and trainees. It seems that Starkville has been in existence for at least 20 years. Dozens of recruits were brought in when they were children from the ages of 10 to 14. In most cases they were matched up with "parents" in their mid twenties, early thirties. They lived together as American families, going to school, playing American football, baseball, acting in school plays and playing in the bands. The parents as well learned skills that would place them well in American society. They became auto mechanics, engineers, teachers, maids, chefs, even policemen and firemen. After three to four years the families were moved out, presumably to their new lives. A deeper dig into passport and visa records, as well as customs accounts, was able to identify as many as 20 "families" that had re-located in the west. Not all were in the U.S. There were three families living in Israel, others in Britain, France, and Australia. Eight families had relocated to the U.S. One was the Crawley family in Indianapolis who had spawned Rod Crawley, otherwise known as Abdul Sadir, and his twin brother Mike, known in his homeland as Mustafa Sadir. They were the two kamikaze pilots - one hit the USS Lincoln, the other Cheyenne Mountain. Their parents were picked up immediately when the pilots were identified - first with the deepest sympathies of the U.S. Government. But when it became obvious this was a coordinated attack, both the Crawley parents were taken into custody and thoroughly grilled for their part in this debacle.

The parents of Mary Cogswell (Leona Mir-So) were brought in to the FBI office in Salt Lake City, and the mother of Joe McMann (Ali Jabara) was being questioned in Las Vegas. Again sympathies were offered because their children had perished in an explosion and fire in the missile silo they were manning. Further investigation revealed the parents were part of the scheme all along. Jabara's father had actually flown the coop out the back door when he saw the FBI drive up to their house. That actually turned out to be a major turning point in the overall investigation.

Maliah Jabara was genuinely distraught when she realized what her son had done. Through the years she had played her role maybe too well. She had come to love Ali as her own and even tried to make the marriage to his father a true American love story. For a while it had worked. They had even had another child after setting up house in Las Vegas. Ali too seemed to have been enthralled with having a younger brother to share his life with. However, lately as the time for the action neared, Ali stopped calling home from his base in Wyoming, did not come home for Thanksgiving as he had in previous years, and basically stopped all communications, at least with his mother. When Maliah tried to talk to her husband about it he became irate and even physical. He slapped Maliah around and told her to just shut up and remember what their mission was. When he boogied out the backdoor when the authorities arrived, Maliah was distraught and a little bit pissed. It took only about 30 minutes for the FBI interrogators to break her down, and when they did she shared an abundance of information that was helpful.

Maliah Jabara was able to identify five of the other "families" in the U.S. that had come from Starkville. One family lived in Atlanta and both father and son worked for Delta Airlines - father as an engine mechanic, and the son as a copilot in the Boeing 767. Another family lived in Lynchburg, Tennessee and their son was an engineer with the Tennessee Valley Authority where he was responsible for dam safety. A third family lived in Sacramento where father and daughter worked for California Power and Gas (CP&G). A fourth family lived in Pittsburgh where the father was a steelworker and the mother a nurse. Finally, the fifth family also lived in Las Vegas. They had been close friends of the Jabaras through the years. Their one child had been killed in an automobile accident shortly after arriving in the states, but the father had worked through the ranks and was a captain in the LVPD. His name was Naresh Hadad, or James Montgomery to the Las Vegas cops.

Maliah's best nugget of intel as far as the Tango Team was concerned was that she had overheard her husband on the phone two nights ago. He was in a heated discussion with whom Maliah assumed was a superior. Her husband had volunteered to go to Germany for what he phrased as "the next phase of the operation." She did not understand what the "phase" might be, and the caller obviously shut down her husband and his wishes. She did however pick up one vital piece of information. Her husband mentioned "the air base" and offered that since he worked on Nellis AFB in Las Vegas, he would have a good knowledge of what needed to be done. Milo Jabara was a civilian firefighter at the Nellis Air Force Base fire department. The person on the other end of the call had apparently denied Milo's request, but Maliah thought he passed on more instructions to her husband. Milo had listened for a long time, then said "Are you sure Naresh can be trusted?" Once again she could tell from her husband's reaction the caller was not happy. Finally her husband simply said "Yes Barak. We will succeed, and let the will of Allah be with you as well." When Maliah had quizzed her husband what the call was all about he struck with his open palm across her face and told her to mind her own business and get out of the room.

CHAPTER NINETEEN

—

OVER THE ATLANTIC OCEAN

Brad and the rest of the deployed Tango Team were catching up on some sleep and had indulged in some of the gourmet food and vintage whiskey the CIA stocked in their Gulfstreams. Cretin got a call from Columbus and woke up the rest of the team to assemble in a lounge in the back of the jet where a Skype system was set up.

"Guys, we have a little info from one of the parents of the explosion in Wyoming. It is very likely that El-Kamani is heading into Germany and to what was overheard as "an air base." Genoa briefed. "We also have found out that there are many more of these families spread around the world who are hell bent on destruction of us and our allies. We're taking care of that part on our end, but we need to narrow down your search. Germany is not one of the countries they have infiltrated, but that doesn't mean they aren't a target. However, the President has brought the German Prime Minister into the loop, and we hope that they can take care of themselves."

"Brad, correct me if I'm wrong, but your boss General Porter says there are three Air Force installations in Germany - Ramstein and Spangdahlen Air Bases and the Landstuhl Hospital, is that right?

"Yes sir. That's correct, though Landstuhl is actually an Army installation. I think the Army has some other facilities in country as well sir." Brad answered.

"So, do you have any thoughts as to what might be the target? Let's not forget guys, we're down to hours now." Genoa cautioned.

Brad thought a minute, then "Sir, They could probably make the biggest splash in the headlines if they take out Landstuhl, especially if we have a lot of patients there. Ramstein is a big base, but probably not as significant as Spangdahlem. We've got three squadrons of fighters at Spang and a nuclear armory. Since the father said something on the phone about an "air base" my guess is it's not Landstuhl, and of the other two, I'd concentrate on Spangdahlem."

"Good point." Columbus came back. "I understand the wing commander is an old friend of yours. I'll brief him in to assist."

"Yes sir. Colonel Kerry Day was my Operations Officer on the raid into North Korea." Brad acknowledged.

"Great! In the meantime I have briefed the German Bundestag Intelligence Minister. He is spearheading the protection of their homeland and he's also working on tracking El-Kamani since he landed in country. We've managed to track him to Berlin and on a train to Dresden. Then we've lost him. The Germans are still looking with Geek and Watchtower riding herd. Good luck on your end." Genoa signed off. "Let me know when you are in position."

Cretin went up to the cockpit to relay the news to Fl;yGirl and they amended their flight plan to land at Spangdahlem Air Base. They touched down about 90 minutes later.

CHAPTER TWENTY

ATLANTA, LYNCHBURG, SACRAMENTO, PITTSBURG, LAS VEGAS

FBI and local authorities were dispatched to the homes and workplaces of the Starkville families reported to be in the U.S. In the cases of the Delta mechanic and pilot son living in Atlanta their apprehension was easy. The son was on a furlough between flights. The father was picked up at Hartsfield International Airport and he surrendered peacefully. A search of their home found explosives and bomb making materials with a pressure cooker bomb that looked like it was ready to go. There was also an explosive vest that conveniently fit the son, the Delta pilot, perfectly. Intense interrogation, aided by the lie that they were given up by their own people in Tehran, revealed that their timeline was targeted for Wednesday - two days from now. The father was to place the bomb and detonate it in the wheel well of a Delta aircraft just before it was to be pushed out for engine start and taxi. Two hundred and fifty passengers, crew and ground crew would have been killed or injured. The son's task was to attempt to hijack the aircraft he was copiloting on that day to Washington. The plan was for him to take over the cockpit when the captain took a potty break, kill the flight attendant who replaced the pilot in the cockpit while he was gone, and fly the jet into the U.S. Capitol building in D.C. If anything went wrong he was to detonate the explosive laden vest he was wearing and bring the jet down with close to 300 folks on board. They were fairly easy to break in interrogation. The FBI had them convinced that they had captured their handler Barak El-Kamani and he had spilled the beans on his "sheep." At first the son would not believe what the authorities were telling him, but when it was pointed out that all of the Starkville graduates had been identified by El-Kamani (true or not), he caved.

In Lynchburg, Tennessee, the home of the upstanding citizens of the community was raided and again an immense amount of explosives and detonating devices were discovered. It turned out that their task was also to be accomplished in two days, and the target was the largest dam in the Tennessee Valley Authority system. Its breach would bring death and destruction downstream that would rival the Johnstown, Pennsylvania flood of years ago. There was no confession by anyone in the family - only resistance and hostility. But the event was successfully diverted.

The raid in Sacramento resulted in the same way. No confessions, but a home filled with C-4 explosives rigged in a dozen or so devices designed to take out the gas and power structure of the California Gas & Power Authority. Again, the timetable pointed to Wednesday.

It was apparent that although something was supposed to happen within a few hours on Monday, based on the original threat, the next phase was for two days later. At least that seemed to be the plan for incidents in the United States. Genoa reminded everyone and the President and SECSTATE that there were cells in Israel, Britain and Australia. No on knew their schedule.

Pittsburgh was a little different. The Mustan family had lived there in their same neighborhood for 15 years. Golan Mustan worked as a steelworker in one of the two mills still in production in the "steel city." His wife was a nurse in Pittsburgh's biggest hospital. They were good, upstanding citizens as far as their neighbors and co-workers knew. They had originally come from Turkey, and about one week ago they left for a vacation back to Istanbul. Questioning of their neighbors and friends revealed that they had a son who was an outstanding soccer player in high school and at Penn State. After graduation he had entered the Navy and went through pilot training in Pensacola. One neighbor thought that within the last three years young Robert Mustan had moved over to the Air Force on a pilot exchange tour and was stationed somewhere in Germany. The puzzling thing about it all was the shape their home was in when the FBI and local police broke in. It was if they had left in a very big hurry. There were dirty dishes on the table, luggage in a store room, their computer was even left on. It did not look like someone who had left for a planned vacation, rather they had left very quickly, like maybe they knew what their son had in mind in his job at the Air Force base in Germany. Their car was tracked to the airport and parked in the short term lot. They had taken a flight out to Paris. From there they disappeared.

The fifth family not involved in the Monday activity was that of the police captain in Las Vegas. The FBI raided his home, but his wife was home alone. She reported that her husband was at work. However, in fact he had never showed up for work today and his co-workers had no idea where he was. An immediate all points bulletin was put out, and as far as the LVPD knew, one of their own was missing.

Milo Jabara had escaped from the raid on his house just in time and he had watched from a desert area near his home while the authorities searched for him and interrogated his wife. He stayed on foot and was able to evade the road blocks, eventually reaching a coffee shop about 6 blocks away from his home. He got on his phone and called Naresh Hadad, known in Las Vegas as James Montgomery, LVPD police captain. Naresh answered his cell on the first ring. It was a call that he had expected for many years. In fact, he was always optimistic that his turn would come. Since the death of his son after they arrived in Las Vegas from Iran, the IRG has basically put Haresh out to pasture. Minimum contact that he had with Barak El-Kamani had at first brought him very little satisfaction. Finally he was given a job to put together with Milo Jabari, his good friend.

"Milo. My brother, what is happening?" Naresh asked

"Naresh, we must meet. My son has performed his duty and the authorities have raided my house. I talked to our big brother. He has instructed us to follow up with our plan tomorrow evening. He has left the country and phase two of the larger plan will happen tonight in Germany. We are phase three. Are you prepared for this? Are you up for this?" Milo had his doubts about the police captain.

"Yes, of course." Naresh responded. "But I just got a call from my wife. The FBI and my own men are searching for me. We need to go underground until it is time."

"I agree Naresh. Let us meet at the Northwest Mosque." Milo suggested. "The Imam will keep us safe until we need to move. Do you have access to the explosives?"

"Yes. I will need some help with them. Meet me at the U-Store It place on Lincoln Avenue, just beyond the intersection with Desert Boulevard. Are you in uniform?"

"Yes. Of course." Milo answered. "I can be there in twenty minutes."

Naresh and Milo met at a public storage facility and Naresh opened the garage size unit he had rented and equipped. It was equipped with a new Ford Explorer baring the paint job and logos of the Las Vegas Police Department. But the paint job was the only thing this vehicle had in common with the rest pf the LVPD fleet. Inside it was loaded and wired with enough C-4 and fertilizer to blow a hole in the desert big enough to build two or three new mega-casinos. They drove the truck on back streets and were able to park it in a garage owned by the Imam at the Northwest Las Vegas Islamic Center, a mosque where they prayed together at least twice a week.

CHAPTER TWENTY ONE

—

SPANGDAHLEM AIR BASE, GERMANY

The Gulfstream touched down as smooth as silk and taxied quickly to a desolate corner of the base. When Brad and the team emerged from the jet the Wing Commander and about a dozen Air Force security police were there to greet them.

"Conan!" The Wing Commander yelled. "I didn't believe it was really going to be you. What are you doing so far away from your cush guard job, and who are these characters with you?" Logically so, the appearance of Ebola, dressed in black sweats and a hoodie, with a full beard, along with the rest of the team not a whole lot less grungy looking, it was enough to raise the eyebrows of any spit and polished Air Force wing commander and a select team of cops. Mitchell was dressed in a flight suit, and Nitro, Jihad and Shooter were in military fatigues. Cretin was in civies - jeans and sweats. All of them looked rough and deadly serious.

"K-Day. Good to see you. I wish it were under better circumstances. I understand you were briefed by our boss on what we're doing here?" Mitchell responded.

"Yeah, sort of. All I got was that you were inbound with a team of folks looking for some bad guys maybe trying to extend the activities of yesterday in the states." Colonel Day said. "That certainly got my attention, but I've gotta tell you, I'm puzzled. Why here? Why us? There's gotta be a lot bigger targets for them to make their splash. And seriously, who are these guys?" Day looked and started to point toward Ebola. But when the assassin met his look with a stare of his own, the colonel diverted his gaze.

"K-Day, you ever heard the term 'if I tell you I have to kill you?' Well, take it literally in this case. I won't kill you, but he certainly could." Conan answered in a whisper while tilting his head toward Ebola. He beckoned for Cretin to join them. "Colonel Day, this is Cretin. Kerry you understand callsigns. In our case we use them because no one has a 'need to know' real names and data. Cretin is our team leader on this operation."

"Ok. 'nuff said. Cretin - good to meet you." Colonel Day said as he shook Cretin's hand. "Where do you want to start."

"I don't really know. Is there anything going on tonight - celebration? Gathering of folks?" Cretin asked.

"No man, it's a Monday evening. Things are pretty quiet. We had a Christmas bazaar over the weekend at the club, but that's over and most folks are resting from the weekend. We have one F-16 squadron deployed to Zaragoza, Spain for training during our shitty weather winters here. Half of our A-10 squadron is in the desert for their normal rotation. Otherwise, nothin' happenin'?"

"Ok. So where are the most crowds? What's the part of the base with the densest population?" Cretin asked

"I guess it would be the Base Operations and what you could call the 'commercial' part of the base." Day responded. "The base exchange, commissary, all ranks club, gas station and convenience store, recreation center and Base Operations are all there in about a three block span. There's also a McDonalds and the dining hall close by. In fact, it's always bothered me that all of that is crammed in together. It's a traffic nightmare a lot of the time. It's all relative though. Nothing like the traffic you have in the D.C. area. Mondays are probably our least populous days here though, because the commissary is closed. I assume that because you are asking that, you believe the target is the populous. Should I be evacuating folks?"

"No. Not yet at least. We don't even know if your base is the right place. Hell, we don't even know if Germany is the right place. All we know is that one of the principals in this agenda was heading this way. Last known location all the way up north in Dresden. No, we'll simply have to set up and spread out a bit and look for anything unusual." Cretin said, then gathered the team around them.

"Shooter, position yourself in some high location where you can look over the most of the populated area. Nitro and Jihad, you all are in uniform so stick together and wander the area. Ebola, you're with me. Colonel, we need to borrow one of your humvees and we'll position ourselves in the center of the parking lot." Cretin dealt out the assignments. "Conan, why don't you stay with your buddy here and just keep a lookout." Cretin pointed to the wing commander as "Conan's buddy." Not exactly an enamoring description of the Wing King, but with the seriousness of the tone of conversation, neither Day or Brad were bothered.

"Ok. Move out. Check in on comm every 15 minutes. If the threat we got on video is correct, we have no more than 4 hours to wait."

CHAPTER TWENTY TWO

SPANGDAHLEM AIR BASE, GERMANY

The Iranian Revolutionary Guard had a very good cyber hacking program. Although they could not hack into the European command structure launch system, they were able to enter the practice scramble schedule of the United States Air Forces Europe (USAFE) command and control center. The practice scenarios were somewhat predictable. Although the system was set up to practice a scramble each and every shift of the alert force, there was some semblance of civility to it. They usually did not blow the horn during dinner or church time, and they limited the middle of the night scrambles to about one a month. The IRG had a timeline they wanted to follow to back up their threat to the U.S. President and the rest of the world. They wanted the next surprise to happen by about 6 PM Monday night. So, the hackers set up a scramble order for 4:35 PM, Central European time. The word was passed through the communications net El-Kamani had set up, and he passed it on to his "soldiers" at their posts on Spangdahlem Air Base.

"Your families will be honored and taken care of for the rest of their lives my brothers." El-Kamani said to his two men parked in their truck near the base commercial complex. "You are heroes and you will be welcomed in the afterlife and seated at the side of Allah. I respect and envy you." El-Kamani signed out with his men and waited for the next apocalypse.

The two men dressed as U.S. firemen drove their car around the parking lot that served the Base Exchange and Commissary and was across the street from the base operations. Then, as they turned to line up with the entrance to the BX, the driver stood on the accelerator and locked his eyes on the door of the complex. They sped up onto the sidewalk and knocked over two pedestrians on their way to the entrance. As they crashed through the glass doors, the passenger flipped a switch that initiated an ignition sequence with the hundreds of pounds of explosives and fertilizer they had in the car. The devastation was massive. The explosion rivaled that at the Murrah Building in Oklahoma City years ago. The Base Exchange was leveled, a crater about 50 yards in diameter formed under a huge cloud of fire and debris. Every building within a three block radius was severely damaged. No pedestrian on any sidewalk within 100 yards was left standing. Several cars were on fire and the gas pumps at the base convenience store and gas station all went off as secondary explosions. There was very little left of the perpetrators and their car. It was all fiery dust. Cretin and Ebola managed to survive solely because of the bulk and armor on the Humvee.

Brad Mitchell and Kerry Day had been driving around the base in the wing commander's staff car. Brad wanted a tour of the premises to look for what could be a target. He had been to Spang several times back in the 80s when he was a pilot flying out of Hahn Air Base, about 40 miles away on the other side of the Mosel River. Hahn was one of the bases closed in 1991 after the thaw to the Cold War supposedly took place. At the time there were three F-16 squadrons at Hahn, sitting nuclear alert and flying low level training missions all over Europe. Brad was a flight commander at the time and way too often he had to divert into Spangdahlem due to bad weather at Hahn. Hahn historically would have low ceiling and visibility when everywhere else in Germany would have at least flyable weather and a 600 foot cloud ceiling. The reason was simple. Hahn was 600' higher in elevation. Invariably in the winter, the ceiling would lift enough about 1 PM to launch the fleet, and more often than not, by 2:30 it would come back down. Each pilot would make one instrument approach down to minimums and if he could see the runway, land and go home to a nice warm bed. If not, he would perform a missed approach and divert to Spangdahlem, Bitburg or Ramstein, one of the other nearby U.S. bases. Unfortunately though, back then there was no time to wander around the base. The Hahn commander would dispatch a "blue goose" (a basic yellow school bus painted blue) to pick them up and bus them back to Hahn to do it all over again tomorrow. Usually fresh crews would be bussed back the next morning to fly a mission from Spang and maybe land back at home base. As a result, Brad figured he'd landed at Spangdahlem a half dozen times and never saw any of the base outside of the base operations and weather shop.

They were about a mile away near one of the fighter squadrons when the bomb went off. Colonel Day stomped on it, laid on his horn and activated his emergency flashers. He wished he had red or blue lights to turn on so folks would get out of his way, but normally the wing commander's car was not classified as an emergency vehicle. They could see the fire and destruction and knew that whatever they had been waiting for had just happen. Os so they thought.

The guardsman in the bushes about 100 yards from the entrance to the Quick Reaction Alert area zeroed in his aim on the security policeman sitting in his truck on the taxiway just outside the gates to the facility. The explosion over a mile away startled both of them, but the American stayed in his truck and picked up his radio microphone to call in to headquarters - what had happened? The sniper took a deep breath, let it half way out, centered up his aim and pulled the trigger. The cop's head basically exploded and spread blood and brains all over the cab of the truck. The sniper dropped his rifle and started moving toward the truck. In the meantime, his partner who was much closer, ran quickly to the truck, searched the bloody corpse for what he needed and pulled the man out onto the taxiway. He found the key, the key to the gates closing in the QRA shelters. He paused and listened and soon he heard the klaxon go off for a scramble alert. He waited until he saw the crews and crew chiefs respond to their jets and calmly went over, unlocked and opened both gates wide. Then he got back to the truck, started it up and picking up his partner, drove down the taxiway and off near the end of the runway toward the base perimeter. They had identified a spot in the perimeter fence that was out of sight of the tower and other activities on base. They ditched the truck in some bushes in the woods, hiked over to the fence and cut a hole big enough for each man to slip through and out into the German countryside. From there they knew the way back to their house where their handler was waiting. The German populous was reacting to the activity - an explosion on base. People stopped their cars, came out of their homes and generally milled around wondering what was happening on base. Many of the folks were Americans living on the economy and they all jumped in their cars and headed into work. The two Iranians were able to commandeer a small pickup that a driver had left running while he rushed up the hill to view the activity. They jumped in, turned it around and eventually made their way back to their house, leaving the truck a few blocks away.

As the Wing Commander and Brad Mitchell streaked up to the scene, Brad's phone went off. It was Genoa. "Columbus, we've been hit here on the base." Conan passed on. "A massive bomb around the commercial area - BX, commissary, convenience store, base ops. It's a mess. A lot of carnage." There was a pause. Genoa was not expecting this. He thought he would be delivering news, not the other way around.

"Jesus. Ok, do what you can to help, but there's something you need to know. One of the families identified in the country from the Iranian Starkville operation has a son who is a navy pilot on an exchange tour there at Spangdahlem. Air Force personnel confirms he's been there about three years, assigned to the 480th fighter squadron. His name is Robert Mustan."

"Copy that. I assume he might have had something to do with this bomb, but it sure doesn't sound like something a pilot would have the expertise to pull off." Brad said. "I'll stick with the wing commander here and brief Cretin to look out for evidence of his involvement."

—

CHAPTER TWENTY THREE

ALERT FACILITY, SPANGDAHLEM AIR BASE, GERMANY

"Klaxon! Klaxon! Klaxon!"

Right on time. Thought Robert Mustan as he scrambled into his flight suit and boots. But even with prior knowledge the sound of the alarm was nerve racking. It wasn't as if they couldn't hear the damn horn going off. How could anyone miss it? There was one outside each bedroom door and several more all around the QRA (Quick Reaction Alert) area. It wasn't the noise or the voice back-up that bothered most pilots, as what it meant.

They were on Victor Alert—the standard term for nuclear alert. It was Monday afternoon. Six pilots were on Victor, assigned to six F-16Cs—each loaded with two wing tanks of fuel, two live AIM-9M heat seeking missiles, an ECM pod (electronic countermeasures) and a B-61 thermonuclear bomb. No matter how many times they'd been scrambled for practice, most pilots never got used to it. You never knew - *Is this the real thing?* The sound of the wail of that horn is enough to send all kinds of thoughts through a fighter pilot's mind. This scenario was very common place in the middle decades of the 20th century during the height of the Cold War. It was the primary mission for air-to-ground tasked squadrons. But in 1991 that had all suddenly come to an end with Glastnost and the crumbling of the Soviet Union. Alerts were over and the nuclear weapons were all shipped back to the states. F-16 squadrons concentrated on conventional bombing and air-to-air training. In fact, as the war in the middle east became the preeminent threat to the U.S., training was tailored more to that environment. Low level missions to avoid Soviet radar contact were no longer the mode of operation. Large package, high altitude ingress missions were more prevalent.

Then in 2010, Russia starting feeling their oats. Their President Gorky was an ex-KGB agent who never really accepted the fall of the USSR. They started quietly building up their military and even their nuclear arsenal against the terms of the treaties they had signed with the U.S. The liberal American administration let things slip and soon the Russians were back acting like they were a super power again. They invaded and took over Crimea, threatened to take over Ukraine, moved in to aid and shore up Assad in Syria, and cozied up to the Iranian regime. So, two years ago the U.S. quietly brought nukes back into Germany, and put Spangdahlem on Victor Alert. It was more of a show of force than anything else. With only 6 bombs ready to go, at least as the USAF in-theatre arsenal, they were hardly a huge threat. However, when you counted the submarine launched missiles in the waters within reach of Mother Russia, and with the nuclear capabilities of U.S. bombers and missiles, America posed enough of a threat to at least slow down the Russian activities. At least that was the hope.

Practice or not, the boys were humping. Their alert operations building was at the edge of the QRA and about a 60 yard sprint for the pilot manning the farthest shelter. They were supposed to be airborne in 15 minutes and especially with the F-16, that was a reasonable expectation. Their jets had been cocked and re-cocked with every oncoming shift. In reality a good pilot in a hot cocked jet could taxi within 5 minutes of his arrival at the aircraft. And for sure, these were good pilots. Usually the most time was spent in copying the message, and about five minutes verifying it with the "cookies" (authenticators) and getting a good inertial navigation (INS) alignment.

The crew chiefs arrived at the Tab Vee (shelters) at the same time as their pilots. They too were on alert shifts, living in the same quarters with the pilots. They stripped the jet of all of its safety flags and helped the pilot strap in, then stood by the fire extinguisher during engine start.

Then they waited, fully expecting an engine shutdown, and they would button their charge back up for the night.

The third player in the game was the close in sentry, an Air Force Security Policeman assigned to guard the jet and the Tab Vee. Number recognition with the close in sentry was always fun. You were never sure that these 19 year old kids with modern issued rifles could: 1. Remember the number of the day, and ; 2. be able to add 2 and 3 and get 5. When whatever combination of addition was made the pilot and crew chief were allowed under the red rope that was strung across the front of the Tab Vee to access the jet. That red rope signified the "two man concept" zone. Inside the rope the pilot and crew chief had to have each other in clear sight at all times around the bomb.

Major Mike Horan, the alert force commander for this shift was just going up the ladder to climb in his jet when he heard the roar of a "goosed" jet engine. An aircraft was taxiing. The unmistakable blast of the engine and acceleration could only mean that a jet was moving. It was "Rogue," one of the other pilots on alert. Horan could see the cop drop the red rope and "Rogue's" jet come out like a filly out of a starting gate. The silver bomb under the left wing gleamed in the reflection of the big spot lights around the area.

"Holy Shit!" Horan exclaimed. He looked at Dan, his crew chief and at his cop. At any other time their expressions would have been funny. Dan's chin was gawking down to his knees, and the sentry's eyes were popping out of his head. He immediately looked at Horan for "What do I do now?" Horan saw that they both understood the situation. He could see the taxiway gates leading out of the QRA. The gates were open! This was no exercise!

The procedures were simple. You jump in the jet, crank the engine if scrambled on a Klaxon (as opposed to just cockpit alert), you copy the message from the Command Post over the radio, read it, verify it's an exercise message, and then shut down the jet. In exercises there were two other fail safes other than the message itself. The security police got a different type of message and they only open one of the gates from the QRA so that only half of the taxiway is accessible, thus an aircraft can't taxi through. The fire department stations one of their big trucks blocking the entrance to the runway. God forbid, the real thing meant different measures. The fire truck was standing by, but not in the way, and both gates were open. Both gates were open now!

Horan and Dan moved into high gear. Just like in practice, they stripped the jet of all its safety pins in no time. Horan glanced at the bomb while he was zipping up his anti-G suit. The "silver bullet" was actually kind of pretty. Long, sleek and God how deadly! This particular one was cranked down to a medium yield, but even that would make Hiroshima and Nagasaki look like popcorn. Up the ladder—Dan was right behind him. Snap in the shoulder harness and a quick pat on the back. Horan could see the fear in the crew chief's eyes. Rightfully so. If we're going to drop nukes on them, what do we think they will do in retaliation? Horan knew that hanging around Hahn would not be too healthy. Just then he thought of his wife and kids. Shit! He just hoped that somehow she got the word and would have the sense to do what they always talked about — throw the kids in the car and high tail it to Switzerland. He did not have much faith in the Air Force's evacuation plans. The way he saw it, the airlift would be too busy bringing troops and arms to the war than to worry about getting folks out.

The ladder was off and the engine was cranking. As soon as he hit the battery switch, the radio was squawking.

"Gringo, Ninety One Dash Five. Are we taxiing?" "Gringo" was the call sign of the Wing Command Post. "Ninety One" was the call sign of the individual jets - "One through Five."

"Negative Ninety One Dash Five. Negative! Prepare to copy Alpha Echo Zero One." That was the title of tonight's scramble message.

"Gringo, something's not right out here."

"Gringo, Ninety One Dash Four. What's going on?"

"Say again Ninety One Dash Four."

"Gringo, get your head out of your ass and tell us what's going on."

"All right, knock it off." Horan had heard enough. One of the "privileges" of being the ranking guy on alert—he was the Alert Force Commander. Besides, all of these guys were in his squadron, and one of his pet peeves was radio discipline.

"Gringo, Ninety One Dash One is up, ready to copy."

"Roger Ninety One Dash One. Sir, is there an aircraft taxiing out there?" The controller was obviously distraught.

"That's affirmative Gringo. Ninety One Dash Two has taxied. Both gates are open, we are ready to copy." There was a long pause, then ....

"Sir this is Gringo. This is an exercise message." Horan's heart stopped. Then what the fuck was "Rogue" doing? Why was the gate open?

"Gringo, read the message." At this point he didn't trust anyone, and he wanted to translate for himself.

"Roger sir, this is Gringo. Prepare to copy Alpha Echo Zero One. Lancer, this is Gringo, prepare to copy Alpha Echo Zero One. Sierra - Two - November - Charlie - Charlie - Mike - Three - Echo - Echo - Two - Zero - Three - Two - Xray - November - all but Charlie Zulu. This is Gringo out." Then he read it one more time. The process was for the pilots to match the numbers and letters to a verification card called a "cookie." The last phrase "All but Charlie Zulu" put limitations or clarifications on the scenario, but the "cookie" would always verify a real or an exercise order.

Horan only half listened to the second reading. He didn't know what to think. It was an exercise message. He felt relieved at that, but what the hell was "Rogue" doing? He reconfirmed the message one more time. There was no mistake, and he didn't see how anyone could interpret it otherwise. Gringo was finished. Each of his wingmen were acknowledging.

"Ninety One Dash Three copies."

"Ninety One Dash Four copies." They knew he was pissed and they didn't want the wrath of "Kahn" (Horan's callsign) down on them for BS radio calls. They had enough to think about.

"Gringo, Ninety One Dash One. OK, we copy. Now why was the gate open and why did Ninety One Dash Two taxi?"

"Sir, I don't know. I've notified Colonel Day. The SPs are investigating the gate. They've been at the BX area. There was an explosion there and the Base Ops area at about the same time as the Klaxon." Horan's heart stopped again. Was there a fire truck blocking the runway? His question was soon answered.

"Ninety One Dash Two, this is Baron. Hold your position. Do you read me?" Horan recognized the voice. It was Jim Varga, Chief of Standardization/Evaluation. It made sense that he would be out here. He plays the Red Baron role as a quasi-launch director on the ramp during exercises. Tonight he was also an exercise evaluator. He must be in the Director of Operations' (DO) truck with the UHF radio, out near the runway, talking to the pilot of the taxied jet.

"Baron, Ninety One Dash One, what's your position?"

"Standby Dash One. Ninety One Dash Two, this is the Baron. Hold! Repeat, Hold! Do not take off!" There was a definite sense of urgency in Jim's voice. Horan felt helpless and there was nothing much he could do with this beast strapped to his rear. It was not time to add to the problem.

"Gringo, this is Ninety One Dash One. We are going to shut down. I'll call you on the land line. Sabres acknowledge."

"Gringo copies sir."

"Dash 3"

"Four"

"Five"

"Six"

"Baron copies. Gringo Ninety One Dash Two just took off. If you haven't already—inform the Wing Commander and the DO." Damn!

The call came in on Colonel Kerry Day's radio and phone. It was the wing command post. "Colonel Day." He responded

"Sir, this is Captain Makula. Sir, we just had a scramble alert at the QRA and one of the aircraft has taxied." The officer on duty relayed the news.

"What do you mean he has taxied? Is it a valid message? Were the gates open?" Day was nervous. With the news Brad Mitchell had brought with him and with what was going on back in the states, he worried that whatever was happening had suddenly escalated. He put the phone on speaker so Brad could listen.

"Sir, it was an exercise message, but he taxied before we even had a chance to transmit it. The gates evidently were open sir. The SPs are breaking loose from the bombing to investigate." Mikula was nervous to say the least.

"Crap!" Day said. "And there is no firetruck at the end of the runway. They are all here fighting fires. We're on our way to the runway. Mikula, re-confirm with USAFE it was an exercise message. Get the Vice Commander in there with you. I'll be out here trying to make sense of all this." He stomped on the gas and pointed toward the flight line. What had happened to his people and his base was catastrophic, but having a nuclear weapon on the loose could be a whole lot worse. Ten seconds later they saw and heard an F-16 in full afterburner take off and climb out to the west. All local flying was over for the day. There was no doubt what aircraft it was.

"Captain Mikula, this is Colonel Brad Mitchell. I just arrived on the scene and I need to know one thing right now. What is the name of the pilot who just took off in that jet"

"Mike - Colonel Mitchell is with me. Tell us what he needs to know." Day said, assuming his controller would be hesitant to give that kind of information out to a stranger.

"Yes sir. It is Captain Robert Mustan" Mikula responded. Conan's heart jumped into his throat.

"Kerry, you have a spare jet in the QRA loaded and cocked, right?" Brad asked. He was thinking fast. He knew that the alert force would have a jet ready to be substituted for any with a maintenance issue. It would have live missiles and a hot gun, wing tanks, everything but the bomb. That would be transferred over as quickly as possible should the jet be needed.

"Yes, of course." Day answered. "Why….? Are you thinking what I think you're thinking?"

"Probably. Take me to that jet and have someone from the alert force bring me their helmet, g-suit and harness." Brad then got on his "bat phone" and called Genoa and Cretin. He relayed to them what had become obvious. As devastating as it was, the bomb and destruction at the base commercial center was a diversion. It diverted the security policemen and the fire department and in so doing allowed a member of the Iranian Revolutionary Guard steal an American F-16 loaded with a thermo nuclear bomb capable massive destruction and death. He told them what he was planning on doing, and suggested that Genoa get the President on the horn to the Russians to try and head off a retaliation should Mustan deliver his weapon.

"Mikula, we're going to the spare aircraft in the QRA. File me a flight plan as Conan 01 with Base Ops. I want a quick climb to One Five Thousand (15,000 ft). Call the center and see if they have the runaway on radar. I'll contact them for a snap vector. Find out which GCI (Ground Controlled Intercept) site I need to talk to. Also, there should be a duplicate line somewhere in someone's vault. I need it delivered to me at the end of the runway. I may have to fly the same route to find him."

"Command Post copies. We have the duplicate lines here in the weapons office safe sir. I can get someone to get it to you" Mikula responded.

"Gringo, this is Baron." Jim Varga had been monitoring the radio. "I'll come and pick it up from you."

"Brad, there's no way you can catch him. He's got a helluva head start." Day said.

"I know that. But listen carefully. My boss back in D.C. is moving ahead of it too. He'll get authorization from USAFE and European Command. If this guy is flying his line, he might have a Time On Target (TOT) in mind. Hopefully there's some orbit time built in. Even if he's on his way, our launching to try to stop him might at least help to convince the Russians that we are serious and that we do not mean to start World War III. That they don't need to counter-attack. I'd bet the President is on the horn talking to the Russians already." Brad's brain was moving at warp speed.

"So what the Hell will you do if you catch him? Shoot him down? A nuke loaded F-16 crashes in Germany?! Jesus, what a mess!" Day was thinking out loud. He knew very well that if this guy was deranged enough to steal his aircraft and fly his line with the intent of executing the mission, he probably would also have the bomb armed and ready to release at any sign of trouble. A nuclear explosion anywhere east of the Ukrainian border would be close enough to affect some Russian forces and be seen as a deliberate attack by all but the most liberal minded Russian hierarchy.

"I don't know, Kerry. I don't expect to catch him at all—at least not going in. But if I can blow his shit away as he's coming out after he's done it, that might be the leverage the President needs to convince someone that this was a mistake. Besides, I'm not so sure he's flying the line. Maybe he's stealing the damn thing." Day hadn't thought of that. In fact, Brad hadn't either until after he said it. Sure enough! Maybe that's it! Back during the Cold War the advertised bonus to a U.S. pilot who would deliver an F-16 was half a million bucks. Who knows what the bomb would bring? Another option? Brad didn't know which was worse, but he suspected that with the current situation in the world, this latter option was the better of two evils. God damned jihadist! Brad knew one thing for sure now—he had to get airborne. Somebody had to stop this bastard and he was the closest to capable as anyone.

"Baron, get the line and elephant feeder. I'll be in EOR in ten minutes." The wing king's car was sliding broadside toward the half open doors of Tab Vee 70. Maintenance had just gotten there and they were opening up.

She fired up like a champ. Brad finished strapping in as he got the INS cooking, and confirmed he was on the Command Post frequency. He trusted the crew chief and the rest of the maintenance folks to strip her down and button up any loose panels. Normally he'd never do that. The one thing a fighter pilot is almost religious about is his walk around inspection of the jet. When he straps it on he knows that no one else is up there to help, and if something goes wrong, it will be a quiet ride down in the parachute. So—a good preflight becomes automatic, though hopefully not so automatic that he overlooks something. Tonight Brad determined that timing dictated trust. One thing Brad did notice before he went up the ladder of aircraft 81-383 -- the name on the canopy rail—Capt. Robert "Rogue" Mustan. How appropriate! He was chasing the prick down in "Rogue's" own jet. Each of 24 to 26 pilots of each squadron had their names painted on a jet. They may never get to fly it but once in a while, but it made for good photo ops. Brad was really starting to hate this guy. He was also pissed at someone for not seeing this coming, or for not somehow stopping it sooner? Isn't that what the Personnel Reliability Program was all about? PRP—the human factors program developed and practiced to keep people who are stressed out, sick, or otherwise not just right from working on or around nuclear weapons. It's an all encompassing program that includes everything from the use of prescription drugs to the two-person control system. What it meant to a fighter squadron commander or operations officer is that they are charged with the responsibility to know everything there is to know about the guys they put on alert. If a pilot is having marital problems, money problems, physical problems, whatever—somebody needs to know about it. Usually that's the flight commander—middle management, but the ultimate responsibility lies at the top. Brad wondered who the squadron leadership was at the 480th.

"She looks good down here, sir." The crew chief was on the headset and ground cord.

"OK Chief! Go ahead and disconnect and pull the chocks. I'm going to give the INS one more minute."

"Right sir, disconnecting. Good luck, sir."

Brad tapped the brakes as he came out of the chocks. He watched the missiles on the wingtips closely until they cleared the Tab Vee walls. They looked sleek and deadly out there and he hoped he wouldn't have to use them tonight. Or did he?

"Gringo, Conan One taxiing now. Any last words?" Brad asked the same question via his phone to his boss back in D.C. He had the fancy radio/phone laying on the side console with one of the ear buds in his ear under the helmet. He wanted whatever intel anyone had immediately.

"Conan, this is Gringo. You are filed. Tower should have the clearance and frequency. Rhein Center has not seen nor heard from our bird. Standby for Falcon One" Captain Mikula sounded stiff and unsure, but at least he was talking about launching.

"Brad, this is K-Day. I'm feeling a bit antsy about this. Having one goof ball out there trying to start a war is bad enough. I'm not sure we need to add to the fray."

"Kerry just hear me out, we don't have time to argue this one. If you're not already, get on the horn to Ramstein. Hopefully they have heard from my folks back home and they will authorize this. If not, I'll abort." Brad then keyed the phone and queried Columbus about the issue.

"First of all, we could have less than 12 minutes if he's flying his line with no planned delays. Two things—I don't think he'd plan this without a delay. Too many things could have gone wrong to slow him up. Two—I don't think he's flying the line. I think he's stealing the damn thing." Brad paused for just a second to let that sink in. He was taking his best shot. "If we accept scenario two, I might have a chance to stop him, or at least destroy the jet before it's towed off to hide in some Russian underground hangar. But we have to assume scenario one—and now with about 10 minutes left, I hope the President has been talking to his buddy, Gorky! I think I'm the only trump card we have. Even if I can't find him, they'll know that we tried. I'll squawk 7700 and yell 'May Day' on guard every 30 seconds if it will help." Brad didn't really mean that. Squawking emergency on his IFF (Identification Friend of Foe) set wouldn't help. It wouldn't be necessary either. The Russian GCI was very good. They would have him tracked and locked into their computers about the time that his wheels came up after takeoff. Yelling on the radio wouldn't help much either. About the only ones that would hear that on a Monday night would be all the airline pilots in between "coffee, tea or me" offers from their over-endowed stewardesses (oops - flight attendants). Wouldn't that be a gas! "Ladies and Gentlemen, this is your captain speaking. According to some nut on our radio—dial channel eight on your armrest control—if you look out the left side of the aircraft you will see a large nuclear explosion in about 30 seconds." No, Brad didn't think he'd advertise this mess on the radio, and he admonished himself for reverting to old macho thinking. Remember ——— PC.

He was pulling into the EOR when the Operations Group Commander's truck slid to a halt beside him. Brad opened the canopy as Major Jim Vargas got out of his truck to place a packet into the elephant feeder box. The feeder was a long pole (about long enough to reach an elephant's mouth without getting too close) with an aluminum box attached to the end. The idea was to reach up to the cockpit of an aircraft with its engine running without getting too close—especially to the jet's intake. The "Hoover" intake of the F-16 hangs below the fuselage, dangerously close to a person's height. It came by its nickname honestly—it sucks! There have been at least three cases of crew chiefs being sucked inside, and Pratt and Whitney fan blades make the Texas Chainsaw Massacre look like kid's stuff. The pilot would normally place his old line and mission materials into the feeder box, and then the Baron would hand him up a new one. In this case Brad had nothing to give. All he wanted was the duplicate of the "Rogue's" line so he knew where to head to try to intercept him. It was a quick "exchange" followed by a "thumbs up" from the major.

"Conan, this is Falcon One" Colonel Day sounded very somber and serious. "This may be your last flight, Brad. So make it count. USAFE says it's a go."

"You've got a go from D.C. Conan. Good Luck." Genoa squawked into his ear lobe.

"Tower, Conan One taking the active. I need a clearance, a frequency and the current weather." Normally you request those things, but Brad was not in the requesting mode right now, and the tower crew obliged. Their tower was partially damaged by the explosion that had taken place below them, and they sensed this was a revenge flight.

"Roger, Conan. Spangdahlem weather measured 400 overcast, two miles visibility, wind calm, altimeter Two Niner Eight Five. You are cleared to Zweibrucken via the Alpha Sierra One Zero departure, quick climb to One Five Thousand is approved. Contact Rhein Radar on Two Niner Four point One and squawk Five Five One One." Alpha Sierra10 was a standard departure routing that would take him down south over the Zweibrucken AB if he flew the whole route. Rhein Radar was the Germans' answer to the local FAA flight following facility. They were on radio frequency 294.1. The 5511 squawk directive was the setting Brad would put in his IFF (Identification Friend or Foe) system that enable Rhein to better identify him

"Conan One, cleared for takeoff." Brad didn't even slow down as he acknowledged, much less stop to run up and check the engine. He had two stages of afterburner cooking before he had her pointing straight down the runway. Three! Four! Five! Oh yeah! There it was again—that same feeling. No matter what else was ever on his mind, there was nothing that matched the feeling that Brad got when he stroked the F-16 into full afterburner for takeoff. Melanie had asked him one time how he liked it. He answered it was "better than sex." He didn't really mean that, and he'd regretted it ever since. But it was close.

CHAPTER TWENTY FOUR

AIRSPACE OVER EUROPE

She didn't see the target right away. She wasn't really paying that much attention. Captain Stephanie Michaels was the duty controller onboard Sentry 41, an AWACS (Airborne Warning and Control) aircraft inbound to Germany from a round robin mission in the Atlantic. They were still a little south of Paris, returning from an orbit off of Lajes, in the Azores, where they had participated in an exercise with the Navy. The fact that Stephanie had to be on the scope at all irked her, but it was her shift. Everyone else in the back of the aircraft was catching up on some sleep so they could hit the ramp running when they got to Ramstein Air Base. Stephanie knew that the Ramstein Officers Club would be hopping, and there was a certain fighter pilot she was hoping to see there in an hour or so. But for now she was pulling scope duty, only because their wing Director of Operations had ordered that another set of eyes was required anytime they were flying in foreign airspace. There had been several close calls and two registered "near misses" in the last few months, and he did not want to lose a multi-million dollar system to a mid-air. So, one of the GCI controllers was always on duty with a "hot scope," backing up the flight crew radar and air traffic control.

Right now Stephanie was tracking a target that was climbing out of central Germany, but not squawking on IFF. That was strange. The bogey was climbing through Flight Level 190 (19,000 ft). He was breaking the rules if he was flying VFR (Visual Flight Rules), and he should be squawking and talking to Rhein Radar. Stephanie knew that the German airspace was very complex, but the basic rule was that anyone flying above 10,000 ft. had to be under IFR (Instrument Flight Rules) and using their IFF, squawking whatever code Rhein issued them.

Captain Michaels tried "bugging" (highlighting with her cross hairs) the target to get some more information. The radar onboard AWACS was as sophisticated as they come, but all she could ascertain was that it was a fighter size target. By tracking back through the target history, she determined that the bogey took off from Spangdahlem Air Base. Stephanie knew her Order of Battle, and she figured that this was most likely an F-16 from the 52cnd Fighter Wing. The target was still 125 miles ahead of them, and she knew that her flight crew would be working with French Air Traffic Control, and have no knowledge of her little game in the back. This bogey was no threat to AWACS, but it was a good mystery to pass the time, and to keep her mind off the Ramstein club. She flipped through the pages of her controllers' guide and found the frequencies for Rhein Radar and a few of the German based GCI facilities.

"Rhein Radar, this is Sentry Four One." Stephanie decided she would have to use the aircraft call sign, rather than her own. After all, she wasn't actively controlling anyone, and Rhein would have no idea who "Steve" was anyway. They would have an inbound flight plan to Ramstein on the AWACS, and they would recognize the "Sentry" call sign.

"Sentry Four One, this is Rhein. Squawk Five One Four One and ident." His reply was automatic. He thought the Sentry was a little early, but if he (or in this case, she) was calling, she must want to land. Things were a bit slow today anyway.

"Negative Rhein. We are still 100 miles out. We will call for recovery in about two zero minutes. I am painting a target climbing out of Spangdahlem, now passing Flight Level Two Six Zero and not squawking. Do you have him?" Just then Stephanie realized her boredom and curiosity was liable to get one of her "Buds" in trouble.

If this guy was an F-16 jock she could be ratting on him and she could get him violated. Too late now.

"Negative, Sentry Four One. We have no traffic in the vicinity of Spangdahlem. What is the position of your target?" This was the second query the Rhein controller had received tonight about traffic from Spangdahlem. The first had been over the phone from the Spangdahlem Command Post, relayed through Eifel Approach Control. He had told them that he had no such target. Now this.

"He's currently 13 miles south of Ramstein, heading south—just about to cross into French airspace. Perhaps I have a false target. Thanks anyway. We will call again soon for our recovery." Stephanie just wanted to disengage now. Something was fishy, but she did not want to get a U.S. fighter pilot in trouble with the Germans. Using the cross hairs on her scope she could pinpoint the location of this bogey to a gnat's ass, and this guy was not flying a normal departure profile. He was about to bust into French airspace, and she knew that the French were bigger assholes about their "sovereign airspace" than the Germans were. She switched frequencies to Strawbasket, the local military ground control intercept (GCI) facility.

"Rhein, Conan One, airborne out of Spangdahlem, quick climb to one five thousand." Brad Mitchell had his Falcon in about a thirty degree climb. He wanted to get up there fast, but he wanted some airspeed at the top too.

"Conan One, radar contact. State your intentions." Now the German really did have a target climbing out of Spangdahlem, but he knew about this one—he had the flight plan. He wondered if the fraulien on AWACS was watching this one too. It would be nice to have the Americans' equipment. The old radar he was stuck with must have been the original—probably invented by Marconi.

"Roger Rhein. Request snap vector to the bogey that climbed out of Spangdahlem about 20 minutes ago. He is most likely at low level. Is there a GCI up tonight?" Brad had the German flustered. He wanted vectors to a target that wasn't there, and he wanted to leave the frequency to talk to GCI while still in controlled airspace.

"Conan One, I have no traffic for you. Strawbasket is available on frequency Three Forty One One or One Three Four Five on VHF. But you must stay on my frequency until you are clear of Frankfurt airspace."

"Rhein, this is an emergency. I must find that bogey. I will switch to Strawbasket on VHF One Three Four decimal Five, and maintain your frequency on UHF." Brad knew there was no time to mess with these guys, and certainly no time to explain. He knew where Frankfurt airspace was, and he would keep himself clear as he headed east. With two radios he could monitor both frequencies at once.

Brad had a nagging feeling about Robert Mustan and what he was up to. Kerry Day had relayed a quick story about Mustan that no one thought much about at the time, but now.... It was during the wing's Operational Readiness Inspection (ORI).

USAFE wings were tested constantly it seemed. There were three types of headquarters inspections and there always seemed to be one just around the corner. The Management Efficiency Inspection (MEI) was a paperwork drill and not much fun for the operators. Those in management positions were wrapped up in showing off their documentation programs in flight safety, personnel reliability (PRP), standardization, and reams of other paperwork that mostly non-flying inspectors wanted to see. The pilots all had to take standardization tests and how each squadron did on those was important, but basically an MEI was proof of the old adage "When the paperwork weighs as much as the airplane, you can go fly." Spangdahlem's last MEI was about two years ago and it passed with flying colors.

The second type of inspection was the NATO Tactical Evaluation (TAC-EVAL). It was a lot more fun and was basically an operational test of the wing's combat readiness. The inspection team was made up of NATO allied officers and augmented with pilots and other skill sets from other wings. The scenario usually was a maximum flying effort to see how many sorties (flights) the wing could generate in a short period of time. Pilots were evaluated on their skill and prowess, and it seemed like the entire remainder of NATO's forces was airborne to test them out. Missions were tasked to all of the local gunnery ranges and air to air airspace, and it was not uncommon to have U.S. F-15s, British Lightnings and Jaguars, German Tornados and F-4s, Dutch F-16s, and even older F-104s try to intercept the force and disrupt the mission. The NATO folks did not task the wing's nuclear capability. They knew that the US Air Force tested their nuke readiness constantly and besides, most of the NATO inspectors were not cleared for the "need to know" classification of the wing's nuke mission. It had been over two years since the last TAC-EVAL at Spang. They were due.

The most important inspection a USAFE wing goes through is a USAFE Operational Readiness Inspection (ORI). It combined the operational paperwork drill and the flying inspection into one scenario and included the nuclear mission, if the wing was so tasked. It usually started off with a simulated base attack and the entire wing immediately went into gas masks. The whole week was spent fighting a war and demonstrating the capability to do so while under chemical attack. The flying usually started off the same as a TAC-EVAL - conventional missions to ranges and simulated attacks. Toward the end however, the scenario changed as if we were losing the war and the mission escalated into the nuclear role. One squadron of F-16s went through uploading of nuclear weapons - REAL nuclear weapons under high security - just like was supposed to be there at the Victor Alert facility tonight. While the maintenance and munitions folks did their thing, the pilots went through preparation to fly their "line" or target mission. A few pilots were selected to "certify" to the Wing Commander, Vice Commender or Director of Operations, just like they had to do to become mission ready in the first place. A "certification" consisted of the pilot briefing the mission from start to finish - scrambling, copying and authenticating the message, take off, the low level flight itself, bomb delivery, and recovery. A cast of about a dozen inspectors and wing staff were there to grill him or her with questions and he/she had better have the right answer. The nuclear part of the ORI had only one passing grade - an A+. The rest of the inspection could have been outstanding with every take off on time, every bomb on target, and zero discrepancies. But if one part of the nuke tasking was a failure it all was a bust. Wing commanders were known to get promoted to general or fired based on their wing's ORI performance.

The nuke load out culminated in a scramble to the jets, start up and message read - just like at Victor tonight. Sometimes there would actually be what was commonly called an "elephant walk," a parade of every jet out to and down the runway, and back to parking. Then the bombs were downloaded and returned to their hideaway dens. Several of the jets would then be reconfigured with practice bombs and pilots would be tasked to fly a simulated mission to one of the local gunnery ranges. The practice bombs were designed to simulate the flight of a B-61 nuke, and in most cases (depending on the target area), the delivery would mimic the real thing. After that, the inspection was usually over and everyone gave a sigh of relief - OR - dreaded what would come next if something had gone wrong.

During the last ORI, just a few months ago, Robert Mustan had been selected to "certify" and also to fly a simulated mission to Siegenberg Range in southeastern Germany. His certification was flawless. In fact, it was lauded as the best seen to date by the inspection team. But as it turned out, rather than fly a simulated flight path to the range, Robert flew the actual flight path of the real target line he had certified on - at least part of it. His certification target was an airfield in western Russia, not too far east of southeastern Germany. He broke the flight off as he approached the border, but he encroached into the "Buffer Zone," a fairly wide swath of airspace in Germany that butted up against the border. Mustan had flown an actual simulated loft attack profile as he approached the border and his recovery had breached the BZ. He surprised the local GCI facility who had been looking to the east with their radar for obvious reasons, but they were able to pick him up and follow his flight path. Robert transitioned quickly over to the Siegenberg Range, made his designated TOT (Time on Target), and delivered his bomb with a "Shack" (direct hit). Siegenberg didn't allow loft deliveries because of the size of their range, but Mustan laid down a perfect strike from level 200 feet at 540 knots (about 600 mph). Then he flew a standard recovery back to Spangdahlem.

The GCI facility in the area relayed their discovery and tracking information back through channels, and the wing knew about Mustan's flight path before he even landed. The simple fact was however, that what he had done was not really a violation - just a "bending of the rules." The common policy was not to fly the actual route of a real nuke attack line. After all, the Russians knew that Spang had nukes, they knew the wing's tasking, and they had good tracking radars. Why give them the "heads up" of a real route of flight of a planned attack? So the normal flight plan was another route that ended up at the range, stayed out of questionable airspace, and was more logical. But there was no directive that determined the route of flight and the pilots were free to make up their own profile. Flying into the BZ was a "no-no," but in fact it happened all the time. The BZ covered a lot of flyable airspace, and especially if the aircraft didn't stray too close to the border, it was not such a big deal. Not a good idea during a headquarters ORI however. As it turned out, the wing decided not to advertise the indiscretion and only told the squadron commander about it. Since Mustan's bomb was a direct hit, all was forgiven - at least as far as the wing hierarchy was concerned.

The squadron commander and Operations officer were also happy about the bomb score, but a little more concerned about the round about way Robert had taken to get there. They questioned him on it, and he simply said he thought he had done nothing wrong and disputed that he had overshot into the BZ. He said he had deviated for some weather and perhaps that was when he strayed. He was admonished and told to be smarter next time. As it turned out, the mission and target that Mustan had certified on that day, and the flight profile he had partially flown was targeted at Finthen Airfield - **the same line he was sitting alert on today.** So he had practice flown two thirds of the route of flight he had in his cockpit tonight. *Christ,* Brad thought. *Why would Mustan want to start a war between the Russians and the U.S.? Then he realized that might just be EXACTLY what Iran might wish.* He tuned his radio to Strawbasket's frequency.

"....just at the end of my radar coverage now anyway. To be honest, we weren't paying any attention to traffic from the west." Brad had tuned into a conversation already in progress. Radio courtesy demanded that he wait for a break to make his call

"Roger Strawbasket. Well, whoever it is, he's into French airspace now, still climbing and still heading south. I sure hope he knows what he's doing. Wait a minute! Now there's another one. This one has climbed back over Ramstein and is heading east at Flight Level One Five Thousand. He's squawking Five Five One One." Captain Michaels onboard AWACS now had Brad on the scope, relaying information to Strawbasket GCI.

"Roger, Sentry. Strawbasket has contact there. Heading Zero Eight Five, angels One Five Five." BINGO!! Brad heard music to his ears. Sentry 41! That was the standard call sign of AWACS. Could we be so lucky as to have an AWACS up tonight, and with radar contact on "Rogue?

CHAPTER TWENTY FIVE

AIRSPACE OVER FRANCE

His real name was Muhammad Mustafa. He was of Lebanese descent, which made the cover story easier—though the cover story was about the farthest from the truth as one could get. His family had been chased from their home in the Bekaa Valley by the Israelis. They had relocated to Iran and because of their deep hatred for Israel and Americans, they were perfect draftees for Starkville.

When they "graduated" from Starkville almost 20 years ago they migrated to the U.S. and settled in Pittsburgh, Pa. Mustafa's father got a job in one of the steel mills and his mother worked as a nurse. Although his parents mellowed a bit through the years, Mustafa did not. He was ultra religious and spent a lot of time with a local Imam. He also went back to Iran twice during his high school days. After high school he got a scholarship to Penn State to play soccer. He was a great player and he also excelled in Naval ROTC, graduating as an Ensign and moving on to flight school in Pensacola. His first assignment was to an F-18 squadron flying off the carrier Nimitz in the Pacific. Then, right according to plan, he took an exchange tour assignment and was assigned to the 480th squadron at Spangdahlem. He went through F-16 upgrade first at Luke AFB in Arizona, and arrived at Spang two years ago with lots of experience.

It took Mustafa four months to upgrade to the F-16 -- with flying colors, and another 9 months after arriving at Spangdahlem to work the arrangements and manipulate the schedule. Finally, the day had come, and the "Rogue" got his chance and he volunteered for a Victor Alert shift. So far it had gone like clockwork. He was now 100 miles into French airspace on a Monday evening. The weather was lousy all over Europe, and even the French would probably let him go. Oh, they would yell at him over the "Guard" frequency to identify himself and squawk an IFF code, but as long as he kept quiet, he believed they would leave him alone. He was right.

CHAPTER TWENTY SIX

RAMSTEIN AIR BASE, GERMANY

At the Ramstein Air Base Officer's Club things were hopping. Although the fighter squadrons had been moved out of Ramstein, there were plenty of fighter pilots in the headquarters staff, and the special ops guys on base were pretty big partiers as well. The weather was lousy so most everyone knocked off early and went to the bar. There was a major Crud match going on, and this time they even managed to talk Brigadier General Chuck Morton into being the referee. Morton was the USAFE Assistant Deputy for Operations (ADO). He had been briefed on the explosion at Spangdahlem but had no particulars yet. He left instructions for the Command Post to contact him as soon as they knew more.

For the past several years the Air Force senior leadership had supported an unofficial drive to de-glamorize alcohol, and subtle hints to be a non-player were often dealt out to senior colonels and general officers. It really rubbed on Morton, for he always was a fighter pilot's fighter pilot. He worked hard and he liked to play hard. He maintained a great level of credibility when he flew, and he had maintained the respect of the youngsters. He felt that his credibility at play was just as important to the camaraderie and esprit de corps. He was not too good for them, and they needed to know that. Tonight most of the other general officers at Ramstein were at the Enlisted Club at an awards banquet or on various trips. The Commander in Chief (CINC) was in the States testifying before Congress about mismanaged funds at the officers clubs, and his own boss, the DO, was in Turkey, flying with a squadron deployed there from Italy. Once again, the "assistant" was left at home to mind the store. But at least he was free to party with the guys without raising too many eyebrows.

Crud is a fighter pilot game held on and around a pool, billiards or snooker table. No one is sure where it was invented, but rumor had it that the Canadians thought it up at their "Maple Flag" training exercises at Cold Lake, Canada. At any rate, the game matched two evenly numbered teams of participants in a contest to knock one ball (the target) into a pocket by hitting it with a cue ball that is rolled by hand (no pool cues), before the target ball stops moving. There are several rules, including the fact that the shooter must be physically positioned at the ends of the table when he or she shoots. Any violation of this rule immediately invokes a call of "Balls" (or "Lips," depending on the shooter's gender) and a "life" on the shooter. Three "lives" and the player is out. "Life" is awarded by being the last shooter with a chance before the target ball goes in, by touching the target ball by hand, by shooting off the table, and a number of other crimes subjectively declared by the referee. The most heinous crime of all is to touch the referee who stands right beside the table at a side pocket. The criminal who suffers that bad luck also gets to buy the ref a drink of his choice. Crud becomes a contact sport, especially as the night wears on and the rivalries heat up. Physically blocking the opponent's access to the ball is not supposed to be legal, but again, the subjective call of the referee is the final word.

Chuck Morton had just awarded a "life" to the the special ops squadron commander for excessive blocking, and he was taking no shortage of grief from the special ops team. Of course the opponents, who were a team of support officers and two visiting reporters were most appreciative. They were getting their asses kicked, both physically and on the score board. General Morton had a little sympathy for them—they were green at this. But only a little sympathy—after all, they asked to play, and he actually enjoyed seeing the one asshole of a reporter get roughed up a bit.

"General Morton. Sir, you have an important phone call from the Command Center." The Club Manager was careful to approach the table between setups. The call had come into the office, and the paging system had failed to produce a response. No wonder. The noise in the bar would drown out a fog horn. The manager knew the general was at the Crud table.

"Shit! OK, thanks. All right you assholes. Take five and get a round on me. 'Mom' must be calling." The general went off to find a phone to a thundering cheer and applause. Fighter pilots love it when someone else is buying. The nearest house phone was in the lobby near the men's room.

"Morton here." He wanted to make sure the Command Center folks knew that this had better be important.

"Sir, this is Captain Wierzbanowski from the USAFE Command Center. Sir, sorry to bother you, but I have Colonel Day on the line from Spangdahlem. Sir, you need to hear this." The captain was obviously shaken.

"Kerry Day. What's new? Have you narrowed down any cause to the explosion?"

"Boss, we have a real problem. I realize that what I'm about to say blows OPSEC all to hell, but you need to get to the Command Center. Suffice it to say that one of our alert birds is airborne. I don't know why and I don't know where to, but I have another aircraft airborne trying to catch him." Day tried not to use the word "nuclear" over the phone. Morton's comeback wasn't quite as responsible.

"Jesus Christ! You mean to tell me that you have a nuclear loaded jet flying around Germany on a Monday night, and another one up trying to shoot him down? You gotta be shittin' me, K-Day!" The general realized right away that he had said too much over the phone. He especially realized it when he saw the reporter from the "Stars and Stripes" newspaper disappear into the men's room, his eyes as wide as his fat gut.

"Wierzbo, I'll be over to the Center in just a minute. Get the ViceCINC out of the Enlisted Club, and get the numbers for the CINC in D.C. Colonel Day, who else knows about this?"

"Pretty much everyone sir. The chase aircraft is piloted by Colonel Brad Mitchell. He was here on a tip that a follow up to the terrorist attacks in the States yesterday was to happen here. I assume you were briefed on the explosion on base today. Evidently Mitchell and his team back home believe that was a diversion to allow this pilot to get airborne. We believe that Washington's on the phone to the Kremlin. Sir, this guy could be flying his line." Colonel Day tried to let that one out softly, realizing that it really didn't matter. The gravity of the situation would hit like a ton of bricks. "Sir, I'm on a secure line here, just waiting to turn the key. We need to go secure for anything more."

"OK! Wierzbo, set it up. Get me on a secure line to Spang. "I'll be right there." Chuck Morton hung up the phone and started running toward the front door. Peter Donald, "Stars and Stripes" reporter, stood off to the side in the hallway and watched, positive that there was a story here.

—

CHAPTER TWENTY SEVEN

AIRSPACE OVER FRANCE

"Break, Break! Strawbasket and Sentry, this is Conan One, airborne out of Spangdahlem at One Five Thousand, Sentry, understand you have contact on our previous bogey?" Brad Mitchell peered into his radar scope to see if he could pick up any traffic out there. He thumbed out to 80 miles, but he knew an F-16 size target would not show up much beyond 25 miles.

"Conan One, Strawbasket. Radar contact. Sir, I have no abnormal traffic out here, but Sentry 41 has a target now heading south over France." The GCI controller wanted to be of help, but he had no one but Mitchell and a few airliners on his scope.

"Conan, this is Sentry Four One backender. Sir, we are still 100 miles west of Ramstein, but I do have a fighter size target, now over Dijon, France at Flight Level Three Three Five, heading south and not squawking. My target history tells me he took off from Spangdahlem at 1700 local." Captain Michaels was trying to decide what was going on.

"Sentry, I love you!" Brad hadn't even met her, but he knew he owed Stephanie Michaels a drink, at least. "Strawbasket, are you sure that no other traffic launched from Spangdahlem and headed east about that time, low level?"

"Negative Conan One. I can't be sure sir. We were looking east at the time. But I have no one out there now." They both knew that if the "Rogue" was out there low level, Strawbasket probably wouldn't see him anyway. The mountains and the ground clutter would mask his radar return. That's why the nuke mission was planned at low level. Surprise.

"Roger that. Sentry Four One, can you go secure?" Brad wanted to talk freely, and use the secure communications available. They had a secure system for both radios. Right now they were talking over VHF (Very High Frequency) radio.

"Yes sir, I can." Came Stephanie's reply.

"OK. First I need you to go through the USAFE Command Center. Get their Have Quick frequency and get a 'Mickey' from them. In the meantime, give me a snap vector to the bogey, and then I'll meet you and Strawbasket up secure Victor." Brad was clicking.

"Roger, Conan One. Come right to One Eight Eight. Bogey bears One Niner Zero degrees for 132 miles, angels Three Three (33,000')." Stephanie flipped through her Controller's Guide to the USAFE frequency list, and dialed her UHF (Ultra High Frequency) radio to 300.4.

"Conan. Right to One Eight Eight and climbing. I'll meet you secure in one minute." Brad then keyed his mike button to the UHF frequency he'd been monitoring—Rhein Radar. "Rhein, Conan One. I am in contact with Sentry Four One. She has my target on radar. I am turning south and climbing, and I MUST leave your frequency to contact the USAFE Command Center. I will attempt re-contact with you later on VHF. If not, be advised I will enter controlled and French airspace. Be advised this is an emergency. I will attempt to keep you informed."

"Roger, Conan One. Can you have Sentry Four One relay information?" The German knew that something was going on, but he didn't want any violations on his watch. At least the fraulein on AWACS could keep him posted.

"Roger Rhein. I will try." Brad switched his VHF to the secure mode, and dialed up the Spangdahlem Command Post on UHF. "Gringo, Conan. Advise the wing commander that our bird is apparently headed south, now over France. Looks like the second scenario we talked about. There is an AWACS up here with radar contact. I am going to contact them and USAFE on Have Quick. It looks like we at least have a little time."

"Thank God for that, Conan." Captain Mikula responded for the Spang Command Post. "I'll pass the message."

No shit, Sherlock! "OK Mike. Since I'm headed south you might get Zaragoza in the loop. I might need someplace to land. Better yet, maybe they can scramble a tanker." Brad was on a roll now. He remembered that one squadron of F-16s had deployed to Zaragoza from Spang to get some good training during the typically lousy winter weather in Germany. That used to be a standard scenario and Zaragoza was a Spanish base with a major USAF presence. Tankers often operated out of there as well to help refuel jets on their way to the Middle East. If any were on alert, they could be airborne to help him chase down the rogue.

The secure mode of the VHF is a scrambler. It normally worked well, except that you had to key the mike and wait a second before you talked, giving the radio time to settle in on its code. It also sounded like you were talking into a tin can, "...Sentry, this Conan One. How do you read me?"

"Conan One, this is Sentry Four One. I have you loud and clear, how me?" Captain Michaels was actually enjoying this, and debating whether she should wake up her supervisor, or keep all the fun to herself. She soon got her answer.

"Sentry, you are loud and clear. OK, listen up. The target you are tracking heading south is a nuclear loaded F-16C off an alert line at Spangdahlem. We believe the pilot is taking the aircraft to a foreign government. Can you divert to keep track of him? I do not expect to be able to catch him unless he slows down." Brad wasn't sure where the AWACS was, but he figured the geometry quickly. She was supposedly over France, and just about anywhere in France was closer to the "Rogue" than he was.

Stephanie swallowed hard. Some game this is! Now it was time to back peddle. "Uh sir. I'm just a backend controller. My supervisors are not even aware of the target. The flight crew isn't either." As she spoke, Stephanie threw her checklist at the nearest sleeping crewman, to wake him and get some help.

"Well Godamnit, make somebody aware! And get the flight crew on frequency. Did you get the USAFE Have Quick frequency?" Brad was pissed, and he didn't have time to mess with this chick now.

"Yes sir. Frequency is Three Zero Zero point Four Two Five. I am ready to pass you a 'Mickey." At least she had done that right.

Have Quick is a secure UHF radio system that involves frequency hopping. The system is keyed by maintenance personnel earlier, and the operator only has to load the Word of the Day (WOD) and Time of Day (TOD) -- "Mickey" for short. Some enterprising young lieutenant must have thought that one up—"Mickey," for Mickey Mouse watch—that's how you get the time of day. Actually, the system gets it by setting up for and receiving a tone from another station. The tone puts the radio into its "ready" mode, and the operator turns a wafer switch to go "active," starting the frequency hopping. As long as all the players got the same "Mickey," and have the same frequencies (WOD) loaded, they will be able to talk to each other as they hop from frequency to frequency. Brad got a good tone and was thankful he had a jet that was ready to go to war. "Roger, Sentry Four One, Conan has a good tone. USAFE, are you on frequency?"

"Conan One, this is the USAFE Command Center, call sign 'Big Star.' Sir, General Morton is on the line to Spangdahlem. Can you standby?" Captain Wierzbanowski was one nervous Jose.

"Roger, Big Star. I can standby, but in the meantime let's all go active." Brad wanted to get the whole group on secure radio. He and the two captains switched their radios to the active mode. By this time, Stephanie Michaels had alerted her flight crew and her watch crew chief. They too came up secure on their own radios.

Brad decided he'd better check in with Genoa. "Columbus, this is Conan, are you on?" He keyed his phone and waited.

"Roger that Conan. We understand your target is heading south. We're working on getting you some help out of Spain. There is a squadron of F-16s at Zaragoza and a few air refuelers. Unfortunately I gotta tell you there is another deployment to worry about." Genoa replied.

"Oh boy. I can't wait. Go ahead." Brad was ready for anything now, but not what he got.

"Evidently there is a squadron of Iranian Air Force fighters in Libya." Genoa relayed. "It's a contingent of Mig 29 Fulcrums. That's not all that unusual. They've been doing that for months helping the corrupt government in Tripoli take out the rebel forces. But the latest news is they have flown in a tanker, an old KC-747 that is now on the ground on a base outside of Tripoli.'

"Great! Yeah, I know about that tanker. I actually refueled off it back when relations were better and we deployed into Shiraz, Iran for 6 weeks of joint training." That thing has got to be 40 years old."

"I suppose it means they could be planning on rendezvousing with the runaway to refuel him."

"Ok. Thanks for the good words." Brad said. "I'll keep you in the loop.

CHAPTER TWENTY EIGHT

RAMSTEIN AIR BASE

Peter Donald knew that something big was happening, and from the conversation he overheard on his way to the men's room, he decided it could be the scoop of a lifetime. He snuck back into the bar and found his partner desperately trying to keep up in a beer chugging contest with a lieutenant twice his size. He decided then and there that the Air Force Times reporter was a lost cause. Besides, why should he share any of this story with someone who already has a good job. Neither one of them was Walter Cronkite, but Peter had dreams and this just might be the story to put him up in lights. They were at Ramstein doing stories on the low level flying issue in Germany. The Germans were up in arms about noise and potential accidents caused by low flying fighters. The crash of the Italian air demonstration team at the Ramstein Air Show several years ago, and a recent crash of an American A-10 into a village had brought the issue to a head. The German government was threatening restrictions, and the various Air Force chiefs were trying to work out a solution. It was a good story, but nothing to match a runaway nuclear weapon.

Donald returned to the lobby of the club, and placed a long distance call to the Washington Post. Within minutes he was talking to the foreign news editor, Marianne Rogers. He made a deal that he would get full credit and byline mention on any story he could pass to them. Then he told Ms. Rogers what he had heard. There were two airplanes airborne from a USAFE base, one of them loaded with a nuclear bomb, the other apparently trying to shoot him down. He suggested that the Pentagon probably knew about it, and probably the White House. Donald hung up the phone and went back to the Ramstein bar, and Marianne Rogers took it from there.

General Chuck Morton hung up the phone with Colonel Kerry Day at Spangdahlem. He had heard enough. He had no time to wait for the ViceCINC to get there from the Enlisted Club. But, before he picked up the phone to the National Military Command Center (NMCC), he wanted to be sure of one thing.

"Conan One, this is Big Star - General Morton. Do you read me?"

"Big Star, Conan reads you loud and clear sir. Sir, do you know the situation?" Brad wanted to get on with the conversation. He would soon fly out of radio range with Ramstein.

"Roger. Now Conan, confirm for me—this bogey heading south is the alert bird from Spang, right? Are you sure? Are you sure our weapon isn't heading east at low level?" Morton wanted to be sure about what he was going to have relayed to the President of the United States.

"Sir, I can't be positive. However, Strawbasket GCI saw nobody, and the only traffic seen at all is this bogey by AWACS. A straight line course and fuel limitations would put him headed to Sardinia. However, my sources at home tell me he may have tanker support out of Libya. Sir, can we get a scramble out of Zaragoza? And sir, you should also know the brass and the President already know about this." Brad did not want to steal the general's thunder, but he didn't want to embarrass him either.

"Ok. Well that makes my life easier. So, Conan, how much play time do you have? How about AWACS?"

"Conan One has a good two hours. I have a hot gun and two Mikes." (heat seeking missiles).

"Sentry Four One has roughly two hours of fuel as well. However, we are inbound to Ramstein, and we run out of crew duty day in one plus 30." The pilot of Sentry 41 wasn't completely up to speed on his backender's game, and he'd just as soon put this beast on the ground.

"All right, Hear This!" Morton was in the ordering mood. Sentry Four One and Conan One, attempt an intercept on the bogey. Plan on landing at Zaragoza. If you can't catch him by then, at least we'll have a good idea of his intended route. I'll get right back to you."

"Conan copies."

"Sentry Four One."

CHAPTER TWENTY NINE

OUTSIDE SPANGDAHLEM AIR BASE

Barak El-Kamani had been working hard. He rigged the house his men had rented with enough explosives to put it into orbit. Along with C-4, TNT and fertilizer, he had rigged up a device that would send out sarin gas - enough to kill everyone in the local town. His two soldiers made it back to the house in about 45 minutes after they snuck off base. El-Kamani lauded them appropriately for doing the "will of Allah." In the meantime, he had communicated with the airborne pilot Mustafa by a secure phone that Mustafa had snuck on board his jet on alert, and relayed orders that help was on the way.

Cretin, Jihad, Shooter, Nitro and Ebola had searched the wreckage around the bombed out area. Nitro was able to narrow down the origin of the explosion to a vehicle that had been driven half way into the entrance to the complex before it went off. There was not much left of the occupants, but they were able to recover a card with an address and a medal that had a symbol of the Islam faith on it. Colonel Day was able to get someone to the base locator office. The address was one of a rental house in a neighboring town off base that was frequently rented to Americans. Cretin and his team borrowed an SUV from the base transportation office and the base security police chief sent a squad of cops to accompany them.

"What is our next move my brother?" One of the IRG members asked El-Kamani. "Are we going to the next event, or are we going to leave the area?"

"As it turns out my brothers, there is no reason for you to go anywhere." You have done your job here and you will be rewarded nicely. I will be leaving presently and have only one task to accomplish." El-Kamani replied as he pulled out his Glock sidearm fitted with a silencer. Before either man could react El-Kamani put a bullet dead center in each forehead sending the men to the promise land. Then he completed rigging the house to blow. He rigged up a shotgun to go off with a trip wire activator located just before the front porch. It was a thin wire stretched between two bushes. With it he also rigged a tape recording of a woman's terrifying scream to go off right after the gun blast. The recording was rigged to activate on sound, a jewel of an electronic device developed by the equivalent of James Bond's "M" in the movie series, who was gainfully employed in Tehran at IRG headquarters. Barak's thinking was whatever invading force there was would be less cautious if they heard a woman screaming for help. Turns out he was right.

Barak started to leave the house when he saw four military vehicles drive up and stop down the road about 100 yards away. He stepped back inside and watched as dozens of men in military fatigue uniforms with protective vests deployed toward the house. El-Kamani quickly slipped out the back of the house and made it across a small pasture to the safety of a grove of pine and spruce trees. There he paused and made sure the way in front of him was not blocked by incursion from the rear. Seeing the coast was clear he moved down the hill toward the village center where he had parked his stolen car when he came in. He was three miles away when the first explosion went off.

Cretin had taken command of the AF cops when they arrived at their parking spot. The lieutenant in charge of the SPs was not excited by the idea, but a direct order from the wing commander made him stop and think that his career was on the line here. Maybe if it was all fucked up it would be better if he could claim ignorance. Cretin divided the force into four teams with himself, Nitro, Jihad, and Ebola each leading three AF cops. He set Shooter up with his long gun on top of a knoll about 100 yards from the house where he had a good view of at least two sides. Nitro and Jihad each took a side of the house while Ebola took the rear. Cretin lead his men toward the front door. They approached cautiously but did not have much cover to be invisible. They figured that if anyone saw them coming they would at least have the place surrounded.

Nitro had reminded everyone about trip wires and other activators that could be employed upon entry to the house. It was a little after sunset in Germany in December, so the wire El-Kamani stretched across their path in front of the house would be difficult to detect. Sure enough, it was effective.

Cretin tripped the wire and froze immediately, signaling his men to stop and yelling, "Wire!" loud enough that at least the teams on the side could hear. It might have been loud enough, but that's not what everyone heard. The shotgun blast followed by the woman screaming got their attention and just about everyone reacted. The cops hit the doors running, guns drawn and ready. Nitro froze in place and Cretin tried in vane to hold his men back. Ebola also froze and his men did as well. As soon as the front door was opened all hell broke loose. There were three huge explosions, annihilating the house and leveling the intruders. Six security policemen including their lieutenant, were killed instantly, most of them blown to pieces of flesh, bone and blood. Cretin too took a frontal blast and was blown back almost ten yards. His face was a mess of melted skin and molten metal. Jihad also was killed by flying debris. Nitro and Ebola and the remaining cops were injured. Two of the cops were bleeding profusely and one had a wooden plank impaled through his torso. Ebola had managed to duck and take most of the blast on his back. Nitro took it on face first but he was mostly shielded by one of his cops who had rushed the house. The cop didn't make it.

Ebola recognized the sarin gas first. It was a rotten smell and burned the eyes badly. He yelled for everyone to take cover and cover their noses and mouth. It was the first words Nitro remembered ever hearing from Ebola. Fortunately the AF cops all had gas masks strapped to their belts as standard procedure. Ebola took a few off the dead cops and got one to Nitro. The gas spread with the breeze and much of the village was affected.

Nitro got one of the security police radios and called into their headquarters on base, telling them what had happened and that there was gas in the air. Then he got on the horn to Columbus back in D.C. and Conan airborne. "Nitro here. The house we were trying to interdict went up in flames and gas. Cretin and Jihad have bought the farm. Ebola and I are injured but functional. Shooter's ok. I've got burns on my hands and face, but it's not too bad. We didn't see any movement in the house and only guess that because it was rigged to blow, the occupants are long gone."

"Columbus copies," Genoa said. "Nitro, get yourself to the hospital and get those burns cared for. Be advised that the German Bundestag Polizei has tracked our principal as stealing a car in Dresden several hours ago. That car was spotted by traffic cams exiting the autobahn just northeast of you earlier today. Since you're down two and so far behind, I'm going to gamble that he is not heading back to Dresden, but probably straight to Berlin or Frankfurt. You, Shooter and Ebola head to the train station in Berlin. Maybe we'll get lucky."

"Nitro copies." The three of them drove back to the Spangdahlem hospital where they joined the line of dozens of burn victims from the earlier explosion on base. Nitro sweet talked a nurse into giving him some bandages and salve and basically treated himself. Then he, Shooter and Ebola jumped back in the SUV they had borrowed and headed east, "borrowing it" some more for a longer outing.

CHAPTER THIRTY

RAMSTEIN AND WASHINGTON

General Morton decided he wasn't going to trust the word of some colonel he didn't know to tell him everyone who was anyone was up to speed back in D.C. He used the joint process to call Washington. CincUSAFE wears several hats, and as a Commander in Chief he has communications direct to the National Military Command Center (NMCC). There is actually an intermediate stop there at SACEUR (Supreme Allied Command Europe), but Chuck Morton decided he had no time to wait. He would let the ViceCINC run those traps later. He did manage to get the Air Force Operations Center on the line as well, so at least he had the service communication link covered. As luck would have it, the Air Force Chief of Staff (General Michelle Porter), the Secretary of the Air Force (Alfred Horowitz), the Chairman of the Joint Chiefs (General Andrew Adams), and the Secretary of Defense (Robert Lucroix) were all in the SECDEF's office when the call came in. Lucroix's Executive Officer (a Marine one star) answered the NMCC Hot Line in his office. It did not take much of an explanation before he came busting in on his boss' conference looking white as a ghost.

"Mr. Secretary, there's a call on the NMCC Hot Line you need to take. They have the USAFE Director of Operations on, and a big time problem." He was normally calm under fire, but he had never had to deal with nukes before. The SECDEF looked to the CSAF, who gave him a shrug and a "I haven't a clue" look. The SECDEF punched on his speaker box.

"This is Bob Lucroix."

"Sir, this is Commander Mathers at the NMCC. I have Brigadier General Charles Morton on the line from USAFE, sir. We need to go secure." The Secretary picked up his phone, turned the key to go secure, and turned off the speaker box. General Porter left the room and went immediately to the NMCC so that she could get in on the conversation.

The news was passed, and after too much discussion the SECDEF agreed that it was time to contact the President and let the generals sort out what else needed to be done. General Porter took over the conversation in the NMCC. The Chairman came in to "help."

"Chuck, this is General Porter. Let me get this straight. You've got a nuke loaded F-16 flying south over France, and another jet and AWACS trying to shoot him down? What the hell's going on over there? Who the fuck's in charge? I assume you have relieved the wing commander at Spangdahlem?"

"Ma'am, I haven't given the order to shoot down anyone. I thought I'd leave that up to you." Chuck Morton was being sarcastic, but he felt the cynicism in the CSAF's voice. He also didn't like being cussed at, even if it was the Chief. "Ma'am, the CINC is there in D.C. with you. The Vice is just now coming into the Command Center. My boss, General Olsen, is in Turkey. No, I haven't fired anyone yet. I think there's time for that later. Ma'am, I beg your pardon, but we don't have much time to be emotional about this. I believe this calls for immediate action, and I am prepared to initiate at this end."

"Sorry Chuck, you're right. The SECDEF and the President will take care of the political end of this. We need to determine the military course. What is your proposal?" The CSAF was thinking a bit more rationally—besides, the Chairman had just slipped into the chair beside her. He put his hand over the microphone and quietly mentioned that with the Tango Team in operation the President probably already knows about this and it would be prudent for the Tango Team to be involved in any planning.

President Jim McDivitt was just leaving his office for the VP Conference Room when one of his communications "gofers" came running up. "Sir! Mr. President. The Secretary of Defense is on the line, sir. He needs to talk to you ASAP. It's an emergency, sir."

"It is always an emergency when Robert wants to talk. All right, son. Lead the way." The President detected an unusual sense of urgency. He followed the sergeant into the comm center, and took his seat at the console. The communications through the center were always secure, and always tape recorded too.

"Hello Robert What's up? Has the D.C. traffic finally brought bureaucracy to a complete halt?"

"Mr. President, we have a situation that calls for immediate communication with the Kremlin, and probably half of our NATO allies." The SECDEF wasted no time in getting to the point. He explained the situation and recommended an immediate call to President Gorky of Russia. He also suggested that a call be placed to the leaders of Britain, Germany, France and Spain. Each would have a vested interest in the proceedings yet to unfold. We would most likely need their help. "Mr. President, I believe we have no choice but to order this aircraft shot down if we cannot force him down. We must assume that the pilot is not doing this on his own. If the Russians are behind it, you must insist on the aircraft and weapon's return immediately. I would suggest we could forfeit the pilot if we could get the bomb back intact."

Jim McDivitt was a political animal. He was not particularly strong willed, but he had done well by himself by appointing a Cabinet of sharp, aggressive and persuasive experts. He felt bad about shutting his SECDEF down. "Hold on Bob. I know all about what's happened. We're working it through the Tango Team. But, you make some good points. Bring the Chairman and the Chiefs into the Situation Room. We'll coordinate there. Just answer me one thing—does the press know about this?" He was reasonably sure there had been no leaks from the Tango Team, but now that half the Pentagon seemed to know, he was nervous.

"Sir, as far as I know, there's only a handful of military people and Secretary Horowitz who know about it—besides you and I." The

SECDEF saw nothing but bad news coming out of the press on this one. "We definitely need to keep it down. I suggest you impress that upon our allies and the Kremlin as well. It will be tough to keep a lid on."

"I agree. Let's get to it." President McDivitt pressed one of the many buttons on his console and spoke to the communications officer. "Get me President Gorky."

Marianne Rogers hung up the phone on the pip squeak from the Stars and Stripes with a smile on her face. Who did he think he was? Guarantees? In the news business? He must be smoking something. She had said just enough to be assured she heard all he had to give her, made lots of empty promises, and then put him off to visions of fame and fortune. She immediately dialed her Pentagon correspondent, Peter Sciapini.

"SkeePee, get your ass in gear. There's something big going down on the Air Force side over in Europe. Evidently there's a runaway nuke over there. Find out! Bend the rules, Ski—there's a big time scoop here." Marianne didn't mince words. But she knew the last order wasn't necessary for Sciapini. He didn't know what rules and ethics were. That's why she had put him in the Pentagon—to scrape and dig, and find as much dirt as he could on the military.

"Will do, boss! I doubt if there's anyone around that would know much. Let me see what I can find out." Sciapini first went to the Public Affairs desk, only to get first a blank stare, and then the standard answer when it comes to nuclear weapons.

"Our policy is to neither confirm nor deny the presence of nuclear weapons in ....what country did you say?" It was obvious this was a lost cause. He hit the hallways. One thing about the halls of the Pentagon, as long as you look like you are in a hurry, have a file or piece of paper to keep glancing at, you can go just about anywhere without anyone challenging you. There were still closed off areas, and one of those surrounds the NMCC, but the SECDEF's office is on an open hallway, as is the nearest snackbar to the NMCC.

There was certainly something going on. There were a number of people running in and out of the SECDEF offices. Many of them he recognized and spoke to. But none would respond to questions, and the

Marine guard on the door was shooting him more than a casual glance. He wasn't supposed to be snooping around here, so he beat a hasty path toward the River Entrance, as if to leave. At the next set of stairs he broke right and down into the bowels of the building and wound his way to the snack bar. This was one of two that was open 24 hours a day, mainly for the shift workers at the various communications and command centers. It was nearly always crowded with folks on a break, and a good place to snoop a scoop. Mid afternoon however, only a few Army folks were there, and they looked just as puzzled as anyone.

"Where is everyone?" Sciapini asked an Army major as he plunked money in the coffee machine. He didn't know any of these people, and they didn't know him. He could be easily mistaken for one of the dozens of civilian computer geeks that kept the comm systems operating.

"I don't know. We were wondering that ourselves. Some Air Force guy came in a few minutes ago yelling about a work recall, and the rest of them disappeared." The Major shrugged, finished his cherry pie, and sauntered off toward the Army hallway. Sciapini decided to have a nice long, drawn out dinner, followed by lots of coffee. This was probably the place to pick up bits and pieces of the puzzle. Even people at war took a break once in a while. He took a cassette recorder out of his pocket, hooked up the earphones, and stuck them in his ears. He reached down, switched on the machine, and started swaying to the music. Except there was no music. The machine was on record, and the earphones were really high powered microphones (pointed out). To anyone looking he appeared to be off in his own world, oblivious. In reality, he was recording every conversation within 100 feet.

CHAPTER THIRTY ONE

RAMSTEIN AIR BASE

General Morton's plan was simple. Much of it was built on Brad Mitchell's suggestion, and Chuck Morton was adding as he went along. He had diverted Sentry 41 to try to intercept the runaway. He had Mitchell trying to chase him down. Neither operation would work unless the "Rogue" turned or set up some kind of orbit. He had too much of a head start for Mitchell, and the F-16 flew up to 100 knots faster than AWACS, without even trying. There was a chance that the French could intercept, but what should we have them do? Shoot him down? If anyone was going to do that, Morton suggested it should be an American. Everyone agreed, and Brad Mitchell (for one) was relieved, because he wanted to do the honors. The next best bet was a scramble launch out of Zaragoza to try to intercept from there. The SAC tankers weren't on alert, but they could get at least two KC-10s airborne within 30-45 minutes. The fighters would take a little longer, because they weren't in Zaragoza on alert. They were there for training. The last jet had been put to bed at 4 pm. The pilots and maintenance crews were spread to the winds by now. The only other option might be the Navy. Commander John Mathers helped out there from the NMCC. A quick look at the Navy status board showed the carrier Truman and her task force still on the Atlantic side of Gibraltar. No other ships were even close. The Truman had been the playmate of Sentry 41 near Lajes.

She did have two F-18s on the ground at Rota, Spain, but not in any condition to help. General Porter broke his train of thought.

"General Morton good work so far. Be advised the President and his Team assembled to deal with the on going threat are on board. We believe you are in the best position to put something together. You may be contacted by Mr. Robinson Genoa. He's the CIA Director of Operations and the Tango Team chief." Porter wasn't sure how much she should divulge but at this point she was convinced this "team" needed to get bigger. "What do you think his intentions are, Chuck?" The Chief of Staff was hunting for clues. *Where was this guy headed?*

"Ma'am, I wish I knew. When he first launched, our first fear was that he had completely gone off the deep end and was flying his line. If that had been true there would be a big mushroom cloud over Finthen airfield right about now, a couple hundred miles southeast of Berlin. All hell would be breaking loose. He could still do something like that, but I think it's more likely that he's trying to steal the damn thing. Back in the 80s there were recurring intelligence reports advertising the going rate for an F-16 delivered to the East Bloc at about $500,000. Who knows what they would pay for a B-61? I don't know what the Ruskies would fork over, and I hope we don't have to find out."

"OK Chuck. Launch the rest of your plan, but keep the French out of it. See if you can get someone up from Zaragoza. Tell Mitchell it's his ball game, but to avoid shooting at all costs. We can't afford for that thing to go off. Keep us advised." Basically Brad Mitchell was being stretched thin between the official Air Force/Pentagon chain of command and the Tango Team. Fortunately the President and Genoa recognized the fact that this had basically turned into a military operation and they need to let the military handle it. With a little help of course. Genoa relayed the guidance to Conan.

"Brad, this has gotten bigger than Tango. You are "chopped" back to the Air Force, specifically USAFE. Keep me in the loop though. There will likely be aspects of all of this needing Tango guidance." Genoa ordered.

CHAPTER THIRTY TWO

MOSCOW

It was early in the morning—the middle of the night—when the aide came to knock on President Gorky's door. He did not relish this. It was a damnable cold night in Moscow, and he had been awakened from under several inches of covers himself. He knew the heat in the old mansion was better in the President's quarters, but still not what it should be. This was important, no doubt, but he wondered how Gorky would react. He had only had to wake a boss once before in the middle of the night—Chernoble.

"Comrade Gorky, I am sorry sir, but we have an urgent message from President McDivitt that you need to see." The aide tried to be as gentle as he could, but the President came out of a deep sleep as if in the middle of a nightmare. It was as if he already knew what was on the communique. Mrs. Gorky awoke with a start and turned on the light. She too was terrified. Only then did the aide realize that they probably both thought they were under attack—that there was a coup. After all, that was the talk these days, especially in the American press. Gorky was in a sweat, but he finally recognized his aide, and took the written communique.

"PRESIDENT GORKY. I REGRET TO INFORM YOU THAT WE HAVE LOST A TACTICAL NUCLEAR WEAPON ON BOARD AN F-16 AIRCRAFT. THE JET SEEMS TO HAVE BEEN HIJACKED AND IS CURRENTLY FLYING SOUTH

OVER FRANCE. WE ARE IN PURSUIT. I WILL KEEP YOU INFORMED. IF YOU HAVE ANY KNOWLEDGE OF THIS OPERATION, I RECOMMEND YOU EXERCISE YOUR INFLUENCE TO HAVE THE WEAPON RETURNED TO US IMMEDIATELY. McDIVITT."

The Russian President was in shock. He did not know whether this was a trick, whether McDivitt actually thought the Russians were behind this stupidity, and especially whether or not there was an immediate threat to the Homeland. "Get Yakonoff here immediately. I will go to the bunker." Gorky ordered his aide as he rolled out of bed. "Damn, it's cold!"

By the time Boris Yakonoff, the Minister for Defense, arrived at the palace bunker, Gorky had been through several cups of strong American coffee and a pack of stronger Russian cigarettes. Yakonoff quickly got up to speed. Gorky had prepared a reply to the Americans, but he wanted his trusted friend and comrade to see it first.

"MY DEAR PRESIDENT McDIVITT. I CANNOT BELIEVE SUCH A THING COULD HAPPEN. REST ASSURED THAT RUSSIA HAS NOTHING TO DO WITH THIS ACTION, THOUGH WE MOST CERTAINLY FEEL THREATENED. AFTER ALL, IT IS OUR HOMELAND THAT THIS BOMB WAS MOST LIKELY TARGETED AGAINST. IS THERE ANYTHING WE CAN DO TO ASSIST YOU? GORKY." Minister Yakonoff read the communique carefully. "Do you feel threatened, my President? Our radar sites confirm that two aircraft took off from one of the bases in Germany this evening. Both are indeed heading south over France. Our national assets identify them as F-16s from Spangdahlem Air Base. This is most assuredly the nuclear base they have re-armed with nuclear weapons, but with them heading south I don't think we are in danger."

The two men agreed that Russia was in no danger as of yet, but it would be prudent to monitor the situation closely. The communique was softened a bit and sent to Washington. In the meantime, a call went out to the Russian Intelligence agencies to see if there was some covert action the two leaders did not know about, to steal an American bomb. It would not be the first time the old KGB had pulled such a stunt, but this was stretching the limits of their charter. The head of the agency, along with the country's top nuclear scientists, were summoned to the bunker. It would be some time before anyone had any answers. The ball was squarely in the Americans' court.

CHAPTER THIRTY THREE

—

THE PENTAGON SNACK BAR

"Jesus, Man. Can you believe this is happening? I heard of some crazy stunts before, but what could this guy be thinking?" The two Air Force sergeants were still in the hallway approaching the basement snackbar. It wasn't until they reached the entrance could they even see who was in the room. A couple of Army officers in line for burgers, a Navy seaman with a tray of at least a half a dozen hot fudge sundaes—he obviously lost the flip in the NMCC—and one of those computer types sucking on a cup of coffee and swaying to his earphones, probably listening to Mozart. He didn't look like the type to be digging M.C. Hammer or Kool and the Gang.

"I don't know Brother, but I ain't seen so many uptight folks. Desert Storm was easier than this. If the fool drops that bomb we might as well go find a deep hole to hide in. I heard the captain say the Prez is talking to Gorky." The two controllers obviously thought that they were among friends, or not in earshot of anyone who would count. These two were from the Air Force Operations Center. They had been monitoring all the calls between the CSAF and USAFE, and they were aware of enough to be dangerous.

"Well, it sounds like General Morton over there is going to take care of business. But I don't understand why not shoot the bastard down. Seems to me nobody would take one of those fuckin' bombs unless they planned on using it. We need to blow his shit away. Maybe those boys from Zaragoza will get him. The two sergeants ordered their chili dogs and cokes, wrapped aluminum foil over the top of the dogs, and disappeared down one of the maze of hallways.

Peter Sciapini reached down, turned the recorder off, unplugged his ears, gathered up his goods and walked out—not knowing whether to smile or to shit.

CHAPTER THIRTY FOUR

SPANGDAHLEM AIR BASE

Back at Spangdahlem Air Base things were hardly normal for a Monday night. Not any more. Colonel Day had recalled the entire wing. The Command Post was rapidly filling up, and although no one came in with a smile on their face— not to worry, there would be nothing to smile about here either. The gravity of the situation became obvious. The first one on the carpet was Colonel Bill Schneider, the top cop on base. He was tough, a previous Army Ranger, and well liked among his people. Right now he was getting his ass chewed.

"You wanna tell me how a God damned cop truck just disappears? What the hell happened out there, Bill? How did the gates get open?" Day wanted answers because everyone up the line wanted answers.

"Sir, I lost a good cop out there with his head blown off. We are scouring the countryside for whoever killed him and took his truck." Schneider answered.

Mitchell turned his inquisition on the Base Commander. "Dan, what do we know from the Base Exchange explosion?"

"Apparently it was a bomb in a car that plowed through the BX door. It took all the fire equipment we had and as much as the Germans could spare to help. We've just now got it contained. Anyway, that's why we responded to the real world fire rather than the scramble. It's wrong, and they know it. But it's tough telling a fireman to let a fire go while they truck out to the runway, when they usually never even see an airplane taxi—much less take off. The OSI and the guys from D.C. that came in on that Gulfstream found some evidence that we confirmed for them, and they went off to search out a house in one of the neighboring towns. Bill sent some of his men with them." The Base Commander nodded toward the top cop.

———

CHAPTER THIRTY FIVE

TRIPOLI, LIBYA

Jowal Rafshanjani was at his post in what used to be Mohammar Khadafi's command bunker outside Tripoli. He was second in command to Barak El-Kamani. He had just heard from his boss that everything was on track. Mustafa had indeed flown off from Spangdahlem Air Base in Germany with a nuclear bomb and he was inbound to Libya. The surprise was that the Americans would send off a chase aircraft, but he didn't worry. Mustafa had a significant lead.

"Launch the tanker and the fighter escort. Execute the Falcon plan as we have briefed. Put our defenses on high alert." Rafshanjani instructed his staff and the Libyan military personnel still around. There was no doubt who was in charge. The Libyans were afraid of the Iranians. Even though Tehran had sent in their forces to help fight the rebel insurgency, the Iranian Revolutionary Guard people were tough to deal with and it seemed, impossible to please.

The launch order came into the Command Bunker at Tripoli airfield. The crews had been assembled earlier, briefed their mission, and were just awaiting news to launch -- news that their pigeon was inbound. The old but recently upgraded KC-747 tanker was the first to launch, followed 15 minutes later by four MIG-29 fighters. The Migs were only armed with heat seeking missiles. The pilots used to train with real armament back when the Shah was in power and afterward for a while. In fact the U.S. had graciously equipped the Iranian Air Force with brand new F-4 and F-14 aircraft back in the 70s, and provided them with Maverick missile for tank killers and Phoenix and Aim 9 heat seekers for air to air. The IAF had managed to keep most of those planes operational, but their training had slacked off. Now, with the U.S. embargo on military gear, as well as food and other equipment, they had to cut back and save the real thing for when it was necessary. They were working on getting new air to air missiles from the Russians, but the sanctions and embargo were limiting the Russian cooperation.

The Migs caught up with the tanker 100 miles northwest of the Libyan coast. They each refueled from the "drogue" basket trailing from the tanker's left wing—just to be sure everything worked, and the five aircraft continued north into the dark toward Sardinia. The refueling boom tucked up underneath the tail of the converted airliner remained stowed—for now.

———

CHAPTER THIRTY SIX

WASHINGTON D.C.

Peter Sciapini finished his story and took it to Marianne Rogers. He was obviously proud of what he had written. She had been waiting impatiently, and she wanted to get the hell out of there for the night. News hawk or not, there was such a thing as family time for everyone.

"How much of this is conjecture, and how much is true, Ski?" Marianne asked after reading the reporter's story.

"Shit Boss! It's all hearsay. I can't stand here and tell you these guys know what they're talking about. I don't even know who they are. But I guarantee something's going on over there and it all fits." Sciapini knew he had a good story. He also knew it was based on rumor, innuendo and guess work. But, what the hell! That's what he gets paid for.

"You mean to tell me these 'Pentagon sources' are just voices in that damn recorder of yours?" Marianne wasn't really pissed, she just wanted the full story before she gave her OK.

"What can I tell ya, Boss?" Sciapini wore a shit eatin' grin as wide as his dirty, ruffled collar. "They talk, I listen. Can I help it if they talk too much?"

"OK, SkeePee. Print it! But I want your ass back over there first thing in the morning. Shit's gonna hit the fan when the morning edition gets out, and I want you there to record every back peddle and waffle the Pentagon comes up with. And get hold of Mark Peterson. Tell him to get to work at the White House. If this is true, I gotta believe

McDivitt has things buzzing there. I want to know what the gist of the conversation with Gorky is." Peterson was the newspaper's White House correspondent.

"Yes Ma'am!"

CHAPTER THIRTY SEVEN

———

AIRSPACE OVER FRANCE

Robert Mustan had now discarded the name in his own mind. He was once again Muhammad Mustafa, and he wanted nothing to do anymore with the western world. He looked forward to being in Libya, amongst his own people and away from the American influence. He had throttled the Falcon back to .85 Mach, settling down into a comfortable cruise speed of about 400 mph that would conserve fuel. One of the beauties of this jet was a computer that would tell you just how fast to fly to conserve fuel, to go the farthest—whatever you wanted it to tell you. It even told you exactly how much gas you would land with at your present cruise setting and altitude. He had a long way to go, and he knew that if his playmates didn't show up on time he would be required to land for gas. He didn't want to have to do that. Explaining his presence, and the configuration of his jet to some official in Sardinia would be difficult. He could explain the bomb as some sort of practice munition, or electronic countermeasures to locals who don't even know what an F-16 is. But explaining the fact that he was there at all without a flight plan, would be pushing it. He would have to feign an emergency. He had of course, planned for every contingency, and he would go into Alghero, on the northwest coast of Sardinia, if necessary. He would stay away from Decimomannu, on the south coast, because the Americans used a training base there. From Alghero to Beni Walid was only 600 miles, easily reached after refueling. He was now just south of Lyon,

France—about over top of Grenoble. As he had suspected, the French had not reacted. They had asked his call sign and intentions several times, but when he never answered, they finally gave up. He would be "feet wet" over the Mediterranean in another 20 minutes.

Brad Mitchell eased the nose of his jet over at 33,000 feet. He kept the power up to let her accelerate, flipped on the "Altitude Hold" function of the auto-pilot, and studied the charts. He knew that the "Rogue" was at least a hundred miles ahead. There was no way he could catch up in a pure tail chase, but he would give it every chance. They were similarly configured. The only thing in his favor was that he wasn't dragging that bomb along. Unfortunately, the "silver bullet" was sleek and clean, and not much drag, so he would not have much of an advantage. He could only hope that the "Rogue" was trying to conserve gas, and that if Zaragoza could launch some tanker support, he would have gas to spare. He considered tapping afterburner, but he knew that the fuel consumption would be way too much, and he would run out before any tankers could offer a refill. He would just have to take what he could get from a slight overtake and hope the "Rogue" would do something stupid. He checked his missiles one more time. They were cooled and ready. He kept the master arm switch in the "Simulate" position for now, allowing him all the fire symbology, but a safety factor so as not to accidentally launch a missile off into the French countryside. He made a mental note to be sure to go to the "Arm" position if he got in close. What he did not need in the heat of the battle was to obtain perfect shoot parameters, mash the "pickle" button, and have nothing happen because he forgot to arm up.

Brad unfolded the map out in the cramped cockpit, and turned on his console flood lights. "Sentry 41, Conan One, give me your best fix on the Bandit right now." He knew that the AWACS controller could pinpoint the position within a mile.

"Roger Conan. Bogey is now One Eight Three degrees for 123 nautical miles, approximately 12 miles south of Lyon, France. Heading is now One Six Five. Angels Three Three. He's currently doing point Eight Five Mach. " Stephanie also had her charts out. She drew a straight line from the bogey on an extended heading in front of him.

The line crossed the French coast halfway between Nice and Marseille, and dissected the island of Sardinia.

"Thanks Sentry. Keep a good eye on him. How far behind are you?" Brad was trying …to get the big picture, locating all the players.

"Conan, we are 82 miles at his four o'clock. We are at your one thirty to two o'clock for seventy miles." Stephanie had the geometry down. "We are maxed out in speed. We are closer to him now than you are, but if we all keep the same speeds and headings, we should merge with you just about the time we hit the coast, and he will be 75 miles ahead."

Mitchell gained more admiration for the female controller, and was sorry he had snapped at her before. He made a quick calculation on his map, laying his pencil down in a straight line from Nice to the east, west and south. If "Rogue" turned east at the coast, he could barely make it to Yugoslavia. Otherwise, it was Italy, Sardinia, Corsica, Majorca or Spain. He just wouldn't have the gas to go any further. It wouldn't make sense that he would suddenly turn east to Yugoslavia or the boot of Italy. If he was going to do that, why not go direct from the beginning? Flying over Switzerland without talking or squawking would have been just as easy as flying over France. It also doesn't make sense to turn west to Spain. Too much chance of intercept from our own guys. No, it had to be Corsica, Sardinia or Majorca. But then what?

"Sentry, Conan, I'm too far out now to reach Ramstein. Do you still have them on frequency?" Brad wanted some help.

"Roger Conan, I have them on HF. My senior controller has been talking to the USAFE Command Center. Standby." HF stood for High Frequency radio. It had a long range, enhanced every time we put another satellite up. Most fighter aircraft were not equipped with it though. "Conan, this is Sentry Four One. I have just spoken to USAFE and they are launching tankers and fighters from Zaragoza to attempt an intercept, and to rendezvous with us. How copy?" This was a new voice—a male with a very official sounding tone.

"Conan copies. Ask USAFE if we have any FG-15s at Decimomannu. If I were a betting man right now, I would say our bogey is headed toward either Corsica or Sardinia. He can't get any farther than that. We should know soon—about the time he goes 'feet wet.' He will need to commit by then. If we have any eagles at Deci, they could intercept easier." Decimomannu was a training base with an Air Combat Maneuvering Instrumentation (ACMI) range. It was used by the NATO forces for good over water air-to-air training. Periodically, F-15s from Lakenheath in England deployed down to Deci for their version of the F-16 training scenario at Zaragoza.

"Roger, standby Conan." There was a long pause while the controller passed the question over the HF to USAFE. The answer came back negative. "Conan, the only forces at Deci right now are Italian Tornados."

Shit! Thought Brad Mitchell. *Eagle drivers were never there when you needed them.*

"OK, I copy that Sentry. Suggest to USAFE that they alert Deci, and consider that a better recovery base for us -- especially if we don't get tanker support. They might also want to tell the Italian authorities to be on the lookout for this guy if he lands in Sardinia or Corsica. Suggest the same alert for Majorca." There was something they must be overlooking, but Brad couldn't figure what it was.

Mustafa pressed back in the seat and tried to stretch. It was going to be at least another two hours before he would see the sands of the Sahara, so he worked his muscles and stretched. It was almost calm enough to sleep up here. He had typed all the coordinates he needed into the INS, and "George" (the autopilot) was in control. But Mustafa was much too professional and too excited to sleep. He wondered what reaction had taken place at Spang. They most likely thought he was flying the line, and they would be looking for him in former East Germany. It was well passed his projected TOT (Time on Target), so he knew they would be very puzzled. What amazed him was that only the French controllers had even questioned his location and identity on the radio, and they had given up early. The Germans never even saw him. He was sure that once he was over the Mediterranean, no one would see him, except those he wanted to. He figured the tanker and the IAF were still about 300-400 miles ahead. He made a quick fuel calculation, put his head back, closed his eyes, and said a prayer to Allah for assistance.

Brad Mitchell safed his ejection seat, raised it until his helmet hit the canopy, and then unstrapped his lower harness buckles. Then he pulled out the ever present "piddle pack." He knew this was going to to be a long night and he wanted to get this over with before things got exciting. Taking a leak in the F-16 is no small feat. There is no relief tube, and the thirty degree inclined seat made it an uphill pee. Brad had to laugh. He had mastered the technique. Ever since he had three kidney stones back in his F-4 days, his bladder would only go for an hour or so—especially when it was constantly being squeezed by an anti-G suit. So Brad always carried one or two "piddle packs" with him, and he used them. A "piddle pack" was a plastic pouch with a sponge inside and a conveniently sized opening. The sponge would soak up the urine until it was saturated, and the rest would fill the pouch. Brad was so famous for having to use these things on almost every sortie, one squadron had tried to change his nickname to "Packman." He laughed to himself. No way! He liked the name "Conan," and he didn't want to be known by any other handle.

The practice of using nicknames is almost as old as flying itself. There are documented nicknames for pilots in every war. No one knows where or why it started, but it is almost a must in today's tactical air forces. Different outfits have different methods of naming their own. Sometimes it is an initiation rite, as it was it Brad's case. Sometimes it just comes naturally. Some nicknames last forever, some are changed when the pilot goes to a new squadron. For a while during and after the Vietnam war, nicknames were used as callsigns over the radio as his was tonight. Thus the term, tactical callsign. A pilot's tactical callsign would be how the flight was managed, and all transmissions would use his callsign instead of "one, two, etc.," his position in the flight. For example, Buick Flight may be scheduled as a flight of four F-4s over North Vietnam. They would talk to controlling agencies as Buick Flight, while amongst themselves they might be "Rowdy, Sawhorse, Boxman and Gopher," the tactical callsigns of the four pilots. This practice had various restrictions laid on over the years until one day an F-4 pilot shot down one of his own wingmen by mistake on a training missile shoot. He couldn't remember his wingman's callsign to warn him to defend against the heat seeking missile. The powers that be determined that tactical callsigns were a partial cause of the accident, and from then on, all radio calls would use only the flight position—ie; One, Two, Three, etc. However, the practice of nicknaming pilots has continued, and Brad remembered well how he got "Conan."

He had been the Squadron Commander of the 80th squadron in Kunsan, Korea. The Headhunters, as the squadron was called, were a spirited bunch of fun loving fighter pilots on probably the Air Force's last "good deal." A remote tour—away from home and the worries of a family, where esprit de corps takes over for loneliness. The "Juvats," another nickname for the squadron, had a time honored tradition of taking their "newbees" down to the local bar district off base on a "Sweep" soon after they arrived in country. There were a set number of bars to be visited, no set number of songs to be sung, and a huge number of beers to be drunk. At one of the stops, the "Old Heads," those two or three pilots who were the next to rotate back home, would name the new guys with their tactical callsigns, or nicknames. Brad Mitchell was a big guy—about 6'4" and 225, with a volatile temper. About that time, the Conan movies were a big hit at the party hooch, and one of the old heads decided that the name "Conan" fit Mitchell. It stuck and he liked it. In his case it wasn't used all the time. Especially not now that he was a wing commander, and had to command some respect from the young guys. But when the temper flared, everyone stood out of "Conan's" way. Obviously, for other reasons Genoa had decided to use callsign and nicknames for the Tango Team as well. Even another logical use of a time honored tradition.

CHAPTER THIRTY EIGHT

ZARAGOZA AIR BASE, SPAIN

The 10th Fighter Squadron was very much at home at Zaragoza. They had been one of the original squadrons at Hahn Air Base in Germany, and deployed to Spain at least once a year to get in some good flying during the lousy weather winter months in Germany. Hahn was one of the bases closed back in 1991 and the 10th was actually deactivated. However, with a Republican administration in power, beefing up the defense budget, and the re-emerging threat from Russia, the Air Force re-opened three fighter squadrons. The 10th was sent back to Germany to Spangdahlem, and was currently on a six week deployment to Zaragoza.

The Sabres were hard at play. In fact, things had gotten so out of hand that they had already been kicked out of the Zaragoza Officers Club twice and they had only been in country for a week. That wasn't all that unusual though. It was almost a ritual. If the squadron wasn't banned from the club at least once in every deployment, they must not have had a good time. Much of the problem was self inflicted by the staff at Zaragoza. The Officers Club had just recently been closed for food because they could not maintain a profit. Clubs in the Air Force were required to be self sufficient. If they weren't, they were "flagged" and brought to the attention of the CINC himself, as if he had nothing better to concentrate on. Ever since a fiasco in the 80s at the Ramstein Club, that ended in Fraud Waste and Abuse accusations from Congress, club activities were always front page news to the legislature, and therefore to the generals who had to answer for them. Since Zaragoza had only a small permanent party corps of officers, they depended on the TDY personnel to make the Club prosper. The same was true with the Enlisted Club, but historically NCO and enlisted clubs do a thriving business. Especially at a base like Zaragoza, where so many of the enlisted force live in the dormitories, they have nowhere else to go for food and entertainment.

The Officers Club at Zaragoza usually just scraped by. But due to gross mismanagement, there had recently been a huge loss in revenue. Spanish employees who had worked there for years were caught with their hands in the till. Firing them proved to be impossible due to various status of forces agreements and lack of proof. As a result, the club went under, and the wing commander couldn't stand his name in lights, the officers were about to lose their club. They were expected to go to the Enlisted Club or the Recreation Center to eat. All that did was piss off the Sabres even more. The old fighter pilot adage "there's a pork chop in every bottle of beer," became the excuse not to walk the quarter to half mile to eat. So tonight they had decided to take out their frustrations on the glasses and furniture.

The Sabres had finished flying for the day at about 4 pm. It had been a good last few days, too. They'd had "Sabre Late Night" at the bar last Friday, and everyone was still in a partying mood. At "Sabre Late Night" the squadron commander, Lt. Colonel Ed "Coach" Howe presided over the informal pilot meeting. Events of the week were covered and the schedule for the rest of the deployment was discussed. There was a lot of good fighter pilot bullshit to pass along, as well as never ending rations to those who had screwed up during the week. The session always ended with the "Coach" awarding the "Bent Sabre" to the member of the squadron who had put his name up in lights the best (or worst) during the week. The "Bent Sabre" was just that—a long sword, bent at about a 30 degree angle halfway along the blade. It was to stay closely guarded in the recipient's possession until the next "Late Night with Sabre One." Lucky defenders of the blade had earned their honor by any number of faux pas. One week a lieutenant had received it for a

string of expletives and cuss words over the radio, not knowing he had
a stuck microphone, while flying in the same formation as the wing
commander. Another had received the sword for a more serious offense
of dropping a bomb off range. The "Coach" himself had won it last
month for explaining how he was going to "take the Wing Director of
Operations to the cleaners" on the golf course the next day, not knowing
the DO had walked in and was standing right behind him. Last Friday
it was "Lucky" Finnegan's turn. Captain Jim Finnegan was the A Flight
Commander. He had come off the range earlier in the week, and hadn't
paid any attention to the tower instructions about a runway change. He
lead his flight of four up for the initial approach the wrong way.

So everyone got a good laugh, Finnegan bought a round of cheer,
there was a move afoot to change his callsign to "Wrongway" Finnegan,
and the group settled down to singing every rendition of filthy fighter
pilot songs they could remember. And for the Sabres, that was a lot of
songs. They had just published a song book that had every aviation song
imaginable—from the World War I and II eras, through Korea and
Vietnam, and several written since. Very few were the kinds of songs
you would sing in church, or in any sort of mixed company—unless
you were a fighter pilot. When they got to singing, and there was liquor
flowing, there was safety in numbers. The basic philosophy was "If you
don't like our songs, fuck you!" Suffice it to say, the one or two women
in the bar left soon after the crooning started. Except of course, for the
women fighter pilots in the squadron. They could hold their own and
a couple of them could really sing. One lady that had left disgusted
was the Zaragoza Wing Commander's wife. She never did like these
goings on much, and she especially had it in for the Sabres. The last
time they were in Zaragoza, in December of last year, they had gone on
one of their rampages and tried to dance with the Officers Wives Club
Christmas tree. The tree fell, and the angel on top ended up on one of
the pilot's face. That little episode cost the squadron $200, and the pilot
a Letter of Reprimand. At any rate, Mrs. Davenport was grossed out
again tonight, and she went straight home to report her disgust to her
husband. He promised to investigate. Actually, Colonel Ron Davenport
just wanted an excuse to go to the club and join in himself. He had only

been home because he knew his wife was supposed to be at an Officers Wives Club (OWC) meeting, and the dog hadn't been out in hours.

By the time Colonel Davenport got to the Club all hell had broken loose. Colonel Joe Ripley, his own wing Operations Group Commander had decided that the heat was too much, and had diplomatically retired to his quarters. One of the things most colonels figure out is that if the boys are getting too rowdy, disappear. Ignorance is bliss. One can always claim he had no idea what was going on. That was the case tonight.

After the "Choir" had all but lost their voices, someone decided that it was time for carrier landings. Tables were pushed together and lathered up with beer, and a wet "runway" 20 feet long was fabricated out of six or seven tables. The drunk fighter pilots would run full speed at the tables and fling themselves belly first onto the "runway," arms out in front of them, and legs bent at the knees. The idea was to catch the cable (a garden hose) with the legs before going off the end of the tables. Someone had found an old bathtub in a pile of junk behind the club, and they brought it in as the "deep blue sea" at the end of the tables. The bathtub had been filled with beer, and had a head on it about two feet thick. The cable operators were two of the flight commanders, and they of course, had complete authority as to whose legs did or did not engage the cable. Suffice it to say that just about everyone got to swim in a tub of San Miguel beer at least once. There were always a few casualties in an operation like this, and tonight was no exception. There were cracked chins from hitting the "runway" too hard, scraped shins from not hitting it hard enough, and one or two welts on the back of the legs from over zealous cable operators. Unfortunately, there were also several busted tables, and a whole tray of glasses, that just happened to be in the way. That's when Colonel Davenport walked in, and the Sabres were "asked" to leave. Ed Howe was told to be in the Wing King's office the next morning at 0730 -- in his dress blues.

Not to be put away wet, the Sabres took their frolicking to the hallways and rooms of Billeting. Someone found a bowling ball in a roommate's closet, and soon a bowling match started up in the hallway, using San Miguel beer bottles for pins. Then the LPA (Lieutenant's Protective Association) decided to go on a "room inversion" rampage.

The LPA was made up of all the squadron lieutenants. Normally lieutenants catch all the flak and shit duties, and they felt there was safety in numbers to be able to yell "Bullshit" in unison if they felt persecuted. Of course, this was never taken seriously by anyone of the rank of captain or above, but a good LPA could bring a lot of laughs and spirit to the organization. Tonight the lieutenants were fired up. They started at one end of the hall and worked their way to the other. Every room that was unattended was "inverted." Everything in the room was turned upside down—bed, chairs, desk, refrigerator, even the contents of the refrigerator. If the occupant of the room happened to be home, and had retired for the evening, Katie bar the door. He probably found himself "walled"—standing on his head against the wall with the bed propped vertically against him.

Above the Sabres, on the second floor, the Zaragoza Tanker Task Force aircrews were trying to get some peace and quiet. They had tankers tapped for an 0200 hours show time for a trip to the Mideast the next day. Unfortunately, their complaints and pleas fell on deaf ears, at least until the call came from the command post.

The call got to the Tanker Alert Force Commander first because there were communications set up for it. Although they were not officially on alert, they often had to move up their schedule to meet some deployment of fighters or short notice missions that needed some gas. "Scramble two tankers ASAP. Contact the USAFE Operations Center for specifics." The Zaragoza Command Post controller had no idea how to scramble any fighters. There were none on alert. He did have the visiting squadron commander's phone numbers and a call was put in to Ed Howe. Another call went out to Colonel Davenport.

Ed Howe did not have a secure phone in his room, so the controller couldn't tell him much—only that USAFE wanted him to get at least four fighters airborne as soon as possible. He threw on a flight suit and went immediately into the squadron hallway. After dodging a bowling ball on its way to pick up a seven-ten split, he called for a Knock-it-Off.

"All right guys, that's enough! Listen up. There's something going on. I just got a phone call to scramble at least four jets ASAP. I'm not sure we can even do that, but we have to try." He looked at his Operations

Officer, Ron Parkins. "Do we have four sober pilots?" Parkins didn't think so, but he would let the "Coach" make that call.

"I don't know sir, but I'll find out. What do you want us to do?" Parkins was as dedicated a professional as there was in the Air Force. He knew something important was happening, and the time for play was now behind them.

"I'm going to the Command Post to get the straight skinny. I need you to get someone over to the enlisted side, find the maintenance folks, and get them prepping six jets as fast as they can. Then, you and your fliers get to the squadron building. I'll meet you there. The tankers are scrambling as well, so pick people who can really hack it, or pick no one at all." Howe had to be sure he covered the bases. A night scramble after a long duty day, and an evening of partying is an accident waiting to happen as it was. Add refueling and an extended mission to it, and someone is asking for trouble.

Howe went to the Command Post and arrived about the same time as Ron Davenport, the host wing commander. They were filled in quickly on the phone by General Morton from Ramstein, and instructed to launch everything they could as soon as possible. The fighters and tankers were to head due east toward Corsica, attempt to intercept the "Rogue," and force him to land at Decimomannu. Once airborne they were to contact Sentry 41 and Conan 1 for directions and to rendezvous. At the very least, a tanker had to be launched to refuel Sentry 41 and Conan to recover them at Zaragoza. One of the colonels was tasked to fly onboard a tanker and act as On Scene Commander.

"Gentlemen, I don't need to tell you there is high visibility out there. The President and the diplomats are already involved. We want this bomb back, but if he won't land, we do not have clearance to shoot him down. Tell your boys to defend themselves as necessary, but not to initiate hostilities. Is that understood?" Morton wanted very badly to be in Zaragoza right now. The ViceCINC was at the controls at Ramstein and dealing with Washington. Chuck Morton wanted to be where the action was.

"Yes sir. I understand and unfortunately I think there's a problem. Sir, our jets are loaded with training ordnance—SUUs and TERs and training missiles. We won't have time to load anything else up. All the base down here has is AIM-9Ps anyway. Our guns are loaded with training rounds. They will do a job on a target, but with no explosive charge and no tracers to track their aim." Howe figured the SUUs (practice bomb dispensers) and TERs (bomb racks) could be downloaded in no time, and that would significantly reduce the drag on the aircraft. However, the missile on the wingtip was for training only—it gave all the symbology and information to the pilot, but it had no rocket motor. It wouldn't shoot. They might have time to load Papas (AIM-9Ps), depending on how fast Colonel Davenport could get his munitions people to respond. There would definitely not be time to download and reload the guns with high explosive rounds.

"Well, get out there and let this bastard know he's not getting away with this. If he lands somewhere, put a flight in there with him. Better arm your guys with sidearms. He's got live missiles and a gun, but there's only one of him. If he shoots first, blow his shit away, even if it is with TP bullets. That oughta be a lot of fun in the dark." Morton knew that it would be close to impossible. Without tracers the pilot would have no idea where his bullets were going. Besides, the "Rogue" would most likely have all his lights off. Another pilot would have to get so close to even see him, that if he shot at that range, he would most likely fly through the explosion (assuming a hit) and blow himself up.

"OK sir. We're on it. Colonel Davenport will run things from here and his Vice will be on the tanker. I will lead my squadron." Howe did not even wait for a reply. He left and went immediately to the squadron building to see how many (if any) sober Sabres there were.

Ron Parkins had done his typical masterful job of organization. He had six pilots ready to go—Howe didn't ask to smell anyone's breath. The Officer In Charge (OIC) of the maintenance unit, Captain Steve Lamond, and his NCOIC, Chief Don Hester, were also there with puzzled looks on their faces.

"Steve, how many jets can you give me for an engine start in 20 minutes?" Howe asked the maintenance officer.

"As many as you need, sir. We were able to get about twenty guys out of their quarters. Half of them aren't in uniform, but they're here.

Do you want bomb droppers or air-to-air jets?" Of the 20 aircraft the squadron had at Zaragoza, twelve were configured with wing tanks and SUUs and TERs for working the air to ground bombing range. The other eight were clean (no external stores) for air-to-air training. Each one had a training missile on it, regardless of the configuration.

"We're going to need the gas. Give us four primary and two spare air-to-mud jets. Drop the SUUs and TERs. If there is time and the local guys deliver missiles, load the Papas, but don't let that hold us up. Arm the guns, and we'll pull all pins in the chocks—no end of runway checks. We'll be hopping." Coach Howe had everyone's attention. They still didn't know what was going on. However, he knew that the maintenance guys would be the long pole in the tent for this one, so he wanted to get the Chief and his Captain on their way. Chief Hester was barking orders into his hand held radio before they even left the building.

Howe turned to Parkins and his suddenly sober Sabres. "Ron, give me a primary four ship and two spares. I will lead. We'll start the spares if the jets are ready, taxi them to EOR, but not take them off unless needed. Here's the situation." The boss quickly explained everything he knew. There wasn't much time. The mission was to get airborne as quickly as possible, head east looking for a lone jet over the Mediterranean, intercept him, and convince him to land at a base in southern Sardinia. Their only help was in the form of an AWACS and some colonel from the National Guard, way back in trail. Howe didn't know that Brad Mitchell was the "some colonel." If he had he might have felt a little better about it. Howe was Brad's number two at Kunsan when Mitchell led the attack on the north. He considered Brad Mitchell as the best squadron commander he ever had and tried to emulate Mitchell in his own methods of command.

There was never any doubt that Ed Howe would take the lead. He was the squadron commander, and he belonged out in front. He knew that, and all of his men knew it. He rounded out the flight with Lt. Jack "Pigpen" Smiley as #2, Capt. "Lucky" Finnegan as #3 and deputy lead, and Capt. Mike "Kujo" Greenwood as #4. The two spares were Major K.C. "Strobe" Shobe and Lt. John "John Boy" Brandon.

They briefed the particulars in the life support room, as they donned G-suits, harnesses, and grabbed their helmets and flashlights. The briefing continued in the crew van on the way down the flight line, and would have to be completed in the air, over the radio. This was not normal business for an F-16 squadron. Although it is a multi-purpose jet, the Air Force primarily uses it as an air to ground fighter, at least in the active service. They did very little night flying, and when they did, it was usually in pairs to a night gunnery range. All of the pilots were qualified in air-to-air intercepts, and most had even flown some intercepts at night—but usually one-vs-one against a wingman with all his lights on bright and flash. This was going to be a demanding mission, and one that would normally take an hour or so to prepare and brief. The "Coach" didn't have an hour. They were lucky if they had time to relieve themselves beside the jet before it was time to be cranking engines.

By the time the van pulled up to the row of Falcons, Chief Hester and Captain Lamond had their maintenance troops in overdrive. Six fighters had the canopies up, and munitions men were dropping suspension equipment. Only one aircraft was ready to go, but there were at least three troops working on each one.

"OK guys. I'll take this one and get it started and on the radio. Start as soon as you can. Check in on squadron common when you're on frequency, and let me know as soon as you are ready to taxi. I'll go with the first four jets that are ready. If necessary, we'll go off two at a time. Questions?" They all had questions—like what the hell is Mustan up to? Is he going to shoot first? But they kept those questions to themselves. "Lucky" Finnegan gave his boss the "two snakes" sign as the "Coach" climbed out of the van. "Two snakes" was another one of the traditions left over from their Headhunter days in Korea. Finnegan had also been in the 80th TFS before their assignments to Hahn. The "two snakes" were the arms encircled over the head like horns, with fists clenched. It was another throwback from the Conan movies, and was a salute of "good luck" and "good hunting." "Coach" Howe reciprocated.

As Ed Howe started his engine the first KC-10 tanker took off. The second one was just starting to taxi. "Zaragoza Command Post, Sabre One is starting, standing by for words."

"Roger Sabre, start is approved, tower is working a clearance for you. Sir, there should be some missiles rolling up there any time now." The command post controller at Zaragoza was excited. He had never been this busy. Normally the ZAB job was one of the dullest in the command and control world. Not tonight. "Sir, we have Sentry Four One on HF radio. She says you need to be airborne within twenty minutes or you will not be able to intercept."

"Tell Sentry we should make that, but it will be close. Is anyone working with the Spanish? We will need to go supersonic to make this work." Howe knew that the Spanish were very protective of their desert. Supersonic over land was taboo anywhere in Europe. Sonic booms tended to mess up the reproductive cycles of cockroaches or something. That was as good an excuse as any. Ed Howe called it the sound of freedom.

"Sabre, don't worry about the Spanish. Don't worry about a clearance either. Let me take care of that from this end. Just consider my scramble order as your license to get the job done." Colonel Davenport had taken over the mike, and obviously he had control. Howe was impressed. The previous "milk toast" colonel had some balls after all.

"Roger that sir. We'll be airborne with four in fifteen minutes." Howe looked down the flight line and saw a trailer pull up to Finnegan's aircraft with about a dozen AIM-9P missiles on it. He made a mental note to find out who got missiles before they took off. It would definitely dictate his tactics once they got in close.

"Sabre Three is ready." Finnegan could see four other strobe lights, meaning at least five of them had started. He had watched the munitions team load a Papa missile on his right wing tip in about 45 seconds. He hoped that they had done it right and all the pins were pulled. Obviously he had no time to preflight the missile. The jet next to him got one too. He thought that was his wingman, "Kujo." In the dark and their hurry to get going, he hadn't paid attention to who had climbed in what jet.

"Sabre Four's ready."

"Roger Sabres. We'll taxi One, Three, Four and Six. Two and Five, taxi when able. Sabres go button two." Howe switched to ground control frequency and called for taxi clearance. Not that it mattered, he was going to taxi tonight even without clearance. Just a habit.

"Roger Sabre One. Taxi to runway Three Zero. Wind is Three Two Zero at one zero, altimeter is Two Niner Niner One. You are cleared quick climb and immediate turn to Zero Niner Zero. Contact departure control on frequency Three One Four decimal Zero, and squawk Four One Zero One." Howe loved it when a plan came together. He repeated the altimeter setting, pushed up the power, tapped the brakes and taxied out of the chocks. As he made the turn onto the taxiway he returned his crew chief's "Two Snakes."

Jim Finnegan's head ached. Not because he was hungover. He had actually only had one swig of the beer he had bought when he had to buy a round earlier in the night. His "wrong way" approach to the traffic pattern that had earned him the Bent Sabre award had pissed him off. Finnegan was a perfectionist, and he hated it when he screwed up. As far as he was concerned, it did not happen very often. At any rate, he had decided to take a week off from booze, and do some hard studying this next week while he had the time. He didn't get the time very often at home. With three kids and a wife who hated Germany, he found himself playing Mr. Mom and Dear Abby most of the time. He relished these TDY trips to hone his fighter pilot skills, and reestablish himself as the squadron Top Gun. Tonight his head hurt though, because he was stupid enough to go off the end of the carrier into the foam of the "deep blue sea" with his head down. He now had a large bump on his head where it struck the far end of the bathtub. He was pissed at himself about that too.

Finnegan's Falcon had stepped through its flight control checks while he finished strapping in. The F-16 is a magnificent machine, with state-of-the-art technology. Some had often described it as ahead of itself. The fly-by-wire flight control system was controlled by a computer. It had to be. The design of the aircraft was such that the location of the center of gravity would put it out of control without the computer. That factor was what allowed the F-16 to turn such a tight circle. The computer limits the turn to nine Gs (nine times the force of gravity), but that restriction is because the pilot would have a hard time taking more than that. The jet could probably withstand 13 - 15 Gs. The flight control check was all done automatically. The pilot just flips a switch and takes his hand off the controls. When the computer is done, a light tells the pilot he's good to go. If not, try the test again. It it doesn't work that time, call a specialist. No calls tonight. Finnegan was prepared to take it even if it hadn't passed it's test.

He turned on the radar and the Radar Warning Receiver (RWR), downloaded the Stores Management System (SMS) of the SUUs and TERs that were no longer there, and loaded the missile. The SMS was another computer that interfaced with what was loaded on the aircraft and the Fire Control Computer (FCC). The SMS did other things too, but basically it was sort of a bookkeeper and helped manage all the little electrons that ran around the system. The Falcon was often called the "electric jet," and very few pilots knew why things happened the way they did—just as long as they happened when they were supposed to. The missile had to be loaded into the computer or the aircraft would never know it was out there on the wingtip. If the system doesn't know it's there, the pilot can never shoot it. This was just another subtlety the pilot realized when he started thinking HE was in control. When the aircraft first came into the inventory the older fighter pilots complained that they weren't really flying the jet—some damned computer was. At that time the side stick controller that replaced the conventional stick between the legs didn't even move. The pilot made an input, the computer would sense the pressure on the stick and the computer would move the flight control surfaces to roll, climb, dive, whatever. Later the stick was changed so it now moves a grand total of ¼ inch, just to let the pilot think that he's in control. Actually there were a number of ways to fool the system, or make a wrong input.

As soon as his INS showed an eight minute alignment, Finnegan went to NAV position and called "Sabre Three's ready" on the radio. As he taxied out, he ran the self test on the RWR gear. He might need it tonight. The RWR detected radar energy and displayed a symbol and an audio signal for the pilot to determine what was looking at him. A very sophisticated "fuzz-buster." Different symbols meant different weapons systems, and it was optimized for the state-of-the-art Russian SAM (Surface to Air Missile) threat. It would also respond to other aircraft radar, and although it would not display distance from the emitter information, the pilot could tell the direction and relative signal strength just by the clock position on the scope and how close to the center the threat was displayed. The Built in Test (BIT) showed everything was working.

Next Finnegan turned down the intensity on his cockpit lights, and looked around to make sure everything was strapped down tight. He wanted no distractions, either from interior lighting or anything flying around the cockpit. He called up the missile and made sure the SMS was on the proper station. The munitions guys did not have enough time to download the training missile, so it was still on the left wing. Just to be safe, Jim downloaded it from the computer. If the jet doesn't know it's there, it won't try to shoot it.

Taxiing out, Ed Howe took inventory and attendance. "OK Sabres, say status and let me know if you have missiles. Lead is green, no missile, hot gun."

"Two needs three minutes to taxi. Flight controls. One missile, hot gun."

"Three's in, one missile, hot gun." Finnegan called up the gun to be sure. 510 rounds.

"Four's in, one missile, hot gun."

"Five's just getting started. No missile, hot gun."

"Six is in, one missile, hot gun." So the answer was that he had four taxiing now, three with missiles, and one to taxi in a couple minutes. Too late

"OK Sabres, go button eight and set up for 'Mickey." He wanted them all on the Command Post frequency and to load the WOD and TOD for Have Quick radio operation.

"Two," "Three," "Four," "Five," "Six." After checking them in on frequency the "Coach" called for a "Mickey" tone from the controller. That accomplished, he sent everyone to the active frequency to be sure it worked. Neither number two nor number six could get a good Have

Quick check. "Damned Lieutenants." Howe thought. It wasn't an easy exercise, but they should be able to do it by now. It couldn't be just coincidence that the only two Have Quick systems that didn't work happened to be on the lieutenants' aircraft. No time to mess with it now. He got everyone back on the normal frequency. By now they were approaching the runway.

"OK. Sabres One, Three and Four will go as planned. Sabre Six, you now become Sabre Two, acknowledge."

"Roger, Six becomes Two." The lieutenant was fourth in line, but numbers 3 and 4 pulled over to the side for him to take his new place in line.

"Twenty second takeoff guys. Expect me to accelerate to 400, and then make an AB climb, right hand turn to Zero Niner Zero. Lots of pitch. I'll continue climb to Flight Level Three Zero Zero. Join when you can, but don't expect me to slow down much. Command Post, we will call you after airborne. Get a UHF or VHF frequency for AWACS for us. Also a frequency for Conan One. Any questions?" The only acknowledgement was from the command post controller, who was behind from word one. The rest were as ready for this as they would ever be. Then it hit the "Coach." *Conan one. That is too familiar. Could the colonel in the chase plane be Brad Mitchell - Conan from their days in Korea? Shit hot!"*

"Sabres go button three—no check in. Let's go." Howe switched to the tower frequency.

"Zaragoza tower, Sabres are rolling with four."

"Roger Sabre One, cleared for takeoff. Wind is Three Three Zero at Twelve knots."

One by one the pilots stroked the afterburner and a bright plume of fire lit the dark Spanish night. The fireballs lifted off into the darkness, stayed low to the ground until almost a mile past the end of the runway, and then rapidly rose into the sky. After a minute or two the plumes blended in with the stars and the noise subsided to just the idling engines of the two ground spares left behind. The time was 6:58 pm -- just one hour and twenty two minutes after Muhammad Mustafa had stolen his aircraft

———

CHAPTER THIRTY NINE

OVER THE MEDITERRANEAN SEA

"Sentry Four One, this is Big Star." Captain Stephanie Michaels recognized the voice as that of General Morton. She had talked to him a few times over the past hour, although usually her supervisor jumped in when it was the headquarters calling. This time her supervisor was relieving himself at the urinal in the back of the airplane. "Steve" answered.

"Go ahead Big Star, Sentry has you loud and clear." That wasn't exactly true. They were talking over secure voice and the distance between them was starting to weaken the signal.

"Sentry, this is Big Star. Make sure you get this. We just received information from the intelligence folks that there is a force airborne out of Libya—a Boeing 747, and four MIG-29s heading northwest, directly on a collision course towards our bogey. We must assume it is a rendezvous they have in mind, not a collision. We must also assume the 747 is outfitted for air refueling. The Iranians deployed all of these jets into Libya just recently. Do you copy?" Morton sounded pissed. Not only was he stuck hundreds of miles from the action, he was forced to rely on information passed through sources he trusted about as far as he could throw them. He knew that the U.S. had satellites airborne that could pinpoint takeoff times and afterburner signatures of any aircraft in anyone's inventory. The satellites are of course, designed to detect Russian ICBMs, but they were also very good at identifying any air breathing afterburner. In fact, it was only the day before that he had to pass on a satellite detected airspace violation to the German authorities. These satellites were so good that they could even highlight a jet on a training mission that just happened to use afterburner. That was a no-no at low altitude over Germany, except for takeoff, unless it was an emergency. So, when a pilot tapped burner because he felt like it, there was a threat that some geek back at DIA would see on his scope and report it. A fighter pilot couldn't get away with anything anymore, and this particular watchdog caused lots of paperwork problems for the USAFE/DO staff.

"Roger Big Star. Sentry copies. What time did the bogeys launch, sir?" Stephanie knew that she was the only one airborne with the big picture. It was now a little after 7 pm, and she saw five different entities on her scope, all heading toward the Mediterranean. Now she was being told that there was another, and although she didn't have this new set of targets on her scope yet, given their launch time and speed, she could predict an intercept point with the "Rogue." Once she had that, she would have a good heading to vector everyone else on.

"It's been about an hour, Sentry. They are presently 100 miles east of Tunis, between Sicily and Tunisia, heading 335 degrees at about 400 knots true (airspeed)." Morton knew what Stephanie was thinking and he wanted to give her all the help he could. It was not a perfect world. "Steve's" geometry told her that the Sabres now pressing supersonic out of Zaragoza could get to the "Rogue" at about the same time the Migs and the Iranian 747 did. But everyone else would be left behind. Conan 1 would be about 50 miles back, assuming the "Rogue" maintained his present speed. The tankers from Zaragoza could get close enough to support her own aircraft or Conan 1, or the flight of four from Zaragoza, but not all three—not as a two ship anyway. Stephanie quickly took charge. She knew that everyone else out there was dependent on her "eyes."

"Esso Seven One, this Sentry Four One. Vector Zero Niner Zero and maintain Flight Level Two Six Zero. Expect Sabre One, flight of four, to pass you on an intercept heading toward the bogey. You are to support Sabre One flight, acknowledge." The lead tanker acknowledged

"Steve's" instructions. They had no choice, and the Zaragoza Vice Commander was on board to give them even more instructions.

"Esso Seven Two, Sentry Four One. Vector Zero Six Niner for rendezvous with us and possibly Conan 1. We need you to split from Esso 71 and come further north. Essos be advised there are Iranian Migs in the air from Libya, heading toward the rendezvous point." This last transmission got everyone's attention on the two tankers. The KC-10 had fairly restricted visibility—especially in comparison to the bubble cockpit of the F-16. But at this point, it really would not have mattered. The encounter soon to ensue was still miles in front of them.

"Sentry Four One, this is Sabre One. We're airborne out of Zaragoza, passing Two Zero Zero for Three Zero Zero, heading east. What do you have for us?" Ed Howe was all business now. He had his Falcon in mid afterburner, climbing at .87 Mach. But all he had in front of him was a black hole. He did have a couple of targets on his scope at 22 and 25 miles, and he suspected they were the two tankers that had taken off just ahead of him.

"Sabre One, this is Sentry Four One. I have you radar contact. Continue present heading and maintain a minimum of One point One Mach on level off. Your intercept point is 286 miles at Zero Niner One. Esso 71 is currently at your twelve o'clock for 23 miles. He will follow. Esso 72 will be vectoring north to rendezvous with us and Conan 1. Sabre One, be advised there are four MIG-29 playmates and a Boeing 747 -- suspected tanker—Iranians airborne out of Libya. They will arrive at the intercept point at about the same time. How copy, Over?" Wow! What a mouthful! "Coach" Howe felt elation when he heard that Brad would get some gas and not be left stranded. And then his heart jumped when he heard there were real bad guys ahead.

"Sabre has you loud and clear, Sentry. Heading Zero Niner One. Radar contact with Esso. Are you talking to Conan?" Howe wanted to hear a voice he recognized and maybe get some insight from Brad Mitchell as to what the fuck was going on!

"Roger Sabre One. Break, Break! Conan 1, Sentry Four One, how do you read?" Stephanie wanted to be sure she had everyone on frequency anyway. In fact she did not. She did not know that Ed Howe was the only one of his flight on the Have Quick frequency. He had tried another "Mickey" and Have Quick check with his wingmen after airborne, but Lt. John Brandon, the new number two in his flight, still could not get a good secure UHF radio check. So, Howe left them on unsecured UHF, communicated with them on his VHF radio, and had come up secure himself with the AWACS controller. It was complicated, but it would soon get worse. Brad Mitchell could hear Stephanie, and he could hear her talking to others, but he was too far away yet to hear Howe or the tankers.

Muhammad Mustafa glanced nervously at his fuel gage, and then back to his radar. He had the scope out to 80 mile scan. He knew that even a tanker size target would not normally bloom in at that distance, but he hoped the Mig escort would be close enough to present one big target. He was starting to worry about his fuel, and he had the sudden urge to want to push it up. He knew that was a mistake though, and he kept his calm, unaware of what was happening at his 6 o'clock and 3 o'clock. He decided to break his radio silence.

"Shepherd, this is the wayward sheep. Shepherd, this is the wayward sheep, over." He reconfirmed he was on the prearranged frequency and repeated the call several times over the next ten minutes. Finally, after what seemed like an eternity, he heard a response.

"Sheep, this is the shepherd. You are loud and clear. At what hour does the moon rise in the east?" This was the authentication code they had worked out months ago.

"When the prophet decrees and the tide is at Mecca." Mustafa had rehearsed this drill in his sleep. He was glued to his radar now. Where are they?

"Roger Sheep. We are inbound with four of our leader's finest. They have you at 43 miles." The MIG-29 radar was optimized for air-to-air, much like, but not near as good as the American F-15. Mustafa breathed a sigh and said a thanks to Allah.

Brad Mitchell could visualize the whole scene in front of him now. He knew the "Rogue" was still out there, rushing to meet four Iranian fighters and a tanker. He looked down at his map and was able to imagine where they all were, and where Ed Howe, and the rest of Sabre

One flight were. He knew about where Stephanie and her AWACS was, and he decided she knew what she was doing with the tankers. This whole drama was unfolding in front of him, and he would probably be too late. He pushed the throttle up a little. He wondered what kind of ordnance, if any, the "Coach" and his Sabres had. Brad knew that Zaragoza was only a training base, and he didn't think they had any missiles. He didn't like the idea of sending unarmed F-16s up against four MIG-29s. The Migs would be loaded for bear, and he was the only F-16 airborne with anything close—other than the "Rogue," and he certainly would be of no help to the good guys. Brad made the decision that he had to get closer and he bet on the come that the "Rogue" would have to slow down to refuel. He reached up to his SMS and selected the two wing tanks for jettison and punched them off. There was a thump as the tanks fell away, and Brad wondered where they would land. The Falcon immediately responded to the reduced drag and started to accelerate. Without tapping afterburner, Brad was soon reading .98 Mach. He fed that information to Stephanie and let her computer do its magic

"Roger Conan. I don't have an accurate fix on the fighters and the 747 yet, but given their reported location, heading and speed, you should catch up ten minutes after they rendezvous with our bogey. Sabre One flight will still arrive ahead of you. Sir, will you have enough gas now to recover?" She was concerned about his jettisoning good fuel.

"Roger Sentry, those tanks were empty. I'll need a top off to make it to Zaragoza, but I can make it to Deci without one, unless I have to do too much afterburner work. Could you get the current weather at Deci and Zaragoza?" Brad wanted to be prepared. Night landings were exciting enough. Night landings in rain and fog were no fun.

"Roger Conan, standby." Captain Michaels delegated that chore to one of her co-workers. Everyone on the AWACS was awake now. Some were working the problem, but since this was the only war in town tonight, most were just standing around watching.

Lt. Colonel Ed Howe had his formation in position now. His wingmen knew better than to take too long getting there, even if their leader was going faster than the speed of sound. They were in a loose route formation, close enough so they could see the plan form change of his aircraft as he banked into turns at night, yet far enough away so they could spend much of their time monitoring their own aircraft and the radar. Each afterburner showed a steady glow as the Sabres were in min AB to keep the speed up. The wing tanks and missiles were a lot of drag, and it took afterburner to keep up the speed to make the intercept work.

They had passed up their tankers several minutes back, and they had gone "feet wet" over the Mediterranean coast. Howe knew that the AWACS controller, somewhere off to his left, had the big picture, but he was anxious to get his own radar contact, and take over the intercept. He had already decided how to do this with the armament he had in the flight. His wingmen all had AIM-9P missiles, he did not. They all had a hot gun, but the gun would do them very little good at night. The "Papa" missile was old and not very sophisticated. Basically, it meant the shooter had to be behind his target, within about 40 degrees of the tailpipes, and that any hard turn or decoy flares would defeat it. They were no match for full up MIG-29s, especially not at night. His plan was to go right up alongside the "Rogue" himself, and place his wingman (Lt. Brandon) in about a 1500 foot trail formation, in perfect position to blow the "Rogue's" shit away. Finnegan and his wingman would fly back at about a two mile trail, and 1500 ft. spread, to look for the oncoming posse. He had briefed this over the radio and everyone said they understood. Easy for them to say, but the "Coach" wondered how much they really comprehended and how much they were scared shitless.

The first intercept of any kind was between Sentry 41 (AWACS) and Esso 72, the second KC-10 tanker. The timing was not good though. Stephanie Michaels was worried that she would miss too much of the picture while the radar was stowed. When the E-3A (AWACS) air refueled, it had to stow its big radar antenna inside the rotating disc. For that period of time Stephanie could not provide any directions to the fighters out in front of her. But she had no choice. They needed fuel, and the pilot made the decisions. She was really just along for the ride. Just before signing off, she updated Conan and the Sabres and the other tanker on the big picture, froze what she had on her scope, and then she just sat and waited for what seemed like an eternity while they took fuel. The AWACS is a big airplane, and it holds lots of gas. Stephanie was able to convince the pilot to take just enough to get them to Zaragoza with a little reserve. There was a war to be fought out there, and she did not want to miss it. She turned on the radar and took a look. She already knew what to expect. Sabre One was in contact with the "Rogue" and the Iranians. At this point the "fight" was a hundred miles ahead of the E-3A and the KC-10, now dropping in formation for later assistance.

"Two has hits twenty left for twenty three, left to right." Lieutenant Brandon was the first Sabre to see the "Rogue" on radar. At least "Coach" Howe assumed it was the "Rogue." Twenty left on the scope would put him north of their flight path, and left to right meant the target was heading basically south. For a second or two he forgave the lieutenant for screwing up the radios. But only for a second. He would have to get everyone on the right frequency now, and they would be broadcasting in the clear. But at this point, that probably didn't matter too much. Hopefully their playmates ahead of them did not know they were coming. It wouldn't be long now.

"OK Sabres. Go tactical and kill the strobes. Dim and steady outside." That was really a leftover call from his F-4 days, but his wingmen got the message. By killing the strobe they turned off the flashing white light on their tail that could be seen for miles. The only lights left on were the red and green position lights on the wingtips and the fuselage. He wanted his wingmen to be able to see each other if at all possible, though he knew that most of their "seeing" tonight would be with the radar. Brandon slid back into about a 2000 ft. formation off Howe's left wing and about 60 degrees back. Finnegan took his two ship back to the briefed trail formation, and number four moved out and back on him.

"Sabre One has contact now. Ten left, eighteen miles, Angels Two Six. Heading is One Seven Two." Howe had the target now. His radar kept breaking lock. They were coming in on a direct beam—the worst possible angle for radar. It can't see any relative acceleration, and it outsmarts itself by believing it has a false target. This was a built in anomaly of all radars to avoid locking on to real "false," or non-moving targets. It was a good thing to know if you are under attack, or even think you might be by a radar guided missile - just keep your threat on your wingtip so his radar has a beam look. But right now it was no help.

"Three has hits forty right for twenty six, Angels Two Four." Finnegan had another set of targets. It had to be the tanker and the Iranian fighters. "Two hits there."

"Roger Three, monitor. Sabres let's use uniform for intercept calls. We need to keep AWACS in the loop. I'll be right there." Howe wanted to be sure that Sentry 41 could hear what they were saying. Since Brandon could not use Have Quick, they couldn't afford to be on different frequencies, and they would need Stephanie's help. He came up on secure voice.

"Sentry Four One, this is Sabre One. Are you still there?"

"Roger Sabre. We just finished refueling. Bringing the radar up now." Stephanie could see that there were a whole lot of airplanes getting closer to one another out there.

"OK Sentry. I've got one bird unable Have Quick. Come up Three One Zero Zero, normal. Is Conan on freq?" Howe wanted all the potential players on one frequency, and he had not heard directly from Brad Mitchell since this thing started.

"Conan is up I'm about thirty miles in trail with the bogey with two Mikes and a hot gun. I've punched my tanks, so I don't have much play time. Going squadron common." Squadron common frequency was 310.0, the frequency the Sabres, and now Sentry 41, were all on.

"Sabres and Sentry check uniform." Howe checked them all in.

"Two."

"Three."

"Four."

"Conan."

"Sentry Four One." "Steve" felt like one of the boys.

"Roger, Conan. We are on Victor One Five. Sentry, keep the tankers off this frequency, but vector them this way. We are going to need some gas." Victor 15 was the channel the Sabres were on with their VHF radios. They would use this one as a back up, and for radio calls the

AWACS didn't need to hear. At least that was the general intent. In the heat of the battle things always went haywire, and even the experienced pilots had trouble pressing the microphone switch the correct way. And that was in PEACETIME battles. Tonight could be a disaster. Howe decided that maybe only having one radio would be better. Technology had outsmarted the man many times in the electric jet. He suddenly remembered another example.

"Sabres, let's break lock until ten miles. No sense in lighting up their RHAW. Maybe our "Rogue" will leave his strobe on for us too." By breaking the radar lock the radar warning receivers in the runaway F-16 and the foe would not detect the radar pulse as easily. The intercept would be more difficult for the Sabres, because they would only have blips on the scope—no information like heading, speed, etc. When they got in close they would have to lock on again to monitor overtake— especially in the dark.

"Green em up Sabres!" Ed Howe called for his flight to arm their missiles and guns.

Chuck Morton was even more pissed. From the minute they had received word that there were Iranian Migs and a tanker heading toward a rendezvous with USAFE aircraft he had asked the basic question— "What are the rules of engagement (ROE)? Were our pilots to shoot first, ask questions later? Hardly likely! Were they allowed to defend themselves? Just how far were they to go to recover the runaway jet and bomb?" So far, the only guidance was with regard to shooting the "Rogue" down. That was a no-no. But that decree also came out when there were no other playmates involved, and we had no idea where he was headed. Now it was obvious. This was a theft or a hijack of an American fighter and a nuclear bomb by a nation dedicated to terrorism and bringing down the U.S. government. At least that's the way Brigadier General Charles Morton, USAF, saw it. So what kind of guidance was he to give the pilots of the five F-16s about to wade into the hornets' nest, outnumbered at least 20 to 5 in missiles alone? He had been asking the question of the ViceCINC and the Vice had been asking Washington, and the Pentagon's only answer was, "We'll get back to you." Morton could not wait any longer. He keyed the microphone in full earshot of the ViceCINC.

"Sentry Four One, this is Big Star, over."

"Big Star, go ahead. The Sabres are within 15 miles of the bogey, and they have contact with the Iranian force." Stephanie made it short and sweet. She did not have any time to fool with headquarters right now.

"Roger that Sentry. Hear me good. The ROE for the Sabres is to defend only. Do not initiate hostilities. Fire only if fired upon. If hostilities appear imminent, retreat. How copy?" Morton glanced at the Vice, and got a nod of approval. His guess was as good as anyone's. The Vice passed the information to the Pentagon. Hopefully, everyone was singing from the same sheet of music.

"Sir, I copy. It is probably too late for imminent hostility detection. Twelve hundred miles of closure with 15 miles separation is pretty imminent. I will pass the ROE." Stephanie had never slammed a general officer before, and she probably wouldn't do it again, but who was he kidding? These guys were about to fly head long into a formation of fighters with only one logical purpose in mind—to protect their stolen treasure. And she was supposed to tell the Sabres to back off if it got too hot? *You gotta be shittin' me!*

"Wayward Sheep, this is the Shepherd. Our fighters have you now at 38 miles. Prepare for rendezvous, and descend to Flight Level Two Four Zero." The tanker pilot was relaying information to Mustafa. The Migs had him on radar, even if he couldn't see them yet.

"Roger Shepherd. I am descending to Two Four Zero. Refueling checks complete." Mustafa was always a creature of habit, and even his years of flying with the U.S. Navy had not cured him of his "by the numbers" flying. His Soviet style training, very much indoctrinated into the Iranian Air Force as well, ensured that everything he did was calculated and by a checklist. For this reason, he had followed his pre-refueling checklist to the letter. He had turned off all energy emitting equipment, including his radar warning receiver. Only his radar was left on for now, until he was in close formation with the tanker, and then he would turn it off too. The idea was that queer electrons running through the system might cause spurious inputs to the tanker flight controls or refueling boom. At any rate, the "Rogue" had turned off his RHAW gear that would have allowed him to detect the Sabre radars looking at him. Besides, if the Migs could detect him, they could surely detect anyone else out there.

"Sheep, this is Tiger One. How do you read me?" The lead MIG-29 Fulcrum pilot was calling him.

"Tiger, this is Sheep. I have you loud and clear."

"Roger Sheep, Tigers are two miles above and behind the tanker. We will join in position on you once you are on the boom. Confirm there is no other traffic with you." Mustafa instinctively looked outside, both sides and behind him. He saw nothing. But when he brought his eyes back in the cockpit, he now had his friends on radar. He rejoiced.

"Negative Tiger. I am alone. I have radar contact on you and the Shepherd now, at 21 and 24 miles. Shepherd, start your turn." There were many ways to do a tanker rendezvous, but the most practiced was from a head on approach, similar to the situation they were in. Who turned to join on whom depended on which way the flight wanted to go afterwards. In this case they all wanted to drive back south, so the tanker and her playmates would turn, and the "Rogue" would fall in behind. Because of his speed and their proximity, the turn was already late in starting, and Mustafa would have to slow down more than usual to keep from overshooting.

"Roger, Shepherd is in the turn, 280 knots." Mustafa's jet was doing about 350 right now, and they would later compromise on about 310 to refuel.

"Sheep, this is Tiger. We have at least two targets approaching from your right, co-altitude, approximately 10 miles from you. Do you have them in sight?" The Mig pilot seemed excited. Mustafa snapped his head to the west, but all he saw were thousands of stars. He checked his RHAW gear, saw it was blank and remembered he had turned it off. He immediately pushed the power button. The system would take some time to warm back up, and BIT check itself. He was annoyed. He did not need this. The refueling rendezvous needed to go well, and he didn't need an airliner or two finding the same piece of Mediterranean sky on the same night. He looked west again. Nothing.

"Negative Tiger. No traffic here. Do you have their altitude?"

The lead Mig pilot had already pushed it up and turned westerly to set an intercept on the intruders. He instructed his aft two-ship to swing to the other side and to offset enough to run a stern conversion on the trailing target. The leader and his wingman would run a collision course on the front target and identify it. If his identification was an enemy they had orders from their supreme commander to shoot. He would give that order, and his aft two-ship would be in position to destroy the trailers. He would then be free to turn back and deal with the lead target. That was how it was theoretically supposed to work. And indeed, it always worked that way in their structured training scenarios. They had practiced for this very same situation for the last two months. The targets always "died" gracefully. What they had not planned for was a fifth target out there, following the flight path of their sheep. Brad Mitchell.

Brad now had it all on his scope. It was too much, even for all of his experience. He had the "Rogue" and what he assumed was the tanker turning in front of the "Rogue." But then he had these other targets fanning out, and apparently heading for Sabre One Flight, who was just appearing on the side of his scope.

"Sabre One, looks like the fighters are targeted on you. Conan is still 15 out."

Captain "Steve" Michaels had it all on her scope too, and she knew exactly what was going on. She had not received a warm response when she passed the ROE on to the Sabres. She couldn't blame them either. They were now in imminent danger.

"Sabre One, looks like the lead entity is targeted on you. The trailers are pinching to the north. Leaders are at Angels Two Six, trailers descending through Two Zero Zero." The aft Migs were diving to use the altitude for acceleration, and to give them more of a surprise entry.

"Sabre copies. Sabres, cameras and tapes on. We know the rules. Keep pressing!" Ed Howe's mouth and throat had gone very dry.

"Shepherd, Sheep has you in sight now. Push it up. Still negative tally on strangers, but I have RHAW at six o'clock and three o'clock." Mustafa's RWR was back among the living, and lighting up like a Christmas tree. There was definitely someone behind him and to his right locked on with air-to-air radar. Obviously not airliners. However, he had the tanker in sight, and it was time to fly his best formation, and rejoin on the boom.

"Sheep, this is Tiger. Continue with refueling and recover to our base, regardless of our fate. We will engage the targets if necessary. Tiger One now has two targets in the front."

"There are two in the rear also." Tiger Three was converting his intercept to the north side of the oncoming targets. He and number four had descended to 18,000 feet, and were now doing 1.4 Mach.

"Tiger One is at five miles now. I see no lights. Tiger Flight turn off your lights also." The Fulcrum leader figured that if the oncoming pilots had turned off their lights, they must be up to no good.

"Enemy! Enemy! Enemy! F-16s! Tiger Three, cleared to fire. One and Two will turn back on these two." The Migs had blown by the F-16s very close aboard. So close that the pilots could see the glow of the interior lights in the other man's cockpit. The Iranian saw all he needed to see—F-16s with what looked like live missiles. He feared the U.S. F-16s. Their missiles were about equal (if the Americans had the AIM-9M), especially since the Russians had not supplied Iranians with the AA-10 radar missile. But he did not want to get into a close-in turning fight with the Falcon. Although the jets were comparable in maneuverability, the American pilot got a lot more practice at "fighting in a phone booth."

"Tiger Three copies enemy. Cleared to fire." The number three Mig had "Lucky" Finnegan in his sight. His missile was ready. His wingman was locked on to Sabre Four—"Kujo" Greenwood.

"Damn! Heads up Three! They just went blowing by us close. Fulcrums, no doubt. Two, you still with me?" Ed Howe had to cringe as the head-on intercept unfolded. The Mig pilot had come very close, obviously to identify him in the dark. The lead Mig had passed him on his right, and the wingman was in close trail. They had taken it up into the vertical after they went by, and Howe could still see the plumes of the Mig afterburners above and behind him.

"Two's in. Tanker's in sight, twelve o'clock for six miles." Lieutenant Brandon was glued to his leader and to his radar, and now the aircraft in front of them. He knew he couldn't afford the luxury of bringing too much into his crosscheck. For now at least, the Migs were not hostile. That description lasted about two more seconds.

"Sabre Three break left! Break left! Missile on the way your left eight o'clock." The call came from Sabre Four. He had been looking to the north for the Migs he knew were there, when all of a sudden the sky lit up with a flash and he could see a missile launch, apparently at his element leader. He rolled his own aircraft into 90 degrees of left bank and pulled hard on the stick. Just then he saw another missile—this one was aimed at him, and his radar warning receiver was screaming. "Two missiles! Two missiles!" He radioed.

"Sabres, punch your tanks. Two, take it up and left. Look for the leaders." Howe was searching the sky above for the original two Migs. It was obvious that saddling up on the "Rogue's" wing was going to have to wait, His playmates just became hostile.

The whole scene unfolded in front of Brad Mitchell with sickening speed. He had seen the Migs coming around on Sabre Three on his radar, but he surely did not think they would shoot. The first missile came off the rail of the number three Mig, and within seconds "Lucky" Finnegan and his F-16 were part of a huge fireball. The second missile streaked toward Sabre Four and exploded close enough that Brad could see the whole silhouette of the Falcon. There was no huge fireball, but it was obviously not a complete miss.

Brad wasted no time. His radar was locked on to the number three Mig all along, and now the Fulcrum was right in front of him, belly up. He uncaged his AIM-9M and the growl turned to a higher pitched wail. He mashed the pickle button and flinched when the sky lit up on his left wing. The missile was away and true to its mark. It impacted the tailpipes and the Mig exploded. He immediately shifted his gaze to look for the wingman. He saw him, but the Mig was much too close to Sabre Four. Obviously the Libyan pilot had not monitored his overtake well, and in the heat of the battle and dark of night, he had almost followed his missile to its target. When the target did not blow up, the Mig pilot pulled hard on his stick, and extended his speed brake to keep from overshooting. By the time Brad picked him up, the two aircraft were side by side, and the Mig was sliding out in front of the Falcon, too close for Mitchell to shoot. He kept his eyes on the two jets wallowing in the sky—one because it had just almost had its shit about blown away, and one because its pilot was ham-fisting it, trying to keep from becoming his target's target. In the meantime, Brad Mitchell flipped his radar into a 10X40 scan to concentrate its search high and in front of the nose. He pulled the nose around to optimize the radar scan to look for the front pair of Migs and Sabre One.

Captain Jim "Lucky" Finnegan never knew what hit him. He had RWR warning, and he had been looking for the Migs, but when his flight lead had called for a "heads up" he had shifted his gaze forward, looking for the front pair of Migs. The "Break" call immediately made him respond, but it was too late. The Russian built missile impacted just behind the cockpit, in the wing root of the F-16. His whole world went up in flames, and though he reached for the ejection handle, he died before the sequence was initiated.

Captain Mike "Kujo" Greenwood was fighting for control. The second missile had exploded by a proximity fuse right behind him. He could hear shrapnel rip into the jet. When he tried to jettison his fuel tanks, they would not blow. He looked quickly at the engine gages and everything seemed ok there. But something was wrong. It was noisy in the cockpit, and there were lights on the telelight panel. Before he could concentrate on the problem, he realized he had a bigger one. The Mig that shot at him was still coming. He had pulled about as hard as he could on the stick to defeat the missile and he didn't have much left. The Mig kept coming, getting bigger in the picture. "Kujo" realized what was happening. The Raghead had pooched it! He was overshooting! That Sonofabitch had just tried to kill him, and the leader had blown away the best flight commander "Kujo" had ever known. He led the turn and rolled hard back to the right, flipping the weapons switch on the throttle to Dogfight—calling up the gun.

The Mig and F-16 were side by side, within 100 feet of one another, canopy to canopy. This is one time in aerial dogfighting that speed is not life. The Fulcrum had at least 100 knots excess speed and he slid out in front. Greenwood rolled the jet back in plane, settled the gun sight on the glow of the mig's canopy and squeezed the trigger. He held the trigger down until the gun noise subsided, and at that time the Mig pitched up in an unorthodox way, and there was a flash of a rocket motor from the cockpit area. The pilot had bailed out. "Kujo" didn't know whether his bullets had found their mark, or if the Iranians were as afraid of the Falcon as the Syrians had been (back in '73) of the Israelis—bailing out just as soon as they became obvious targets. There was no time to gloat. His own jet had problems.

Ed Howe and Lieutenant John Brandon pulled their jets into the vertical and toward where they thought the lead Migs would be. They were correct. Two missiles were in the air almost simultaneously.

"Go idle, Two, Break left!" He yelled. By decreasing the power to idle the engine would put off significantly less heat, and the heat seeking missile would have to work harder to find their target. It worked! Both missiles missed by a long shot. But Howe did not like the odds. He had no missiles. His wingman had one, and he had no idea what or who even was left behind him. These were not smart odds.

"OK Two. Stay with me! We're going to jam 'em and then get outta here." They kept their turn going and passed close aboard to the Migs. Then Howe unloaded his jet to zero G and let it accelerate in full afterburner, diving toward clear airspace away from the threat. Just about then another missile blew up near the Migs. "Thank you somebody!"

Brad Mitchell had locked onto a target, but he had no way of knowing whether it was the lead Mig or his wingman, or "Coach" Howe. He could hear the chatter on the radio, and since the "Coach" was breaking up and left, and his target was pointing down and right, he uncaged the one remaining AIM-9M. Then the target lit up in his face as it fired its own missile. That was all the confirmation he needed. Missile away! This one was not so true. It streaked by the first target and blew up between the two Migs. All he really managed to do was highlight himself to the Fulcrum pilots, and fire off his last missile. He too decided it was time to vacate the premises. He looked for Sabre Four—the wounded bird who was squawking for help on the radio. Brad again used the 10X40 scan of the radar and found "Kujo" on a southwesterly heading, away from the fight and descending.

"Sabre Four, Conan - Buddy Lock!" Mitchell was telling Greenwood that he had just locked his radar onto what he thought was a friendly target. He wanted confirmation from "Kujo" that his RWR had just sounded a warning.

"Roger, that's me! I've lost pressurization in the cockpit, and I've got one generator out. I'm also losing fuel. Where's the tanker?" Greenwood was shook up.

"Sabre Four, vector Two Niner Zero for the nearest tanker. He's at 70 miles." Stephanie Michaels had watched the whole battle in helpless awe. She saw it all happen, but she could do nothing to help. It was all too fast. Now at least, she could help get them home. "Conan 1, Four is at your one o'clock for eight miles, Angels One Niner."

"Conan has contact. I'll join on him. Bring the tanker in toward us." Brad sensed that "Kujo" would need some gas fast.

"Roger sir. Break, Break! Sabre One, Sentry Four One. I have you southeast of the bogeys, sir. The bogey tanker and runaway are at your four o'clock for eleven miles. Migs are joining on them from behind. What are your intentions, sir?" Stephanie knew that it would not be wise for Ed Howe and his wingman to fly back through the enemy to get home, if they could help it. Ed Howe was way ahead of her.

"Roger Sentry. Sabre One and Two are going to Decimomannu. We don't have enough gas to outflank these guys and find the tanker. Conan can you escort Four to the tanker and try to get him to Zaragoza, or a piece of concrete somewhere? Sentry, give them all the help they need, but also follow this gaggle of Ragheads at a safe distance and see if you can pinpoint where they land. Suggest you take the other tanker with you and recover at Deci."

"Break, Break! Sabre Four, understand we lost Three? Did anyone get a beeper?" Each pilot checked to see that he had his guard receiver on so that he would hear the beeper sound of the survival radio beacon automatically triggered if there is an ejection. No beeper.

"Negative sir. No beeper. It was a huge fireball, and I saw no chute. The Mig driver I shot did bail out though." Greenwood was regaining his composure and almost smiling about his first "kill." He wasn't sure he wanted any more, though.

"OK. Sentry, see if you can raise any Italian rescue. Pass to USAFE we lost one F-16 -- Sabre Three, Captain Jim Finnegan. I don't have a clue what his tail number was. We shot down at least two Migs. Understand you still have two up there joining on our 'Rogue?'" Howe sounded tired and pissed.

"That's affirm sir. There are two of them still with the tanker and the F-16." Stephanie reflected his mood.

"Right! Pass the word and do what you can. We need to know where they take that thing. Sabre One is outta here." Coach Howe set up a glide into Decimomannu, and the two of them landed uneventfully. The base was ready for them. Their phones had been ringing off the hook for the last hour.

Greenwood determined that the leak was in his internal wing tanks. He probably had holes all over the wings and fuselage. But the jet flew ok, and their best bet was to stay with the tanker. Sabre Four, escorted by Conan 1 stayed with Esso 71 all the way back to Zaragoza. Greenwood was ok until he lowered the landing gear. Then he lost hydraulic pressure and had to engage the departure end cable. The jet was pretty much done in, but he walked away.

The AWACS stayed about 100 miles behind the Iranians and their new toy. As they approached Libyan airspace the AWACS took up an orbit, and Capt. Michaels just watched. The Iranian force landed at Beni Walid Airfield, about 100 miles west of Tripoli, nestled up next to one of the few mountain ridges in Libya. At 2:30 am, 16 hours after they had originally taken off, a very tired AWACS crew climbed out of their airplane on the ramp at Decimomannu, Sardinia. Ed Howe was there to meet Captain Stephanie Michaels with a cold beer. Although the bad guys had won the first round, the good guys had gone down fighting, and much of it they owed to this gutsy GCI controller called "Steve."

CHAPTER FORTY

BERLIN, GERMANY

El-Kamani decided there was no need to return to Berlin the way he came, through Dresden. He had stolen the car and he was in a bit of a hurry to get to Tempelhof Airport. He knew his number two man in the IRG was in Libya running that part of the operation but he wanted nothing to go wrong and always followed the adage that if you want something done right, you do it yourself. At the same time, he didn't want to call attention to himself by being in too much of a hurry. He didn't know whether the Americans had identified him or not. The fact that they showed up at the house near Spangdahlem could have been simply that they had tracked the men who worked for him there.

To be safe, he drove into the city of Berlin and checked into a moderately priced hotel near the commercial center. He needed to do some shopping. He dumped the car in a parking lot adjacent to another hotel and walked to a men's clothing shop. There he bought a nice suit, shirt, tie and pair of Italian shoes. On the way to the hotel he stopped at a convenience store and bought some toiletries including a razor. In his hotel room he first checked in with the airlines. There was nothing from Berlin direct to Tripoli. He could go through Cairo, but that was a non-starter. El-Kamani would be very welcomed in Egypt. In fact, the Egytian security forces would love to welcome him either to their jails or to their morgue. In the recent past he had led an assassination attempt on an Egyptian cleric who had publicly chided the Ayatollah Khomenei.

The operation was a success but along with the cleric, twenty one other members of his family and inner circle were brutally murdered in their mosque. The Egyptians had actually captured El-Kamani and two of his henchmen as they were making their departure. However, another group of IRG commandos was able to raid a safe house where the Egyptians were holding their captives prior to transferring them to headquarters. El-Kamani got away, but not before the Egyptians had photoed and fingerprinted him.

Before that time El-Kamani had been a ghost to western intelligence agencies. They knew he was out there but no one, even the Mossad in Israel, could place a name to a photo or in any way identify him. When he returned to Iran from Cairo after that mission he went through significant plastic surgery and had his fingerprints removed. The only problem with that was that a man with no fingerprints stirred up almost as many questions as a man with the prints of a notorious terrorist. So he hooked up with a genius plastic surgeon who had patented a new process - attaching a very thin layer of skin with a set of fingerprints to the fingers. It took almost a month for the process to set up, but at the end of that month, when he took off the white cotton gloves he had worn for weeks, he had the fingerprints of a man who had died a few months prior. The new prints were attached with an equivalent of gorilla glue. They weren't going anywhere, but they were very susceptible to heat. El-Kamani had to remember not to handle extremely hot cups of tea or coffee or touch anything hot without gloves on. The process was a complete success. His only problem was that although they kept the whole operation secret, hidden from even his co-workers at the Revolutionary Guard, there was one person who knew - the doctor who performed the "miracle." El-Kamani had a solution to that however. Late one night, while driving home from his laboratory, the doctor had a fatal accident as his car ran off a highway into a ditch and he was killed instantly.

Barak found an Aer Lingus flight that left in three hours and flew direct to Marakesh. From there he knew he could get into Libya fairly easily. He should be at Beni Walid airfield by early morning. He shaved his beard, shaved his head completely, dressed in his newly purchased clothes, and stepped out to take an Uber car to Tempelhof airport.

Nitro, Shooter and Ebola had arrived at the Bahnhof in central Berlin within two hours after leaving the hospital at Spangdahlem. They checked the inbound train schedule from the north and west. Ebola set himself up as a scruffy homeless man on a stoop that looked over all of the passengers coming up out of the rail platforms. Shooter set up on one of the stairwell overpasses with his rifle tucked under an overcoat. Since it was cold in December in Berlin, no one thought he looked out of place. Nitro paced up and down the platforms of trains coming in from Dresden, Bonn, and Cologne. Neither of them knew who they were really looking for, but they had a general description of El-Kamani from earlier intelligence reports, and a tip that he would be coming by train. That tip was bogus.

Trains came and went. There were several potential players, but soon the Americans realized this was a lost cause and called in to Genoa in D.C. "Ok. Let's shift to his departure rather than arrival." Columbus said. "We know the F-16 is on its way to Africa. Since the Iranian Air Force is coming out of Libya to escort him in, we should assume Libya is his destination. Geek has done some diving into airline schedules. There are three departures that he could jump on to get close. An Egypt Air to Cairo, an Egypt Air to Alexandria, and Aer Lingus to Marakesh. They all could connect with flights into Tripoli. You guys head out to Tempelhof. We'll do some surveillance and digging from here and let you know when you get there what to look for. I'll have a contact in the Bundestag Polizei hook up when you get out there. You might need more eyes."

When they got to the airport, Nitro checked in with Columbus again. "Here's what we got. We're going to gamble he won't go through Egypt. He has a history there and although connections into Tripoli are better through Cairo, we're thinking he'll avoid the Egyptian authorities." Genoa relayed. "So, let's look at Marakesh. I've got three German special forces types at the gate already. They're supposed to be masquerading as passengers - a couple, man and wife, and an older man with a cane. Good luck."

Nitro and Ebola got through security at Tempelhof ok, though without tickets. It took some arguing and checking by the German version of TSA. They let the two of them through, but they would not let Shooter go through with his rifle. In fact, they detained him while Nitro and Ebola ran ahead.

El-Kamani got to the airport with an hour to spare. He stopped to get a yogurt and a roll, and a cup of coffee at a fast food stand. Unfortunately the coffee was hot and he did not have his gloves on. He got one of those sleeves to go on the cup that helped, but he still had to handle the cup very carefully. He walked to the gate, found a seat with a wide open view of the gate area, and sat down to eat his snack. His educated eye picked up an older gentleman who seemed to be very nervous, or at least he was looking for someone. He walked with a slight limp and used a cane in his left hand. Barak looked around for others but couldn't spot anyone strange. Pretty soon a disheveled looking man who looked filthy, almost like a beggar off the streets, came into the area and simply squatted by the gate door. The Aer Lingus attendant behind the desk became agitated with his constant coughing and finally had enough. She went to the man and asked to see his boarding pass. When he couldn't produce one she told him he would have to leave and told her co-worker to call security. The bum got up and was about to leave when the elderly gentleman came up to the attendant and said something to her. They gestured toward the grubby man who then went back to his position by the gate. As the elderly gentleman walked away, El-Kamani realized he had the cane in the other hand and walked with an opposite limp. Not exactly a practiced operative.

Ok. El-Kamani thought. *There's two. The old man with the cane, and the homeless looking guy sitting on his haunches with the attendant's permission. Who else?* He got up to throw away his trash, but was not careful with the cup. He bumped it against the side of the receptacle and spilled some coffee on his hand. His reaction was one of what later he chided himself as unfounded panic. He shook his hand and yelped and quickly ran to the men's room to dry his hands. He got the attention of everyone at the gate.

There was no reason for Nitro, Ebola or their German cohorts to suspect anything more than it looked like - some clumsy oaf spilled coffee on himself. They continued their perusal of the crowd. The German couple of agents who looked to be traveling together had zeroed in on a middle aged man with a full beard and a very quiet demeanor. They sat in two seats beside him and the woman struck up a conversation. She was surprised he spoke German like a native. He was very forthcoming, not at all showing something to hide. Soon she looked at Nitro and gave a slight shake of her head - not a good bet.

Nitro got an idea. Why not be offensive about this. He made the rounds to communicate his plan to his team quietly, meeting the old man and the husband of the couple in the mens room and quietly passing Ebola a note. They positioned themselves so that they could each watch at least 20% of the gate area, so amongst them they had everyone covered. Nitro then went to a customer relations phone and made a request.

"Mr. El-Kamani, Mr. Barak El-Kamani, please meet your party at Gate 47B. Mr. Barak El-Kamani go to Gate 47B." The announcement went loud all over the B concourse.

Barak El-Kamani looked up sharply. When he did he met the gaze of the wife of the German Intelligence couple. She stared hard at him - too hard. El-Kamani quickly averted his stare and looked around for the others. The old man with the cane was searching another section of the seating area, as was the hobo. He looked back at the woman and saw her elbow her "husband" seated next to her and whisper in his ear. The man looked directly at El-Kamani and he knew he'd been made.

Timing is everything. Just then the gate agent announced the boarding of the flight to Marakesh. El-Kamani got up immediately and merged into the crowd as they lined up. Typical of Germans, or all Europeans for that matter, there was no regimen to their waiting in line. They just didn't like to, so they funneled in together and pushed forward, eventually arriving at the head of line. El-Kamani was persistent and pushy. As Nitro fell in behind him he likened the whole experience to waiting in ski lift lines in Val d' Sere, France. Katie bar the door.

Ebola was next to the gate in his crouched over position. He was able to maneuver in ahead of El-Kamani, but because he had no boarding pass he was forcefully pushed aside by the gate agent and one of the passengers. Bad move on their part. With the speed of greased lightning Ebola pushed the gate agent back to the gate, grabbed the boarding pass from the passenger and left the passenger stooped over puking on the floor by the gate from a well placed short but powerful jab to the kidneys. He then boarded the plane. All this happened just ahead of El-Kamani and he didn't really see what had happened. He could feel the other agents behind him and pushed himself on through the gate to the causeway.

The old man with the cane ended up about 15 passengers behind the target, with Nitro and the couple 15 or so back from there. Nitro thought that even if this wasn't the right guy, they would be at least on the way to the right part of the world. Boarding passes were a problem though. Only Ebola had one, and that one would soon be contested when the passenger he mauled recovered. While pressing bodies down the causeway he called Genoa and quickly explained where they were.

"Right. Nitro, press on. We have comm with the lead German agent. He's an elderly gentleman who walks with a limp. He'll clear things for you with the gate agent. We need this guy alive though. In fact, unless taking him alive isn't possible, let him go and follow him." Columbus said. "We don't know who's really pulling the strings on this operation. Maybe he'll point the way."

Ebola got the the plane first. He checked the boarding pass he had absconded with off the the passenger in line. Figures - it was first class. So he had to turn left and go towards the front of the plane while most everyone else was turning right back to the "cattle car" section. He found his seat and stood there watching the door. El-Kamani entered the door of the plane and immediately pulled a gun and put it to the head of the pretty head flight attendant. Ebola thought German TSA wasn't as good as they thought they were. Shooter's rifle couldn't go through, but this guy had a big semi-automatic pistol.

El-Kamani had seen Ebola turn towards first class ahead of him. He kept the fight attendant between him and Ebola. He yelled his orders in

German. "Halt!" he said to the passengers trying to load behind him. To the male flight attendant nearby, "Close the door. Now! I will kill her first and then you!"

The male attendant obeyed. He closed the door and locked it shut. The door to the cockpit was open. The co-pilot was still out doing his walk-around check of the plane. Nobody expected a plane to be hijacked before it even taxied. The captain was busy copying instructions from the tower and had not noticed what was going on behind him. El-Kamani forced the attendant to the front of the first class section. Then he ordered everyone to the rear of the plane, paying special attention to Ebola. Once they were all at least beyond the entrance door he shoved the attendant into the cockpit and told her to sit in the copilot's seat. That got the captain's attention.

"Captain, listen to me very carefully." El-Kamani said, pressing the gun against the captain's neck. "There are twelve people on this airplane other than you me and your new copilot here. The door is closed and locked. You will have the ground crew push you away from the gate, start the engines. taxi and takeoff to the south. If not and if you try any tricks to stop me, you should know I am a licensed commercial pilot and I have several hundred hours in this type of jet. No tricks. I will be standing here in the door watching your every move and listening to your calls on the radio." He snatched the headset from the copilot's position and plugged it in beside the door in what used to be a flight engineer's position. When the aircraft flew overseas for longer than 8 hours they had a third crew member in the flight engineer's seat. Tonight's flight was only supposed to be five hours and wasn't scheduled for a flight engineer, but the communications in his position were the same as the pilots'.

The captain did as he was told. He called the tower and the maintenance crew on the ground. In the meantime, El-Kamani summoned the male flight attendant. "Bring me one of your other attendants and herd everyone else back into seats in the middle but forward of the wing escape hatches." He ordered. A pretty young flight attendant looking like she was no more than 20 years old came forward. She was trembling with fear. *All the better.* Barak thought. He summoned the male attendant forward again. Then he told the pilot to turn around and watch him. He took his gun, placed it next to the girl's temple and pulled the trigger.

There were muffled screams of terror and hatred from the pilot and the crew and passengers. "Now, all of you …. understand me. I will kill anyone who tries anything funny or maybe just because I'm bored and I just want to kill someone. You will all do as I say or I will kill each and every one of you, but in some cases I will make it much more slow and painful." He looked at the captain. "Are there any questions?" The captain shook his head and turned back to the cockpit duties. The female flight attendant in the copilot's seat burst out crying, as did a few of the women passengers and remaining flight attendants. Everyone was distraught except Ebola.

Ebola tried to settle himself in the middle of the sparse crowd, but his appearance and terrifying looks scared the hell out of everyone. Half of them figured he must be in cahoots with the madman up front. No one would sit near him. He was able to use his "bat phone" and called Columbus. In fact he had turned it on with a hands free function and Genoa got to listen to the whole tirade by El-Kamani. "Ebola, I hear it loud and clear. Don't try to talk so you don't get caught. Click the mic twice for yes and once for no and I'll only ask you yes - no questions, got it?" Two clicks.

"Are you the only one of the team who made it on board?" Two clicks.

"Is he on to you?" Two clicks.

"Shit. Ok, we are recommending to the Germans that they let hm go. This guy's history tells us he will follow up on any threat. So try to keep your phone hidden and keep me in the loop. Otherwise - good luck. You're on your own." Two clicks.

The Germans cooperated. In fact to El-Kamani's way of thinking, it was too easy. The ground crew buttoned up the jet and pushed it back from the gate. The pilot cranked up the engines and the tower issued taxi and take off instructions. They were airborne with 15 minutes. Barak told the captain to put Tripoli in his nav system cross hairs for now. The flight attendant in the copilot's seat was a blubbering mess.

Once they were airborne and climbing out to the south, El-Kamani pulled her out of the seat and sent her back to the rest of the sheep in the back. He walked back about two seats into first class and stopped. From there he could still see what the captain was doing and monitor the passengers and crew as well. He then had each passenger and crew member come forward to him and back one at a time. Most of them were scared to death, expecting the same fate as the previous young flight attendant. Barak loved that they feared him.

Ebola tried to avoid his trip to the front. He kept pushing others in front of him. Finally however Barak forced the issue. He stopped the parade and got on the intercom. "Agent dressed as a homeless person. I know what you are. Come forward immediately or I will kill another woman. Do not try to be a hero or I will kill all the women."

Ebola ditched his phone and shuffled to the front. He buried his black eyes deep in a stare down with El-Kamani. Neither man would flinch or even blink. Finally El-Kamani had enough. He slammed his pistol across Ebola's face, drawing blood and chipping a couple teeth. "Don't fall over." He said as he grabbed Ebola's arm. He forced hm up into the cockpit and told him to sit in the copilot's seat. Then he took some duct tape the flight attendant had brought him and taped Ebola's hands and ankles to the copilot seat. "Now I have you where I can watch you." He said. "Have you ever been to Libya. American?"

CHAPTER FORTY ONE

―

WASHINGTON D.C.

The Italian rescue effort failed to locate any sign of "Lucky" Finnegan. There were pieces of airplane all over the Mediterranean, most at the bottom. One Iranian pilot was rescued, however he was unconscious and appeared to have a broken back, probably from the ejection. He was in the hospital in Corsica, and initial indication was that the Italians had offered political asylum.

In Washington the mood was solemn. As reports came in from USAFE headquarters and Zaragoza, it became clear that the U. S. had fought and lost a major air battle. The kill ratio may be 2:1 in favor of the Americans, but the Iranians had accomplished their objective. The Iranians now had a nuclear loaded F-16 and a pilot who knew how to employ it. All that was missing were their intentions.

"AIR FORCE LAUNCHES, LOSES NUCLEAR BOMB" read the headline in Tuesday's Washington Post. The story actually was fairly accurate, although by the time it came out, much more had unfolded. Peter Sciapini basically wrote the story that no one knew where the aircraft was headed, and that BG Charles Morton had disclosed information about the incident. By Saturday morning of course, the F-16 and its cargo were on the ground in Libya, the air battle had taken place, and all of Sciapini's news was old. All that is, but the fact that Chuck Morton had afforded him information. That tidbit of sensationalism brought a rise out of the White House, the SECDEF, and every echelon of command below. It only took a phone call or two to understand that Morton had not purposely divulged anything, but his loose lips in the lobby of the Ramstein Officers' Club had found the ears of a nosey reporter. BG Chuck Morton was removed from the fray, told to keep a low profile, to talk to no one. He was basically "shit canned." His boss, Major General Manfred "Ollie" Olsen, was recalled from Turkey and sent directly to Zaragoza.

In the meantime, Pete Wilson, Pentagon Chief of Media Relations, was busy preparing a statement for the press. There was no sense in covering up anything. Too much had already happened, the Italian press was swarming all over Sardinia and Corsica, and the French, Germans and Spanish were all asking pointed questions. Wilson worked with the Chief of Staff, and it was decided that Secretary Lucroix would hold a press conference at 10 a.m. to explain the situation.

The first order of business was a meeting of all the major players at the White House. The President, the SECDEF, the Chairman of the JCS, the National Security Advisor Admiral, and the Secretary of State were all in attendance at 7 am Tuesday morning. The Chiefs of all four branches of the service were there, as was Robinson Genoa.

"OK folks. What do we know so far?" The President appeared remarkably calm and rested for a man who had not slept the night before.

"Sir, you know what transpired last night." The SECDEF started off. "We have two healthy F-16s and an AWACS on the deck at Decimomannu, Sardinia. The rest have returned safely to Zaragoza. One of the F-16s there was pretty badly shot up. Of course we lost the one jet, and apparently the pilot. The Italian rescue choppers are still out there, but it doesn't look like there was an ejection. They did pick up one badly injured Iranian pilot. However, he is in critical condition, and the Italians indicate they will not allow us access to him. Paul's State Department folks are working on that end of it. The runaway jet is on the ground in Libya at a base called Beni Walid, about 100 miles west of Tripoli." As he spoke, General Adams pointed to the base that had been highlighted on a map for all to see.

"Do we know what they are going to do with it?" The President studied the map with intense interest.

"Sir, we have launched two more AWACS down to the area." The Chairman answered this one. "One is ours that was in the U.K. for an exercise. The other is a NATO AWACS. Our crew on the deck at Decimomannu will be able to fly again this evening. We are going to try to maintain around the clock surveillance as best we can. We can't get very close without violating what Libya calls their 'sovereign airspace,' so I have ordered the Navy to maintain combat air patrol (CAP) protection for the AWACS. The carrier Truman is just about here." He indicated a point just east of Gibraltar. "She will keep F-18s and F-35s up as long as we have AWACS up. If they fly the aircraft from Beni Walid, we should be able to tell."

"We have also diverted our satellite assets to keep constant surveillance. Whatever flies from any base in Libya will have an instant signature transferred to Bolling AFB. Sir, we don't know what they plan. For now they are being very quiet, both in Tripoli and in Tehran." Secretary Lucroix was showing signs of the long night with little rest. He desperately needed a shower and a shave, but what he craved was a long nap.

"Mr. President, I have here a communique for you to send through the German embassies in Tripoli and in Tehran." SECSTATE Wisnewski handed the President a red folder. "Basically it condemns the theft of one of our aircraft and the bomb, and demands the immediate return. The Brits and the Germans are also prepared to follow up with a condemnation of their own. As you know, only the Germans have a consulate in Libya. The French are balking, and the Spanish are still trying to sort out what happened. The Italians appear to be blaming the whole thing on us. As Roger said, I have Ambassador Wright in Rome working on that. Apparently everybody who is anybody in the Italian government is playing dumb and pointing fingers elsewhere."

"Why doesn't that surprise me?" The President tried to smile. He read through the communique quickly, nodded, initialed it, and handed it back to the SECSTATE. Wisnewski left the room for a minute.

"So what do we suppose the Ragheads have up their sleeves? Who are they going to nuke? Chad? Israel? I guess this is the next step we were warned about. Nothing else has happened since our twenty four hour threat, correct?" Eyebrows raised all around the table. The President had a point there. Part of the ultimatum given on the video was a complete dismemberment of Israel. However, to a man, everyone in the room realized that the real threat was not what terrorists would do with this one nuclear bomb against Israel, but what the Israelis would do if they felt genuinely threatened. A very uncomfortable feeling had set in.

"Paul, I think you'd better get your traveling bag out of the closet again. You'd better get to Jerusalem." The President addressed the SECSTATE who had just returned after giving the communique to an aide to send.

"Yes sir. I had thought of that. I have an aircraft scheduled out this evening."

"Well, does anybody have any suggestions?" The President looked around the room.

"We need to either get the damn thing back or blow it off the face of the earth right where it is. And we need to do it fast." Richard Henry had not spoken during the whole preceding conversation. He had appeared deep in thought. As the National Security Advisor he had the reputation of being somewhat of a hawk—to be expected from an ex military man. He was another of the President's brilliant appointments, and he served to offset the extreme anti-military theme too often set forth by the White House Chief of Staff and the Vice President.

"Don't you think that's a little harsh Richard? A nuclear explosion, even in Libya, deliberately set off, would turn world opinion against us." President McDivitt respected Henry's exceptional intellect, but he was surprised at his firm statement.

"Sir, these bombs need to be armed to really go off. At the worst, a low order secondary explosion would expose a small amount of radiation. Nothing to worry about. It could be taken out by some well placed explosives. No, I believe we cannot sit around on this one. We must act immediately. We know where the aircraft is right now. They could move it at any time. More importantly though, we are entrusted with half the world's arsenal of nuclear weapons. If we give the impression that we cannot keep them under control, we lose tremendous credibility. This is the ultimate in a terrorist act. It is what everyone in the civilized world has feared for years, and depending on how the Iranians play it, chaos could be widespread. And I should point out, we don't even know if the government of Iran is behind all of this or if this El-Kamani character is acting on his own as a loose canon. Lady and gentlemen, I submit we do everything in our power to get this weapon back or destroy it, as soon as possible." Henry was finished. He definitely had been deep in thought.

"I agree, but we can't expect him to leave the jet out in the open where it can be blown away." General Porter pulled out a packet of satellite photos. "He has so far. These are photos from the first satellite pass after sunrise this morning, Libya time. The jet is parked here in front of this third generation shelter. They appear to be servicing it. If you look very closely in front of the right wing, you can see that the bomb is still there." The President and his staff huddled around the pictures, each observing with his own level of expertise, most having to take General Porter's word for it. "But our intel folks tell us that these taxiways here lead into underground hangars buried in this ridge line. This is probably Libya's best fortified air base. It's the only one with any contour to it. They took full advantage of the terrain. I would expect them to move the jet underground if they feel threatened. If they do that it would be difficult for us to bomb it from the air. We couldn't guarantee hitting the F-16." The general leaned back so that the rest could look closely at the maps and photos.

"We could get it with a SEAL team." Admiral Rogers said. "Slip them in off a sub at night. The Libyan security is hardly state-of-the-art. I'd bet we could get a good team of 5 or 6 in there and blow that jet to Timbuktu. Do we have any indigenous 'friends' we can rely on in Libya?"

"We had help in '85 with the bombing raid. We'd need to check with CIA for specifics." The SECDEF answered. "I don't know how fast we could scramble a team of SEALs in there. I'm also worried they wouldn't know what to look for."

"There are SEALs on every carrier at sea on standby all the time. The Truman has a contingent of Seal Team Four. We could put them ashore faster than the Air Force could muster a bombing raid." The Admiral countered. "If we're worried about identification, send one of the pilots in with the team. Genoa immediately thought of Brad Mitchell.

"Any other ideas?" Asked the President.

"Sir, I recommend we do both. We form a task force in the Med and we prepare to blow this airfield off the face of the earth if need be. If the F-16 is in the open, we get it first. In the meantime, we send in a team of SEALs to pinpoint the location, and if necessary, take out the jet and the bomb. We should be able to coordinate the whole thing." Henry was thinking off the cuff, but he was a fast and complete military thinker. "The idea of sending one of the Air Force guys in with the SEALs is a good one. If that bomb is downloaded from the jet, we'll need someone who can positively identify it. Who better than a pilot who is qualified to fly it?"

"That all makes sense to me." Chimed in the SECDEF. "In the meantime we give Tripoli and Tehran an ultimatum. They need to release the aircraft to us and we fly it out. I don't think we can afford to take their word for it that they will peacefully fly it to us. If that jet takes off headed for friendly territory with an Iranian or Libyan pilot at the controls, we cannot afford to let him get there."

"I agree. How much time do we give them?" The President asked.

"It would take us 72 hours to get a sufficient task force in place. It would be at least that long for a SEAL team to get ashore and make it over land to Beni Walid. The Chairman was checking his calendar watch and making notes. "We could strike Friday night."

"Sir, I recommend an ultimatum of noon Thursday - Libya time. That will give us two days to work the diplomatic end. We may need that time to hold back a few of our allies." Secretary Wisnewski was of course, referring to the Israelis.

"Begging your pardon Mr. President, but I think we have just the pilot to go in with the SEALS. He's on the Tango Team now." Genoa spoke up.

"Ah yes Robby. I know who you mean." The President got up and paced the room a bit. "Michelle, what's the pilot's name—the one we lost last night?"

The CSAF referred to her notes. "Captain James Finnegan sir. His wife and three children are at Spangdahlem Air Base. His parents are in Colorado."

"What will be the funeral plan?"

"Standard procedure would be a memorial service wherever the wife wants one. If they have one at Spangdahlem, there will be just a small one back here—assuming he's buried at Arlington. I assume we will make every effort to find the body before a service here. Sir, you need to know that there were at least 200 other casualties in this thing. The explosion at Spangdahlem Air Base was devastating. Also, the security policeman guarding the alert force gate was murdered." Porter explained.

"Make sure my staff gets all the phone numbers and names, ages of kids, all that stuff. The list of calls for me to make is getting awfully long folks. Have the CINC over in Europe attend any service they might have at Spangdahlem. Regardless of how big they do it up, we will put on a real dog and pony show here. Encourage the families to have them buried at Arlington. I will attend. And if we lose any more before this thing is over, we'll do the same." The President turned from the window he was staring out of and faced the group. "Ok folks, we will do it your way. General Adams, form your task force. Launch this SEAL team. Coordinate with Mr. Genoa and his team. Friday night it is. In the meantime Mike, direct our press folks to keep any comments today very generic." This last comment was pointed at White House Chief of Staff Mike Mulroney. "I will hold a presidential news conference tomorrow or Thursday. I need to speak to the Armed Services Committee Chairmen first.

"Listen to me folks. We can't let these bastards get away with this!" The President pounded his fist on the table. "But there is another issue we have been forgetting. Unless I'm mistaken we still have two missing Iranian ass holes running around loose in Las Vegas - one masquerading as a police captain and one as a fireman. Any news on that front?" He looked at Genoa, who nodded in the affirmative but did not speak. "Robby, let's go get me up to speed with Tango." The President and Genoa then left the room. The others surmised that the meeting was adjourned.

CHAPTER FORTY TWO

———

WHITE HOUSE VICE PRESIDENT'S CONFERENCE ROOM

"Mr. President, as you so rightly pointed out in the Situation Room, we believe there is an incident in the making in Las Vegas." Genoa explained to the Boss. "When the threat came through on the video it was obvious there would be some attack at least once every 24 hours. The first four all happened on Sunday - the missile silo explosion in Wyoming, the attack on Cheyenne Mountain, the sinking of the Abraham Lincoln, and the aborted attack on you here in the White House. Within the 24 hour time frame alluded to in the video we had a bombing at an American Air Base in Germany that looks very much to be a diversion so that they could steal one of our aircraft and bomb."

"So, that takes care of Sunday and Monday. Now, when we raided all the homes of the terrorist teams in Atlanta, Lynchburg, Sacramento, and Pittsburgh we discovered that they all had targeted dates of Wednesday. So, what happens today, Tuesday? We believe that the two operatives on the loose in Las Vegas have something planned for today, I have dispatched two of our team out there to try and figure out what the plan is." Genoa laid out his thoughts.

Yusef and Longbow had landed in the Sin City via one of the FBI executive jets. Their first task was to take Maliah Jabara and Leona Hadad into custody. Their husbands had evidently flown the coop - Milo, the Nellis AFB fireman and Naresh, the captain in the LVPD were in the wind somewhere, in uniform and with a suspected plan of no good. The two women were brought into the local FBI office but kept apart, neither knowing of the other's presence.

Leona Hadad was easy to talk to. She had become numb to the cause since her son was killed, and in fact she had personally sworn off the cause of jihad. She had in fact melded into the American way of life and no longer believed in the path she and her husband were supposed to take. The fact that Naresh had gone off the deep end in the past few days seemed more of a mystery to her than anything. She did however reveal that her husband had become more and more active in the Southwest Las Vegas Mosque and that he swore by the teachings and guidance of the Imam. Yusef was able to get up close to Leona and gain her confidence, speaking her language and sounding sympathetic. He became convinced that Naresh was at the mosque.

Maliah Jabara was another story. She was defiant and determined not to talk at all. Even by trying to work on the emotions of losing her son in a suicide bomb in Wyoming, the team was getting nowhere. Her son and her husband had become more and more distant in the past few months and she simply didn't seem to care. She did reveal that Milo had contacted Naresh on Sunday night and she thought they might be together somewhere, but she had nothing else to say because she didn't seem to give a shit what her husband was up to.

They decided that Yusef would enter the mosque alone. After all, he is a muslim, looks like a muslim, talks the talk, and today he dressed the part. He entered looking for a place to pray. Longbnow, being a woman couldn't go the place that Yusef could even if she looked the part - which she didn't. She looked more the part of a California surfer girl - long blond hair and fair complexion. She maintained her distance, and set up with a clear shot of what looked like a garage exit from the mosque with the tools of her trade - a long rifle with a big scope and silencer.

Yusef took his time with his prayers and looked around the mosque. It was not a real busy time - midday on a Tuesday, so he couldn't melt into a crowd anywhere. He feigned looking for a rest room and opened several doors in the rear of the great prayer hall. When he opened the last door down one hall he struck it rich. It was a garage and there behind the door to the outside was a Ford Explorer with the paint job of the Las Vegas police. It had all the bells, whistles and lights, but a closer inspection revealed something else. There were enough explosives and bomb materials in the back cargo area to wipe out half the city. Yusef opened the rear cargo hatch and hadn't heard a door close behind him. As he was taking a photo with his I-phone, a hard piece of steel came down on the back of his head and he immediately went to his knees. Before blacking out he thought he saw the uniform of an LVPD cop.

Milo and Naresh weren't sure what to do. They obviously had been discovered, but they certainly had the upper hand. This man who looked like he belonged in the mosque was either just too curious or he was a cop of some sort. They had both been trying to contact their handler for the last two days to no avail. El-Kamani was evidently too busy to deal with them. They had their orders and even if this was someone to be feared, they couldn't let him stop them. They decided to simply tie the man up, throw him in the back of the car, and let him die with the rest of the infidels.

It had been an hour since Yusef entered the mosque. Longbow was nervous and worried. She called Genoa. "Yusef is inside the mosque, but he's been in there too long. I don't want to call him on the phone. It might give him away. Any guidance?" Columbus had seen that Yusef had turned on the GPS function of his phone.

"He probably only did that because he was in some sort of trouble." He said to Longbow. "The signal comes from an area in the back northeast corner of the building. That looks to be in the vicinity of a garage. Isn't that where you're set up?"

"Yes. I've got it covered but it looks pretty quiet." Longbow replied.

"It is time my brother." Naresh said to Milo. "Let us do the bidding of our God almighty." He got behind the wheel of the Explorer while Milo opened the garage door. Naresh pulled out and waited for Milo to get in. When he did so they were both in full view of Longbow behind her scope. She had studied enough photos of the men provided both by the Las Vegas police and the Nellis AFB personnel system to know she had her targets. But where was Yusef? She had the chance right now to stop whatever they had in mind. But where was Yusef? And would it not be better to find out what these guys are planning first? She knew she didn't have time to contact Genoa, to think about it at all. She waited.

Naresh peeled out of the back street behind the mosque and headed for the center of town - at least the part where the action is - the Strip. He drove fast but not so fast as to attract attention. No lights and siren. He was not responding to a terrible crash, he WAS the terrible crash. Milo had climbed into the back seat. He had armed the explosives and wired everything together. He climbed back up front, looked at Naresh and said "Let the dark rain fall."

Naresh turned in toward the entrance to the MGM Grand, drove onto the sidewalk when he got abeam the concrete barriers strategically placed to stop exactly what he was doing, he stomped on the accelerator and the Ford crashed through the first set of glass doors and exploded. The destruction was catastrophic. The building basically imploded on itself. Over 700 people were killed, hundreds more seriously injured.

Longbow sat near the mosque with her head down. The GPS signal from Yusef's phone was coming from the car. She heard a huge explosion and saw the fiery cloud mushroom up from the strip area. She had blown it.

Back in Washington the Tango Team had real time coverage. The phone line to Longbow was still open. She relayed to Columbus that there was an explosion and that Yusef's phone was in the middle of it. Genoa had the team call the LVPD and request a search of the mosque for Yusef and directed Longbow to join the search. He hung up the phone with a sick feeling in his stomach. He picked up the phone to the President.

"God damnit!" the President exclaimed. "We can't win one! Shit Robby. What's next?"

Genoa had no answers. As the numbers came in from Las Vegas it was obvious that there were going to be a lot more funerals to attend and phone calls for the President to make. He vowed to himself that they would somehow turn the tide.

CHAPTER FORTY THREE

BENI WALID AIRFIELD, LIBYA

Muhammad Mustafa was welcomed with a warm embrace and typical Moslem greeting by the third in command of the Revolutionary Guard, Jubal Goreng. "You have done well, my friend. I only regret that we lost two of our finest fighters. The Americans responded quicker than we thought. I find it gratifying however, that we also shot down one of their fighters and the rest turned tail and ran." Goreng also congratulated the two Mig pilots and the crew of the tanker. "The bomb is now ours and we have the world at bay. With your background and knowledge of the Americans, what do you think they will do now?"

"Sir, I would not presume to suggest such high decisions. However, I do believe the Americans will try to get the bomb back or destroy it. They could have shot me down from their perch before the battle ensued last night, but I am sure they did not want to face the consequences of a nuclear bomb falling into the sea or onto Sardinia. However, now that it is on the ground, I do not believe they would hesitate to destroy it, if they could. They have very good precision guided bombs that could pinpoint the Falcon and destroy it from the air." Mustafa also believed that if he or any other pilot took off with the bomb, the Air Force or the Navy would not hesitate to shoot it down this time. They would have to consider it a threat. He did not express this concern, however. He knew El-Kamani's plan, and he was prepared to sacrifice himself for the cause if necessary.

"As we expected." Goreng turned to his military assistant. "Is the decoy in position?"

"Yes my brother. The decoy is in full view with maintenance men performing simulated work on it. The aircraft and the bomb are in the underground shelter, being readied to fly. The defenses around Beni Walid are at their peak readiness. We have moved every excess anti-aircraft battery and missile system in to enhance the defenses. Our radar tells us that the Americans have an AWACS aircraft airborne just outside our airspace. We believe there are also fighters there to protect it. The aircraft carrier Truman and its flotilla are approaching from the west." The general replied.

"Excellent!" Goreng shouted in an almost maniacal way. "Give them something to do! Make runs at their AWACS with our fighters, but turn around short of leaving our airspace. Keep their pilots busy and tired."

"Sire, if you remember, Libya tried that before and their fighters were shot down. The U.S. does not recognize the 200 mile territorial airspace limit. They will protect their AWACS at all cost." The general was nervous. He did not like conversing with the Goreng in this state of mind. Goreng had always been a hot head, but he also was very close to the Ayatollah - something like a godson to the leader.

"I understand fool! I remember very well that Libya's fighter pilots became disoriented and strayed too close." Goreng shot back. "Do not let that happen to our pilots! Be sure that they turn around before the American fighters can get to them."

"Yes my brother."

"Now Muhammed, are you prepared for phase two of the operation?" Goreng returned his attention to his young hero.

"Of course Sir. I need to do some target study, but I can be ready to fly in a matter of hours. There is one decision yet to be made, Sir. The yield on the bomb is adjustable. Right now it is set on a low yield for the target I was to fly against in western Russia. However, it can be turned to one of many settings." Mustafa did not know his intentions. Were they to annihilate an entire population, or to just make a point?

"How big an explosion will it make?" Goreng asked.

"Enough to wipe out the entire city of Tel Aviv. Ten times that of Nagasaki and Hiroshima."

"Good then. Turn it all the way up. And do not worry. You will have plenty of time for your study. We will wait until our leader Barak arrives and I believe he intends on giving the Americans another ultimatum." Goreng dismissed everyone but Mustafa. When they were all gone he once again addressed the young protege.

"Muhammed, you have done well and made us very proud. Now I must ask you one more thing. I am holding you fully responsible for the security and and operation of the F-16 and the bomb. This is not a punishment. Quite the opposite. We cannot trust anyone else. I believe there is a move amongst the staff to overthrow El-Kamani and myself. I know there is resistance to this particular adventure, and I am afraid someone will use the opportunity to unseat Barak. This must not happen. How we are perceived in this operation is paramount. We must deal with the Americans and Israelis from a position of complete power. Do you understand?" Goreng's eyes were deep and penetrating as he watched Mustafa's reaction.

"Certainly sir. I am honored that you placed this trust in me. I will not let you down." Muhammad's response was quick and unhalting. It was almost as if he were in a trance.

CHAPTER FORTY FOUR

WHITE HOUSE PRESS ROOM

"Ladies and Gentlemen, in a moment Secretary Lucroix and General Adams will address you with reference to last night's activities and the report in this morning's Washington Post." Pete Wilson, White House Press Secretary, zeroed in on Peter Sciapini who squirmed a little in his chair. He knew that his story was old news, but they were the only paper to run it. "Secretary Lucroix will read a prepared statement and General Adams will point out locations on the map. Afterwards they will entertain your questions. Secretary Lucroix."

"Thank you Pete. Yesterday, at approximately noon Washington time, an F-16C loaded with a B-61 nuclear bomb was flown from a base in Germany, apparently by the U.S. pilot on alert at that time. There was a scramble exercise and a series of incidents that compromised our fail safe system. The most serious of which was a car bomb that was detonated at the base exchange area, killing hundreds of people. There was obviously a conspiracy of some sort, and the jet was allowed to launch. Another quick thinking pilot from a team on site from here in D.C. launched about a half hour later to attempt a tail chase, and an E-3A AWACS aircraft just happened to be airborne. The runaway jet was detected heading south and we launched an intercept force from Spain. None of these other U.S. aircraft were fully armed because they were not on any operational alert status. Apparently the Iranian Air Force launched an air refueling aircraft and four MIG-29 fighters from

"

Libya to rendezvous with the F-16. All the players arrived over a point in the Mediterranean at about the same time." General Adams was following the saga along by pointing to the flight paths on the chart. "Our fighters had orders not to fire unless fired upon. We attempted to intercept and force the runaway to land. We were fired upon first and we lost one F-16 and probably its pilot. Another was severely damaged, but it recovered back at Zaragoza, Spain. Our pilots defended themselves and shot down two Migs. However the runaway F-16, the tanker, and the remaining Migs escaped and are now on the ground in Libya." The Chairmen did not point out the location of Beni Walid. There was no reason to give away more intelligence data than is necessary. "That completes my statement. I will now entertain your questions."

"There were many questions, at first dwelling on General Morton and the allegation that he had released information. That was handled rather abruptly by General Adams. "General Morton has been relieved of his position."

The rest of the questions centered on the air battle, and the situation at Spangdahlem. The SECDEF handled most with plain answers. When they got to the big question of what was to be done about the whole thing, Lucroix answered.

"The President will make a statement tomorrow or Thursday. I will leave the answer to that one to him. Now, if you will excuse us, we have work to do."

CHAPTER FORTY FIVE

———

AIRSPACE OVER THE MEDITERRANEAN

Barak El-Kamani was tired. He had not slept in close to 30 hours. He rechecked the duct tape on Ebola and also taped the pilots feet to his seat. Pilots don't used their feet in these big jets to control the rudder like back in the old days. Especially now when a computer is handling the flight controls most of the time, the feet are just along for the ride until it's time to come up on the brakes after landing. He wanted the pilot somewhat immobile as well as he went back and talked to the passengers.

"You have seen what I am capable of. It is too bad I had to kill such an innocent young woman." He explained. "But I needed to get your attention. I assume now that I have it." He looked at each passenger and saw nothing but fear in their eyes. Maybe a little hate too, but definitely fear.

"Good. Now rest assured this is not a suicide mission. We are not going to fly this aircraft into some building. We are merely flying to where I want to get off. At that time what I do with you depends on how you handle yourselves here. Do not try any heroics and you may just live to see your loved ones again." He left the passengers calmer than how he found them, but not exactly with warm, fuzzy feelings.

About 90 minutes later the Aer Lingus Aerbus 334 crossed over the northern coast of Libya. Two Iranian Mig 29s intercepted them and flew in a loose formation off the right wing. El-Kamani handed the pilot a piece of paper with the coordinates of Beni Walid Airfield written on it. He instructed the pilot to make an immediate descent and landing on the main runway. They touched down with a nice smooth landing and rolled out to the end of the runway and turned around. Barak directed the pilot to only shutdown the left side engine, then he unstrapped Ebola from his seat, but backed away and made the flight attendant tape Ebola's hands behind his back. He had radioed ahead to his comrades on the base and they were able to bring out a set of stairs to the left side of the jet. They were smaller than what normally would fit for an Airbus 334, but it was only about a ten foot drop down to the stairwell platform from the forward entrance door of the airliner.

In the meantime several IRG members scrambled underneath the Aerbus and fixed several pounds of C-4 explosive in the two main wheel wells with a radio cell phone controlled activation device. The captain and passengers were unaware of what was going on down there. Barak had the flight attendant open the cabin door. He pushed Ebola out the door onto the stairwell platform. With his hands taped up Ebola could not maintain his balance and fell hard against the steel railing. IRG forces took him with them and El-Kamani then went up to the cockpit.

"Captain, you still have enough fuel to make it to Marakesh, your previous destination. You could also fly over to Tripoli if you'd rather. It matters not to me. When I depart the aircraft you will restart your engine and depart. I must thank you for the exciting ride, and I hope you find the rest of your trip smooth and a little less eventful." With that, El-Kamani walked back to the door, waved a fond farewell and smiled at the passengers, and then jumped down to the stairs.

The stairs were rolled away and El-Kamani stood and watched the pilot through his cockpit window. The captain started the engine and in a few minutes, he looked at Barak on the ground and gave him a "wind it up" signal - one finger pointed up and motioned around and around. El-Kamani and his men backed up and watched the big jet start a slow roll down the runway. The engines wound up to full power and because the jet was fairly light on fuel and passengers, it lifted off the runway with close to 4000' remaining.

Barak El-Kamani stood for a while and watched the jet climb out and head to the northwest. His third in command, Jubal Goreng, had joined and welcomed him and handed him a cell phone. El-Kamani waited until the flashing navigation lights of the airliner were faded in the distance and he mashed the call button on the phone. There was an explosion in the sky from the direction of the Aerbus. The blast had sheared through the right wing and the jet quickly fell out of the sky, exploding again when it hit the ground. He smiled. *An unscheduled, but still another bitter pill for the so called 'Free World' to swallow.*

CHAPTER FORTY SIX

UNITED STATES AIR FORCES EUROPE (USAFE)

The rapid reaction capability of the U.S. arsenal was tested. Wheels were put in motion all over the country and Europe. Recall rosters were utilized and the Air Force, Navy, and even some Army Special Forces personnel were called in to work all night. The force list was created at the Pentagon, and the chain of command established. Major General "Ollie" Olsen, the USAFE Director of Operations was appointed Task Force Commander. He arrived in Zaragoza from Turkey Tuesday afternoon. A number of his own staff from headquarters at Ramstein were assembled and flown down via two small transport aircraft. He had planners, weapons and tactics specialists, logisticians, and command and control types—everyone he needed to put together a small war. Their movements were quiet and easy to hide. Even their wives were unaware of their whereabouts.

The first deployment of any size was the 493rd Fighter Squadron of 24 F-15s from Lakenheath Air Base, England to Decimomannu. They arrived at 11 am Wednesday morning, followed by three C-130 cargo planes worth of their maintainers and equipment. It was billed as a routine deployment into Deci for training. It was easy to sell, since there was no U.S. unit at the training site, and it was just about time for such a rotation. Coincidentally, the 493rd had just completed a unique and classified deployment to northern Germany where they had the chance to train and fight with former East German MIG-29s, flown by Luftwaffe pilots. They were perhaps the most current and well trained F-15 pilots in the Air Force right now, and General Olsen wanted every edge he could get. As it was, both the Air Force and the Navy were restricted in their armament. The advanced radar missiles (AMRAMS) deployed on the F-15, F-22 and the new F-35, and on some versions of the F-18 and F-16 were basically grounded. There was a major flaw that had brought down two F-15s flying out of Edwards AFB, Nevada. There was a major refurbishment underway, but presently only aircraft fighting in the desert (Afghanistan, Iraq and Syria), and aircraft on air defense alert in the States were equipped with the most modern weapons. The force being assembled for this mission would be equipped with only AIM-7 radar guided missiles and the latest AIM-9 heat seekers. Not the best situation, but certainly enough to defeat the Iranian arsenal.

So the 493rd bedded down for what looked like a standard six week deployment to Deci. Actually, only 22 of them landed at Deci. The Lakenheath Wing commander and a weapons tactics officer came directly into Zaragoza to participate in the planning and briefings.

The only other daytime movement in the first few days was the SEAL team off the Truman. Eight Navy SEALs were picked up and flown to Rota AB, in southern Spain. They arrived on Tuesday afternoon. They were to bed down there and would be joined Monday morning by Brad Mitchell, before being transported for the next leg of their journey.

Another coincidence of normal scheduling helped disguise more of the force assembly. Eight F-16s flying the Wild Weasel mission from the 22cnd Fighter Squadron at Spangdahlem AB had arrived at Zaragoza Monday morning. They were due to swap out with the 10th squadron F-16s, and were the supposed advance party of the rest of their squadron to come later. The Weasel is the Air Force's electronic jamming and attack aircraft. It can detect a radar warning and potential surface to air missile launch and fire missiles at the emitter to destroy it or the missile before it gets off the ground. At least that's the theory, but it obviously depended on how many missiles were being launched. Additionally, through the night on Tuesday and into Wednesday morning, three

EA-6s off the Truman, two more AWACS E-3A aircraft, and six more KC-10 tankers arrived at Zaragoza. The EA-6 was the flying "jammer" that the Navy used to shut down enemy radars and communications. By noon on Wednesday, there were almost 75 aircraft assembled at Zaragoza and Decimomannu. There was only one ingredient left, and during the night on Wednesday, eight F-22 Stealth Fighters arrived from their base in Virginia.

General Olsen would have liked to have more. Jamming platforms and JSTARS command and control aircraft would be nice, and he wanted more night attack capability. But the decision was made to keep things as low key as possible. Seventy five visible aircraft at the two bases were not all that uncommon, but any more would have tipped off the not-so-casual observer. So the task force was formed and the planning was well underway. The operation was named "DIRECT RECOVERY."

The Navy flew into Zaragoza Wednesday morning with a P-2C and two F-18s off the USS Truman. The Truman's "Air Boss," Captain Josh Patillo brought his tactics experts along too. The basic plan was put together by the USAFE/DO staff planners, with help from the various experts, and it was decided that Ed Howe, Sabre Lead, would be the overall Mission Commander—at least of the Air Force side. The plan followed somewhat like the 1985 raid on Libya. The Navy would take one AOR (Area of Responsibility), and the Air Force the other. However, there would need to be split-second timing coordination, and the main targets for the Navy were communications and other military targets around Tripoli. The object was to be sure that what was about to happen at Beni Walid airfield would be unannounced for a specified period of time—long enough to find and destroy the F-16 and its deadly cargo.

Ed Howe had of course returned from Decimomannu to Zaragoza. He had been in on the intricate planning of DIRECT RECOVERY from the time he hit the ground. Brad Mitchell was involved both from his tactical background side and his experience in Korea, but also as the liaison with Tango. Brad and Howe of course were old friends and had flown together many times, both as commander/Ops Officer and as just plain wingmen.

"What's the latest on Finnegan?" Brad asked Ed when he came into the squadron area.

"Nothing much. They've found a lot of pieces. Enough to know the jet completely blew apart at altitude. There's not much of anything even bigger than a foot square. Brad, they plan on having a memorial service at Spang on Thursday. I know you'd want to be there too." Howe realized that Mitchell couldn't be at Spangdahlem and somewhere in the Mediterranean with a bunch of Navy kamikazis at the same time.

"Are you going to go?"

"I hope so. It depends on how much of this planning we get done. Right now I plan on taking a jet up and back on Thursday."

"That's good enough. I'll do a lot more for 'Lucky' on this mission than I ever would praying for him." Brad pulled out his wallet and took out a folded up, yellowing piece of paper. "Here, take this with you. It's a poem I once heard at a memorial service. It means a lot. Marie may like you to read it at the service."

CHAPTER FORTY SEVEN

WHITE HOUSE OVAL OFFICE

"My fellow Americans, as you know, Friday night we had an F-16 Falcon aircraft and a nuclear bomb stolen from the Air Force and flown to Libya." The President of the United States looked tired and very serious on TV. It was 9 AM, Wednesday morning, and he had not had much sleep since Sunday night. "Hundreds of brave young men and women died in a diversion explosion and act of terrorism, and we lost another F-16 in an air battle over the Mediterranean. We also shot down two Iranian Air Force MIG-29 fighters. At this time we don't know why this criminal act was performed, nor do we know what the enemy intends to do with the aircraft or the weapon. In fact, we still don't know for certain who this terrorist regime is that has brought death and destruction to our homeland and abroad. At this time we suspect it is the government of Iran and we must suspect the worst. I have sent Secretary Wisnewski to the Middle East to try to negotiate both the return of the Falcon and its cargo, and the rational response of our allies in the area. The mere thought of a nuclear weapon in the hands of a man like the Ayatollah is frightening. I want to make it perfectly clear that we will not take this lying down. I am hereby setting a deadline of 6 PM Washington time, tomorrow, for the return of our aircraft and its weapon—intact. I am not prepared at this time to discuss the consequences, but let me assure you and the world we will not limit our response. One way or another we will get back what is ours and once again make the world safe from this menace. Thank you, and may God bless America and our fighting men and women."

The questions were the normal, "What if …. " and "How did this …. " and mostly were deflected, rather than answered. President McDivitt was not about to give away anything, much to the chagrin of people like Peter Sciapini and Marianne Rogers. They knew the Pentagon was up to something, and they desperately wanted to scoop the story. The President did acknowledge that the aircraft carrier Truman and her armada were in the Mediterranean and would stay on scene until further notice. He also said the Air Force units deployed to Spain would remain in country a little while longer.

CHAPTER FORTY EIGHT

ROTA NAVAL AIR BASE, SPAIN

At 6:30 Thursday morning the P-2C touched down at Rota, Spain. A tired Brad Mitchell and Major Ron Edwards, USAFE Plans, were welcomed by the local detachment commander. Rota was usually a ghost town. It was a huge base with a very long runway, and that was its reason for continued existence. Rota had been the primary first recovery base and alternate landing sight for the space shuttle. So, whenever there was a shuttle launch from Florida, Rota got busy. Otherwise, a staff of about 80 folks, mostly Navy and Air Force, kept the place running.

Brad and Edwards were deposited at Billeting where the SEAL team was waiting for them, along with a civilian from the Defense Intelligence Agency (DIA). They were escorted to a small conference room with a guard posted outside, offered some coffee, and introductions were made.

Ron Edwards was an intelligence specialist who had spent most of the night with Brad, Ed Howe, General Olsen, and the rest of the USAFE staff at Zaragoza, going over this part of the operation. He was detailed to the USAFE Plans staff because of his incredible accuracy in predicting events that were occurring in Eastern Europe. His kind of insight made it easier to forecast the threat, and build the budget and the force structure to meet it. He was brought along on this operation because Olsen wanted the best crystal ball gazer the Intel community had to predict the Libyan response. Edwards had with him the latest satellite photos of Beni Walid, and the intended shore landing site, codes and instructions for the SEAL team leader.

Mr. Wilbur Marsh was the spook from DIA. He was an expert on North Africa, particularly Libya. He also knew everything there was to know about the Iranian regime and its opposition, but more importantly, the friendly indigenous forces in the Libyan area. He was sort of a pompous asshole, as far as Brad could see, and he acted like he thought he was in charge. That was the only problem with this august group. Nobody knew who was in charge.

"Sir, I'm Lieutenant Jack Lee. I'm Alpha Team Leader. I wish we could say we are happy to have you along with us, but, I have to be honest, sir. We have a lot of territory to cover and a tough mission ahead of us. I don't relish nurse-maiding an out of shape Air Force fighter jock even if he is a colonel." The wiry little lieutenant was certainly blunt. One thing Brad noticed right off the bat—he had a hand shake grip that would put Hulk Hogan to shame. Surprising for such a small man.

"Glad to meet you too, Jack." Brad lied. "I'm sorry you feel that way. Believe me, I don't relish this either, but we're stuck with each other. I may not be in the shape you guys are, but I run a bit, and I'll leg wrestle anyone here. We've got about eight hours for you guys to teach me everything you can. If I can't keep up after that, I guess you'll just have to shoot me."

The lieutenant warmed a little to that prospect and actually cracked a smile. "Yes sir. Would you like to meet the rest of the team?"

"Sure."

"Chief Petty Officer Bob Roach. He's what you guys call the NCO In Charge. Twenty Five years as a SEAL. He's my number two man—and the truth be told, he's really in charge." The Chief was a burly man. Only about 5'8" but solid as a rock at about 200 pounds. At least he grinned when he shook Brad's hand—another bone crusher.

"Some things don't change from service to service. A good Chief equals two or three officers. My pleasure, Chief." Brad turned to the rest of them.

"John Davis—our comm man. We call him 'Radio.' Steve Lundick—explosives. 'Blaster's' his handle. Manny Molina—lead scout. 'Scout' for short. Dave Bushime—back up to 'Blaster' and a little first aid. Call him 'Medic.' Louis Leitow—second scout, usually in the rear, so we call him 'Wipe.' And Ahab Anam—he's new on this trip. He's our intelligence guy and fluid in the language. We'll call him 'Spook.' By the way sir, 'Blaster' speaks a little of the language too." Brad shook hands with each one, and when he was done he almost asked "Medic" for a splint for his crippled hand. He decided the SEALs must have a secret handshake that's designed to cripple the other guy. Not many of them smiled or even grunted an acknowledgement. It was obvious they all felt the same as their leader. They didn't want this soft Air Force fighter jock in the way.

"Sir, unless you have an objection, we'll call you 'Air Force.' We need short, descriptive names out there in the dark." The lieutenant was patronizing again.

"Well, I've got one a little shorter that I go by in my job and in the Air Force. How about 'Conan?" Brad shot back. "Hopefully, you'll not be disappointed." Lee looked at his team. Most of them snickered and there was some muffled comment about slaying dragons and screwing sorcerers. But eventually they just shrugged an "I don't give a shit" shrug.

"Conan it is then."

"Gentlemen. I suggest we get down to business. All this is well and good, but we have a lot of ground to cover." It was the DIA spook, Wilbur Marsh, astride his high horse and not real impressed with all this muscle flexing. The men acknowledged he was right, and settled down for two hours of briefing and training.

The team covered the terrain features, the photos, the codes to be used, the timetable, their insert plan, and most importantly, their pick-up plan. They were to be inserted as close as possible by submarine tonight, go ashore by raft, dig in, and wait. Their indigenous contact was a single Libyan, code named "Fox," who would find them and get them to Beni Walid. They were to locate the jet and the bomb, coordinate with the strike package by radio, and then dig in to stay out of the way. If the Falcon and its cargo were hidden and/or not destroyed, the SEALs were to get the job done any way they could. As a bonus, they were to attempt to locate Robert Mustan and bring him back. The Navy would pick them up by Sea King chopper, 40 minutes after the first strike. The pick up point was memorized by each. This was not going to be a cake walk by any means. The chances of them getting ashore undetected were pretty good. But to travel the fifty or so miles to the airfield, penetrate the defenses and find a single aircraft under heavy guard was another. Top that off with enough ordnance from the sky to blow a city away, and things would get real hot before it was over. Brad looked around at this team of trained animals. They each had a gleam in their eye. They were looking forward to this! He was scared shitless.

Over the next six hours Brad went through as much training as Chief Roach could shove down his throat. He was issued a 9 mm automatic, which he already knew how to use, an Uzi semi-automatic machine gun that he had only seen on TV, and the biggest knife he had ever seen. He guessed it was a Bowie. He got a chance to fire each weapon at the base firing range, and he got some elementary hand-to-hand combat training that included use of the knife. The intricacies of where and how to cut a man open quickly so he doesn't make a sound chilled him to the bone. Brad was determined though, not to show he was apprehensive. He took everything in and made an effort to at least look excited. The basic plan was for him to stick close to the Chief, not wander off, and not do anything stupid. At 1600 hours they all got dressed in wet suits. Flightsuits and fatigues went into waterproof bags, along with the weapons. Brad followed everyone else's lead and strapped the knife onto his right calf. He laughed to himself as he wondered what Arnold Schwarzenegger would think of "Conan" now.

Towards the end of the day Brad got a call from Genoa back in D.C. Brad updated him on what he thought was their readiness. Then Columbus dropped a bomb on him.

"Brad, I've had to send Melanie into Libya. There apparently is a problem with the indigenous contact who is supposed to meet and lead your team in. As you know, Melanie conducted a short operation in that same area a couple years ago. She knows the area and she knows Beni Walid. She'll hopefully meet you all when you land. Good luck." Genoa hung up before Brad had a chance to respond. He knew about his wife's talents and her experience in Libya, but that didn't mean he wanted her in the middle of this action. He would have liked to at least talked to her, but he assumed he would get the opportunity sooner than later.

CHAPTER FORTY NINE

SPANGDAHLEM AIR BASE, GERMANY

Over the next few days the Air Force proved it knows how to take care of its own. The fact that 122 personnel were killed in the bomb attack was devastating. Each surviving family member was accorded the same benefits and handled with the utmost of sensitivity. None more so than Marie Finnegan, wife of the lost fighter pilot. Squadron wives pitched in to stay with her and the kids. Normally the wing commander and his wife would be deeply involved. They did make an appearance, but with 122 plus casualties, Colonel Day had to spread himself around. Legal representatives contacted Marie Finnegan through the squadron commander's wife and explained all the procedures and benefits. A check for $3000 for immediate expenses—no questions asked—was issued. Arrangements were made for trips home and for memorial services. It was decided there would be one service for all of the deceased on Thursday at noon, with a "missing man" fly by for Jim. Marie and the kids would leave Friday, and one of the officers in another squadron was appointed to take care of packing them out later. The bottom line was simple. All three children were financially set through college, and Marie herself got all the financial benefits she needed to complete any schooling she wanted. The kids were actually put in a special category for appointment to the Air Force Academy, if they wanted to go there later. Jim had been a "Zoomie," so it was a pretty good bet that at least one of them would want to follow their Dad, much to Marie's chagrin right now.

Through all of this, Marie was sheltered from most of the red tape and left to herself. The wives took care of everything. The children each took the news differently. Margo was the oldest at 11. She took it hard. She barely came out of her room, and when she did it was no fun for the rest of them. Robbie was seven, and he sat down with his Legos and toys and pretty much played very quietly by himself. Thad was only three and not old enough to understand. Marie was a different story. She was a mess. She was very dependent on Jim, and deeply in love with him. All she knew was how much she hated the Air Force, and how she wanted to go home. Her mother arrived on Wednesday to help on the trip.

It was another typical Spangdahlem winter weather day. Five hundred foot ceiling, fog and drizzle, tops of the clouds about 5000 feet, clear above. The weatherman, as always, predicted possible clearing in the afternoon for a little while. It was barely flyable in the morning, so at least the memorial flight was able to take off. The five "Stingers" from the 22cnd FS launched off at 1150, ten minutes before the start of the ceremony. All flying for the day had been canceled, except for the memorial flight, and although the forecast was hardly good enough for a fly-by that anyone on the ground would see, the decision was made to launch anyway, just in case. Weathermen at Spang had a reputation for being wrong a majority of the time. Besides, the USAFE Commander in Chief (CINC) was on base for the ceremony, and the wing commander couldn't stand the embarrassment if it did clear. The "Stingers" didn't mind. It was sunny and clear above the clouds, and at least they got to fly. Most of them would rather fly than go to a memorial ceremony anyway. No disrespect there—it was the fighter pilot way of showing respect. Demonstrate what the deceased did best.

Chapel #2 was full. Only one coffin was in front of the pews, draped with an American flag. Another ceremony had taken place an hour earlier at one of the base hangars where dozens of coffins were honored. The decision was made not to slight anyone, but to include everyone in this ceremony, even if only Jim Finnegan's coffin was on display. There were plenty of flowers, and the usual Sunday organist was playing some morbid song to put everyone in the right mood. The relatives that had come over were seated up front, each with an escort from their squadron. As it turned out only a few of the families of those killed in the blast wanted a service on base. They had elected not to come over to Germany, but to meet the coffins when they arrived in the States. Most of them were to be shipped out on Friday to Dover AFB in Delaware. The aisles of the church were full of people, and there were more standing outside.

Marie Finnegan did not have a black dress. She never thought she'd need one, and she wasn't about to go shopping over the last few days. She wore a dark blue suit and sunglasses to cover her swollen eyes. The kids were all dressed in their best outfits. Nancy Howe, Ed's wife, sat next to her, and Rex Milican, a pilot from the 23rd sat with them as an escort. Marie's mother sat next to her also, escorted by another pilot. Rex Millican and Jim Finnegan had been roommates at the Academy, and had also gone through pilot training together. Until Rex and his wife Becky had divorced two years earlier, the Milicans and Finnegans had been very close. It was natural for Marie to ask Rex to escort her. He would also take care of the official aspects, and escort the body to D.C.

On the stage sat the USAFE Commander in Chief, Colonel Kerry Day (the Wing Commander), Chaplain John Tremain, and Ed Howe. When the crowd was as big as it was going to get, and everyone in the front rows had been seated, the chaplain started off the ceremony. There were the standard "Dearly Beloveds," and prayers, and words of consolation. Colonel Day was next and he had some good things to say about Jim and about the rest of his wing's dearly departed. He had done his homework (or someone had done it for him), and he did a very classy job building up each of the fallen members he spoke about individually in the eyes of all that knew them. His words about "Lucky Finnegan" were short, because he knew that Ed Howe was to follow.

The "Coach" had flown up from Zaragoza, and actually had to land at Ramstein Air Base because of the weather. He got a U-Drive truck from the Ramstein motor pool, and made it in just in time for the ceremony. After it was over, he planned on about five minutes of "good luck" words with Marie, a run home to see his kids, get some clean clothes, kiss Nancy, and then head back to Ramstein so he could make it to Zaragoza before the 12 hour duty day was up. He stood and went to the podium, unfolding a piece of faded yellow paper.

"This week will probably not go down in the history books as a time of glory for the United States or the free world. We may never know what happened out there on our ramp, and we may never know what led up to the bomb at the BX. We know what happened over the Mediterranean when Jim Finnegan was killed while trying a peaceful intercept on one of our own jets. And we know that all of these warriors did not die in vain." Many winced at that remark, and those close to her could feel Marie Finnegan cringe as well. Ed Howe went on.

"These people died as heroes, doing their duties for God and their country. James Finnegan will always be a hero to me. We called him 'Lucky,' but there was no luck involved. His was pure dedication and aggressive perseverance. He was without a doubt, the best flight commander any group of pilots ever had. He cared for his people, and he led by example. He was the Top Gun in the Sabres in air-to-ground, Top Gun in air-to-air, and he has always been Top Gun amongst fighter pilots." Howe continued his words with a close eye on Marie. He didn't want to say anything that would make her too uncomfortable. "But more importantly to most of this audience, Jim Finnegan was Top Gun at home too. He was Top Gun Little League coach, scoutmaster, father and husband. There was nothing he wouldn't do for his wife Marie and his children, Margo, Robbie and Thad. Before we close I would like to read a poem for Marie. It will be followed by a special song sung by Mrs. Linda Orsam, wife of Lt. Colonel Hank Orsam. They express the feelings felt toward the loss of all these fallen heroes."
Last Flight (1)

If only I had bid you stay. Yet I know of your need to be,

to leave the earth, to touch the sky, and become free.

And of your need to come back again to me. . . . But somewhere in that eternity you ceased to be, And never again came back to me.

1) Written by Paula G. Morton, after her father, Major Victor Morton and 11 comrades were killed in a DC-7 aerial tanker crash, September 14, 1979, near Klamath Falls, Oregon

The poem was actually much longer and very gut wrenching. After the third line Ed looked up and saw that Marie was about tho lose it. He decided to cut to the last two lines and left it there.

As if the poem wasn't gut wrenching enough, when Ed Howe was finished Linda Orsam, wife of the 23rd Fighter Squadron Commander, got up slowly and walked to the podium. She was wearing a peach colored suit, and her hair was pulled back into a pony tail. She looked beautiful, but she also looked tired and worried. As the crowd quieted she glanced quickly at Marie, and then fixed her eyes on a point on the back wall. She wondered if she could make it through this. Then, with a voice of an angel, she sang the Bette Midler song, "You Are the Wind Beneath My Wings." After the second or third line little Thad Finnegan stood up and saluted his Dad's coffin. He remained standing there, and seeing that, Margo and Robbie also stood up. In a moment Marie was standing. Rex Milican didn't know what to do. He looked around quickly and saw that all eyes were on Marie and the kids. He too stood, and soon the whole chapel audience was standing. Linda almost lost it. She didn't expect this, and it was hard enough to get through the song. She swallowed hard and made it through the last strands with the lasting tone and quality to her voice that brought tears to every eye in the building.

When the song was over, the family and immediate friends were escorted outside. Everyone else followed. It had stopped raining, and in fact a strange thing happened to the weather. It was almost as if the sky parted right over Spangdahlem, and a large break in the clouds formed parallel to the runway for about five or six miles. Airborne, Lt. Colonel Hank Orsam, commander and leader of the memorial flight of five F-16s, had his flight in a tight orbit, eight miles to the northeast. On cue by radio from Lt. Colonel Jim Reed (the wing Assistant Director of Operations) they departed the orbit in a descending path toward the base and the chapel. Reed was in the chapel parking lot in the DO truck, and when the crowd was outside he cleared the flight to proceed. Orsam cleared #5 (the spare) off to stay out of the way, and rocked the rest of the flight into a tight formation. He set his throttle for a nice comfortable 330 knots and looked for the chapel. He didn't believe this weather. Somebody up there was definitely watching today and blessed the crowd and the event. When the flight was one half mile from directly overhead the crowd, Orsam keyed the mike button and said "Now!" Don Locke, flying the #3 position abruptly pulled the nose of his Falcon into the vertical, selected full afterburner, and climbed completely out of sight, accelerating as he went. The noise was deafening, and the formation left behind included the empty slot of the wingman—otherwise known as the "missing man." Almost as quickly as they parted, the clouds began to reform and before the crowd could disperse, it was completely overcast again.

Marie Finnegan watched the jets fly over while she gripped Thad's hand tightly. Margo stood tall and straight, almost defiant, and did not hold back the tears as she thought once again of her dad, the fighter pilot. Robbie just stared after the missing jet, trying so hard to follow it up into the vertical climb, that he almost fell over backwards. When it was over, Marie took one or two greetings of condolence and then retreated to Rex Milican's car. She and the kids and her mother left the base then, and they left Germany the next day. Marie was sure that she never wanted to see Spangdahlem Air Base again for the rest of her life.

CHAPTER FIFTY

ZARAGOZA AIR BASE, SPAIN

"Be seated!" General Olsen had walked into the room like George Patton. All the way to the front with the entire room at attention, turned and faced them all, looked them all in the eye, and then finally told them to relax and sit down. They were crowded into the main briefing room of the Weapons Training Detachment building at the northwest end of Zaragoza. The commanders or liaisons for each organization in the Task Force were there. Even the Operations Officer of the F-22 outfit had arrived earlier in the day. His pilots and planes would come in later that night. AWACS was represented by Captain Stephanie Michaels and her crew. The refuelers were there, the Navy, the Intel community, and all the fighters that had gathered in the area were represented. Captain Josh Patillo, Commander of the USS Truman Air Group, Colonel Ron Davenport, Zaragoza Wing Commander, Colonel Pete Trask, Lakenheath (F-15) Wing Commander, and a host of other colonels or equivalents sat up front.

"Ladies and Gentlemen, I assume you all know why we are here." Olsen began. "I also assume you all saw or read of the President's news conference yesterday. So far, there has been no reaction from Iran or Libya, but we must assume they intend to use this new weapon they have acquired. Our job—your job - is to destroy it, assuming the State Department fails to get it back. We have assembled a formidable task force. I would like to have more, however we have been told to keep a low profile. Once our force is complete this evening, with the arrival of the F-22s, we will be ready. Your mission is to blow the hell out of everything that even smacks of a military target in and around Beni Walid airfield. Hopefully, the first F-22 will take out the Falcon and its bomb. The rest of you will have specific designated impact points, but the object is to make it hurt. Make them remember! Make them believe that this was a big mistake! Punish them! Colonel Howe."

General Olsen introduced Ed Howe. As Mission Commander, "Coach" would conduct the briefing. This was a coordination briefing. The specifics of how to and where to would be left up to each individual formation leader. The purpose of the coordination briefing was to get all the players on the same sheet of music and to make sure the timing was right. Avoiding fratricide and running into each other in the dark are paramount considerations in a large force attack like this.

"Thank you sir. Let's start off with a time hack. I have 30 seconds to 1304. While we are waiting, a reminder to be sure and get an updated hack from the Zaragoza command post or AWACS prior to your push off time. Fifteen seconds. You Navy guys may have to get yours from AWACS airborne. Five, four, three, two, one, Hack! 1304. Does anyone need another?" Ed looked around the room and then turned to the weatherman. "Weather."

"Yes sir. The forecast for Saturday morning here is good. Basically clear with some patchy fog in the valleys. Decimomannu may have some low stratus associated with a warm front just about here." The sergeant was nervous. This was big time for Zaragoza, and he had never briefed anything other than the basic range mission. His pointer shook as he outlined the weather patterns on the map portrayed on the wall. "Also, in the Med around the fleet you can expect low ceilings, around 1000 feet. Tops should be around 7000, and it clears out as you approach the coast. Weather in the target area looks good. Clear to partly cloudy at around four to five thousand feet. Winds out of the northwest at 10 to 15 knots. Moon will be down by your Time on Target. It will be about 50% earlier in the night. For your recovery, expect clear and windy back here, winds 350 at 20 to 30 knots. Deci and the Truman will have the same low ceilings with some possible rain, visibilities in the rain down to as low as a half mile. Any questions?" The forecast for Decimomannu and the fleet raised a question or two, but nobody thought an Air Force weatherman could forecast out two days in advance anyway. So, the questions were academic.

"Ok, thanks. Intel?" Howe beckoned the intelligence folks to come forward for their brief. The lights went out and the slide projector showed a picture of an airfield with a single runway, several hardened shelters, several hangars and buildings, and one taxiway that seemed to dead end in some shrubbery.

"This is Beni Walid as of six months ago." The intelligence captain was very confident and comfortable speaking. This is what she trained for. She felt honored to be part of the operation. She was Linda Halterson, the 10th Fighter Squadron's own IN officer. "The runway orients north-south. There are 10 hardened revetments, and most of them are out in the open." She pointed out features as she briefed. "This taxiway actually leads into an underground facility here. This is a straight top down satellite shot, so it doesn't show the contour well. However, this ridge line is fairly steep, and it parallels the runway. We don't know how large a facility is in there, but we think it's extensive." She clicked the projector forward. "This is one of the three air vents in the ridge line that indicate the complex could run the entire length of the runway." She reversed the projector to the original shot and pointed to the three locations along the ridge. "These may also be vulnerable targets. Copies of these shots, along with more recent photos of the airfield and defenses are in the packages given to each flight lead." Captain Halterson turned off the slides and turned on an overhead viewgraph projector, also projecting a photo on the screen. "Here, in front of this revetment, you can see the F-16. The bomb is still attached. Now, with the protection of an underground facility, it doesn't make sense that they would keep the Falcon out on a pad—unless they were getting ready to fly it soon."

The intelligence briefing went on for another 15 minutes. Linda pointed out all the new missile systems and anti-aircraft batteries around the airfield, and the other targets to be hit. She also reviewed the capabilities of the Iranian fighters and their missiles. By the time she was done, everyone in the room could have logged off six months' worth of current intelligence training. It was a good show.

"Thanks Linda. Any questions for Intel?" Ed Howe scanned the audience. "OK. In your packets is a timing card. Timing is critical for this operation. Sunrise down there is 0547 Zulu (Greenwich Mean Time) tomorrow. There will be enough light for us daytime kind of guys to do our job at about 0530. The ridge keeps the airfield in the shadows in the morning. The TOT for the first bomb on Beni Walid is 0525, with F-22s hitting these four Tab Vees and the three vents to the underground shelter." Howe pointed to the targets on the map that was projected on the wall again. "Navy, your TOT is at 0520 at this communications site in Tripoli, and spread out for the next hour at various military sites around there. At 0535 the main wave of F-16s hits targets all over Beni Walid. The object is to leave it a parking lot. Make your take off times match to your orbit push-off times. Tankers will be on orbit here, here and here, and AWACS will set up two orbits—here and here." Howe used a big picture map of the Mediterranean.

"There shouldn't be any conflict between forces, unless there is an air-to-air threat that gets the F-15s involved near the carrier. AWACS should help there. There are no real SAFE areas, but a lot of deserted land. Best option in case of trouble is to get 'feet wet.' We're going to have a modified C-130 on orbit as a Search And Rescue (SAR) 'Duckbutt,' and the Navy might be able to muster up a sub to help you if you're in the water." Howe didn't like briefing this part of a mission. Sometimes he felt that if you talk about something enough, it might happen. But it was necessary. "If you do go in around Beni Walid, there is a pick-up point for our SEAL team right here, on the back side of this ridge, at the intersection of two roads. The pick-up is 40 minutes after TOT, or 0610. Be there or be left behind."

"There are codewords in your packet for all our radio frequencies. However, the Air Force plans on using Have Quick. Use the codewords as a back-up, or in case something goes wrong with 'Mickey.' There are also codes for pushing the TOT, low fuel states, etc. We need to keep the chatter down. Expect quick-flow, comm-out refueling. Any problem there from the tanker folks?" Howe looked to the KC-10 squadron

Operations Officer, who gave him a thumbs up. "Handle recoveries and emergencies in your own way. Each aircraft is different. Should we end up with a mixed formation, 160 knots on final should cover all of us. Any questions before I get to the Rules of Engagement?"

"ROE is simple. Positively IDd as a bad guy, shoot it! Remember, it's going to be dark out there going in. Although he doesn't have a great radar missile, you may not want to wait for a visual ID to shoot. However, I'll leave that up to you Eagle and F-18 drivers and your special gadgets. Coming out's another story. Navy, you take care of your own, and you can expect us Viper drivers to swing to air-to-air as soon as our bombs are gone. You'll have our egress route. Look for us there. Expect anyone else to be a Bandit. We won't have a whole lot of play time off the target. We'll need to get to the tanker. So, if you see us turning more than about 45 degrees on egress, expect we have company. You are welcome to come help. Are there any questions?" There were a few, and Howe and the various experts cleared them all up. The briefing broke up after some more words of encouragement from General Olsen, and the direction to get together on the radio and/or phone for a last minute update and time hack at 1 am Saturday morning

CHAPTER FIFTY ONE

WEDNESDAY NIGHT, AL JAZEERAH TV, WORLDWIDE

"My friends and Islamic brothers of the world. I speak to you today from a position of power. At this time in the nation of Libya we have in our possession a weapon for bargaining. God has been good to us, and he has given us guidance. He has delivered to us an aircraft and a bomb, and we have been instructed to use it if necessary. Let everyone in the world know that we will not hesitate to do so, and that any act by the United States or any other infidel nation to deny the people of Islam what is theirs will only serve to accelerate a catastrophe." Barak El-Kamani was speaking on Al Jazeerah television and radio, and it was carried by many of the large worldwide networks. The speech had been advertised through the Iranian government, and most of the embassies in Tripoli.

"To the government of Israel I issue a direct and immediate warning. You will release all Arab and Islamic prisoners at once. You will remove all presence from the occupied territories and the West Bank. You will pay a restitution for crimes against the people of Islam an amount equal to ten billion U.S. dollars to the government of Iran, through the embassy of Lebanon in Tel Aviv. You will pay this money and release all prisoners by Friday of this week, and you will also agree to the other demands by then. All Israeli presence in Arab land will be removed by the end of this month. That includes your presence in Jerusalem." El-Kamani's eyes were sagging and tired. It was almost as if he were speaking in a trance. But he looked directly into the camera, and did not refer to notes or falter. The English translator reading the prepared text made it even more trance-like. "The consequences for refusing our demands will be catastrophic for the people of Israel. Many will die, Jew and Arab alike. But the objective will be reached. Israel will no longer exist. To the people of the world, do not misunderstand me. I believe the nation of Israel can coexist with Arabs and the nation of Islam. However, not under the present and past circumstances. We will not go on as we have in the past! Do not doubt our resolve! You need only to look at the mountain in Colorado, to the plains of Wyoming, to the casino in Las Vegas, to the rubble of the American base in Germany, and to the wreckage of the American aircraft carrier off the coast of Bahrain to understand our resolve." The speech was over. The world shuddered to a cold feeling up its spine.

CHAPTER FIFTY TWO

—

2400 HOURS, THE MEDITERRANEAN SEA

The *Augusta* was a fast attack submarine of the Navy's Mediterranean Fleet. As such, there wasn't a whole lot of extra room for passengers. Fortunately, Brad Mitchell and the SEALs were not aboard for long. They were choppered out to sea from Rota and dropped onto the sharply rocking deck of the boat at a rendezvous point that maximized the reach of the helicopter and minimized the run of the sub toward the Libyan shore. The boarding itself was terrifying to Brad. Whereas the SEALs did this kind of thing all the time, he didn't even like going on Zip lines. To be honest, Brad was somewhat afraid of heights. That was always surprising to most of his "buds," seeing as he had no problem at 50,000 feet in a bubble cockpit, looking down on the curvature of the earth. It was the fact that he felt like he had no control of the situation when he jumped out of a helicopter tethered to a rope. In fact, Brad had always said he never understood how anyone in the parachute or sky diving business could jump out of a perfectly good flying machine. He had to jump out of one that wasn't perfectly good in Korea and he never wanted to do it again. They managed to get aboard without getting too wet and had a few hours of "leisure time" aboard the *Augusta* going over their plan and intel one more time while drinking mugs of what the Navy called coffee. When it came time to depart, the *Augusta* surfaced again and her nine passengers were put off on two hard rubber boats, each fitted out with a small electric engine.

It was not the kind of night that SEALs liked. The sky was mostly clear and the moon was bright. Anyone looking close could spot their rubber rafts as they approached the shore. It was also windy and the sea was rough and rolling. It was not going to be an easy trip. The submarine could only get as close as a mile and a half to shore. The Med shallows quickly off the coast of North Africa, and the captain did not want to be caught on the surface. Brad barely had time to clamor into his boat and get seated when the sub had submerged again. Chief Roach, Brad, "Radio" Davis and "Wipe" Leitow were in one raft. The other four SEALs and their lieutenant were crammed into the other. There was no more room to spare in Brad's raft either. They had all the radio equipment with them. The chief and the lieutenant each started their engine and headed their rafts for shore. The engine was so quiet that Brad could not even hear it over the wind and the crash of the waves.

About a half a mile off shore they shut off the engine and each man grabbed a small paddle. It was hard work, and Brad was thankful for the wetsuit. The Med may be ok to swim in this time of year, but not at this time of night. It was 0100 hours when they had surfaced in the sub. Brad guessed it was close to 0200 now.

The coastline was rocky, although not impassable. There were stretches of sand in between the rocks. Actually, it was more like dirt—a dark, hard sand. Not the kind of place where you would find a lot of bikinis. The infiltrators were happy about that too. They didn't need to be sneaking ashore in the middle of a beach resort area. Brad wondered if there were any of those in Libya. He really expected barbed wire and minefields. He guessed that even Khadafi, back in his days, wasn't worried too much about this part of the coastline. They were miles from any civilization, and hopefully, miles from any human being—except one. They were supposed to meet up with someone code named "Fox," probably Melanie Mitchell.

The first thing they did was drag the rafts onto the sand and while four of them dug two large holes in the sand, two others quietly let the air out of the rafts. Rafts, engines, paddles and all went into the holes. Then they were covered up, and the whole area was dragged with shrub branches, erasing footprints and any evidence they had been there. During all of this, Lieutenant Lee and Chief Roach climbed to the top of the nearest high point to survey the area. Brad sat in the sand with the others, each with their own chore to do. "Radio" checked out the equipment to be sure it was dry. "Medic" and "Spook" inventoried the first aid kit, and each of them went over their weapons with a fine toothed comb. Brad did the same, though he wasn't sure what to look for. His gear and flight suit had been in a water tight bag, and the bag had done its job.

The Lieutenant returned and ordered them to change and "dress up." Brad obliged and stripped off his wet suit, and donned the flightsuit. The rest of them changed into their camos. "Wipe" buried all the wet suits while they all re-applied their "makeup." They had used different shades of black, gray, green and tan to camouflage themselves before they even left the sub. However, the salt water washed some of it off, and changing to a new uniform exposed more skin. Brad was a complete novice at this, so he let "Radio" fix him up. They wore no watches or jewelry, and if the moon hadn't been so bright they would have melted into the landscape. Soon, the chief appeared beside Brad—so quietly Brad almost jumped out of his skin. He'd been concentrating so hard just trying to see everyone in the dark, he had forgotten the chief was out there.

"Easy! Easy there!" The chief patted his shoulder, then to the lieutenant, "All set, Skipper. Looks clear."

"OK! Let's move out. We should be about a mile from the contact point." The lieutenant whispered, and in single file they moved quickly up the rise in front of them and out into the desert. "Scout" went first, followed almost 30 yards back by the lieutenant, "Radio," "Blaster," ""Medic," the chief, Brad, "Spook," and "Wipe," about 20 yards back. Brad marveled that he couldn't hear a thing from any of them, but he kept tripping, crunching and stumbling along himself. He wondered how much they could hear him.

After what seemed like an hour—he didn't have time to dig for his watch in his pocket—they came to a road. At least it used to be a road at one time. It was just two tracks in the sand, winding around the rocks and shrubs, parallel the coastline. They dug in on the inland side of the road where there were several large rocks. "Wipe" and the chief went back and swept tracks for a hundred yards or so. Then it got real quiet. Brad had time to pull out his watch -- 3:15 am. He also followed the example of the others and tried some of the rations they had. He wasn't sure what he had selected. It looked like a granola bar, had the texture of jerky, and tasted like zucchini. He hated zucchini! His second helping was a little better—chocolate. He knew he had two of those in his packet, so he'd better ration what tasted good. Within a minute or two the chief, who had plopped down beside Brad, was snoring! Brad wondered how he could even close his eyes. His own were as wide as saucers.

After an hour or so, Brad felt a strange feeling—like the hair on the back of his neck was standing up. He felt like he was being watched. From his "hole" he could see the chief, and four of the others. He knew the rest of them were on the other side of the rock he was half under. The only one south of him was the chief, and he was very still. Slowly he turned his head, and sure enough—no less than two yards away was a figure of a man, sitting on his haunches, very still. Brad's heart stopped and his mouth went very dry. He didn't know what to do. The chief wasn't in kicking distance, and he was the closest "good guy" to Brad. He turned his head again and this time the figure was standing, and holding a gun. Brad decided they were all about to die. His semi-automatic was still on his shoulder. He rolled onto that shoulder toward the chief and pulled at the 9MM in his holster. Before he could even get his hand around the grip, the chief's big hairy hand closed around his and another one had him by the chin. By the time Brad had finished his roll he was flat on his back, with one arm under him, and the chief lying on top of him.

"Fox." The chief whispered, and slowly shook his head. He had been watching all the time, and had the visitor in his sights for about 20 minutes. Brad realized what had happened, and nodded in terrified amazement. Their contact had snuck up on them—he thought, and was just standing up to make contact when Brad had decided to react. The chief was in complete control. It was then that Brad recognized

Melanie as "Fox," and realized how he had come so close to shooting his own wife.

"Spook" and "Fox" spoke briefly, and then the lieutenant and chief joined in. Brad acknowledged that Melanie was his wife and that he'd suspected that since she was alone there was a problem with the real "Fox." They took a minute to hug and kiss like normal husband and wife, but only a minute. The team members were not happy at all about this situation, but the lieutenant realized it was what it was and they had a mission to do. "Ok guys. This lady knows more about this area than all of us combined, so we're putting our destiny in her hands. Our best course of action is to be sure she is protected. Let's move out!"

For an hour and a half they half ran, half walked in a crouch. Brad was tired, but what hurt the most was his back. He wasn't sure why they ran bent over either. It wasn't as if they were hiding from anyone in particular that would see them. He decided it was just the SEAL way of running, and he also decided he was a lousy SEAL. So, he straightened up to give his back a break and promptly got clotheslined by a branch of one of the few trees in the Sahara. He now knew for sure why he had joined the Air Force and not the Army or Marines, and especially not the SEALs. Shortly after his encounter with the tree they abruptly stopped and sprawled face first into the sand. From the south there were the headlights of a vehicle. It was about a mile down a road that stretched out about a hundred yards in front of them. The vehicle was a military truck and it went by about a mile or so north of their position, and then turned west and stopped. Brad could see the gleam of a chain link fence in the truck's headlights when it stopped. Someone got out, opened a gate, let the truck through and then closed the gate again. They watched the taillights of the truck climb what appeared to be a fairly high ridge and then disappear over the top, at least five miles away. Only then did Melanie move. This time they were up and running as fast as they could.

The road the truck had passed by on was probably a major highway for Libya. It was a two lane, hard surface road with wide shoulders of hard gravel. The fence was just to the west of the road and appeared to parallel it as far as they could see in either direction. Unfortunately, it was not just your standard chain link. It was about ten feet high and had rolled barbed wire on top of it. "Blaster" looked it over very thoroughly and nodded to the lieutenant. He worked quickly, and then rolled out of the way. There was a muffled explosion that sounded more like a good hit in a pillow fight, and a little dust and sand. When it settled there was a hole in the base of the fence just about big enough for a dog to squirt through. One by one Brad watched Melanie and his compatriots skinny through. Determined not to be left behind, he was amazed at how thin he could make himself. He did manage to take a few scratches, one good one on his left shoulder, ripping his flightsuit and drawing blood. While "Blaster" repaired the hole in the fence with wire and pliers, "Medic" applied a quick dressing to Brad's shoulder. Whatever he sprinkled on there stung worse than the original cut.

A half hour later they were at the base of the ridge the truck had ascended. None too soon either. The sun was coming up, and they needed to find a place to hide. Melanie led them south along the ridge, slowly climbing as they went. In another half hour the sun was almost above the horizon, and it was already hot. They came to a small stream where a dam had formed a pond. It looked too good to be true, and in fact, they didn't want to be too close to what was sure to be the gathering place of every critter in the desert—two legged as well as four legged. They found some fairly lush foliage around the base of a large boulder. Melanie and "Scout" had pulled the bushes away, and there was an entrance to a small cave. The lieutenant was hesitant, but after a fairly heated discussion with Melanie and "Spook," he ordered the party into the cave. "Wipe" stayed outside for the first watch. They were to stay there all day, so the plan was to get some sleep. It would be a long night.

After the sun went down they waited until it was good and dark. Brad guessed it was about 2300 hours. The moon was out again, and too damn bright. It was only about half full, but there wasn't a cloud in the sky and the stars seemed like they were very close. Brad remembered from the weather briefing they got on the sub that the moon would be going down Saturday morning before the shit hit the fan. But right now it was their enemy. They moved in the shadows of rocks and scrub trees whenever they could. Since they were climbing the ridge that was steep at times, they did a lot of zig-zagging back and forth. It was difficult to keep track of everybody. Brad decided to just concentrate on the chief, though his mind wandered forward to where he knew Melanie was leading the pack.

They climbed for about two hours. Not straight up, but more at an angle towards the south. Finally, they reached the top of the ridge and stopped to see what was on the other side. Brad was amazed. There before him was a huge airfield complex. Two runways, taxiways, several state-of-the-art Tab Vees, and a few low buildings. It was sparsely lit, but there were pockets of activity at some of the the Tab Vees with high-powered light-alls (mobile generators that drove spotlights). From their vantage point they couldn't make out what was tucked up next to the ridge, because the rocks and trees got in the way. Brad could see that the main taxiway came right up toward the ridge and was probably the one that led to the underground shelter. He could also see that they would have to get closer to get a fix on the Falcon and her cargo (assuming it was still out in the open). The lieutenant was way ahead of him and the group started making their way down the ridge.

They settled on a spot that nestled up near some rocks, about fifty yards from the fence. They didn't dare get any closer. There were guard towers along the fence about every two hundred yards. Spotlights wandered the hillside sporadically, and their trek down to their final position took almost two hours while they dodged the lights. Brad, Melanie and the lieutenant crawled to the top of one rock, shielded from the nearest guard tower by another. The lieutenant produced night vision glasses (infrared binoculars), and they took turns scanning the airfield.

There were several more buildings up near the ridge line and a control tower near the intersection of two taxiways. On the way down the hill they had passed by one of the air vents for the underground facility, and Brad could see the other two. He counted ten Tab Vees. There was work going on at three of them, but when he looked there with the IR glasses it was all washed out—too bright. Melanie was looking through regular binoculars. She grunted and handed them to

Brad, pointing to a Tab Vee that was right in the middle of the complex. He looked that way and his initial reaction was elation. The F-16 was out there in broad daylight—well, not exactly—it was night, but they had it lit up like the outside of the Academy Awards' theater. There were several men working on the jet and Brad could see what looked like the bomb under the right wing.

"Wait a Minute!" He almost thought out loud. "The Rogue's bomb was on the LEFT wing!" He knew it was, because he could still see it as the bastard took off from Spangdahlem. Why would they switch it? He grabbed the binoculars back from Melanie. It was hard to see the bomb at all with all those "gomers" crawling all over it. But it was for sure on the RIGHT wing. Then his heart stopped. It seemed to have been doing that a lot lately.

There was no RIGHT wing. There was no wing at all. In fact, there was no profile at all to this "airplane." It was a decoy! He had almost missed it because of the angle they were looking down on the complex. This was just a wooden shape of an F-16, cleverly outfitted with the plan forms of wing tanks and a bomb—on the RIGHT wing! In this case it was the wrong wing. Brad almost had to laugh at the show being put on out there by this army of maintenance men pretending to service the false Falcon. But it wasn't funny.

The Israelis were the first to use decoys during their various wars in the Middle East. It was very successful, and just about every nation in the world used them now. From just about any altitude above, the decoys are almost impossible to pick out from the real thing. An aircraft on a bombing run would have little chance of discerning the real target. That was obviously what the Iranians wanted, and after searching the rest of the Tab Vees from their vantage point, it was obvious that the real Falcon must be underground.

Soon after they made their discovery, a flight of two MIG-29s came in and landed. Brad watched intensely to see where the hub of activity was. The jets were taxied to an open ramp in front of one of the large, low buildings near the fence line. The pilots turned their steeds over to maintenance personnel who immediately towed the aircraft down the taxiway toward the ridge line. A huge steel door opened in the side of the mountain, and for that time span there was a flood of light out onto the tarmac. The inside of the underground complex was ablaze with light. The doors only stayed open long enough to tow the two Migs in, then it got dark again. Brad was watching the pilots, however. They went into the closest low building, and after several minutes came out again minus their life support gear (parachute harness, G-suit, etc). That was either the squadron building, or a maintenance debrief building where they also stored their gear. They walked next door to a well lit, two story building that looked a lot like a dormitory. There were several pilots moving in and out of there, all wearing flight suits. As the crow flies, he was about 200 yards away, with a fence and a guard tower in the way.

CHAPTER FIFTY THREE

BENI WALID AIRFIELD

Barak El-Kamani watched as the explosion and fire from the downed airliner subsided. He dispatched a squad of guards to check to be sure there were no survivors, then pushing Ebola in front of him he joined Goreng and Mustafa in the huge hangar complex in the mountain. He congratulated Mustafa for his daring feat and expressed his praise to the Iranian pilots that were hanging around as well. He stopped by to admire the sleek F-16 and even sleeker bomb.

"Sire, you need to decide what yield you want on the bomb." Goreng said. "Mustafa can set a wide range of scenarios." Mustafa then explained how the weapon could be set, asking also about what target he needs to be studying.

"The middle of Tel Aviv, specifically the government center. Make the yield high enough to wipe out the whole city, but limit damage to the countryside. Remember, we want to live there eventually after the Jews are gone." Barak responded. Then he directed his men to take Ebola to someplace quiet and private. "I am going to enjoy getting whatever information this infidel has that might help our cause. Bring there as well my satchel with all my instruments."

CHAPTER FIFTY FOUR

WASHINGTON D.C.

Peter Sciapini was frustrated. He knew something was going on, he just didn't know what. All of his sources had clammed up. Mum was the word around the Pentagon. This was as well kept a secret as the existence of the stealth fighter for so many years. His story over the weekend had made him both well known among his peers -- a good thing, and well known among the people at the Pentagon -- not so good a thing. They had been well briefed to stay clear of the Washington Post reporter, or more brilliant careers like BG Chuck Morton's would go down the drain. Still, Sciapini smelled a good story. He wouldn't accept that all the U.S. was doing was waiting. Marianne Rogers was breathing down his neck to come up with something to hang the shingle on. Pete Wilson's daily briefings were too "milk toast" and noncommittal. Keep digging. There's got to be something!

He had it! Jim Danzig! There was his source. After all, he had the goods on Danzig and he could ruin the Air Force captain's career. Sciapini was not above a little blackmail -- all in the name of freedom of the press, of course.

Captain Jim Danzig was one of the 19 military personnel on the White House Staff. Most were communicators and command and control types that manned the White House Situation Room on an around-the-clock basis. But a few of the officers had more important duties. The President had a Marine lieutenant colonel for his Military

Aide. The VP had an Army major. Jim Danzig was the Military Assistant to the White House Chief of Staff -- Mike Mulroney. He didn't like the job much. Mulroney was too anti-military. Danzig was often the sounding board for his boss' frustrations with the SECDEF and the National Security Advisor. His duties varied from personal confidant and the resident "expert" on just about anything military, to just plain gopher and "water boy." It was a two year assignment and it meant almost automatic early promotion if he kept his nose clean. Not bad for a guy who was a logistician by trade.

Jim Danzig and Mike Mulroney had one very important thing in common, though he didn't think his boss knew it. They both had a very liberal view on gay rights and homosexuals in the military. Captain Jim Danzig was gay. With only a few "excursions," he had kept his personal life very private and though he had gotten the standard "how come you're not married?" questions from his co-workers and bosses in the Air Force, as far as he knew, his secret was still "in the closet." There was one person that knew however, and Danzig needed to fear him right now. Peter Sciapini and Jim Danzig had been lovers at one time -- for almost a year.

Before his assignment to the White House, Captain Danzig had been the Logistics Plans Officer at Bolling AFB. He periodically frequented a gay bar in Georgetown, and had struck up many relationships there. Most of his "friends" were professionals -- lawyers, doctors, Congressional staffers, but a few years ago Jim Danzig met Peter Sciapini. Peter was new in town. He had been a reporter in San Francisco, but he had made the move to D.C. to be "where the action was." That was his story, and it was partially true. Sciapini had also become a little too emotionally involved with the large gay community in Frisco, and his rather conservative (at least conservative for San Francisco) boss canned him. He had threatened to sue his old paper, and the compromise was a well hyped up recommendation to other newspapers -- some truth, a lot of lies, and nothing about his sexual preferences. The Washington Post hired him on as beat reporter, and Marianne Rogers assigned him to the Pentagon.

Their relationship initially consisted of a series of one night stands. But after a few months they became full blown lovers and roommates. In fact it was Sciapini that clued Danzig in to the White House job when the incumbent was fired for getting pissed off and telling Mulroney where to get off. Danzig was tall, rugged looking, and handsome -- appealing. What sold him though, was that he was from Mulroney's home state of Colorado. Danzig was born and raised (and corrupted to his current sexual status) in Aspen.

Sciapini and Danzig stayed together for almost a year, each feeding off the other -- in more ways than one. Danzig would freely discuss innocent happenings that Sciapini often used for leverage on his other sources of news. Peter would pass on tidbits of gossip (and some truth) that Danzig used to keep his boss informed and forever grateful. This love-love relationship eventually ended with more or less a mutual agreement. Sciapini wanted to play the field more -- for professional (a debatable word) as well as sexual reasons. And Danzig had tired of the boorish and rough nature of his uncouth lover. Sciapini moved out, and although they ran into one another at their favorite night spot now and then, and they occasionally walked the same halls of the Pentagon, to the casual observer they were total strangers. Not for long!

Sciapini was waiting in the easy chair in Jim's Alexandria, Virginia apartment Wednesday evening. He had "forgotten" to return the key when he moved out. Danzig got home about 6 pm. "What are you doing here, Peter? How did you get in?" Sciapini dangled the keys and put on his shit-eatingest grin.

"Magic, Jamey my love. How are you? I haven't seen you at the Palace lately." Peter tossed the key to a rather perturbed homeowner. "Sorry Jim, but I really needed to see you. You're looking great, by the way."

"Thanks Pete, but you should know I'm seeing someone now and I don't want to start anything with you. No offense, but it's just not there. I thought you felt that way too." Danzig hung up his AF blue jacket and loosened his tie. "Want a drink? I think I'll have a daiquiri. It's been a long day."

"Yeah thanks." SkeePee nodded. "Hey! Not to worry, Big Fella. I do feel the same. Not that I wouldn't like to take a tumble with you, but what I really wanted to see you about is that long day you just had. I need some info, Jim. What's going on with this F-16 thing? What is the Pentagon planning? Are we going to invade Libya? I know your boss must be up to his ass in this thing, and I know he talks to you. So let's have it, Jimbo. What's cookin'?

"Peter, I couldn't tell you anything, even if I knew anything. There's a tight lid on this. You knew that or you would have been able to get something out of your regular sources." Danzig plopped the limeade into the blender, added some frozen strawberries and a little rum.

"That's why I came to you, Jimmy. Everybody is being too tight lipped. That's why I know there's something going on. Don't worry. I won't make you break security, and I'll hold my story until it's appropriate. I just want to be first. Come on Jimmy. You owe me." Sciapini was trying the nice guy tactic first, looking for sympathy. In his case, that word is found in the dictionary somewhere around "shit" and "syphilis."

"I'm sorry Pete. I just can't. I don't know much anyway, but if I told you anything it would be the end of my career. I could even get busted." Jim was getting nervous. He poured the daiquiris, handed one to Sciapini and nervously looked at his watch. "Hey, I've got a dinner date down town in an hour. Mind if I go and get ready? You can finish your drink if you'd like, but I really must hit the shower."

"Sure. Don't mind me. But I really think you need to tell me what you know Jim. After all they couldn't do anything more to you than if they found out you are queer." Sciapini let the bomb drop. And it stopped Danzig dead in his tracks. He looked like a whipped pup at his former lover.

"What do you mean by that?"

"Simple, Jimmy my love. You tell me what I want to know and I go on my merry way. The world will never know any more than they do now about their beautiful specimen of a man from the Rockies. But if you keep me in the dark, then I open the closet door ... or is it the Pandora's box? I wonder what Secretary of Defense Robert Lucroix would do with the information that his dreaded enemy Mike Mulroney has a queer AF captain for a Military Assistant? How far would your career go then, Jimmy darling?" SkeePee was no longer the nice guy.

"Damn Peter! That's blackmail. Besides, how could you do this without implicating yourself? The Post would can you in a heartbeat." Danzig was grasping for straws.

"Shit, Jimmy. Half the city knows I'm gay. My boss definitely knows. I think she likes the idea. It makes her look good with the ACLU and Gay Rights. She hates my guts, but I get results, and she likes that." Sciapini took a long draw on his daiquiri. "Hey Jimmy. These are good. You haven't lost your touch with the blender. You could always get into my pants after a few of these."

Danzig was flustered. He put his own drink down. The last thing he wanted right now was to get into Sciapini's pants. "Peter, I'm not going to stand for this. I'll go to the authorities. I'll just deny everything and tell them you are trying to blackmail me. Besides, as you know, the Pentagon is taking a more liberal stance about the LGBT thing these days. Now get out of my house! Take your drink with you. Maybe you can use it to get into someone else's pants." He fought back.

"I'm sorry you feel that way, Jamie." Peter was ready for this reaction. He pulled out an envelope and tossed it in Jim's direction. It hit the floor and the contents spilled out. Photographs. A dozen or so. Very explicit, very graphic, very disgusting to the straight, heterosexual community. They had obviously been taken from a camera in the ceiling of the bedroom of this very apartment. "What do you think of my photography? Pretty neat, huh? You never knew there was a switch on our nightstand, did you. Remember when I put up the mirror on our ceiling? You thought it was kinky, but you didn't complain much. Of course, you didn't know I put a video camera behind it, did you? You see these are just stills made from the video. I've got the whole thing in movies, complete with all the graphic sounds. Ah, we made beautiful music together, Jimmy."

Danzig was in pain. He looked at the photos with both disdain and fear. He didn't know what to do or say. "You - you wouldn't really use these would you?"

"Why not? A story like this would be almost as good as one about the operation. I get my by-line on it anyway. I can see it now -- 'WHITE HOUSE STAFF INFILTRATED BY GAY MILITARY OFFICER,' or 'MY LOVE LIFE WITH MIKE MULRONEY'S AIR FORCE GOPHER.' How do you think it will sell in the five-sided building? They supposedly have backed off the bash the gay process, but I doubt they would like this situation." Sciapini was turning the screw.

"Why do you want to do this to me, Peter? Is a story so important to you? I thought we meant something to each other." Danzig was turning into a blubbering idiot. Sciapini had him right where he wanted him.

"Don't give me that Bullshit, Danzig" Peter was merciless. "You were on your way out to blow some twit's cock after dinner at Pierre's. I don't mean anything to you and you don't mean anything to me -- except a story. And I'm tired of waiting. Either you spill the beans on what you know about the operation against Libya, or I go public with these photos and all the gory details of Captain James Danzig, USAF, and his love life. With the first story nobody knows a thing about who my source is. You're off the hook. With the second story, you're history -- another queer booted out of the Service, and even your liberal asshole of a boss won't lift a hand to help you. So which is it Jamie Boy?"

Jim Danzig had no choice. He knew an awful lot because Mike Mulroney was in on every meeting after the first one. Because it was a military operation he relied on Jim quite a bit to translate military jargon, fetch records and paperwork, and just generally make him look and sound like he knew what he was talking about when dealing with Lucroix and General Adams. He told Peter enough to get rid of him, but not everything. He confirmed that there was an air attack being planned, but he convinced the slimy reporter that he did not know the actual time. He got Peter off that subject by telling him about the SEAL team and an F-16 pilot that were on the ground in Libya. Sciapini jumped on that bit of information like flies on cow dung. Finally, after Peter thought he had enough for a Pulitzer Prize, and because he wanted to make the deadline for Wednesday's issue, he left a blithering idiot of an Air Force captain about 8 pm. It was a good thing Danzig didn't really have a dinner date that night. He drowned himself in another batch of daiquiris. Only these were much more potent with rum.

"ATTACK ON IRANIANS IN LIBYA IMMINENT. SPECIAL FORCES ALREADY IN PLACE!" The Friday headline of the Washington Post hit the Pentagon like Mustafa's bomb. The story took the whole front page. It was rather vague about the attack, though the reporter had done his homework, and he knew which squadrons from which bases in Europe were in place at Zaragoza and Decimomannu, and what forces the Truman had with her on station in the Med. The Task Force, with General Olsen at the helm was fairly accurately portrayed. The only thing missing was the formations to be flown and the Time on Target. He did not name the actual target base, but he stated that the U.S. knew exactly where the F-16 was located. The part that got the most attention was the description of the SEAL team and the unidentified pilot with them. He even stated that there was an indigenous contact, that the team had made contact, and that they were in place, ready to strike. It was a kiss of death for Brad Mitchell and his compatriots. All this information was credited to a "high White House source." Sciapini was a hero at the Press Club.

The reaction from the Pentagon was swift and two pronged. Immediately a signal was sent out via Norfolk and a satellite hook-up to a submarine in the Mediterranean. It positioned itself for the best possible communications with the SEAL team and surfaced to expose the antennas. Unfortunately, the team's radios were off, not expecting any incoming communications. "Radio" had the set tucked away in his forty pound back pack. Their instructions were to make contact at 1800 hours Friday evening, unless they had reason to do so sooner. The messages sent inland from the sub were in vain, but the boat was ordered to stay in place and to keep trying.

The other Pentagon attack went via the SECDEF to the White House. Who was this "high White House source?" Secretary Lucroix begged the President to call an immediate meeting of his staff to ferret out the source and put it to sleep. There was no telling how much damage was done at this point, but they certainly needed no more. The President agreed.

It was determined that the operation would continue as planned. Although the Iranians would certainly know where any strike would originate, and what forces would be taking part, they probably knew or would suspect the same information anyway. The actual timing and vector of attack were not divulged by the Post article. Those were the important points. Nevertheless, General Olsen was alerted of the compromise, and the word was passed to the various locations involved. Security was tightened at Zaragoza and Decimomannu even more. There were no phone calls allowed off base without going through the Command Posts. Host nation workers were given a "holiday" and each base was buttoned up tight. Perimeter guards were doubled, vehicles were searched both ways at the gates. It became blatantly obvious to anyone that something big was about to happen, but at least any potential intelligence agents with big ears and eyes were screened.

Everyone on duty at the White House was called to the Situation Room. Some that had been on duty and all that had been off duty the night before were asked to come in. Mulroney did the calling personally. He could tell his boss was pissed and so was he. This was a first for most of these people. There were cooks, bottle washers, gardeners and drivers, all mixed with the National Security Advisor, the Chief of Staff, the Vice President, the First Lady. Some of these people had not even personally seen the President. The White House was a big place and the movement of most of the workers was as restricted as that of the tourists allowed to visit each day. But now they were all shoved in a room that was not nearly big enough. It was lunchtime on Wednesday in Washington, but this was not to be a company picnic.

"Sit down if you can find a seat!" The President was obviously not in a good mood. He didn't even smile at his wife as he took a position beside her at the head of the long briefing table. He threw a copy of the Washington Post down on the table. "Is there anyone who hasn't seen this?" Many had not, but they didn't dare admit it.

"Apparently we have someone in this staff who talks too much about information he or she has no business discussing, whether true or not." The President's eyes made contact with everyone in the room, pausing for affect on each person. When he looked at Jim Danzig the Captain swallowed hard. It seemed like President McDivitt looked at him twice as long as anyone else. "Now I know that most of you are not privy to what goes on in this room or in the privacy of any other chamber where I or any of my senior staff are going about the business of running this country. But I also know that most of you see and hear things that even the dumbest among you can translate into classified information. You all have at least a SECRET clearance or you couldn't have gotten a job here. With that kind of clearance and the background required to get it, you should know what you can and cannot discuss outside these grounds -- or even inside these grounds for that matter. Especially with piddlin pimps like this dirt ball from the Washington Post!" Robbins pounded his fist for emphasis. He made his point with at least one in the audience. Danzig squirmed in his seat and looked around to see if anyone was watching him in particular. His palms got very sweaty and his mouth became very dry.

"Much of the information in this article is a lie." The President went on. "I'm not going to honor any of you with the distinction of knowing what is and what is not true -- especially since one of you is evidently a traitor. And I use that word carefully. Whether or not the United States of America is planning an attack on Libya is nobody's business but mine and a few of my trusted Cabinet right now. Freedom of the press does not entitle the world to know the depth and breadth of our military operations preparation. Furthermore, if there were U.S. soldiers on the ground in Libya, in contact with an indigenous agent and poised to strike at the location of our runaway jet -- how long do you think they have to live now -- after this?" He picked up the newspaper and threw it across the room. "I'm am not standing here and confirming that there are such forces in being, but if there were, I'm convinced they would be dead by now. I would expect to see Iranians parading their corpses around the streets of Tehran. Even more frightening is that it would give the terrorists an excuse to execute whatever it is they are threatening to do. How would you like to have the death of millions of innocent people somewhere in the world all attributed to your seemingly innocent slip of the tongue? One of you can claim that responsibility, and I only hope for your sake that it was just that -- an innocent slip of the tongue. Because if we find out that one of this staff is deliberately divulging information to this bastard Sciapini, or any other member of the press, I will personally see to it that the traitor is prosecuted to the full extent of the law. Is that clear?" McDivitt was screaming and shaking with anger. There were no comments.

"General Henry do you have anything to add?" The President turned to his National Security Advisor. Henry shook his head quietly.

"Mr. Mulroney?" Robbins passed up his Vice President either purposely or without thinking.

"No sir. I think you covered the problem adequately. If anyone has knowledge of who our leak may be, they may speak to me privately in my office." The Chief of Staff looked around the room as he spoke, but not directly at his own Military Assistant.

"I thank you all for coming to this meeting. Carry on with what's left of your lunch time and have a nice day." The President actually smiled at a few of them in a complete change of tone. He had said what he wanted to say. No sense in dwelling on it further. There was a country to run and they all had a small part in it. Those that had been seated stood as the President and Mrs. McDivitt departed. Captain Jim Danzig wiped tears from his eyes with a very sweaty palm. He went to his cubby hole of an office, locked the door, and sat down in his chair, shaking uncontrollably.

About an hour later a gunshot rang out through the halls of the White House basement. The Marine Guards down the hall from the Chief of Staff's office responded with guns drawn to a locked door at the end of the hall. A big burly marine with what he always called the "master key" -- a size 15 boot -- kicked in the door with one kick. He and his partner rolled through the opening like two gymnasts, ending up on their knees, back to back, scanning all angles of the small office. Another Marine stood in the door sweeping the room with his aim and his cocked automatic rifle. Slumped onto the desk was Captain James Danzig, USAF, a small hole in his right temple, and a huge gaping one above his left ear. The desk and wall to his left were splattered with blood, brains and gun powder. Clutched in the Captain's hand was an old 45 automatic pistol. There was no note or any other evidence as to why the captain had taken his own life.

———

CHAPTER FIFTY FIVE

BENI WALID AIR BASE

Brad Mitchell knew that he had to try to get a message to the Task Force that the target out in the open that looked like the Falcon was a decoy. They had spent the rest of Tuesday night positioning themselves for a long wait, yet a good look at everything visible. Initially Brad, Lt. Lee, Chief Roach, "Radio" Davis, "Spook," Anam, and Melanie had retreated back up the ridge line a ways, behind what shelter they could find, and far enough away that they could talk. They left the rest of the team down close to the fence in a defensive observation posture.

"We need to get word to my guys that the real target must be underground. That thing's a decoy. A good one too. It almost had me fooled, and we were a lot closer than those guys are going to be 4500 feet up, doing 500 knots. They'll never know it's not real." Brad said. He admired the Iranians for their obvious talents at concealment, but he wondered which of those "crew chiefs" were really Soviet agents.

"Easy sir. You forget that our job is to take out the aircraft and the bomb if your flyboys can't. That's what we're here for. Besides, so what if they blow away the dummy? As long as they get the real thing too, what difference does it make?" The lieutenant made a lot of sense.

"But we don't even know where the real airplane is. I figure it's gotta be right underneath us, underground. That opening we saw earlier when the two Fulcrums came in is obviously the main access, but it must be huge under there. Unless we concentrate all our firepower on blowing away what's under this ridge, we'll have no way of knowing whether we got the Falcon. Even then I'm not so sure we'd get it. Our bombs make a big boom, but they don't blow away mountains. Anyway, there is no sense wasting a couple of two thousand pounders on that piece of plywood if we can redirect it onto something more lucrative." Mitchell was making more sense.

"He's right Lieutenant. If the Air Force wants to do any real damage here, they're going to have to go through those big air vents and in that cave door. A couple of those buildings and barracks may be good targets, but they will go pretty quickly too." Anam was showing off his intelligence expertise. That's why he was added to the team back in Norfolk.

"Shit!" The chief threw in his two cents' worth. "If you want something taken out under here, we're going to have to do it. We'll have to get in there and use some of 'Blasters' good stuff. Fox, is there away through the fence?" He asked Melanie.

Melanie was not that familiar with the perimeter fence, but she thought that for sure there would not be any breaks in it. The Libyans and Iranians were almost paranoid about their security. After a little more discussion, it was decided that they would try to get a message out that there was a decoy and to concentrate the attack on the underground facility and the two or three structures near the entrance. Then they would position themselves for concealment, and yet be in the best observation position available throughout the day as they waited for the next night. Brad stayed with "Radio," Melanie, and the lieutenant. The rest went back down the ridge to settle in before daylight. It was decided that they would not attempt contact until about 2 pm local time. They did not want to risk the transmission being intercepted in time to do something about the attack. At the same time, Brad had successfully argued that the Task Force needed time to change the designated targets and tactics. He found a comfortable spot to stretch out, under a large rock and behind a hedge-like row of bushes. The lieutenant and "Radio" found similar spots on the other side of the rock, and Melanie squatted on her haunches a little further up the ridge, keeping the first watch.

Sometime later—and Brad had no idea when—he woke up with a slight start to the warm breath and soft lips of a kiss. He opened his eyes to see Melanie on her hands and knees over him, her hair down and flowing over his face, and a fierce, burning desire in her eyes. Brad was almost frightened at first. Here was this camouflaged person in fatigues straddling him, looking almost threatening. Then he remembered, *oh yeah! It's just my wife.* When Melanie saw he was startled she smiled, put a finger to her lips for him to not speak, and gently settled her body onto his. She spread her legs over his hips and he could immediately feel himself respond. Their kiss was long and passionate, and in almost no time they had undressed each other and had rolled further beneath the rock he was half under. Brad did not even have time to think about what the lieutenant and "Radio" were doing, much less ask Melanie. The encounter was over quickly. Neither of them held anything back and they were both totally drained in a few short minutes. Melanie rolled off him and was laying beside him, half in - half out of her clothes. Brad heard the crackle of Davis' radio from the other side of the rock. A land speed record was set by both parties in disengaging and getting dressed. Before Mitchell could even finish zipping his flight suit he turned around and Melanie was the "Fox" again, perched on her haunches twenty yards away.

Brad checked his watch and realized it was 2 o'clock. He crawled around to where Lieutenant Lee and "Radio" were setting up shop. "Where's the 'Fox?" She didn't wake any of us up for guard shift. Is she still here?" Lee asked when he saw Mitchell.

"Yeah. She's squatting about halfway up the ridge line on the other side of the rock. She must have thought we needed the sleep. I know I sure enjoyed it." Mitchell had to almost laugh as he said that.

"Me too. We needed it, but we almost missed our comm window. How's it going 'Radio'?" The lieutenant turned to Davis.

"Ready sir." The fold-up antenna stuck up about twenty feet, but the rest of the set was very compact and state-of-the-art. It was all digital and had the capacity to talk on HF (High Frequency),VHF, UHF or FM.

They made contact in no time. Both Davis and the lieutenant were surprised about that. They expected to have to make several tries to raise the sub. It was soon apparent why contact was quick. Davis relayed the information to be passed to the Task Force about the decoy and the recommended targets. Then the submarine communicator passed on his information. The team had been compromised in the press. Their presence was public knowledge, even that they had a local contact. Their mission was to continue and the timetable was unchanged, but the wishes of CINCLANT were that they "be careful." That got a chuckle. A next contact time was established, and both parties signed off. Lee and Davis decided to bury the radio in a nearby spot, in case they were found, so that others of the team could use it if they weren't all captured (or worse).

As they were completing the cover up of the radio, Melanie appeared out of nowhere at Lieutenant Lee's shoulder. She pointed off in the distance, and they all could see a convoy of trucks on the other side of the airfield. They split up and crossed the runway in three columns— one at each end and one across a center taxiway. There were three to four trucks in each column and they came to screeching halts on the near side, next to the perimeter fence. Army soldiers with weapons scrambled out of each truck and congregated around three points near the fence. One group was just on the other side of the fence from where most of the SEAL team was hiding out the day. Another was directly abeam of Mitchell, Melanie and the two SEALs, though a good 150 yards away, since the Americans were halfway up the ridge. The third and larger group of soldiers was surrounding the terrain immediately around the taxiway opening to the underground facility. Each group had a leader shouting orders and Brad could see through binoculars that they were all looking toward the ridge line, as if searching for something. After the news they just got on the radio, it did not take a rocket scientist to figure out what (or who) the soldiers were looking for. The problem was how to alert the others who were fat, dumb and happy, nestled up near the fence, not knowing what the ruckus was about. Of the six men down there, Lee could locate four with his binoculars. He had a pretty good idea where a fifth was, but he could not account for all six. "I've got to move the men." He whispered. "They'll be picked off like ducks on a pond if those gooks come looking. But we could never get down there without being seen."

"I will go." Melanie whispered quietly, and before anyone could comment or restrain her, she was twenty yards down the hill, flat on her stomach and she disappeared from view. Brad felt a strong pang of fear for her. He took the binoculars, crawled to a higher vantage point and tried to pick her out on her descent down the hill. Every once in a while he could see a bush move or some dust being stirred up. Once he even saw her crouched form cross an open space and then disappear again behind a cluster of boulders. Soon after that, all hell broke loose.

The soldiers near the barracks and just beneath the SEALs came through a gate and spread out along the fence line on the uphill side. They trained their weapons ahead of them and stood there waiting. Brad did not know there had been a gate, but he guessed it didn't make much difference. It would be locked. The important thing now was that the enemy was on our side of the fence and obviously looking for "our side." Lieutenant Lee saw the commotion too and settled in beside Mitchell, his own binoculars trained on his men. Davis was behind them, looking anxiously with his naked eye. "What's going on?" He asked.

"I don't know, but it doesn't look good. They have spread out all along the fence. It looks like they are just waiting for a signal to move, or maybe they are just going to stand there all day and night. If that's the case we are going to play hell getting to that aircraft." Lee replied.

"Lieutenant. How about us going down one of these vents?" Davis was referring to the three large ventilation shafts that service the underground hangar. The closest one was about parallel to the three of them and two hundred yards south.

"We would have to do it before the attack, and then we would be in there when the bombs start hitting." Brad said. He had been trying to find Melanie through his glasses. She must have stopped. "Those shafts will be the first things hit by the F-22s. Those guys don't miss and I wouldn't want to be stuck in some air conditioning unit when a 2000 pound bomb comes whistling down my tube."

"You gotta point there, 'Conan." Davis said. It was actually the first time any of them had used his "handle." "Oh well. Sounded like a good idea at the time."

"It still may be, 'Radio.' If that's the only way in there, we'll try it." Lee remarked. "That's our job. But I think the colonel's right. We'd better wait until after the bombs fly. Besides, maybe the hole will be big enough to get your fat ass down there 'Radio." Brad looked at Davis. He sure didn't look fat.

Just then there was a shot from further up the fence line. It was a signal, and sure enough, the whole line of soldiers started up the ridge. Someone in Tripoli reads the Washington Post. Mitchell, Lee and Davis watched in horror as the group of SEALs below them protected themselves. What ensued was a short, bloody gun battle. The Americans went out fighting, because there were Libyan soldiers dying right and left. But the sheer numbers eventually took their toll. Lieutenant Lee saw four of his men go down; three by gunfire, and a fourth—it looked like Chief Roach—executed at the hands of a Libyan officer. The chief was mortally wounded by a grenade and blown clear of his weapon. When the Libyans finally overran the American's position, he was still alive—kicking and spitting and trying hard to fight. The apparent leader of the attackers approached from behind the Chief, grabbed him by the hair and cut his throat with a long scepter-like sword. It was over in minutes.

"Radio" came unglued. He wanted to charge from his position and defend the honor of his fallen comrades. Lieutenant Lee was remarkably calm. He watched the whole brief battle through the glasses, never even wincing. He grabbed Davis' shoulder and shoved him back to the rocks. "Sit tight Radio. There is nothing we can do but die along with them."

"That's better than sitting up here doing nothing. I'd rather die than go home and tell the chief's kid that I watched her daddy butchered and I did nothing about it." The comm man was beside himself.

"We will do something about it. But let's wait until the odds are in our favor. Besides, I only see four of our guys down there. There are two more and the "Fox" down there somewhere." Lee went back to his binoculars.

Mitchell had been looking for the "Fox" during all of this. She was nowhere in sight. But he did find the other two SEALs. They had been positioned further along the fence toward the cave entrance. The line of soldiers hadn't gotten to them when the fighting down the line took place. The soldiers had all flocked to the action like rats to cheese. "Blaster" and "Wipe" scrambled further up the mountain when they had the chance. That's when Brad saw them. He pointed them out to the lieutenant, then he went back to looking for Melanie. It was as if she had completely disappeared. Soon "Blaster" and "Wipe" faded from view as well. Then, about ten minutes later all three of them materialized from behind Brad and the lieutenant almost like ghosts.

"What the?.... How'd you guys get away from that." Lee asked.

Blaster pointed to Melanie, "She basically showed us how to be desert rats boss. She knows every rock and where to hide under it. We just kept climbing and sure enough, we showed up here. What happened to the others? We couldn't see from where we were."

When the lieutenant told them they too wanted to wade into the masses guns a-blazin. Melanie was the calming voice among them all. "There was nothing anyone could do. But while I was down there I think I saw a way we can get close to the hangar entrance."

Nothing much happened the rest of the afternoon and evening. A crew came and put up a temporary fence, and a patrol came out and cleaned up what weapons and ammunition was left strewn around the terrain. But it appeared the Iranians had decided that they must have found all of the perpetrators. The Americans were safe for now.

After dark they slid down to where Melanie led them, close to where "Blaster" and "Wipe" were hiding earlier. It was decided that Mitchell and "Blaster" would work their way over to the side of the hill just beside the opening to the underground facility. If they had to get in there after the attack, "Blasters" talents may be the only way through the fence, and he would definitely be needed to destroy the Falcon. Lieutenant Lee, Melanie, and "Radio" stayed where they were, not too far from where the comm gear was buried. They had to make the midnight contact, and probably one more. "Wipe" was sent down closer to the fence to warn if any more soldiers came a-callin'.

The foliage around the entrance to the underground hangar was much thicker than elsewhere on the hill, but there were no rocks to hide behind. Brad and "Blaster" camouflaged themselves with bushes and branches and settled in just beyond the fence and about 30 yards to one side of where the taxiway disappeared into the ridge. Brad had a good view of the entrance (if it was ever open) and the approaches to it—both the taxiway and sidewalks from the barracks area. He settled down for another sleepless night. He wondered if this would be his last. In his loneliness he had time to think about a lot of things. The Falcon. Mustan. Melanie. Kristi. Whether or not they would ever get out of here alive.

—

CHAPTER FIFTY SIX

ZARAGOZA AIR BASE, SPAIN

"Three, Two, One, Hack! Twenty Three Oh Two. Anyone need another hack?" Ed Howe was addressing a room full of people, most of them pretty tired. They had only had a couple of days to try to get their bodies on a night cycle, and the anticipation of the pending mission had kept most of them awake all afternoon and evening. It was 11 p.m. at night, Friday—Show Time! The crew members of the F-16s, F-22s, and EA-6s were seated in the front middle section of the Weapons Detachment briefing room. General Olsen and a few of the colonels were up front, but the rest of the "non players" were seated or standing on the sides or in the back. The room was packed. The AWACS and tanker crews had already stepped to their aircraft, and some had already launched. Ed Howe had been "officially" on duty since 9:30 pm to "fit" the crew rest rules. He did most of the coordination with the support crews, the F-15 squadron at Decimomannu, and the Navy via the phone. What he couldn't get done was done for him by the members of General Olsen's mission planning staff. They had been at it for hours. Since they weren't going to fly the mission, crew rest was not an issue. Some of them had been at work since they stepped off the plane that brought them down from Germany three days ago. They slept when they could, but theirs was a tough task. They were all pilots and navigators, and they wanted badly to be in the fight, but it wasn't their turn. This was the price they paid for the "privilege" of having a staff job.

"OK, you heard the weather." Howe continued. "Not as bad as earlier forecast, but it could be a factor. In the target area we should have no problem getting to our parameters, and the mid level deck of clouds will make it tougher for the ragheads to see us. However, those same clouds are going to make it tougher to fly formation. Brief your radar work well. In the air refueling track is where I expect the most trouble. I talked to the tanker folks, and they will seek clear airspace. But we can't move the track much. We need to keep the tankers out of the 200 mile buffer the Libyans believe in, and we can't fly in Italian airspace over land. The Italians are being ass holes about this whole thing. They are still pissed at us about the air battle over Sardinia the other night, and they want to know everything that's going on or they will take their ball and go home. Obviously we are not going to tell them our plan, so stay out of their airspace, unless you have an emergency and have to go into Sigonella (Sicily) or Deci. At any rate, brief your instrument rendezvous and refueling techniques well. If we are in the weather and we have to go onto the tankers in flights of four maximum, we will have to spread out the refueling, rendezvous under the weather, and end up recovering at Deci or Sigonella. Flight leaders, the timing and directions for each flight are on your lineup cards. The bottom line is we are not going to change anything except the TOT and the recovery base. Because it will take longer for us to all get gas, and the first guys on and off the tanker will be the most skosh later, we will bump the TOT with the code word 'Omega' plus a number of minutes. I'll want an acknowledgement to that. That should be the only break in radio silence all morning, and hopefully you won't hear it. Any questions on that? Your directions on where to land and an ETA to shoot for are on the card. It keeps the flow even and steady into both bases. Believe me, if we put 54 jets on those two ramps, they will be maxed out. Anybody volunteer to go land on the Truman instead?" That got a chuckle, and actually one of the F-22 guys raised his hand. He was a Navy exchange pilot flying F-22s with the AF, and he was once used to landing on a pitching deck, but in an F-18. Of course the EA-6 guys raised their hands. The Truman was "home" for them. The rest of the Air Force guys would just as soon leave carrier landings to the swabbies. Besides, the Truman was going to be busy launching and recovering her own force of F/A-18s, EA-6s and tankers. "Right. Intel, an update please."

Linda Halterson got up and walked to the podium. The lights went down and she switched on the overhead projector. "Thank you sir. Gentlemen, there have been a few changes. We had contact with the SEALs that are just outside the perimeter. At least we hope they still are. We are holding our breath until the next contact time, in just about an hour. As you may know, there was a compromise to their existence via the Washington Post this morning, and the Iranians probably are looking for them. At any rate, the information we have is that this target..." Captain Halterson pointed to the shape of an F-16 in a satellite photo. "...is a decoy. It's a good one too. In fact, we think that any aircraft you see in the open and not moving is probably a fake. Evidently this underground storage facility is larger than we thought, and they keep their whole fleet in there. In fact, we know their 747 tanker landed at Beni Walid and no one has seen it depart, It's not out in the open so it must be in this mountain as well. So, we have re-designated some of your points of impact. You will find on your mission data cards, and the photos in your packets, the main targets are the air vents," She put up another picture and pointed to the ventilation ducts on the side of the ridge, and then followed her briefing with her pointer. "the defenses, these barracks-like buildings, and the entrance to the cave. The F-16s will also hit the shelters and the decoys, just for good measure. They have brought in more defenses. There is an SA-15 site here, and one here, and a new triple-A site here. We expect that they may also have one of the new Russian SA-400s. If they do, watch out. That thing is deadly. Those of you targeted on the SAMs and guns have your work cut out for you. Again, your best bail out is feet wet. If you do go down in the target area, here is the pickup point for the SEAL team, shooting for a time of 0620. Questions?" There were none and the Captain sat down.

"Thanks Linda." Howe again took the lead. "Lady and Gentlemen, you each have a lineup card with take off times, refueling times, times on target and landing times. It also has code words for pushing the

TOT, requests from the eagles for help and going feet wet coming out of Libya. That last one is the only word I hope to hear all night and morning, and I only want to hear it from my last four ship. 'Bonkers' is the word, and if everything goes right, when Sabre 41 flight squawks 'Bonkers' we all know that everyone is past the coast outbound. Obviously, the important times are the TOTs and the tanker times. Colonel Burton, you can certainly vary your take off time as necessary. Just be off the tanker when the gorilla gets there." Howe was addressing the F-22 Operations Officer, who was leading the contingent of stealth fighters in first. "Our timing on and off the tanker is critical." Howe continued. "The main air refueling track is here. The tankers will be stacked at two thousand foot intervals from 18,000 through 26,000. They will feed themselves from the central refueling track, here, and the Navy will be using the east track, here." Howe was using a big map of the Mediterranean and Libya. "Your missed refueling base will be Sigonella, Zero Eight Zero for 120 miles. We've got Deci on the way to the track and back as an emergency alternate. There is also Tunis, about 70 miles southwest of the track, but I would not expect them to be real receptive to our dropping in there. It is an option though. OK, on the way out we will buddy launch with tankers from here and refuel just Southeast of Majorca, so there's another missed refueling and alternate field if necessary." Howe pointed to Palma de Majorca on the island of Majorca. Those tankers will also be there when we come home and buddy in with us as necessary to top us off. Questions so far?" Howe paused.

"You will have plenty of time to go over flight details later." The "Coach" continued. "All right, impact points. Colonel Burton, you guys need two bombs each down these three ventilation shafts, and then one on each of these six defensive sites. The object is to keep their heads down and cripple their SAMs for the big wave of F-16s right behind you, and to also take advantage of your pinpoint accuracy to see if we can't take out what ever is underground." The Stealth guys nodded their heads.

"Weasels, you get the rest of whatever comes up to meet us." Howe directed the F-16 weasels' attack. Go ahead and give us your 'Shotgun' or 'Magnum' call over the radio when you do launch a missile. That way we won't get so excited when we see this big ball of flame streaking through the sky." The F-16 Wild Weasel aircraft had an array of HARM and SHRIKE missiles that could be launched against most radar and defense sites when they so much as turned on their equipment.

"The rest of us will be hitting selected targets all over the airfield. We will concentrate on the buildings and structures, and keep an eye and ear open for the cavern entrance. If you hear me or anyone else yell 'Sesame,' that's the code word on your card that means the door is open. Put everything you can into that opening. Obviously that's one more break in comm silence, but one we hope to hear. Questions?" Howe surveyed the crowd one more time.

"OK, that's all I have for the group. General Olsen, it's over to you, sir. When the boss is done we will break up into aircraft specific groups. F-16 guys stay in this room." Howe sat down and Ollie Olsen stepped up. He stood there a while, chewing on an unlit cigar, looking very tired, but with bright and beady little eyes.

"I'd like to stand here and make reference to 'wading into them,' and 'crap through a goose,' but somebody already said all that." Olsen said, making reference to George C. Scott in the movie "Patton." "You sons of bitches! I want to be there with you. There's no doubt in my mind that this mission will succeed. But I want you to look around the room. A few of these guys sitting next to you won't be back tomorrow." THAT got their attention

"The Iranians didn't take this jet and bomb to sit by and let us take it back without a fight. And thanks to that bastard in the Washington Post, they know we're coming. You can be sure that every aircraft and every missile and every gun in Libya has got your name on it. Check your Goddamn Six, and check your buddy's too. Good luck! Carry on!" Olsen walked out, followed by his entourage of colonels and staff. Even though he had said to continue, the whole room stood at attention until he was gone anyway. They broke up into different rooms to continue briefing. The EA-6 and F-16 weasel flight leaders conferred with Howe more closely, because they were to be mixed into the same formation as the main force of F-16s—one big gorilla of airplanes. The F-22s would be on their own and out in front.

The game plan was complex, yet easy to follow. The F-22s would launch about 0230 with their own tanker. They would start and taxi all eight jets, and launch seven. Number eight would be a ground spare, and could actually launch if one had a problem right after takeoff. The seven would buddy launch with a KC-10 tanker, refuel east of Majorca, and six would press on. The seventh jet would wait to see that the primary six could all take gas, spare in if not, and recover back at Zaragoza if all went well. The primary flight of six would continue on to the main refueling track, just outside the 200 mile radius, due north of Libya. There they would top off again, and continue on for their attack. Lt. Colonel Mike Burton led the flight of F-22s.

A flight of four F-15s from Decimomannu, led by the 48th Wing Commander, Colonel Pete Trask, was to launch to refuel and precede the F-22s in a low altitude sweep, so as not to arouse suspicion, and then hang back in a Combat Air Patrol (CAP), 85 miles north of the coast. There they would be able to respond if needed, and they would also be positioned between the enemy and AWACS, who was on station just to the north. These would be the first players in the area. It was not normal for a wing commander to lead or even fly in these kind of missions. After all, he had a myriad of other duties than being a line pilot, and supposedly would not be as up to speed as the guys in the squadron. But Trask was different. He was an "up front" kind of leader, and in fact he had won every top gun competition the 48th had in the last two years. He had another reason to be in this fight too. Pete Trask and Brad Mitchell were roommates in Southeast Asia as Forward Air Controllers (FACs) flying the OV-10. Trask and Mitchell were best men for each other's wedding and Pete was Kristi Mitchell's godfather. He wanted to be there for his "bud."

The F-22 had replaced the F-117 stealth fighter in its mission, but it was a fighter and as good if not better than either the F-15 or F-16. Because of the stealth technology they planned a medium altitude ingress that had worked for years against Iraqi, Syrian and our own defenses. For that reason, the Stealth pilots did not want the F-15 support to escort and highlight their presence. The enemy radar could see the F-15 at 16,000 feet, but not the F-22. So the Eagles were to make their sweep at low altitude and in a different direction to see if they could scare up anyone. Then they were to settle into their CAP and wait for calls for help.

The Navy was next. Their task was to launch F-18s as close together as possible, refuel in the east track and hit strategic targets in and around Tripoli, 5 minutes before the first F-22 bombs impacted. They had their own tankers, plus Air Force KC-10 help, and they had F-15 support if needed. The object was two-fold—make lots of noise and fuss to draw the attention towards Tripoli, and to knock out as much of the command, control and communications network as possible. It was to be a low level ingress, to a one pass attack for fourteen aircraft.

The main force from Zaragoza was to launch at 3:15. They too had tankers to top off with on the way out. There were 20 F-16s, eight with two MK-84 (2000 pound) bombs, eight with six MK-82 (500 pound) bombs, and four with CBU-71 cluster bombs. There were two airborne spares. As it turned out, six of the eight F-16 Weasels were flyable, with two down for maintenance. All six were to be launched. Three of the four E-6s electronic combat aircraft were also part of the gorilla. They were all to rendezvous with 12 F-15 Eagles at the refueling track. Another four Eagles manned another CAP, and the original four, led by Pete Trask, was to refuel and back up the CAP after the F-22s egressed.

The formation Howe chose was fairly standard for modern Air Force tactics. The ingress of the gorilla was to be at low altitude—as low as they could stand it over water at night. The idea was to come in under radar coverage until a certain point—usually about eight miles from the target—then pop up to a higher altitude to convert to their dive parameters needed to put bombs on target. Some, like the Weasels and EA-6s would start their fly-up sooner, be able to react to the threat and launch their missiles, or to jam the enemy radars that detected them. Leading the pack would be a flight of four F-15s as a sweep of the area. The Eagles had the best air-to-air radars, and could detect any threat the Iranians launched in front of them. They would break off the sweep at the coast and then set up low altitude CAPs to cover the egress of bombers coming out. The F-15 guys didn't like flying low level much, especially not at night. The F-15C had no radar altimeter, and it was difficult to watch out for the water or rocks and pay attention to the radar at the same time. They were happy to set up their CAPs and let the enemy try their luck.

Next would be Ed Howe and the first four F-16s in a box formation. Once it got light enough, the wingmen would widen out to about 6000-8000 feet from their element leader, and number three would be about a mile to a mile and a half behind Howe. While it was still dark, the wingmen would have to tighten it up to fly a visual formation, and the element lead would maintain his mile trail on the radar. By the time they got to the coast it would be light enough to open it up. Behind Howe's flight would be the first EA-6s, followed by the first two F-16 weasels. Spacing between each flight was the same 1-1.5 miles. Four more Falcons, followed by another EA-6 came next. Flying outrigger on that EA-6 would be another flight of F-15s—two on each side. Four more F-16s, two Weasels, four F-16s, the last EA-6s, two weasels and the last flight of four Falcons completed the train. There were four more Eagles flying outrigger on the tail end. It was a formation of 41 aircraft, all going the same way, same time. It was affectionately known as a "gorilla."

In the target area things were to be very compressed. The F-22s were to hit at 5:25 am with the first bombs on the SAM sites and AAA positions. Their last bombs were to be down the chutes of the ventilation shafts by 5:31, and hopefully they would be on their way out. The EA-6s would offset and jam any other emitter that opened up, and the F-16 weasels would fly up to launch on anything left standing. Howe's flight of F-16s was carrying the CBU, and the hope was to catch the garage door still open and to fling the bomblets toward the hole. If not, the closest barracks to the entrance was their backup target. The next two flights of Falcons had the 2000 pounders, and each pilot had a separate Tab Vee to aim for. The leader of the third flight had the decoy target. The next flight had MK-82 bombs—a string of six each—to deliver on the buildings and what looked to the intel folks as a command post.

If the cave was open, they were to divert their bombs on it. The whole attack, from start to finish was to take a little less than 15 minutes.

Howe had picked a simple, but camouflaged route in. The initial vector was toward a spot on the coast halfway between Beni Walid and Tripoli. With the Navy making noise in downtown Tripoli, any radar or set of eyes that saw the gorilla break the coast would think it was going for the capitol. From there they were to head southwest for 30 miles and then turn north for the attack. They actually would approach Beni Walid from the south-southeast, taking advantage of the masking from the ridge line, the surprise of coming opposite the sea, and the added benny of an attack out of the sun. Egress off target was due north, back down in the dirt, and as fast as their buggies would fly. It was a well thought out and planned attack. Should be a piece of cake. HmmmmmmF!

The launch was completely comm out. In fact, the whole mission was supposed to be chatter free. That did two things—it kept snooping ears from hearing what's coming, and it left the radio open to important things like AWACS calls on the threat, emergency calls, and calls like "Lead, break left, or your jet's on fire." Even the refueling was comm out. The Air Force had become proficient in what was known as "quick flow." The first one in line just flies right up to the refueling boom, taking his cues from director lights underneath the tanker. They vector him up, down, forward and back, and the boomer did the rest. Once plugged in, the boomer could talk to the pilot via his intercom, but normally they did not even do that. Refueling looks difficult and sounds scary to the ground pounder who doesn't know. But in reality, it is one of the easiest things pilots do, so they don't need a lot of jabber on the radio. The next fighter is right there on the wing when the first one finishes his drink, and they just cycle through very quickly.

The tower personnel at Zaragoza and Decimomannu were in on the briefing. They had take off times and tail numbers written down, so there was no need for calls to taxi and takeoff. The assumption was a "green light" unless the pilot looked to the tower and saw a red one. The Spanish and Italian airspace controllers were kept in the dark until the last minute, and then they were advised that they should just be quiet, and it would all be over soon. Convincing them was very easy when there was an Air Force security policeman posted in each area.

The F-22 launch went as smooth as silk. Things didn't go quite as well for the mass launch. The number two Weasel developed a massive hydraulic leak right after start and never made it. There were no Weasel spares, so they went with five. The number eight F-16, Sabre 14 had an afterburner blowout on takeoff, and aborted on the runway. That held up the launch for a couple of minutes until he cleared the runway. He was spared out by one of the two airborne spares. Two flights back had a problem with the number three man. Sabre 33 could not get his landing gear to come up after takeoff. That's not a big deal, as long as they are down and locked for landing, but it means a mission abort. Nine hundred miles one way is a long way to fly with the wheels hanging. He too was spared out and they pressed on. However, during the first refueling, the spare could not take gas. The in-flight refueling door would not open all the way, and when the boomer tried to force it open with the boom, she just made things worse. He too was an abort, and since Ed Howe did not want to take a flight of four into combat with only one formation leader, he told number four (Sabre 34) to sympathetic abort and escort his element leader back to Zaragoza. So the gorilla pressed on minus one F-16 Weasel and two regular F-16s. Their escort had a little trouble as well, and they only ended up with a flight of two as outriggers in the middle of the formation.

Other than the problems encountered by Sabre 33 in the first track, the refueling went smooth. The weather was at 12,000 to 18,000 feet and all they did was raise the altitudes by 2000 feet for each cell. The weather actually cleared out as they got closer to the coast, and over the target area it was clear. The farther north one went from the refueling, the worse it got however. Decimomannu had a 2000 foot ceiling—not a problem for launch and recovery. The Truman was sitting under about a 1000 foot deck with some light rain. Again, not a problem for launch, but if it did not clear up by recovery time it would stretch out the landing chain a bit. Each aircraft would need an instrument approach—at least until under the weather and in sight of the ship, and the radar scopes were limited. It was something the Navy practiced all the time, but they didn't have to like it.

The Navy launch went like clockwork. They lost one bomber to maintenance, and one F-18 cap jet had radar problems. He stayed out of the fray and capped the tanker track visually. They hit their targets right on time and created havoc all over Tripoli. Most of the collateral damage was held to a minimum. However, in one location the government had moved a hospital right beside a large communication site. In the dark, the crew couldn't see any crosses, or signs of a hospital, and dozens of patients were killed or wounded. In another area, a bomb went astray and hit short of its target, impacting a school. Since it was before hours no one was hurt, but the school was leveled.

"Get me Beni Walid. Hurry!" Jowal Rafshanjani yelled to his communications officer. Someone was testing his resolve. It had to be the Americans. "We will show them that I am not a man to be toyed with."

"Sire, I cannot get through. All of our network seems to be down." The young officer said meekly. He tried desperately to raise the other bases on radio, teletype and phone. The Navy bombs had found their marks, and the Libyan command and control network was destroyed.

"What about communication with our own airfield here? Can we scramble fighters?" The general was showing signs of concern.

"Yes Sire. We have commercial phone contact." The Deputy for Air Defense spoke up. "Six fighters scrambled upon the first warning. They are checking in and chasing the attackers. There are two more being readied to launch, and several other aircraft on standby."

At Beni Walid, El-Kamani was informed of the attack on Tripoli. "Get our fighters airborne. This could be a diversion. Lock down this airfield and man the air defense systems. Mustafa!" He yelled at the Rogue.

"Ye sir." Muhammed responded while standing at erect attention.

"Go to your jet. Launch as planned." El-Kamani ordered. "Obviously the American President wasn't listening. Hit Tel Aviv and may Allah be with you." To his second in command he said, "Jubal I am leaving you here to lead the defense of the Americans attack us. I am going to roust our tanker crew and get airborne as soon as possible to Tehran. I must survive to conduct a follow on attack on the infidels."

CHAPTER FIFTY SEVEN

WHITE HOUSE SITUATION ROOM

The room was quiet for the number of people in attendance. Everyone was watching the TV screens and listening to the chatter. Actually there was very little chatter. The attack package was basically comm out. There was a liaison on the lead KC-10 tanker, communications with AWACS, and a link in to General Olsen's command center in Zaragoza. Basically it was Lt. Colonel Ed Howe's show and no one outside of his gorilla could affect any of the tactics or determine the outcome. They didn't need any last minute "GO" direction from Washington. They already had it.

President McDivitt, the VP, SECDEF, National Security Advisor, all the Chiefs of the branches of the Armed Forces, the Chairman of the JCS, the White House Chief of Staff, and Robby Genoa were all there. While they had some time to spare before "showtime," the President asked, "Robby, where are we on the loose ends of this overall threat? Has your team uncovered any information about this attack or any other?"

"No sir. Our team member in Las Vegas had a chance to take out the two attackers on the MGM Grand, but she hesitated not knowing where her partner was. That obviously was a devastating mistake. She is on her way back here. The two wives of the Vegas attackers are in custody, as are all of the family members of the other potential attacks. It looks like we staved off attacks in Sacramento, Atlanta, Tennessee, and Pittsburgh. We have not uncovered any other families that have infiltrated from the Iranian training town called Starkville. We are coordinating with our allies though - the ones specifically targeted by Starkville alumni." Genoa was ticking off items from a prepared list.

"The man we believe behind all of this is Barak El-Kamani, Operations Director of the Iranian Revolutionary Guard. We came close to grabbing him at Tempelhof airport, but he managed to hijack an Aer Lingus Aerbus 334 and flew it yesterday to the airfield we are about to attack. You probably were read in on that action. We had one operative - the man you met named "Ebola" onboard that jet. The rest were not able to board or stop the aircraft. Unfortunately we believe that aircraft has been lost as I think you were briefed this morning. Aer Lingus got a communique from their pilot that he was released to fly out of Libya and he was on his way to Marakesh, their original destination. All communication was lost a short time later and our satellite imagery detected a large airborne explosion about 20 miles west of this airfield." He pointed to the map displayed for the attack. "The pilot did say that the Iranian forced one of the passengers to go with him. We have no idea who it is, but we don't hold out any hope it is our guy. We are assuming that if this attack on Beni Walid is successful the chances of El-Kamani surviving it are slim. However, if anyone can survive, it would be him."

"What about the SEAL Team?" What have we heard from them?" The President asked the Chairman of the Joint Chiefs.

"Sir, we got one message from them that the F-16 and bomb we see on satellite imagery and from our drone reconnaissance flights is a dummy. It's a plywood mockup, and a good one. They even have maintenance personnel pretending to work around it. Evidently the real jet and bomb are in the underground hangar. If the attack underway doesn't get it, the SEALs are prepared to go in and hopefully destroy it. We were also able to alert the team that they were compromised by the Washington Post article." General Adams answered.

"Mr. President, there is one thing you should know about the SEAL Team." Genoa added. "Their contact on the ground is actually our own Melanie Mitchell, Colonel Mitchell's wife. You will remember she has extensive knowledge of the region as a CIA operative. We thought we had an indigenous contact to guide our team in, and Melanie was simply to contact him for coordination with the seals and then get out of town herself. Unfortunately, when she arrived in Tripoli, the contact was not there. She was able to track him down and found that he got cold feet when he heard we were dealing with Iranians. His beef was with the Libyan regime and actually was more on the Iranians' side in this whole operation. Mrs. Mitchell had to eliminate him and she has taken on the task of guiding the team herself. It makes one more we have to recover at the end, but to be honest, the chances of getting all of this team out of Libya are pretty slim."

"Unfortunately I have to agree with you Robby." The President said. "I'd like to think we could pull off this whole operation with no casualties, but that's probably a bit optimistic. One more thing though folks…. what do we do about this town called Starkville?"

"We have some ideas there sir." Genoa said as he looked at his CIA boss and at the Chairman. Then looking back at the President… "I'll brief you on it later." President McDivitt got the idea and nodded agreement.

"Sir the first bombs should be dropping right about now." General Adams announced.

"Let the **dark rain** fall. God Bless our warriors." McDivitt said solemnly.

CHAPTER FIFTY EIGHT

BENI WALID AIR BASE

The tail end attackers on the Navy side detected an airborne threat on their radar warning receivers. AWACS was too far west and the smaller Navy version saw nothing in the ground clutter. But the wingman in the rear element of F/A-18s got nervous. His RWR gear was chirping, and although they were doing the speed of heat, he wanted to be sure. He called for a break turn—a fatal mistake. The leader had no choice but to turn. When you're in that situation you have to trust your wingman and assume he sees something back there. They both pulled into a hard turn. Through 90 degrees they looked back and saw nothing. In the confusion that followed, no one could tell exactly what happened. By turning, they helped solve the geometry problem for the MIG-29s that were in the tail chase. They were able to close the gap and rapidly reach shoot parameters for their heat seekers. About that time, the cavalry arrived in the form of two more F-18s. The lead F-18 pilot had the whole thing sorted on his radar, and he thought he knew who was who out there. His wingman however was inexperienced, and in his haste, he locked his radar onto the wrong target—another F-18.

The first missile flew from an F-18, targeted and true on the number two Mig. Unfortunately, the AIM-7 missile did not impact before both the Migs fired their heat seekers at the Hornets. The Fulcrum driver died first, followed shortly thereafter by the lead F-18 pilot. The number two F-18 pilot was able to defeat the incoming Russian made missile with a combination of idle power, hard turn and flares. But he was now dead in the water for airspeed, and when he turned back around to try to get out of Dodge, he took an AIM-7 from the rookie friendly F-18 pilot right down the snot locker. It all happened in a matter of seconds and there were three fireballs descending into the water. There were four more Migs coming on fast, but when they saw all the fireworks in front of them, they turned west to avoid the action until they could sort out the targets. The lead Mig of the original pair kept on coming however, and he tried to ram the remaining lead F-18. The Hornet pilot had his hands full in a hurry, first avoiding the kamikaze attack, and then trying to keep the Mig form converting to his six o'clock. He was not alone however, and it soon became four vs. one. It was not a pretty sight, and the Mig driver was yelling for help as loud as he could when he died. His buddies were ten miles away by then, and they never even saw the AIM-9 missile that impacted just aft of the Fulcrum's cockpit.

The rest of the Navy forces got away clean, and the four remaining Migs turned back south, not sure what to do now. They understood their orders, so they looked for targets of opportunity. For now, the score was U.S. Navy - 2, Iran - 2. The fact that the American rookie shot down one of his own guys would be worked out later.

Ed Howe was ready. The adrenaline was pumping. They had just left the tanker track, dove down through the weather, and were in a combat descent to low level. He had not heard anything on the radio, so he assumed everyone was still there. He had decided to leave his lights on bright so that his wingmen could still see him. He would turn them off later. He searched the radar for any traffic out there and he knew the F-15 pilots just ahead of him were doing the same. Right now he was most concerned about running over the F-22s as he dove his formation down through their altitude. The F-22s had a direct route to the target, not the round about route of the gorilla. Therefore, about 30 miles north of the Libyan coast, they were projected to pass. Just as he always knew, Howe could see nothing of the F-22s on the radar. That's why they call it "Stealth." The enemy can't see it, but neither can the good guys. He had planned their routes to be separated a little, but with the size of his formation spread all over the Med, it was still a matter of concern. He started his level off, and initially settled at 1000 feet above the water, then easing down to about 500 feet. That was as far as his comfort level would allow him while it was still dark.

A quick sweep with his ground map display on the radar showed the coast. Howe refined his steering, picking out the exact spot where they should break land, noted his inertial nav system was off about a mile, and set his switches to do a flyover update. He had briefed his flight to do the same. There are a number of ways to do it in the F-16 -- by flying over the known point and updating the system, by designating from a radar display, designating in the HUD (Heads Up Display), or by using electronic aids. At any rate, the object was to tweak the system to the best possible accuracy. They had one more spot closer to the target to update on again, if they needed it. It would be light enough to see the actual landmark then too. Howe switched back to air-to-air.

Right on cue, the F-15s broke out of the formation and swung to the west as the gorilla approached the coast. Each four ship set up a counter-rotating CAP, initially at low altitude to avoid detection. At 5:30 they would climb to a more comfortable altitude and one which gave them more radar coverage themselves. The theory was that after 5:20 it wouldn't matter who saw them. The show would have begun. Their CAPs were 10-12 miles long, and manned so that there was always a two-ship pointing at the threat. They flew at 450 Knots while inbound, at 1000 feet above the water. The outbound pair flew at 500 feet to provide some deconfliction, and because they didn't have to spend so much time in the radar.

As Howe's F-16 crossed the coast he could see the explosions and flashes in the sky from the Navy attack on Tripoli, thirty miles to the east. The Navy was on a separate radio frequency, so they did not hear the chatter about the Migs chasing the F-18s north. Howe knew that AWACS was up there someplace, and he hoped they were watching. No news might be good news, but he sure was curious to know if there was any reaction. He turned his formation southwest, called up his air-to-ground mode, confirming his bombs were selected and he was armed. He also took another glance at his quiet RWR gear. The silence was finally broken.

"Bandits, Bullseye Zero Eight Five, Sixty." It was Stephanie Michaels aboard Sentry 41, the closest AWACS. She had just announced the presence of bad guy aircraft, 60 miles east of the target, Beni Walid. From the formation's present position, that was their six o'clock for 20 miles, after they all completed the turn to the southwest. Howe knew though, that they were only about halfway through the turn, and the bandits would be a threat to the trailing elements. They pressed on. There was no telling if the bandits had them in sight or on radar, and that's what the Eagles were there for. Each pilot had to fly his own jet though, and if he felt threatened, he was cleared to react.

"Bulldogs contact. Committed." The nearest F-15 CAP was reacting to the threat. They had been oriented north-south in their CAP and this threat had come from the east. They did not have much time to set up an attack.

"Roger Bulldog, from you, Zero Niner Five for Twelve." Captain Michaels directed. "Two there. Two more Zero Eight Zero Twenty Two." There were at least four enemy aircraft out there.

"Bulldogs contact both entities. Committed on the leaders. Sentry watch the stragglers." The F-15 leader was taking on the lead two-ship of bogeys. Howe figured *the trailers must not be threatening or the Eagles would elect to take them all on, leaders on trailers and visa versa. Maybe there was enough room to take them both on two at a time, without being threatened yourself.* Howe changed the subject. He had enough to worry about ahead of him, without pondering the fate of what's going on back there. They were approaching the turn back to the north. It was just a spot in the desert, no particular landmark. However, twelve miles to the west of the turn was another Libyan airfield, Okba Ibn Nafa. The order of battle said there were Libyan Mig-21s and French built Mirages stationed there, and likely someIranian Fulcrums. Howe expanded his radar search.

It was starting to get light. Lt. Colonel Mike Burton could just make out the shadows of his target as he rolled his F-22 in for the attack. His laser designator was locked on and tracking. He was in "the basket" of parameters. He mashed the "pickle" button and felt the jolt as the bombs released. He went heads down into his scope and tracked the SAM site with the laser. His bombs went off right on target. He blinked away the flash, came outside to clear for his wingmen, and saw explosions all over the area. Ten of their twelve bombs looked to be right on target. The other two must have missed the SAM site they were destined for. Just east of another fireball the ground lit up with the very distinguishable flame of a missile launch.

"Batman, SAMs 10 o'clock. Heads up!" Burton yelled for his wingmen. In each cockpit pilots were busy defending themselves. Their electronic countermeasures reacted automatically, but to be sure, each pilot activated his switch. Infrared flares popped out all over the sky, and the jets dove for the protection of terrain as they turned to keep the incoming missile in sight. A second launch followed the first. Neither missile found its mark. One decoyed on a flare, and the other went ballistic out into the desert. The F-22s got away.

Howe heard the call from Batman and immediately went on the offensive.

"Weasel One, deploy." He commanded the first F-16 weasel in his chain to commence her maneuver early to try and take out the missile site that was playing havoc with the F-22s. Captain Maria Johnson, flying the lead Weasel, tapped her afterburners and started a thirty degree climb out of the formation, put the target area on the nose, and climbed to 6000 feet. Unfortunately, she had lost her wingman back at Zaragoza with hydraulic problems, so she was a single aircraft for now. The other four Weasels were farther back in the pack, but they would be along shortly.

"Bulldogs, Bandit, Bandit! Three, cleared to kill." The lead F-15 had identified the closest airborne threat back near the coast. In reality the poor Mig drivers never even knew they were there. They had been the tail end part of the tail chase of the Navy forces that had hit Tripoli. They had just turned around to head south and ....Whoosh! Two F-15s, right in the face! Both Iranians reacted instinctively by turning their heads to watch the Eagles go by, and they both started to turn their jets to keep the adversary in sight. Neither pilot saw the missiles coming. At least they died relaxed.

"Splash, Bulldog Three."

"Bulldogs, additional bogeys Zero Six Zero, Fifteen and Zero Five Five, Twenty Five." Stephanie had handed this fight off to one of her co-workers in the AWACS and she was concentrating on the force attacking Beni Walid. But they were all on the same frequency.

Shortly after pulling her jet into about an eight mile arc of the target and leveled off at 6000 feet, Johnson jammed the throttles forward and rolled into a hard turn to put the SAM site on the nose. Before she even rolled out she let the HARM missile go. "Magnum, Weasel One." Johnson called over the radio. She fired another missile and broke off the attack, power to idle, a hard turn, and eyeballed the missile site. The SAM operators never even had a chance to fire. They soon got very close to Allah.

"Coach" Howe was into his pop. He had his steed doing 500 knots plus before he started a thirty degree climb. He did not want to use the afterburner if he could avoid it. For one, it made a nice IR signature for a heat seeking missile, and for another thing, it was still dark enough that the attackers would be tough to see from below—unless they had a plume of fire sticking out their rear end. He saw the weasels' missiles streak through the sky and find their mark. *What a way to die.* He thought. With a flick of the thumb on the throttle he was in the air-to-ground mode. The target locator line in the HUD pointed down to the right, just as it should. He had designated over a known Visual Reference Point (VRP) on the ground and followed the steering. At the top of his pop, about 5800 feet on the altimeter, he rolled over on his back and pulled toward the target. One quick look outside and he saw his wingman in perfect position. A look into the HUD. The Target Designator (TD) Box was just short of the barracks. Although it was the backup target, it was short of the cave opening. It was a lot easier to correct parameters to a longer target than it was to increase dive angle to hit a target shorter than where you were aiming.

Howe looked to the target's twelve o'clock, found the taxiway, and followed it to the ridge line. The cavern door was partially open. "Sesame! Sesame!" He called over the radio. Quickly he pushed another button and his system was in Constant Computing Impact Point (CCIP), the normal bombing mode of the F-16 computer. He pulled the flight path marker up past the hangar door, laid the bomb fall line right over it, and let the pipper (affectionately known as the "death dot") track up to the target. His CBUs were set to release in three pairs, 100 feet apart. He was actually almost level to nose high as he lofted the bombs. As they released he rolled hard to the left and sliced back down toward the ground, avoiding the ridge line, but getting back down where the earth protected them from electronic eyes. Another look for his wingman. Good! He's there. Then a look back to see how the rest of the flight was doing.

The MK-84 bombs from the second flight actually went off first. They had a shorter, more direct flight path to their different Tab Vee targets. There were still fires all over the place from the F-22 bombs. Howe saw the flashes of his own bombs. The idea was to try to spread the CBU bomblets into the cave, where they could create all kinds of havoc. He had been a little short, but at least half of the string had found their marks. It looked like his wingy was even further off, spraying the mountainside. Howe hoped that Brad Mitchell wasn't any where near there. Three and Four were right on target though. The mouth of the underground facility lit up like the Washington Monument on the Fourth of July.

The Weasels fired just two more missiles, and it looked as if their surprise attack direction and mass had been more than a match for the defenses. There was some AAA fire, but sporadic and wild, none doing any damage. The entire gorilla was on and off target as planned, but they were not alone.

"Sabres, Bandits Bullseye, One Seven Zero, Eighteen." Stephanie saw the Migs take off from Okba Ibn Nafa on her radar scope. The last of the gorilla had just made the turn from the south and was inbound to the target. The F-22 bombs had just gone off.

Major K.C. Shobe, the Assistant Operations Officer, was flying the number three position of the trailing four ship. He and his wingman were to be the last ones in, off and home. He immediately snapped his head to the west. Nothing. It was getting light, but he couldn't even see the airfield from his vantage point down on the deck. He just hoped that the Migs couldn't see him either. He pressed on. He couldn't push up the speed any more. There were dozens of aircraft in front of him going the same way, same day, same speed. They had to maintain their separation.

"Bogeys three miles, seven o'clock to Sabre 43." Captain Michaels warned.

"Shit!" Shobe thought. He turned his RWR volume up, checked to see that his flares were armed and switched them to singles. He did not want to lose all the flares with one or two punches of the activator because they were in the program mode. It was programmed to defeat the ground defenses by systematically puking out flares, several in a string. Shobe didn't want that. He didn't want them to come out until he commanded it, one at a time to defeat any incoming heat seeking missile. He kept his head on a swivel, and hoped that Sabre 44 was doing the same. This Mig driver could put a real cramp in their style.

Two Mirages with Libyan pilots had scrambled from a Okba Ibn Nafa, and they did not even know the gorilla was right in front of them until after they were airborne. All of a sudden the sky lit up from the F-22 bombs hitting Beni Walid. They turned toward the action and descended to low altitude to maximize their radars, looking up. There on their scopes were more targets than either pilot had ever seen in any ten intercept missions put together. The closest target was a little over three miles ahead, moving very fast. They were at least a mile and a half out of range, so they pushed up the power and settled into a tail chase.

"Sabre Four Three, Bogeys now six o'clock, three and a half, holding steady." Michaels wished she had a big fly swatter and could reach out and get rid of this pest.

"Four Four, keep it low and heads up." Shobe called to his tail end wingman over their dedicated VHF frequency.

"Four." Came the short, nervous response. Soon the whole world lit up in front of them from bombs and missiles going off in the target area. It was difficult to concentrate on the threat from behind, get set up for the attack ahead, and fly formation off of 40 other aircraft.

Stephanie Michaels didn't like the set up. She calculated that the bad guys trailing the gorilla would catch up to shoot parameters during the attack. She knew the F-16s would slow down and be exposed during their climb to achieve attack altitude.

"Shogun, Sentry. Commit One Niner Zero. Bandits One Eight Five, heading north, three miles behind Sabre." She ordered the western most F-15 flight out of their CAP.

"Shogun copies. One Niner Zero. Multiple contacts. Bogey dope." The leader of Shogun Flight responded and the F-15s broke out of the CAP two plus two, six miles in trail. There were so many F-16s, F-22s and EA-6s on their scopes that they could not possibly pick out two that were not so friendly. "Bogey dope" was a request to keep the information coming from AWACS.

"Roger. One Eight Six, thirty miles. Currently stagnated three miles in trail." Stephanie complied.

Shobe and his wingman followed their lead element through the twenty degree offset turn and into the pop. He had looked hard to the rear in the turn. He knew the turn would help to solve the geometry problem for the ragheads behind them. Into the pop—hold the afterburner. He definitely didn't want to show his tailpipe to an ATOLL missile. He thought about even pulling back the power to reduce the signature even more, but speed was life right now, and they couldn't afford to slow down and complete the equation for Ali Baba back there.

"Four Three break right! Break right! Bogey your six o'clock, two miles." The break call was from Sabre Four Four. In the pop he'd picked up the Mig. He wasn't even sure how close it was, but it was bearing down on his element leader.

"Roger! Jettison, jettison! No tally!" Shobe reacted. Two miles might be out of range, but he couldn't afford to trust his wingman's range estimates at this point. If the lieutenant thought there was a threat, he had to react. He quickly switched to Manual delivery and mashed the pickle button to get rid of his bombs. Since he was set up to drop, all he had to do was hold it until the six bombs released. It was about a second that seemed like an hour. Then he rolled into 120 degrees of bank to the right, pulled his power to idle to cool off the signature while he rotated the lethal cone away from any incoming missile, and popped four quick flares out. After about thirty degrees of turn he brought the power back into full afterburner. He needed the power now to keep the speed up, and the angle should be good enough for a trade off. He grunted back the G forces and searched the sky behind him for the bandit. Nothing!

Sabre Four Four forgot about his bombs in his maneuver. He mashed the pickle button, but didn't wait the one or two seconds to release and was loaded up with Gs in the turn when they came off. Two of the 500 pound bombs hung up on the left wing. Two more collided with each other and went off thirty feet behind him. Shrapnel ripped through his elevator and rudder assembly, tearing hydraulic and flight control lines. The good news was that the missile fired from the number two Fulcrum that nobody saw, impacted the explosion of the bombs. The bad news was the Falcon was helpless. It pitched up, did a slow roll over and plummeted to the ground, impacting the ridge line, short of the runway. Lieutenant Paul Morgan bailed out just in time, and was able to guide his chute away from the wreckage.

K.C. Shobe never even saw what happened to his wingy. It all took place behind him, and he had his hands full with the second missile and the Mig that fired it. "Four Three's tally ho. Missiles away. Flares, flares Four." He still kept his wingman in his thoughts, not knowing the lieutenant was in the silk below him. He defeated the missile and was soon pitching up to avoid the incoming fighter's gun attack. He took it straight up and stroked full afterburner, rolling the Falcon on its back, and pulling hard for the Mig's six o'clock.

"Sabre, you have another one at your five o'clock for a mile. Keep coming right." Shogun Lead sounded calm and collected. The F-15s had arrived and sorted the fight, but they couldn't fire yet without endangering the Falcon.

"Roger, Tally Ho. There's one under my belly and slightly in front too." Shobe yelled as he pulled hard to the right again, keeping his eyes "padlocked" on this new threat.

"Roger. Two, that one's yours when you can get a good shot. I'll take the trailer." The Eagles were rolling in for the kill. Shogun Two had positioned himself perfectly 4000 feet behind the lead Mig who was floundering for airspeed after reacting to Shobe's defensive move.

One quick AIM-9M up the ass and he was a goner. He too bailed out, and his craft fell into the desert.

Shobe met the trailing Mig almost beak to beak, no chance for either to shoot. Then he saw a beautiful sight -- something that an F-16 pilot will not admit to very often. The big Eagle of Shogun One had saddled up to the Mirage at about 1000 feet, and the F-15's gun was blazing away. Shobe pulled up into the vertical to watch and saw the Mirage disintegrate, from the canopy to the tail. This guy never had a chance to bail out. The first one hundred bullets penetrated his cockpit, his body and his life. K.C. Shobe unloaded, headed north, and in the escort of his two new friends, endeavored to catch up to the gorilla. He soon realized that he had lost a wingman, when there was no answer on the radio.

"Bonkers, Sabre Four Three!" He called when they crossed the coast outbound. Only then did K.C. Shobe have time to reflect and to wonder whether Lieutenant Paul Morgan made it. He passed the news on to AWACS and Sabre One.

There were a few other commitments of fighters against the Iranians and Libyans, but in most cases no contact. The Libyans seemed to be flying around in circles, or lost. If they were not a threat they were left alone. When it was all said and done, the U.S. had lost two F-18s, one F-16 and one F-15 that had apparently hit the water in the CAP, not in enemy contact. But it was not all said and done.

CHAPTER FIFTY NINE

EARLIER, ON THE RIDGE ADJACENT TO BENI WALID

The Libyan sky was turning a lighter shade of gray. Brad Mitchell didn't think he had slept at all. His mind was still racing, thinking of what had happened earlier, and what was about to happen. He checked his watch -- 5 am. He kicked "Blaster" to wake the seal from what was obviously another restless night. The demolition man had tossed and turned and even talked in his sleep once. Seeing his buddies killed would be a lasting memory for this young boy from Arkansas.

"Blaster! It's almost time. We need to dig in good. Looks like the entrance is open—at least a little bit. I don't know for sure, but the guys will probably try to hit it, and we'll be awfully close." Brad had not been in on much of the mission planning. He wished he knew at least what direction the jets would come from.

"There's a cluster of rocks down there, but it's damn close to the fence." Lundick pointed to a large group of boulders farther down the hill. The fence actually had to be diverted around them, and unfortunately there was a guard tower just on the other side. They would be sitting ducks trying to get to the rocks.

"Let's just sit tight until the fireworks start. Then, hopefully those ragheads in the tower will have their hands full and we can get down there." Mitchell was even starting to think like a SEAL. It was scary.

The first bombs hit the SAMs and AAA sites right on time. The ventilation shafts were next. The WOOMPH noise they made was different than any of the men on the ground had heard before. The bombs entered the shafts and penetrated yards of aluminum and rock before actually exploding, muffling the sound to the outside. But inside the cavern was a different story. The air circulation system in the facility was attached to the ceiling, with miles of ducting. Each of the three shafts was a straight shot through to a separate cooling system, suspended from the ceiling. The first bombs down each shaft went off as they impacted the machinery, spewing death and casualties. Fortunately for the Libyans and Iranians, there were partitions in the facility and much of the damage was contained to the immediate vicinity of the shaft. The second bomb down each shaft went off on the explosion of its mate, making more of a blast on the outside, sending fire and rock both directions. One of the shafts was very close to where the F-16 was parked. However the Falcon was inside a smaller enclosure where it could be guarded, and the ceiling of its "igloo" held true.

Brad could see bombs going off on the other side of the field, and the AAA and SAM reaction. He could see that the F-22s were not all right on target, that much of the air defense was still intact, and he crossed his fingers for Ed Howe and the rest of the Sabres. The noise and confusion did enable them to move. The guards in the tower in front of them scrambled and ran as soon as the first bomb went off. "Blaster" and Brad slid down the ridge to the boulders just in time. Brad was looking to the north for the F-16s when they attacked from the south and the first cluster bombs went off behind him. They had a good vantage point to see the opening to the cave from where they were. The first set of CBU was a little short, but on the right line. Almost simultaneously the ridge line where they had just spent the night lit up like the fourth of July. Sabre Two's aim was a little off and he sprayed the whole mountainside with bomblets. Brad and "Blaster" sprawled face down in the dirt, hands over their heads and cussing the Air Force—both of them. The dirt and debris impacted all around them, but the boulders sheltered them from any major damage. Brad snuck a peak to see that the next two fighters atoned for the miss. Sabre Three and Sabre Four were right on the mark with their clusters. A series of explosions kept going off in and around the hangar door for minutes after the whole attack was over. Brad could not tell how much damage was done, and if the F-16 and its bomb were hit. He didn't have time to think about it.

Mark-84 2000# bombs were going off all over the airfield. Then the barracks and other buildings lit up. Brad got his glasses on the nearest building just before it turned into a scene from a "Die Hard" movie. From the side door several men were running toward the cavern entrance. There was a personnel door of some kind short of the taxiway, and it was still functional. One of the men running looked familiar. Brad focused the binoculars as the light from the explosions helped him out. It was Mustan. Brad recognized him from the photos he had seen, even though he was wearing a funny looking flight suit. Mustan was carrying his helmet bag and harness, and Mitchell made a quick decision. He did not know if the traitor was just trying to protect his gear from the onslaught, or if he was getting ready to go fly.

"Blaster, get us through this fence. We've got to get inside." Brad yelled over the din of the attack.

"You gotta be shittin' me, sir!" Lundick was convinced this Air Force jock was nuts. What they needed was to get away, not any closer.

"The pilot who took the jet just went into that cave ready to fly. I don't know if there's anything in there left to fly or not, but we've got to find out. Our job is supposed to be to destroy the jet and the bomb, remember? Now blow this Goddamn fence!" Just as Brad finished his speech the sky exploded from Sabre 44's jet and the two Migs. Brad could see the silk of the pilot's, but he was at least a mile or two away, down the ridge. There was nothing Brad could do to help. He just hoped that the guys had been briefed on the pick-up point. The way things were going, the downed pilot might be the only one to pick up.

"Blaster" had plastic explosives wrapped strategically around the fence in less than two minutes. The explosion was soft and unnoticeable, with everything else going off high order. They slid through the opening and ran along the fence to the edge of the cavern door. They stopped and looked in on what could only be described as chaos. There were fires all over the place. Several aircraft were burning, fuel was spilled, ammunition was going off. Men were running every which way—moving jets out of harm's way, fighting fires, and just plain running. Just as Brad thought it would be easy to join the melee unnoticed, the big doors started to open the rest of the way. They had only been half open when the attack hit, and miraculously, the mechanism was unscathed. As the door opened two MIG-29s came hurtling out. The second one was actually trailing flames from its right main landing gear area. They made their way out to the runway, avoiding wrecks, craters and debris, and took off. The fire on the one landing gear put itself out once airborne.

Brad looked into the cavern again and there it was. About 50 yards inside and along the side of the hangar he could see the F-16, with the B-61 still attached. He could also see Mustan, talking frantically with another man, who looked to be someone of importance. The Rogue had his helmet out of the bag, and Brad was convinced he was getting ready to launch.

"Blaster. There! See it? Get your satchel ready to blow. Let's go!" Brad pointed to the jet and started running, pulling the demolition man with him. They got into the facility and about half way down the side toward the Falcon when they were discovered. The single Iranian guard shot first, asked questions later. "Blaster's" legs were ripped out from under him and he sprawled head long into the wall. His satchel of explosives went down with him. Brad saw the gunman just in time to duck. He had been gripping his 9MM and now he knew it was time to use it. He rolled behind a tug used to pull the jets, cocked his weapon, rested it on the wheel of the tug, and emptied four rounds into the face of the oncoming guard. Then he puked. Brad Mitchell had never killed anyone face to face before. He did not give himself much time to recover. One look at "Blaster" told Brad that he was on his own. He also knew that he didn't have a clue how to rig explosives.

Mitchell looked for Mustan. "The Rogue" had seen the gun play and was half way up the ladder into his cockpit. Brad had only one choice. He ran wildly at the Falcon, emptying his clip into the crew chief and toward the traitor. The crew chief died quickly, not even knowing what was going on. "The Rogue" was luckier. The only shot his way shattered his helmet, but missed him. He jumped down to meet

Mitchell head on. By the time Brad got to the front of the jet he was out of ammo, and he faced a determined Mustan with a long saber-like knife. A quiet smile appeared on the traitor's face, as he realized he had the advantage. Brad threw his pistol away and groped desperately to get at the Bowie knife that was strapped to his boot.

The man Mustan had been talking to came around from the left side of the jet. He was holding a gun to the head of a disheveled, scruffy looking guy that Brad recognized immediately. It was Ebola. His hands were fastened behind his back and he was bloodied and weak from successive beatings. "Drop your knife American." El-Kamani yelled over the noise of the attacks. "Or I will kill this infidel. You will come with me." He motioned deeper into the hangar. There, tucked in an unscathed - as much as you can "tuck in" a Boeing 747 - was the Iranian tanker, pointed in the other direction. Beyond it the huge doors of a second entrance into the ridge line hangar started to open.

Just then a secondary explosion rocked the inside of the cave. One of the bombs must have set off munitions store inside. It got everyone's attention except Ebola's. He used the diversion to launch an attack on El-Kamani, first with a head butt that splattered the Iranian's nose all over his face. Then he swept El-Kamani's feet from under him with a series of kicks that would put Bruce Lee to shame. Soon he had the Iranian on the floor and was straddling him. Brad ran up and with his Bowie knife cut the flex ties that were binding Ebola's wrists. Then Brad turned again to face Mustan who had returned to prepping himself to fly.

Mitchell's advantage was his size. He was 6'4" and he weighed 225. Mustafa's advantage was his weapon. He swung it wildly and caught Brad a glancing blow on the shoulder. Even a glancing blow with a sword that big did damage. Brad felt the pain immediately and saw half of his left shoulder laid open. He still had use of the arm, and he was able to grab his attacker's arm on the next thrust. Fortunately for Brad, "The Rogue" had not kept up his saber practice while working for Uncle Sam. He was clumsy with it, and the struggle soon turned into a close in, entangled fight. Brad knew that if he could keep Mustan wrapped up, he couldn't swing with the big knife. But Mitchell was losing a lot of blood and he was weakening. They rolled around underneath the jet and Brad was finally able to dislodge the saber from Mustan's grip. It clattered safely across the hangar floor, but Brad was not able to get a clean attack with his own knife. Mustan was gouging at Brad's eyes and trying to swing at the wound to weaken him even more. Mitchell eventually pushed his attacker to arms length and then used the best weapon he figured he had—his size 13 boot. He kicked hard, right on the mark and Mustan doubled over, both hands on his groin. Brad's next kick was to the face, and he gave it everything he had. Mustan wheeled over backwards and sprawled on the tarmac. Brad was on the traitor like a wild man. He was determined to finish this, and he was in real pain. He had the knife against Mustan's throat, remembering everything the Chief had taught him—where and how to kill a man, remembering the Chief, remembering the rest of the SEALs, remembering Melanie, and then—remembering he couldn't do this. Mustan's half open, half closed eyes told Brad the fight was over. All he needed to do was get away.

Mitchell clubbed Mustan hard with the butt of the knife then turned his attention to Ebola and El-Kamani. Ebola was slumped on the hangar floor, his chin hanging down on his chest which had a whole in it the size of a soccer ball. El-Kamani was nowhere to be seen. Ebola weakly raised his right hand and waved Brad on, to leave, to get the jet out of there. Then he fell over still on the floor.

Brad scrambled up into the cockpit of the Falcon. Mustan's helmet was shattered from the gunshot, and would be of no use. He couldn't find the harness to strap in with, so he closed the canopy and tried the Jet Fuel Starter (JFS). The familiar whine was a lot louder than usual, because he had no helmet and the ear protection that comes with it. But Brad did not care. He had kicked the chocks out from under the wheels before he climbed aboard. He had thrown the ladder clear of the wheels, and the scene ahead of him looked barely passable for the Falcon to taxi. There were few people near the entrance. Other aircraft had taxied out during their fight, and the rest of the ground crew were toward the rear of the facility trying to control the fires and busy around the tanker. Brad goosed the engine, not waiting for any warm up time. He decided that he did not have time to do anything more than to reach down and be sure that every switch was in the "on" or "armed" position. He almost made it clear. One wingtip clipped a section of the ventilation that had crashed to the floor, and the missile on that side took the brunt of it. The missile was mangled, but the wingtip itself was ok.

The pain in Mitchell's shoulder was getting worse. He had grabbed a rag from a pile near the chocks and stuffed it up under his flight suit, but his left arm was a bloody mess. He rolled the Falcon out onto the runway, passing several gunners and ground crew who hadn't a clue as what the aircraft was, much less who he was. He stroked the afterburner and lifted off, turning sharply to what he figured was north, keeping down on the deck and pushing it to Mach 1.3 (close to 800 mph). As he lifted off he noticed the huge form of the 747 emerge from the hangar and taxi to the runway.

CHAPTER SIXTY

FROM THE OUTSIDE, BENI WALID

Halfway up the ridge line, Lieutenant Lee, Wipe, Radio, and Melanie watched the whole show. The first bombs down the ventilator shaft were the closest they came to any action. They had seen Brad and "Blaster" go into the cavern, and they saw the F-16 come out. Lee had no idea who was driving the jet, but he guessed their job was over, and they had been unsuccessful, but Melanie thought it was Brad. At least she hoped it was. There was nothing else they could do, except try to help out the pilot of Sabre 44, who bailed out just about a half mile from them. They went back to where the radio was stashed and got off a quick message...."The Falcon has flown. Unknown destination. Five personnel to extract."

Lieutenant Jack Lee, "Radio" Davis, "Wipe" Leitao, Melanie Mitchell, and Lieutenant Paul Morgan were picked up right on time by a Navy Sea King helicopter. The chopper stayed down against the desert and sea and was able to evade the few Migs that were around. The Libyans and Iranians had no workable command and control network, and they did not know where to look for the enemy. None of them much wanted to venture out to sea and take on the whole US Navy. The Sea King was refueled on the way and deposited its weary passengers on the Truman.

A quick tally showed that the damage to Beni Walid was substantial. Several aircraft were destroyed. Defenses were at least neutralized.

Almost every structure suffered major damage, and the underground facility would take massive reconstruction. The number of killed or wounded exceeded 400. The American attack had sent its message. However, satellite IR imaging recorded two takeoffs from the airfield after the attack was over. One was the signature of a fighter size target that flew due north over the Mediterranean. The other was the huge signature of a Boeing 747 that flew from Libya to Tehran, Iran.

CHAPTER SIXTY ONE

—

OVER THE MED, AN INSIDE EIGHT

Colonel Pete Trask had been busy. As his flight of four F-15s swept the area before the F-22s there was nothing to see—either on the radar, or outside. It was too dark outside and he was glad to break it off and set up a CAP. At least then they could fly at a reasonable altitude and not have to worry so much about making a big splash in the Med. Once in the CAP they were able to watch and listen to the whole thing. AWACS kept everyone abreast of the Iranian reaction and Trask's flight was committed once to intercept two Migs approaching from the northeast. The unsuspecting Fulcrum drivers had been in the tail chase with the Navy, as had the MIGs that had met their fate at the hands of the flight Trask had relieved on CAP. When the Iranians broke off their chase and headed west, they waded right into a bee's nest. They did not even realize there was anything going on outside the attack on Tripoli. The Eagles intercepted the Migs just after sunrise, converting from the west, outside radar coverage of the Migs'. Even if the Libyan ground control radar saw them coming, there were no communications left intact to alert the pilots of their impending peril. Pete kept his flight low on the intercept and swooped up from the Fulcrum's eight o'clock position, taxied right into shoot parameters at the Iranian's six, and Trask and his wingman became one-fifth aces with one push of the pickle button.

There were other contacts out there, but the Bulldogs had to refuel. They had been up the longest, and there was timing criteria to make.

Ed Howe had given them tanker times so that they would be on and off the boom before the first wave of attackers returned to the track on their way home. Trask left his CAP with just enough time to make it to the tanker, top off and then return for the final portion of the mission. They were to man the eastern close-in CAP for the last part of the egress of the gorilla, and then stick around for as long as needed to protect AWACS. Refueling was uneventful, and they saw the attacking force rumble into the tanker track, minus only a few airplanes. It was a sight to see. That many airplanes in one piece of sky at once was confusing. He didn't have much time to enjoy the sight, however.

"Bulldogs, bogeys One Eight Five, thirty miles. Looks to be two entities, five miles apart, chasing the gaggle." Stephanie Michaels had not had so much work since the last time her squadron played in a Red Flag exercise in Nevada. This was great! Red Flag was the closest thing to real war that peacetime fighter pilots got to fly in. It was a huge exercise flown on the ranges and in the airspace in northern Nevada. The main contingents usually flew from Nellis AFB in Las Vegas, but other nearby bases of both the Air Force and Navy participated in the scenario usually held three times per year. The AWACs aircraft usually deployed closer to Nevada as well, but sometimes even flew Red Flag missions from their home base in Oklahoma City. Stephanie liked it when they deployed into Nellis. Having that many fighter pilots in one bar was definitely a target rich environment for a good looking single girl. Red Flag was great training for everyone and it gave the American and allied pilots the edge over their adversaries.

There were two flights of Migs following the gorilla out. They did not have a chance of catching anyone. They were at least ten miles back. K.C. Shobe in the last F-16 and Shogun flight of two F-15s from the west CAP were doing the speed of heat, and the bad guys had a long way to go to chase them down.

"Bulldogs, contact there, One Three split now." Trask ordered his second element to outflank the targets to the left side, he and his wingman would take the right. Each pilot selected minimum afterburner to push the speed up to just above the Mach. Trask dove for the deck with his two ship, and Bulldog One Three, seeing that, kept his element up. They would use the vertical to split the targets as well. This complicated things for the Migs. Assuming they even knew they were targeted, they would have to look to both sides, and both high and low. "Bulldog One One has the trailers, One Three, you have the leaders." Trask directed the target sort.

"One Three. I have two contacts there, Eight thousand." The element lead acknowledged.

"That checks. Leaders are at eight, trailers at six." Stephanie chimed in.

The Iranian pilots were all in MIG-29s. They had just launched off from Beni Walid during and after the attack, having been safe in the underground hangar. Or at least they thought they were safe. They had scrambled to their jets when the bombs hit, and had managed to get airborne around explosions, fuel spills, fires and craters. They weren't sure what to do. They could contact no one in their command and control system. However, they had targets on the radar, heading north, and they knew that it had to be the jets that had just bombed their base. The lead pilot in the second formation was the squadron commander and he was bound and determined to get even for the death and destruction just levied on his squadron. It was soon obvious however, that this was one race they couldn't win. The targets were too far ahead and going much too fast. But wait! There were targets coming back toward them.

"Tiger Two Six, this is Tiger Lead. You have targets at your one o'clock for one five miles. Do you see them?" The commander radioed his fellow pilot in the lead pair of Migs.

"Affirmative Sire. I have two sets of targets, one left and one right." The young pilot knew he was about to have his hands full. "Which ones should we take, Sire?"

"Neither. At twelve miles take your flight and drag back to the south. Bring them back towards me and avoid their radar missile." The older pilot was borrowing on his experience and everything he knew about the F-15 and the AIM-7 missile. He could only assume these were F-15s, and if they were, he knew that at about ten to twelve miles the Eagles could fire their missile, well before the Fulcrum became a threat. He wished the Russians had given them their own version of a Beyond Visual Range (BVR) weapon. "Now Ben Ahmed, Now!" The commander directed.

Bulldog One Three had locked onto his target and his wingman had sorted on the other lead MIG. They were waiting for a shoot cue when the targets abruptly changed course. Trask saw it too on his radar. "Lead bogeys are dragging out." He chirped on the radio.

"Roger Bulldogs, and the trailers have split." Stephanie Michaels saw the whole chess game develop. The Eagles had the first pair of Migs outflanked and were about to shoot when the bogeys did a split-S maneuver and ran back down the middle. In the meantime the back pair of Migs split, each heading 90 degrees to the incoming threat. A gutsy move, taking all information off the radar scope, and not very tactically sound. Or was it?

"Bulldog One One has the split. Two stay with me, we'll take the one heading west. One Three, you have the one going east. Watch the draggers and Sentry keep us advised." Trask made a quick and sound decision. His paired targets had spilt, each going away from the center. If there was any tactic to this it was to get him to split up his own formation and go one-on-one with the Migs. He knew that each fight would be close to an even match, but that's not the way the Air Force wanted to fight. Numerical superiority was always the goal. It was much better to go two-vs-one, kill one and have both good guys survive, than to risk losing one or both by going it alone. Besides, they had the advantage of AWACS to keep track of the pair of Migs that was running. He pulled lead on the target that was heading west and locked him up. One Three did the same on the target heading east.

The Iranian squadron commander was a smart tactician. He had been well trained by the Soviets and was regarded as the best pilot in the Iranian Air Force. He knew exactly what he was doing. He knew that he was taking a chance, and that he might have to sacrifice a wingman, but that he was going to be victorious today. He had split the flight and put the incoming attackers directly on the beam. He wanted to present as much problem as possible for the F-15 radar and missile.

"Tiger Two. Tell me when you get a warning on your receiver. Tiger Two Six, be prepared to come back when I call you." The Iranian had a plan, and if everything worked, he should be able to at least isolate two of the F-15s with three Migs. His wingmen acknowledged his commands, prepared to fly by the numbers, doing just as they were told. Just then his own radar warning receiver chirped a warning. He looked down. The symbol was more toward the eight o'clock position on his scope as he headed east. He pumped out two bundles of chaff into the air and turned to put the threat directly on the beam. It worked! The scope went clean and quiet. The F-15 radar had locked onto the aluminum chaff floating harmlessly in the atmosphere. He looked hard for the oncoming Eagles. He had given himself the extra advantage of turning east, so that when he turned back into the fight he would have the sun behind him. There! Two F-15s, nine o'clock high. He pulled hard up and into the attack. "Tiger Two Six, come back to the north-northeast, NOW!"

Pete Trask had trouble locking on to his bogey heading west, but he finally got it to take. He wished he had one of the AMRAAMs, the "grounded" missiles. This would not be a good shot for the AIM-7, especially looking down into the ground clutter, and on the beam. He would wait until well inside the envelope. "Bulldog One Two, lag him, set up for a heat shot." Trask ordered his wingman to convert more to the bandit's six o'clock and be in position for a quick kill with the AIM-9.

"Bulldogs, trailers are pitching back towards the east. Heads up, Bulldog One Three." Stephanie saw the Migs that were running suddenly turn back into the fray. She also saw the lead MIG turn hard into Bulldog One Three, the attacker to the east.

"Roger, One Three's engaged with one bandit. Four take it up!" Trask's other element soon had their hands full. They could not get their radars to maintain a lock coming in, at first they couldn't see the MIG, but now all of a sudden they had a windscreen full of Fulcrum. They had stayed too close together coming in, and it was easy for the MIG driver to keep both in sight as he turned into them. He jammed the lead Eagle by passing him close aboard—very close, and then continued over the top in full afterburner, using God's G forces to slowly convert toward Bulldog One Four's six o'clock. He had one more trick up his sleeve. He pulled lead, and though well out of parameters for a good shot, fired a heat missile at the defending F-15. Then he unloaded the MIG and raced to the north, jamming the lead Eagle one more time. Then the Iranian appeared to be running. It was all in the timing.

The lieutenant flying Bulldog One Four had never seen a real MIG-29 before. He and his element leader had stayed in the CAP when their flight leader had intercepted the first two earlier this morning. Now he had seen more MIG-29 than he ever wanted to see. This guy was good! He thought he was doing ok holding him off when all of a sudden the Mig's wing root lit up and a missile was tracking toward him. Idle, flares, pull hard! Damn! That was close! The missile went harmlessly ballistic and the lieutenant was feeling much better. Now, where did that bastard go? "Four's lost tally, no visual." He had no one in sight. Not the Mig, nor his leader.

"Roger, he's just jammed me again and he's buggin' out to the north. Come hard to Three Six Zero. I should be at your twelve for one mile after the turn." The element leader had his eyes padlocked on the fleeing Mig, trying desperately to get turned around so he could get a shot off before the Fulcrum was out of range.

"Bulldog One Four, the trailers are closing at your six...." Stephanie Michaels made her first major mistake of the week. She was too late with that call.

The original lead pair of Migs that had dragged back through the formation had done just what they were told. They pitched back to the north, and sure enough—there was a fur ball of fighters right in front of them. Their squadron commander had managed to turn the F-15s he was on enough to run them out of airspeed, and then they turned their tailpipes to present a great heat source. The lead Mig signaled to his wingman to take the farthest Eagle. He himself held off using his radar so as not to alert the F-15 of his presence. He pulled his power back, fanned his speed brakes and slid right into the saddle -- 1000 feet behind the wallowing lieutenant. It only took a short burst of the Mig's gun and the F-15 was out of control, one wing gone, and the canopy riddled. The American never even had the chance to bail out. The second Mig was just as successful. The captain driving Bulldog One Three was so engrossed in shooting the fleeing Mig squadron commander that had almost rammed him twice that he never even heard his RWR gear go off. The heat seeking missile impacted his left engine, blew his left vertical stabilizer off and forced the Eagle into an uncontrollable yaw and spin to the left. After two rotations and passing 3000 feet on the altimeter, the American jumped out. He was able to get out a "May Day" call on the radio, and Pete Trask knew that he had lost at least one wingman.

The Iranian driving west with Pete Trask bearing down on him was also a good soldier. "Tiger Two has warning at three o'clock." He radioed his squadron commander.

"Roger, turn hard to the right. Look for them. Use chaff!" The Iranian leader was flying everyone's jet at once. The obedient wingman turned hard to the right, and looked up for the threat he knew was there somewhere. But Trask and his wingman had converted from below.

Pete Trask finally got a good lock and was just about to shoot when the bandit turned hard into him. He was suddenly pressing minimum range for the Sparrow missile. He came off the pickle button. "He's yours, Two. Cleared to fire!" Trask pulled up and rolled over the top to watch his wingman complete his stern conversion with a vertical maneuver, pull lead and fire an AIM-9M. The missile was true and the Mig blew into a thousand pieces. Trask did not wait around to look for a chute. Just then he heard the "May Day" call from Bulldog One Three.

"Sentry, Bulldog One One, snap to One Three!" Trask asked for a quick vector toward the other fight. Stephanie obliged.

"Roger One One. One Zero Zero for One Five. Sir, I think we've lost Bulldog One Four too. The bandits are now Zero Niner Five for One Six—a two ship there, and Zero Six Five for Two Zero, a single." Trask realized that he was now out numbered. He took up an intercept course on the nearest two bogeys.

"Bulldogs, contact on the nose for twelve. Committed there. Sentry, watch the other one. Two, sort side side." Trask was in no mood to fool around. He took the one on his side of the formation, directing his wingy to take the other bandit.

"Two."

"Sentry copies. Single is now arcing south. Looks like he's heading home." Michaels made one more mistake. The Libyan squadron commander was not going home.

The two other Mig drivers were still basking in their glory, each having shot down an American F-15. Their squadron commander reminded them that there were more out here, however. Just then their warning receivers said the same thing. They both snapped their heads to the west just in time to see two great white telephone poles streaking toward them. The AIM-7 missile is about that big, and hurts a lot more. One missile found its mark, impacting by proximity just below the Mig and destroying the flight controls. The Fulcrum pitched up and rolled over into a death spiral, the pilot ejecting just before it hit the water. The second missile was not as true, and what Pete Trask saw next he would never forget.

Trask's missile is the one that missed. His wingman had scored a hit and had followed the missile in toward the targets. Trask had pulled off to convert toward the stern of his bogey and cussed at the miss. What happened next was hard for him to believe. "Two, I don't think mine sees me. He's pointing at you. Keep him turning." Trask ordered his wingman to pass close aboard the Mig, getting him to turn and set him up for the kill. But it did not happen that way. The Mig kept forcing the issue, pulling lead and staying on a collision course. Bulldog One Two never had a chance. He tried a last ditch evasive maneuver, but the two jets collided head on—with more than 1200 knots closure. The Mig plowed right through the aft fuselage from the belly as the Eagle had tried to pull up out of the way. The Iranian died instantly as his cockpit impacted the F-15. The American had time to eject and cleared the wreckage easily, watching both aircraft splash beneath him. Trask felt suddenly alone.

"Bulldogs, another contact—high speed, low level, One Niner Zero for 18 miles. He's heading due north." This was even another target and Stephanie was still watching the Mig squadron commander too.

He was still arcing the fight at about fifteen miles, but not threatening right now.

"Copy Sentry. Be advised we just lost another one. One Two is in the drink, good chute. Mid air with a Fulcrum. Two Migs down as well. I think I'm by myself up here now. Any other help?" Trask was pissed. He had lost three good wingmen. The fact that they only had three Migs to show for it made it worse. He horsed his steed around toward the south to meet this next threat coming in. A quick check of his fuel showed he only had another 15 minutes of play time. He also only had three missiles left—one AIM-7 Sparrow and two AIM-9s.

Brad Mitchell was ass-holes and elbows, and a sore shoulder. He had no inertial navigation to speak of. He managed to get an in flight alignment enough to give him an instrument platform. At least his artificial horizon would show right side up when he was. But that was all he had. He didn't know where to head either, but he thought that if need be, he would take this thing out to sea and ditch it in the Med. It would be politically embarrassing to have an American nuke at the bottom of the sea, but at least the Iranians would not have his toy any more. The radar was tied to the INS too. He would not get good information, though it would show targets. He just would not be able to read the other guy's heading and speed, etc. He broke the coast and started an easy climb, keeping his speed up. He knew he would have to keep it below about 15,000 feet. Without a helmet he not only had no communications ability, he had no oxygen mask. His training in the altitude chamber every three years reinforced that though every pilot reacts a little differently to lack of oxygen, his personal capability started to get fuzzy with hypoxia after several minutes above 15,000. Standard Air Force procedure was to mandate oxygen above 10,000 feet, but Brad knew he could take it a little higher without any measurable issues, and this whole scenario certainly was not "standard AF procedure." He had checked the gas tanks and they had been filled. That was good. Except for the navigation system and the one missile, everything else seemed to work. Wait a minute! The other missile was worthless too. It still had its seeker head cover on. Marvelous! He did not really have time to preflight the jet before he launched. He wondered if the gun was hot.

He armed it up and squeezed the trigger and got his answer. It worked. Either the Libyans did not know how to safe it up, or Mustan had got that much of his preflight done before Brad had arrived. So—here he was. Blasting north into the empty sky with no missiles, a hot gun and a nuclear bomb. He was wrong about one thing—it was not an empty sky.

Trask locked up the target at 13 miles, put him on a collision course and called up his last AIM-7. He was not going to let this one get away. "Sentry, Bulldog's Judy on this one. Where's the original Mig that left to the east?" The term "Judy" was telling Stephanie that he would handle this intercept. All he wanted from her was the location of the leftover Mig from the previous fight.

"He's still southeast at one five miles, heading west." Michaels replied.

Ali Makba, the Iranian squadron commander, lamented the loss of his three wingmen, but he did not want to wade back into the fight without an advantage. The F-15's radar missile was a formidable foe. He had fooled the Americans once. He did not think it would happen again. Wait! What's this? Another countryman heading to the north? He had Brad Mitchell on his radar and thought that he must be another Mig heading into the fight. He tried to call the "friend" on their common radio frequency, but he got no response. Not to worry. He would just intercept him on the way north and they would join forces to seek out the remaining Americans. He pulled the Fulcrum into a lead pursuit and pushed up his power.

Mitchell saw the F-15 on the radar about the time he passed through 5000 feet. He assumed it was an F-15 or a Navy F-18. Nobody else would be north and intercepting a target coming from the south. This guy was definitely setting up an intercept too. He got a radar warning symbol just seconds later. He had to keep looking at the scope because he couldn't hear anything without a headset. Shit! Just what he needed! To be blown away by one of his own. He reached way down in his bag of tricks. He knew the AIM-7 was susceptible to the notch maneuver if he could put it on the beam. He pulled hard to the east, putting the RWR "bat wing" symbol at the nine o'clock position on the scope. Brad had no idea what worked, if this beam maneuver was really legitimate. He figured that if not, he was probably already dead. He squinted hard into the northern sky. He had only one trick up his sleeve, and he hoped the oncoming American fighter pilot remembered what the distress signals were. Mitchell rolled the throttle to idle, extended his speed brake as he came through the Mach, and kept turning to keep the "bat wing" on the beam. Just then he noticed two symbols—the other came from the other side, but it was weaker and intermittent. Oh well, one at a time. He was over deep water now, although he'd rather get farther off shore, he had no qualms about leaving this jet in the drink. Then he realized *Shit! I can't even bail out of this thing. I don't have the harness on so I'm not connected to the ejection seat and parachute.* Ditching definitely is not one of the emergency scenarios practiced or even talked about much. *Oh well. First things first.* Passing 250 knots, Brad dropped the landing gear and turned the landing light switch on, then he started as hard a turn as he could get at 250 knots, into the attacker. He suddenly became aware that his left arm was becoming numb. When he grasped the landing light switch he couldn't feel his fingers.

Trask couldn't believe it. Twice in the same day some raghead had taken him into the beam and then an "Inside Eight" jamming maneuver. This time he wasn't going to bite though. He worked hard and kept his lock.

"Bulldog, original Mig has turned back in. He's now One Six Zero for 10 miles." Stephanie Michaels was concerned. Trask was out there going one vs. two. She had no one else to send him. The first flight of F-15s off the tanker had been diverted back, but they were 80 miles away.

"OK, I'm going to come off this guy and go for the trailer. This one has slowed down. I'm going to jam him and take the trailer." The presence of the MIG-29 probably saved Brad Mitchell's life. Trask threw his radar into the boresight mode, searched for the trailing Mig and locked him up, just about the same time he saw Brad Mitchell. He couldn't believe it! A landing light! This guy was nuts. He couldn't tell what kind of aircraft it was yet. He kept one eye on the radar, and one on the oncoming light. Suddenly the target started rocking its wings, and Trask realized it was an F-16.

"Sentry, this first bogey is an F-16 with his gear down. Do we have any stragglers from the attack out here?" Pete asked as he rolled up on one wing, passing over top the Falcon. He had no time to think about an answer. His other target was five miles off. Now he was confused. He sure did not want to shoot down an F-16. He decided he'd better ID this other guy.

"Negative Bulldog. All Falcons are accounted for." It hadn't dawned on either of them that this might be the runaway. "Your other bogey is now southeast for three miles."

Squadron Commander Makba saw the Falcon's beam maneuver on his radar, and commended his unknown companion for his tactics. It also helped him catch up. He soon saw the attacking target from the north, and sorted to his satisfaction that there was only one. He smiled. Then he became very puzzled. His new wingman had slowed drastically. What a stupid move! He was going to have to take on this Eagle by himself. He dove for the water to get some vertical turning room. He would attack from below and launch a heat seeker with blue sky background. It was then that he looked up and caught a glimpse of the F-16, it's landing gear extended, and the unmistakable shape of the bomb hanging under the wing. He had inspected it very closely back at Beni Walid, and there was no doubt in his mind that this was the same aircraft. Had Muhammad Mustafa stolen the aircraft again? Was he flying it back to the American's? Why were the wheels down? He too had no time to think. He was soon in the knife fight of his life.

Mitchell saw the F-15 come off his attack and breathed a sigh of relief. So far so good. He watched the Eagle cross over the top as he reached for the gear handle. He raised the gear and pushed the throttle up to give the F-15 driver some speed to play with as he would come around to join. Then Brad remembered the other RWR signal. He started a right turn to keep the Eagle in sight and looked for what he thought had to be the F-15's wingman. His eyes widened and his heart sunk as he saw the MIG-29 screaming up from below. Mitchell was helpless. He was a sitting duck for either one of the fighters turning around him, and in no position to help the F-15. He had only a gun and very little airspeed. He unloaded the Falcon to zero G and stroked the afterburner. In the meantime he kept his eyes glued on the ballet going on behind him.

Trask saw the MIG-29 just as he crossed over the top of the F-16. The Fulcrum was coming up at him, and had a good shot. Trask yanked his power to idle to reduce the IR signature, pumped out four flares in quick succession, and rolled down hard into the Mig. They crossed canopy to canopy, no more than one hundred feet apart. Pete rolled again and pulled for all he could get out of his Eagle. Across the circle, the Iranian was doing the same. He had more airspeed when they met at the merge and he was determined to use it to his advantage, not his detriment. If they both kept going straight up, Makba would be out in front—the wrong place to be in a dogfight. He rolled into the horizontal and pulled toward the Eagle's six. Trask was ready for this maneuver. He unloaded while going straight up, got some separation, then pulled over toward the Fulcrum's belly. The Iranian countered—these two were evenly matched. He pulled back into the vertical and slammed on the rudder to roll hard over the top. They soon degenerated into a slow speed fight, and this is where the Mig has an advantage. Both pilots knew it and Trask worked hard at keeping his speed up. However, he had gotten into a position that the Iranian was able to keep his nose tracking around and Trask could not disengage with out getting shot at on the way out of the fur ball.

Brad Mitchell watched in horror as the two big jets seemed to stop in mid air, both going straight up, in a scissors. They were no more than half a mile away from him. He had accelerated his own craft to about 350 knots and just kept turning to keep the fight in front of him. He saw that it was only a matter of time before the Fulcrum would be able to slide back to the Eagle's tail. The Mig has outstanding slow speed characteristics. He had seen it in the Paris Air Show actually slide backwards, downhill, after running out of airspeed. The Eagle could not do that. It would roll off on a wing and accelerate or go uncontrollably into a spin first. Neither was a good option here. If he rolled off to accelerate he would solve the Iranian's final problem, placing the Fulcrum at dead six for the kill. If the F-15 went into a spin at this altitude—they were at 5000 - 6000 feet—Trask could never recover it in time. He would have to bail out. Mitchell decided to try to help. He put the Fulcrum in the middle of his HUD and drove straight into the phone booth with his gun blazing. The sound of the gun was deafening. He had forgotten he had no helmet. He figured he was about deaf now anyway. He also had no radar lock and very little gun sight help. His tracers all went short.

Ali Makba was just beginning to believe he had it made. He had dragged the fight down where he wanted it—low and slow, and he was getting the advantage. He flipped his hands on switch to the guns position and he took one quick look for the whereabouts of the F-16. That was his second to last mistake. He saw the wing root of the F-16 on fire with the gun flashes, and the tracers arcing toward him. He rolled hard into the attack and pulled toward the water. That was his last mistake. Although the Fulcrum will maneuver at slow airspeed, it will not recover without sufficient altitude. He wallowed through the turn and found himself inverted, in a 40 degree dive, at less than 2000 feet above the water. The Iranian saw his mistake, rolled the Mig over and pulled as hard as he could.

Bulldog One One had watched the Mig slide towards his six o'clock, glanced quickly at his altitude, and decided on his last ditch jink out maneuver to avoid what was sure to be an impending gun shot. Then the Fulcrum rolled abruptly and dove toward the water. Trask did not know what had happened, but he was thankful. He eased his mount over and kept his eyes glued to the Mig. It only lasted a few seconds more, but it seemed like an eternity. The Iranian jet flattened out and almost made the pull out of the dive. Instead, it pancaked twice on the waves, breaking up on the second impact. There was no indication of a chute. Just then, the F-16 pulled up in front of Trask with its afterburner lit up and did a perfect four point victory roll. It was then that Pete Trask noticed the Falcon pilot had no helmet.

The two jets joined up and Mitchell patted his shoulder with his other hand, grimacing from the pain as he did. That was the signal that he wanted to land on Trask's wing. He really didn't, but they did not have signals for "I've stolen this jet, take me back home." He also gave the fuel signal—thumb extending toward the mouth from a clenched fist, relaying that he wanted a tanker. Trask nodded and then moved in closer. He knew this guy! It was Brad Mitchell! Brad did not know who was driving the Eagle—the guy had a helmet on, like he was supposed to. But Pete Trask recognized Mitchell immediately. He also saw that his friend was in a lot of pain.

They rendezvoused with a tanker and then went directly to Sigonella, Sicily. By the time they landed, Brad Mitchell had lost all feeling in his left arm. He managed to get the wheels down and pull the power to idle to land. That's the last thing he remembered before blacking out from the loss of blood at the end of Sigonella's runway. A fireman opened the canopy from the outside, climbed over the wing of the jet, reached in and shut it down. The Falcon had returned to American hands.

CHAPTER SIXTY TWO

MISSION ACCOMPLISHED

The Falcon had been tightly secured on the Sigonella ramp. The cops put a cordon around it, and four guards. There was an armored personnel carrier nearby, and all other traffic was diverted around that area of the ramp. By Sunday afternoon a C-17 had been diverted in, and four nuclear certified weapons loaders were flown in from the 10th squadron at Zaragoza. The bomb was downloaded and flown back to Spangdahlem on the C-17. Brad wanted to catch a ride on it, but even he wasn't allowed on a nuke loaded airlifter. Besides, the doctor wanted him to stick around another day.

Two maintenance men and one of the pilots from the Sabres were also brought in from Zaragoza, and the jet was given the once over. The bent missile was removed from the right wing, and the other one was safed up for a ferry flight. An escort two-ship of F-15s from Pete Trask's Bulldog squadron was flown in from Decimomannu, and the three of them flew out to Zaragoza on Monday.

Melanie Mitchell was able to get the Navy to chopper her to Sigonella so she and Brad could have well deserved break and time together. "Jack Lee, Radio and Wipe all send their regards, Brad. We didn't know you had gotten out until after the chopper deposited us on the Truman They're probably on their way back to Norfolk by now. The Lieutenant we rescued is back in Zaragoza with his squadron." Melanie informed him.

"Thanks Hon. I guess Lee, Radio and Wipe are all that's left of their team. We lost a lot of good men— just trying to get back one airplane. I'm glad you made it out." Brad hugged Melanie for all he was worth. "Now I think it's time that we both get out of the game. We have a daughter to raise."

Melanie smiled. "We'll see" She said.

CHAPTER SIXTY THREE

VP'S CONFERENCE ROOM, THE WHITE HOUSE

What was left of the Tango Team was gathered. They had lost Cretin, Shooter, Yusef, Blaster and Ebola. Brad and Nitro were wounded but functional. They were sitting and discussing the overall mission and decided it was only partially successful. The U.S. had taken a lot of hits, lost a lot of citizens, and although they had dealt a significant blow to Iran and Libya, the feeling wasn't all that warm and fuzzy. Drone surveillance followed the Iranian tanker out of Beni Walid and watched as it landed and unloaded in Tehran. Facial recognition confirmed that one of the few passengers that deplaned was Barak El-Kamani, which meant the mastermind of the entire operation was still alive and able to fight another day. In addition, Robert Mustan, known in Tehran as Muhammed Mustafa had escaped Beni Walid with not much more than a severe headache but was labeled a traitor in Iran. Even though he had valiantly escaped with an American jet and a nuclear weapon, the Americans had recovered it. The regime had to have someone to blame and El-Kamani made sure it wouldn't be him. Mustafa was executed in his sleep the first night back.

President McDivitt came into the room. "Please, take your seats." He said in response to everyone jumping up. Are we set?" He asked Genoa.

"Yes sir, we're about four minutes out." They had set up a video feed from the Situation Room and we're watching dual footage - one from a drone covering a town in the desert somewhere, and one from the cockpit of a B-2 Spirit bomber.

"Quarterback, this is Wide Out. We have target in sight looking for clearance." the pilot of the B-2 radioed in. Everyone looked at the President.

President McDivitt looked hard at the footage from the drone. It showed what looked like a town in the mid-west U.S. - schools, churches, shopping centers, ball fields, hospital, middle class homes. He could see people moving around, including children. He reached up and caressed his temples as if he had a bad headache. Then he looked at the feed from the bomber and said.......".Let the **Dark Rain** fall. Wide Out, cleared to engage."

Three B-2 bombers laid down a blanket of Mk-82 500 pound bombs that completely covered the expanse of Starkville, Iran, making it a basic parking lot in the desert. The coverage from the drone showed complete destruction, and although there may be survivors, their "home away from home" was no more.

The President then looked up and said, "Folks, as you know this mission never happened. You and the aircrews are the only ones who know about it. We need to keep it that way. Now, let's go to the White House Briefing Room. We have a ceremony to attend."

The remainder of the SEAL team were at the front of the room when Peter Sciapini basically accosted Lieutenant Lee. "So Lieutenant, what does it feel like to have lost several of your men in the operation?" Always a stupid question - how do you think someone would feel after losing friends and co-workers? Lee just looked at him and then asked, "Are you the reporter who broke the story to the Washington Post about our raid?"

"I am." Sciapini replied with a smug and a smirk, to which Lee let him have it with a roundhouse to the nose, plastering it all over his face, knocking him to the floor.

"So, Mr. reporter, how does it feel to lose the part of your face that keeps getting in your way?" Lee asked. Then he walked back to his team and nodded to Brad and the Tango Team who had just come in.

Sciapini was very still, bleeding from the lip and nose. There was a deathly silence. Mike Mulroney, the White House Chief of Staff was the first to react. He ran up to Lee screaming. "What do you think you are doing? Lieutenant, you will leave this function at once. You can expect charges to be…"

"Just a minute, Mr. Mulroney." It was General Richard Henry, the National Security Advisor. He stepped up to protect Lee.

"Ladies and Gentlemen, the President of the United States and Mrs. MvDivitt." The announcement came from the entrance to the Oval Office. Everyone stood and faced the President. Everyone that is, except Peter Sciapini. He was still out cold, bleeding profusely on the white carpet. McDivitt walked directly to the center of the room and looked down at the pathetic figure on the floor.

"Mr. President. We will take care of this. The man responsible will be punished and an apology will be issued to the Washington Post." Mulroney offered a note of explanation. The President looked again at Sciapini.

"You mean that is the Washington Post reporter?" The President asked.

"Yes sir. That's Peter Sciapini." Henry answered. "Looks pretty good, doesn't he?"

"He looks marvelous. I just want to know what he's doing here. Mike, if I didn't give you orders to keep this slime ball out of my sight, I am now." McDivitt scowled at his Chief of Staff. "Now, who did this terrible thing?" He turned to the honorees.

"I did sir. Lieutenant Jack Lee. I'm sorry, I just could not take his line of questioning. I knew who he was and what he has written." The SEAL stepped forward to take his medicine.

"Aren't you the leader of the SEAL Team?" The President asked.

"Yes sir."

"Lieutenant you have just done your country another great service. That's getting to be quite a habit with you." The President shook Lee's hand vigorously. "I don't know which medal I'm giving you here in a few minutes, but there ought to be another one for silencing that little traitor. I'm just sorry I did not come in a little sooner to see it.

But I'm sure some of his cohorts here got it all on film." The President looked scornfully at the pool of reporters and cameramen, who were all busy writing and taking photos. Sciapini was completely ignored, and continued to bleed on the carpet.

The ceremony was very well done. Each of the recipients was personally decorated by the President as the citation was read. There were many photos and hand shakes. Brad received the Medal of Honor. Ed Howe, Pete Trask and Jack Lee each received the Silver Star. The others received medals of less rank, but just as important to them and to their President. Melanie, as a civilian, received the Presidential Medal of Freedom. Brad also received the Purple Heart, and the amount of praise and descriptions of "Hero" lavished upon him was almost embarrassing. "Your country owes you a tremendous debt of gratitude, Colonel." McDivitt told him.

TWO YEARS LATER, TEHRAN, IRAN

Barak El-Kamani had kept a relatively low profile since his return from Beni Walid. Though he was hailed as a hero by the regime for the devastation he had brought on the United States, he blamed himself for the failure to bring the U.S. to its knees and the survival of Israel. The U.S. increased the sanctions and blockades on Iran. He vowed to continue the fight and was deeply involved in planning new attacks. Even though the Iranian state run press, as well as Al Jazeerah blamed the Americans for the destruction of Starkville and the "murder" of "innocent" women and children, El-Kamani knew that he could bring more terror and destruction on the western world. He had a flat in downtown Tehran, but spent a lot of time at a lake house about an hour out of town. He had built a Russian Dacha style mansion and kept a harem of young men and boys there to satisfy his every need.

The CIA and portions of Tango Team worked long and hard to locate El-Kamani, and with Geek's expertise they were able to do so. On a dark and moonless night in October, satellites confirmed he was in his Dacha. A U.S. Navy destroyer in the Straits of Hormuz launched two Tomahawk missiles. Each missile was stenciled with the words "Remember the Lincoln," crossed into Iran and made a very low level ingress to the Dacha. An Air Force drone was high overhead making movies and with President McDivitt and his cadre of trusted staff, Robinson Genoa, Brad Mitchell and other members of Tango, gathered in the White House Situation Room to watch, Barak El-Kamani's Dacha was pulverized.

Satellite and drone coverage confirmed there was very little left of the complex, and though never confirmed, it was assumed that there were no survivors. Brad Mitchell wasn't so sure. President McDivitt was in the last year of his second term and really didn't care too much about any political repercussions that could come from taking out a serious terrorist threat without at least informing congress first, however he used the moment to crow the praises of the men and women in the armed forces. He cashed in some political green stamps there - at least with the men and women of the military.

Brad Mitchell had recently retired from the Air Force. He was taking some well earned time off, before starting a new job. Robinson Genoa had moved up to take over as Director of the CIA, and Brad had been appointed to the Operations Directorate as the new Tango Team Leader. It seemed there was always something cooking in the world to keep Tango busy.

Melanie decided to fully retire and play the role of housewife, mother and lover. Brad thought that was a good idea too, although from time to time he'd be relying on her counsel and expertise.

Colonel Pete Trask had returned to his job as wing commander at Lakenheath Air Base in Great Britain. By all rights he should have made General at the next go around, but it seemed that too many of his superiors thought he should have given the leadership of the F-15 part of the task force to one of the majors or Lt. Colonels in the Bulldog squadron. The fact that he was the best F-15 pilot in the wing, bar none, didn't matter to the brass. He was passed over for General and sent to Randolph AFB in Texas as the Chief of Safety for the Training Command. After a year of pushing papers Trask retired and lives in northern Texas with his wife, two daughters, and four grandkids.

Lt. Colonel Ed Howe was promoted early to Colonel and assigned to Hill AFB in Idaho as the Vice Commender. Within a year he moved up to commander and became the Air Force's youngest wing commander in history. He was on his way. However, he got wind that with the next promotion he would be assigned to D.C. to be the Secretary of Defense's military aide as a one star general. Howe said no thanks, and to the chagrin of everyone one of his superiors, he retired and moved to

Colorado. His golf game is getting better and he does a lot of volunteer work in the area.

Brigadier General Chuck Morton was basically run out of town on a rail for his loose lips with a reporter around. Ironically he was assigned to the Pentagon as the Air Force Public Affairs Director, dealing personally with the Washington Post, the New York times, CNN, MSNBC and the rest of the military hating media. He only lasted six months in that job before he too retired to Kentucky, where he bought a ranch in his childhood home and raises horses.

Very soon after the action was over there were hundreds of ceremonies and funerals all through the country. Many of the deceased were buried in Arlington Cemetery, but hundreds were interred in their small home towns all over the country. The military put on a good show with missing man formations, riderless horses, bagpipers, flag presentations, 21 gun salutes, and the ever present (and Precious) bugler playing Taps. President McDivitt attended everyone of the ceremonies in the D.C. area. The Vice President, Secretary of Defense, Chairman of the Joint Chiefs, or the affected Chief of the armed service made sure that one of them at least attended the rest. There was no celebration by anyone. America had been dealt another low blow. How many more would there be to follow?

THE END

ABOUT THE AUTHOR

Colonel Dana Duthie's career as an Air Force fighter pilot is the basis for many of the experiences in "Dark Rain." His Air Force career spanned 24 years, from pilot training in Georgia and instructor in Texas to the skies over Southeast Asia, and from the F-4 phantom in Germany to the F-16 Falcon in South Carolina, Korea and Germany. He also "paid his dues" with three headquarters assignments and professional schooling. Some of the story in "Dark Rain" is true, though perhaps embellished just a bit. Colonel Duthie retired in 1992. He lives in Broomfield and Steamboat Springs, Colorado with his wife, and two children and four grandchildren nearby. One grandson is currently serving on the USS Harry Truman, an aircraft carrier off Iran in the neighborhood of "Dark Rain."

www.ingramcontent.com/pod-product-compliance
Lightning Source LLC
Chambersburg PA
CBHW051609100726

47898CB00001B/289